The

Gatecrashers

Selected Historical Fiction Published by McBooks Press

BY ALEXANDER KENT
Midshipman Bolitho
Stand Into Danger
In Gallant Company
Sloop of War
To Glory We Steer
Command a King's Ship
Passage to Mutiny
With All Despatch
Form Line of Battle!
Enemy in Sight!
The Flag Captain
Signal–Close Action!
The Inshore Squadron
A Tradition of Victory
Success to the Brave
Colours Aloft!
Honour This Day
The Only Victor
Beyond the Reef
The Darkening Sea
For My Country's Freedom
Cross of St George
Sword of Honour
Second to None
Relentless Pursuit
Man of War
Band of Brothers

BY PHILIP McCUTCHAN
Halfhyde at the Bight
of Benin
Halfhyde's Island
Halfhyde and the
Guns of Arrest
Halfhyde to the Narrows
Halfhyde for the Queen
Halfhyde Ordered South
Halfhyde on Zanatu

BY JAN NEEDLE
A Fine Boy for Killing
The Wicked Trade
The Spithead Nymph

BY JAMES L. NELSON
The Only Life That
Mattered

BY JAMES DUFFY
Sand of the Arena

BY DEWEY LAMBDIN
The French Admiral
Jester's Fortune
What Lies Buried

BY BROOS CAMPBELL
No Quarter

BY DUDLEY POPE
Ramage
Ramage & The Drumbeat
Ramage & The Freebooters
Governor Ramage R.N.
Ramage's Prize
Ramage & The Guillotine
Ramage's Diamond
Ramage's Mutiny
Ramage & The Rebels
The Ramage Touch
Ramage's Signal
Ramage & The Renegades
Ramage's Devil
Ramage's Trial
Ramage's Challenge
Ramage at Trafalgar
Ramage & The Saracens
Ramage & The Dido

BY FREDERICK MARRYAT
Frank Mildmay or
The Naval Officer
Mr Midshipman Easy
Newton Forster or
The Merchant Service
Snarleyyow or
The Dog Fiend
The Privateersman

BY V.A. STUART
Victors and Lords
The Sepoy Mutiny
Massacre at Cawnpore
The Cannons of Lucknow
The Heroic Garrison
The Valiant Sailors
The Brave Captains
Hazard's Command
Hazard of Huntress
Hazard in Circassia
Victory at Sebastopol
Guns to the Far East
Escape from Hell

BY JULIAN STOCKWIN
Mutiny
Quarterdeck

BY JOHN BIGGINS
A Sailor of Austria
The Emperor's Coloured
Coat

BY ALEXANDER FULLERTON
Storm Force to Narvik
Last Lift from Crete
All the Drowning Seas
A Share of Honour
The Torch Bearers
The Gatecrashers

BY C.N. PARKINSON
The Guernseyman
Devil to Pay
The Fireship
Touch and Go
So Near So Far
Dead Reckoning
The Life and Times of
Horatio Hornblower

BY NICHOLAS NICASTRO
The Eighteenth Captain
Between Two Fires

BY DOUGLAS REEMAN
Badge of Glory
First to Land
The Horizon
Dust on the Sea
Knife Edge
Twelve Seconds to Live
Battlecruiser
The White Guns
A Prayer for the Ship
For Valour

BY DAVID DONACHIE
The Devil's Own Luck
The Dying Trade
A Hanging Matter
An Element of Chance
The Scent of Betrayal
A Game of Bones
On a Making Tide
Tested by Fate
Breaking the Line

The Gatecrashers

ALEXANDER FULLERTON

THE NICHOLS EVERARD
WORLD WAR II SAGA, BOOK 6

MCBOOKS PRESS, INC.
ITHACA, NEW YORK

Published by McBooks Press, Inc. 2006
Copyright © Alexander Fullerton 1984
First Published in Great Britain by Michael Joseph Limited

Cover painting by Paul Wright

Library of Congress Cataloging-in-Publication Data

Fullerton, Alexander, 1924-
    The gatecrashers / by Alexander Fullerton.
        p. cm. — (The Nicholas Everard WWII saga ; bk. 6)
    ISBN-13: 978-1-59013-100-8 (trade pbk. : alk. paper)
    ISBN-10: 1-59013-100-2
    1. Everard, Nick (Fictitious character)—Fiction. 2. Great Britain—History,
    Naval—20th century—Fiction. 3. World War, 1939–1945—Fiction. I. Title.
    PR6056.U435G37 2006
    823'.914—dc22
                                                                    2005033940

Distributed to the trade by National Book Network, Inc.,
15200 NBN Way, Blue Ridge Summit, PA 17214
800-462-6420

Additional copies of this book may be ordered from any bookstore
or directly from McBooks Press, Inc., ID Booth Building,
520 North Meadow St., Ithaca, NY 14850. Please include $5.00 postage
and handling with mail orders. New York State residents must add sales tax to
total remittance (books & shipping). All McBooks Press publications can also
be ordered by calling toll-free 1-888-BOOKS11 (1-888-266-5711).
Please call to request a free catalog.

Visit the McBooks Press website at www.mcbooks.com.

Printed in the United States of America

9   8   7   6   5   4   3   2   1

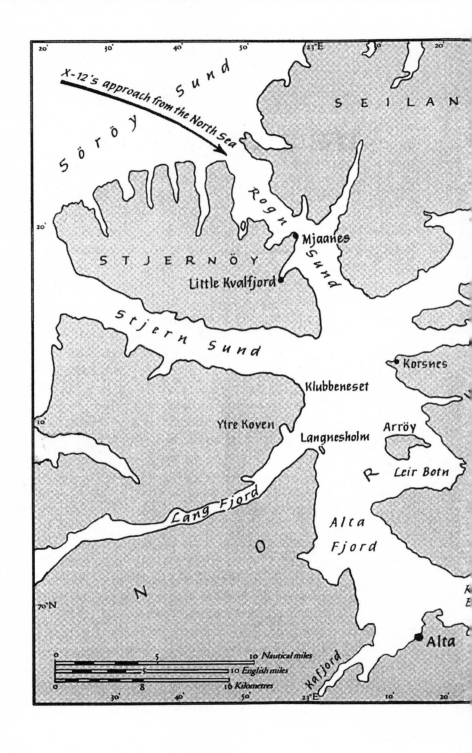

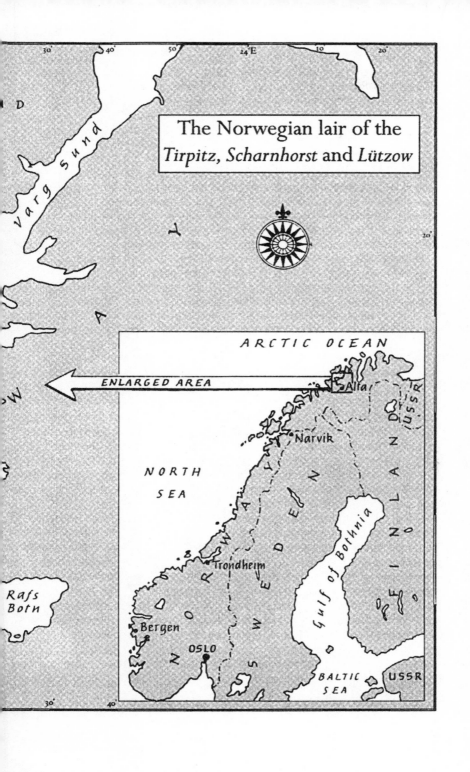

The Norwegian lair of the
Tirpitz, Scharnhorst and *Lützow*

CHAPTER ONE

·   ·   ·

God Almighty, he thought, this is impossible! X-12 pounding, thrashing her thirty-nine tons around like a whale having an epileptic fit! Paul Everard, his hands clamped to solid fittings and muscles straining to hold himself in place against the midget submarine's frantic porpoising, saw Jazz Lanchberry, the engineer, open-mouthed and wide-eyed as he fought the wheel and tried at the same time to stay in his seat. His left shoulder had slammed against the end of the storage locker, and he was dragging himself back into place now, a snarl of anger taking over from the shock in his dark face: he'd momentarily lost control of the wheel and the boat's wild cavorting had acquired a lateral component as well as the plungings and soarings. At sixty feet she was fighting the tow-rope like a huge fish with a barbed hook in its mouth instead of a very, very small submarine with a steel coupling in her snout. Not a damn thing you could do about it, for the moment . . .

Well, there was. In fact there were two things. One, you could release the tow-rope—it could be done from inside, by winding a handle in the bow compartment—and start the motor, surface. But that wouldn't achieve anything except short-term relief, because this exercise did have to be completed and you'd only have delayed it. With annoyance to a lot of people, since the practising was just about finished now, the operation imminent . . . The other option—Paul didn't like it, in fact all his submariner's instincts were against it, but he'd have to try some damn thing before she shook herself to death. He looked round, met Dick Eaton's sideways glance from the first lieutenant's seat a few feet aft: Eaton looked desperate, the violent motion too savage for his hydroplanes to cope with—and X-12 shooting upwards with a steep bow-up angle on her. You couldn't blame him for not having countered it; the upward lunge had been caused by the tow-rope, slack or at any rate unstrained at one moment and then in the next tugging upwards at the midget's stem. Paul yelled over the noise of the sea and thumping steel, "Flood for'ard!"

Eaton's head turning: then he was hesitating. He couldn't not have heard. Presumably he was wondering if he'd heard right, knowing this was a manoeuvre Paul had sworn to avoid. Paul was opening his mouth to repeat the order when the sub-lieutenant acted—pushing the trim-lever forward to pump ballast from the after trimming tank to the bow one, shifting weight into her forepart so she'd lean on the tow and maintain an even strain on it.

That was the theory, how it was supposed to work. The price was to be trimmed heavy for'ard, which in professional terms was unseamanlike, in plainer language bloody dangerous. Other X-craft COs had made a practice of it: Paul realised that until now he'd just been lucky, had had no worse than moderate weather for his own towing exercises.

Stench of diesel, and wet salt smell from the bilges, a slight odour of disinfectant from the wet-and-dry compartment—known as the W and D—which also contained the heads, or lavatory. Bomber Brazier, the man crouching in there with a vaguely startled expression as the boat threw herself around, was this crew's diver . . . The flooding of the bow tank was already taking some effect, though, leaving her light aft, so the stern had a tendency to float upward; to counter this, Eaton pulled the lever back and shoved it over to port to admit seawater from outside into the midships trim-tank. Sweat gleamed on Eaton's narrow, intelligent face, and Paul was remembering that split-second delay in carrying out his "Flood for'ard" order. If he was given the operational command of this boat, he wouldn't have Dick Eaton on the team. And he would—please God—get the operational command. He couldn't exactly count on it for certain, but—

If the medical gentry had rumbled him? If they knew about the nightmares?

Christ . . . But they couldn't. He'd have been told. At least, given some indication . . .

It was working: the shift of ballast had taken all the viciousness out of her motion. Midget submarine X-12—she was forty-eight feet long (internally, more like thirty-five) and had a maximum internal diameter of five-and-a-half feet—was riding quite comfortably, now. You could feel the tugging surges of the tow, but the weight being permanently on the tow-line was cushioning it, dampening-down the jerking around which only a minute ago had been frightful. The towing ship—in today's exercise it was HM Submarine *Scourge*—was on the surface, and with the sea kicking up as it was this afternoon she'd have a lot of movement on her, which was what imparted that violent upward snatching routine. It would be a lot better when *Scourge* herself dived and got under the surface turbulence.

He thought, touching wood—this end of the storage locker—Oh, not the passage-crew chore . . .

There was a chance he'd draw either passage or operational. Most of his training had been for the operational job, but there was still no certainty about it. Passage crews would man the X-craft for the long haul to the target area, and then operational teams would take over for the actual assault—which was likely to be short, sharp and frightening, but considerably less of an ordeal, Paul thought, than eight days of towing—eight days like this. Three men elbow to elbow, with so little space there was hardly anywhere they could squeeze past each other. Right here amidships, at the CO's position near the periscope, a small man could just stand upright under the dome of the main hatch; but Paul wasn't all that small.

She was towing quite easily still. Eaton had adjusted the trim—her bodily weight in the sea, and her fore-and-aft balance. Balance was easily upset in these midgets: you could move a tin of baked beans from the storage for'ard to the gluepot, which with an electric kettle comprised the boat's cookery equipment, and see an immediate shift of the bubble in the spirit-level . . . But a trim that produced this milder reaction to the rough handling from above still went dead against the grain, against all submarine training and experience and common sense. The reason was that if you ran into trouble when you were heavy in the bow, the boat could go down like a stone before you could do anything to check her.

Ten knots showing on the log. Porpoising a little still, but depth only varying between about fifty-five and sixty-five feet. Eaton was using as little hydroplane-angle as possible, so as to encourage her to settle down. There was a varying list as well as depth, a slight rolling as she gently porpoised. Paul watching points carefully all the time—watching Eaton's work, just a few feet aft in the first lieutenant's position, and Jazz Lanchberry's on the helmsman's seat. Lanchberry stolid, silent, rock-like: and Brazier watching from his crouched position in the W and D.

A sharp buzz and a flashing point of light: Paul grabbed the telephone. "Everard."

"All right down there?"

It was Vallance—captain of *Scourge*. The telephone wire was enclosed in the centre of the tow-line, which was 600 feet long and made of heavy Manilla rope. Nylon rope was infinitely better—stronger and less heavy— but nylon came only from the USA and was hard to get. Whatever the material, each rope had to be specially made, built around the central telephone wire. A few of the other X-craft did have nylon tows, but X-12 was not one of those lucky ones.

She'd jerked hard to starboard. Lanchberry countering with rudder. That would have been a sudden yaw on the part of *Scourge* . . . Paul had staggered, grabbed at an overhead pipe for support: he told Vallance, "Not too good when you do that to us. It was very lively for a while, but easier now I've weighted her for'ard. It's the way your stern tugs at the rope that makes for problems. But we're surviving."

"Good show . . . I'll make the ninety-degree turn to port now—OK?"

"All right."

"Then I'll dive. Putting Scutson on this line now."

"Aye aye, sir." He told the others, "About to turn ninety degrees to port."

A nod from Eaton. Lanchberry lifted a hand, without looking round. He was an ERA, engineroom artificer. He'd steer her round, as he felt the pull developing, and Eaton would watch for the tendency to angle upwards on the swing, resulting from the flow of water sliding in under her forepart. But the weight for'ard might be expected to counter that, on this occasion. Some course and speed alterations were part of the drill for this exercise, and in themselves they presented no problems, but on the new course *Scourge* would be battling directly into wind and sea—wind force four, sea rough. There'd be a lot more movement on her, and it would be inflicted on X-12 too, via the tow-line from that heavily pitching stern. Might need a few more gallons in the for'ard tank . . .

But the weight in the bow was already a danger. If she went out of control for some reason—for instance, if the tow parted—she'd be in a nosedive heading for the sea-bed.

He decided he'd use human ballast instead of liquid. Quicker to shift back in an emergency: and self-propelled, at that . . . "Bomber" Brazier, sub-lieutenant RNVR and X-12's diver, weighed close to 200 pounds, and if Brazier moved from the W and D into the bow compartment where the battery was housed, that considerable weight would be shifted about twelve feet.

Paul warned him that he might be required to transfer for'ard quickly. Brazier raised a thumb the size of a banana. "OK, skipper."

A voice over the telephone announced, "Ten degrees of port wheel on!"

That was the voice of *Scourge's* navigator, Willy Scutson. Paul acknowledged, "All set, Willy."

"Bumpy, is it?"

She'd lurched again. Lanchberry spinning his wheel back, muttering soft curses. Paul told Scutson, "Be easier if you kept your bloody ship still."

In a minute *Scourge* would be headed to sea.

A number of full-sized submarines, S and T class and all of them fitted with the special towing gear, had visited Loch Cairnbawn for exercises like this one and for more elaborate rehearsals as well. Then they'd departed, to continue their natural warlike functions elsewhere. But now the whole group was assembling—eight of them, and each would sail with a midget in tow and a thousand miles to cover. Originally the plan had allowed for only six, and the whole team had trained on X-5, 6, 7, 8, 9 and 10. X-11 and X-12 were recent deliveries, and HM Submarines *Setter* and *Scourge* had been added to increase the towing flotilla equivalently.

X-12 turning now, the Manilla dragging her round. It was becoming a jerky, erratic pull, though. Getting worse ... She was behaving like a hooked fish that had been lying doggo for a while and was now starting a fresh attempt at breaking the line.

"All right, are you? X-12?"

"So far."

He gestured to Brazier, who turned to move for'ard, like a big dog in a small kennel. He was built like a heavyweight wrestler. The W and D was a closet-sized compartment with a hatch in the top of it and flooding and pumping controls inside. The diver, wearing a rubber suit and oxygen mask, could shut its two doors and flood it—by a pump working to and from number two main ballast—then open the hatch and go outside, usually to cut through anti-torpedo nets and let the boat slide through to its target. When she'd passed through, the diver would climb back in, shut the hatch and drain the W and D down again.

Jazz Lanchberry glanced round. "Be all right if it don't get worse, skipper."

Compared to that earlier knocking-about, the motion wasn't too bad—thanks to one displaced body and the shift of ballast. But you could still feel the towline snatching at her as *Scourge*'s stern swung up and down.

"You OK, X-12?"

"No problems at the moment."

"We'll be diving in a minute."

"Roger."

"Thirty feet for five minutes, then sixty. Captain suggests you go to a hundred."

You wouldn't want to be towed right in the larger ship's slipstream. He told Dick Eaton, "She's about to dive. Periscope depth for five minutes, then sixty feet. We'll stay where we are for the time being, then go down to a hundred."

The first lieutenant's position was an aircraft-type seat a few feet aft, set transversely and surrounded by controls for the hydroplanes, main motor and trimming pump. He could even steer from there as well, if the ERA happened to be busy with some other task. Paul told Eaton, "You'll have to be quick to pump as soon as the motion eases. Normal trim quick as we can get it."

"Aye, sir." A sideways jerk of the narrow head. Eaton was dressed in serge battledress trousers and white submarine sweater. Paul was in similar gear except he had on waterproof over-trousers; he'd dumped the waterproof jacket near him. It was very essential protection for riding on top of an X-craft if the sea was anything but dead smooth . . . The telephone warned, "Stand by. Diving." He repeated it to Eaton, who was watching his hydroplane position indicator and the depthgauge and the bubble in the spirit-level—which would be a couple of degrees aft of the centreline, because of the bow-down trim. The hydroplanes—just one pair, right aft behind the single propeller which was now idling, with no power on it, out there in the dark water about twenty feet from where Paul crouched with his backside against the warm casing of the gyro-compass motor—were in effect horizontal rudders. The murmuring, moving sea was all around you—within just inches, this steel cocoon like a bubble in it, held and compressed by its enclosing weight. Paul crouching, peering through the W and D, through the open doors in its two bulkheads, to where Bomber Brazier's hunched body seemed to fill the whole of the bow compartment.

Brazier grinned. "Wotcher, skips."

"*Scourge*'ll be diving now. When I beckon, move back." Brazier nodded. Paul asked the ERA, "OK, Jazz?"

"Lovely grub." Eyes on the gyro repeater inches from his face, hands resting on the wheel. It was like a car's steering wheel, about that size too. There was no other kind of ship in which an engine-room artificer would double as helmsman. But Jasper Lanchberry also had the blowing panel—high-pressure air valves to numbers one and three main ballast, and main vent levers, and the pump for emptying number two main ballast, which was a kingston tank and had no high pressure blow—right at his elbow. Besides which his province was the entire boat, the whole complicated bag of tricks tightly packed into the tiny space.

Paul was edging back into his position amidships, when it happened. Simultaneously with the squawk from the telephone—"Diving!"—a very strong jerk, upwards, at the midget's stem. Then recoil, as the tow-rope slackened and the weight of her bow took charge, forepart slamming down, bow-down angle growing fast and depthgauge needle beginning to swing round its dial: sixty-five feet, seventy, seventy-five, eighty . . . Brazier was heaving his bulk into the W and D: and Eaton had the pump running—the trim-lever pushed right back, aft, switching the pump to suck on the for'ard tank. Too little and too slow, to have any useful effect on the immediate crisis. Paul shouted at Lanchberry over the din of external sea-noise, "Blow number one main ballast!" Then into the telephone as X-12 snouted downward—"Willy?"

Silence.

He'd only been checking, confirming that the tow had parted, the Manilla rope and its wire core snapped. X-12 standing on her nose, and rate of dive increasing—120 feet now, steep and aiming for the sea-bed, which wasn't so far away by this time, maybe 160 feet, or less . . . High pressure air was blasting into the for'ard main ballast tank, though—Lanchberry turning his head to see Brazier emerging on this after side of the W and D bulkhead. Paul ordered, "Shut the shallow gauge." A reminder to Eaton—who'd have done it anyway, since the shallow depthgauge would have bust a gut if it hadn't been shut off pretty soon. But the blowing was taking effect—that, and Brazier's move: she was levelling, and the needle's swing was slowing. Bow finally coming up . . . None too soon, in fact: the sea-bed might be soft here but you might have had the bad luck to find a rock-patch too, and X-12's forty tons of deadweight had been heading for it like a truck driving into a wall.

"Stop blowing. Main motor full ahead, group up."

There'd been nothing to be gained by using the motor while she'd been bow-down; a forward thrust would only have driven her deeper. But now she had her snout up, that screw at full power would combine with the effect of the hydroplanes to push her up.

Eaton had slammed the field-switch shut and turned the hand-wheel clockwise to its full extent. Those main motor controls were sited close to his right hand.

"Motor's full ahead group up, sir."

"Periscope depth." She was acquiring a pronounced bow-up angle now, and the trim-pump was still running. Paul told Lanchberry, "Open number one main vent."

You heard it bang open, and the rush of escaping air. Eaton meanwhile pulling the trim-pump lever back, then pushing it over to starboard, which would start it sucking on the midships tank. It was a four-position lever, a very neatly arranged control; the first part of each movement opened or shut the necessary valves, and the second part started or stopped the pump.

"Back in your hutch, Bomber."

That too would help to level her. Paul realised that his pulse had been racing, that he was slightly breathless. Until now he'd been too busy to know it. Lanchberry muttered, craning round, "Nasty. Highly insalubrious, you might say. *Scourge* must've stuck her arse up like a bleeding duck, and . . ."

"Right." X–12 was quivering under the motor's thrust. Paul told Eaton, "Group down. Half ahead."

It was a lesson learnt, a lesson mostly for *Scourge* and for Vallance her captain, primarily that in anything approaching rough weather he had to take care to dive in slow time when he had a midget in tow. *Scourge* had been head to sea, she'd been diving into a lot of turbulence, and—well, Jazz Lanchberry had summed it up well enough . . . Lanchberry added a minute later, when X–12 was lifting slowly, in excellent control again and not as yet high enough to come into the influence of the waves, "No bloody stopping her, I reckoned. Could've hit the putty, smashed up good an' proper!"

"Still had about forty feet under us when we checked her, Jazz."

The ERA's head turned. Crewcut dark head, blue-black jaw, a derisive slant to the thin, wide mouth. Paul added, pressing the "rise" button of the periscope and watching as the tube slid up to its full nine-foot extension, "Thirty, anyway."

Lanchberry let out a snort of amusement, and winked at Brazier. Brazier's head poking out of the W and D like a tortoise's from its shell. Eaton reported, "Periscope depth, sir."

Eaton was a fairly new sub-lieutenant, and he used the word "sir" a lot. Ordinary, full-sized submarines were less formal than surface ships—no less well disciplined, but not as pompous about it—and X-craft crews were slightly more relaxed still. More socially relaxed than *Scourge,* for instance, could afford to be. Paul didn't want to embarrass Eaton, and he hadn't said anything about it yet; left to himself, he'd catch on, soon enough. Paul had his eye at the periscope, scanning grey-green wave slopes. "Bring her up to eight feet, Dick." Nine feet was all right in flat conditions, in harbour conditions, fjord conditions such as they'd expect to have on this operation. In truly smooth water you'd only need an inch of glass showing above it. Now he needed an extra foot or so, to see over the waves. No higher than necessary, because the shallower you were the more you got slammed around, but he did need to see where *Scourge* was before he surfaced.

Shortly after that, passing a new tow, he'd be getting very, very wet, despite the waterproof suit.

Lanchberry muttered as he turned back to his wheel and gyro display, "I dunno . . ."

Referring, presumably, to Paul's equanamity over X-12's recent dash towards the sea-bed. But it truly hadn't worried him. The accident had been foreseeable, and he'd accepted the risk of it when he'd told Eaton to shift the weight for'ard. Then it had happened, and he'd been ready for it and dealt with it, with no more hesitation than a man driving fast on a wet road would have in reacting to the beginning of a skid. Afterwards, there was time to be scared.

And for dreams. The nightmares were bastards. He'd never suffered from anything of the sort before: and they did, frankly, worry him. It was the suspicion that they had to mean something, that there could be a canker of fear inside you. The theory of "no smoke without fire," and dread that some day it might show itself—in waking hours.

Bloody silly. He'd been a submariner long enough to know he didn't have even the slightest tinge of claustrophobia. The nightmares recurred, he told himself, only because he allowed himself to think about them. It was tantamount to inviting them back. And if people got to know about it—in view of the strict medical and psychiatric supervision of all the X-craft personnel—well, if the medical department realised it, he'd be out of this operation like a dose of salts!

He told himself, Forget it.

That was the one good answer. The basis of the worry was that old spectre, fear of fear. You could only beat it by ignoring it.

Jane knew. Since the night he'd woken screaming in her arms . . .

Scourge had just surfaced, emerging streaming from the suds a couple of hundred yards away, her stern towards X-12's periscope—which was about as thick as a walking stick. A sharp underwater thud, followed by two more, was Vallance's three-grenade signal telling Paul to come on up. Vallance was no doubt anxious, scared that X-12 might not be capable of coming on up . . . Paul pressed the other periscope-control button—they were both enclosed in a rubber bag on the end of a wandering lead, and you had to select the right one by feel—and sent the tube sliding down.

"Stand by to surface."

She was rolling now, feeling the waves. And there was a very strenuous and uncomfortable half hour or so to come, getting a new tow passed and secured. All good practice, because it could become necessary on the way to the target area too. When the balloon went up, the eight midgets would be setting off with their towing ships on the surface and themselves at forty or fifty feet, but closer to the target area—which was in the Arctic Circle— the whole outfit would duck out of sight. Closer still, the tows would be slipped and the X-craft would go in under their own power.

A thousand miles of underwater tow was an astonishing thing to contemplate. You just had to accept the fact you were going to do it. Then, penetrate nets, defended anchorages . . .

Plugging in towards Loch Cairnbawn four hours later, following *Scourge* but no longer in tow from her, X-12 was more in the waves than on them. Paul, standing on his boat's flat top—the midgets had no conning towers—stood upright, swaying and bending to the rise and fall, with one arm wrapped around the raised induction trunk. The trunk was a man-high pipe that hinged at deck level and when raised acted as a conduit of air for the diesel engine intake, also as the communication link between himself up here and the dry, warmer people down inside. The hatch was shut: it had to be, or the boat would have filled, since the sea was sluicing right over her, swirling around Paul's legs. All that mattered was that the top of the pipe was clear. Diesel pounding throatily, exhaust spluttering through the froth astern, fumes unpleasant on the following wind. The engine was a four-cylinder, forty horsepower Gardner diesel, the same one that drove London buses.

Any crofter on that headland, as X-12 approached the entrance to the loch, would either have sworn to give up the malt or rushed straight home for a restorative dram. All he'd have seen, with the midget's low, flat top hidden in the waves, would have been a man not only walking on the water but gliding over it at a smart 10 knots . . . Not, in fact, that there could have been any bemused shepherd to have seen it. Security was tight, Loch Cairnbawn and its surroundings a restricted area. Precautions had been intensive right from the start, but from the first day of this month—September of 1943—the clamp-down had become total. No leave was being granted, no private telephone calls were allowed, and no mail was being taken ashore. You could write your love-letters but they wouldn't be posted—for a while.

So Jane could write—he'd had a letter from her only yesterday—but she wouldn't be hearing from him. He'd warned her it would happen, that for a certain period he'd be incommunicado . . .

"How long?"

"Absolutely not the faintest."

She'd frowned. "That's exactly what Louis said."

Louis being the man—Louis himself believed—who really counted in her life.

"What is it all about, Paul?"

She didn't know anything at all about the X-craft, didn't even know such things existed. Only a small handful of people did know any-thing—that they'd been designed for breaking into enemy harbours and anchorages, destroying major warships that couldn't be got at any other way. For a long time Paul and his friends hadn't known in any detail what their objective was to be: there'd been guesses and assumptions, but no certainty. They knew they'd been training for one specific operation, and that it had originally scheduled for March, then postponed for six months.

Training had continued: and now they all knew that their primary target was the *Tirpitz*—43,000 tons, 800 feet long, ten decks deep, clad in armour plating fifteen inches thick, carrying a devastating punch and currently lurking—with *Scharnhorst* and *Lützow* and a big pack of destroyers—in a deep fjord in the remote north of Norway, out of range of bombing or any other kind of attack.

Except by midget submarines—if they could gatecrash the anchorage. One part of her that was not armoured was her belly: and this was where you'd hit her. But—a thousand miles away, and in a narrow fjord approachable only through other narrow fjords, guarded by minefields, steel nets, acoustic detection gear, patrol craft, shore guns and probably fixed torpedo batteries.

Paul's father, Nick Everard, had asked him—in a London restaurant, about eight weeks ago—"What are you up to now? You're not standing-by *Ultra* in her refit, are you?"

Ultra was the submarine Paul had served in, in the Malta flotilla. She'd been near-missed by a bomb off Sfax on the Tunisian coast last November, a fortnight after the "Torch" landings, and she'd been sent back to the UK for major refit. In the week that she'd reached the Clyde there'd been an invitation to junior submarine officers to volunteer for "special and hazardous duty," and having no idea what his next job might be, Paul had rather casually put his name in. At about the same time his promotion to lieutenant had come through.

He'd answered that question of his father's, "No, I'm in—another flotilla, up there." He'd hesitated. The secrecy surrounding the X-craft had a capital S on it: the message had been driven home a dozen times, secrecy was total. So, even when you were talking to Captain Sir Nicholas Everard, Bart., DSO★★★ DSC★ RN . . . An older, heavier version of himself, gazing quizzically at him across the table. Paul had mumbled in some embarrassment, "Careless Talk—all that stuff?"

Kate, Nick's new Australian wife, had laughed. Nick told her, "But he's right. In fact I shouldn't have asked, in a public place like this."

"My, can't we be stuffy!"

She'd said it to Paul, teasing Nick. Paul shook his head. "I never thought so." Hesitating again: "In fact, all things considered"—he'd glanced at his father's medal ribbons—"I'd say rather amazingly unstuffy."

"And bully for you." Kate's hand patted Paul's, on the white tablecloth. "I quite like him too, would you believe it?"

Kate was very attractive, Paul thought. His father had told him in a letter ages ago that she had a look of Ingrid Bergman, and it was a fact, the resemblance was striking. Paul remarked on it, and saw that she liked it; he liked her . . . It had been a happy lunch, with an air of celebration about it—despite a certain background tension—and there was reason for celebration, too. Earlier, walking to the restaurant through a light summer drizzle, he'd asked his father whether he was on leave now.

"No. Just playing truant." Nick had told him, "They've given me a cruiser. She's finishing a bottom-scrape at Chatham, and I've dragged Kate down here just for a couple of days. From my point of view it's a bit of a pierhead jump. The ship's *Calliope*—*Dido* class."

"Well, congratulations!"

Kate said, "Wait till you hear the rest of it."

"It's supposed to be a temporary appointment only." Nick explained, "I'm really just filling in. Hence the short notice, etcetera. The fact is—look, this is a secret now—"

"OK"

His father drew a breath. "It suits Their Lordships to keep me busy for a few months, because after that I'm in line for a cruiser squadron. Taking it east."

"Squadron . . ." Paul did a quick double-take. "My God, you mean—"

Kate nodded proudly. "Promotion."

"Rear-Admiral?"

"Isn't it incredible?"

Kate objected, "Not in the least!" They all laughed. Paul began, "Well, double those congratulations. And I agree, Kate, it's not at all—"

"But it is." Nick Everard shrugged. "Hasn't happened yet, anyway—I'll believe it when it does. But considering I left the service between the wars—with consequent loss of seniority, plus the fact Their Lordships never entirely forgive a man for walking out on them . . ."

"Obviously you've made up for it."

"More than made up for it." Kate had broken in. "Exactly what I've been telling him. It's time they let him take a rest!"

Her eyes were on Nick, and she meant it. Paul was surprised. A moment ago she'd been proud of Nick's achievement, and now she'd have rather seen him shunted into some desk job?

Nick told him, "Kate has some loony idea about my luck running out."

"Oh. Well . . ."

"Don't you agree he's been through enough, Paul?"

He nodded. "I couldn't disagree with that. On the other hand I can't imagine him putting his feet up. Even if they'd let him." He could see she was seriously concerned; he tried to make light of it. "Anyway, cats have nine lives, Kate."

"Miaow," Paul's father said. "He's right. I'm a survivor. Case-hardened. Believe me, I have more reason now to stay alive than I ever had before. Another thing—very few flag officers get drowned. So really all I have to do is last out the next few months, and I'm home and dry." He too, Paul realised, was trying to allay Kate's fears by sounding as if he didn't take them seriously. Then explaining—by way of changing the subject: "But the delay, Paul—this is the secret you have to keep—is because there's a plan to send a contingent of ships to join the Yanks and Aussies in the Pacific. We can't do it right away, partly because we have to keep powerful forces up north—in Scapa and so on—to guard against any break-out by the *Tirpitz* and others into the Atlantic. Presumably there's some expectation of eliminating that threat before long. Don't ask me how . . ."

Paul hadn't enlightened him, although he had a pretty good idea of at least one answer. It was intriguing how the various factors meshed, forming a cohesive and logical pattern which had a surprising simplicity to it. Destroy the *Tirpitz* and you'd free major fleet units which could then be sent to the other side of the world to add their weight to a different struggle against another enemy. In the same blow you'd be removing the major threat to the Arctic convoys—which were vital to the whole strategy of the war—and to the transatlantic supply routes; and the trick would have been pulled by a handful of submersible bathtubs manned by young amateurs like Paul Everard . . .

He shouted down the induction pipe, "Starboard ten!"

Loch Cairnbawn's afforested northern slopes loomed to port against grey sky. Entering sheltered water, at last. Ahead, farther up, lay the cluster of moored ships which included the X-craft depot ship *Bonaventure* and the other one, the old *Titania,* who'd arrived more recently to mother the towing submarines. Around them, dotted about in the rippling grey water of the loch, were smaller ships of various shapes and sizes, the rest of the Twelfth Flotilla's entourage.

"Midships!"

The quiet, mist-shrouded scene was fascinating—when you knew what it was for, how carefully the secret had been guarded and what a far-reaching effect the operation's success would have.

CHAPTER TWO

·   ·   ·

From Norway Pilot, Volume III:

> Altenfjord. General Remarks. Altenfjord is entered between
> Klubbenes (70 12′ N, 22 58′ E) and Korsnes light-structure
> about 4? miles eastward; together with Kafjord and Rafsbotn,
> its continuations, it is the largest fjord in the western part of
> Finmark and indents the mainland for about 17 miles . . . The
> shores are irregular, forming several large bays and small inlets
> . . . Altenfjord is accessible for large vessels.

Even for the largest afloat, for a 43,000-ton battleship . . . Which had put
to sea—slipped out and vanished, during the dark hours!

The man on the church tower stared for a few more seconds through
his binoculars. Focussing on Kafjord, the main waterway's southwestern
extremity and innermost recess. It was barely daylight yet—dawn came at
about 0200 here, at this time of year—and visibility was tricky, but of one
thing there was no doubt: where yesterday at dusk the *Tirpitz*'s great bulk
had lain at rest in the flat, reflective water, now there was nothing except
a rectangular enclosure of buoys supporting steel anti-torpedo nets. The
monster was no longer in her lair.

One floating object which the observer could make out was an anchored battle-practice target; and against the far shore he could distinguish
the shapes of a lighter and a tug at the landing place just north of the
empty nets. If *Lützow* was still in her berth she wouldn't have been visible
from here in any case, since her box of nets was hidden by a spur of land
on the inlet's southern side.

Pushing the glasses inside his coat, the Norwegian turned away, hur-
ried to the belfry stairs and down them spiralling to street level. Emerging,

he crossed the churchyard and turned right into the street: then stopped abruptly, drew back into the shadow . . .

A blacked-out saloon came racing. Brakes squealed as it juddered to a halt. His mind racing too, providing answers to questions he'd be faced with now: what he was doing in the street at this hour, where he'd been, where he was going, what for . . .

He told himself, Calm down, now. There's no problem . . . A visit to the church: a private prayer. Even a German would accept that—he hoped—as damn-all to do with the Master Race . . . The car halted just across from where he stood motionless with his back against the grey stone wall, rigidly defensive. Then he saw the face at the window as the driver wound it down and peered out at him: his breath fogged the air in a whoosh of relief.

"I'll be damned. That old bus of yours looked like a Mercedes Benz, for Christ's sake! It's the light, I suppose." He was at the car, stooping to the window. "What if you're caught on the road at this hour?"

"I had a job. Official. Little diversion here, is all . . . You got the message, eh?"

The driver's home was on the shore of Kafjord, he ran this old banger as a taxi and regularly drove *Tirpitz* officers into and out of town—this town being Alta, at the south end of the main fjord. The other man asked him. "Where's she gone?"

"God knows. All I know is what I see. Or rather, don't see. But your question should be where have they gone."

"The others too?"

"*Lützow*'s still here, but *Scharnhorst*'s out and so are ten destroyers."

"How do we know that? *Scharnhorst,* I mean?"

The 26,000-ton *Scharnhorst*'s berth was in Langefjord, ten miles away. The driver said, "Young Wielding Christoffersen. He was crewing in the Ellefsens' boat. Played truant yesterday—his mother's furious, but—"

"He's a fine kid. But he'd better be damn careful . . . Listen, does Torstein know?"

A nod. "Just left him. He'll be putting the news out—right away, not waiting for the routine time."

"Dangerous."

"Well. It's an emergency, if ever there was . . ."

"Funny we didn't get even a whisper of this in advance, isn't it?"

"Last-minute orders, maybe. A convoy at sea, or something. The girls surely didn't know a thing, they were on their way down to the landing-stage before they realised."

By "the girls" he meant some local women whom the Germans employed on board their battleships as cleaners and cooks. They made sure of hearing whatever was being said, they read every notice that was pinned to the bulletin boards, and whatever they picked up went off to London over clandestine radio the same night. The wireless was operated by the man these two had referred to as "Torstein." A couple of years ago the Gestapo had been getting close to him and his underground activities, and he'd escaped to Sweden and from there to London, where he'd been trained, equipped and sent back. Now he lived in Alta and had a job in the Highways Department; he'd set up his transmitter in that building, linking it before each transmission to a German officer's private receiving aerial. His sources of information included the taxi-driver and the women workers, and also some crew members of boats which supplied *Tirpitz* with fresh provisions. The bits and pieces, when they were strung together, added up to a substantial flow of valuable intelligence, and in recent months London had absorbed every single item and still begged for more. Even the smallest detail of shipboard routine in the German squadron seemed to be of profound interest to the British.

He straightened from the taxi's window. There'd be a Bosch patrol along at any minute, and there was no point in hanging around now.

"See you this evening?"

"Yup." A gloved hand lifted. "Maybe we'll have had news."

"Only that single fact, sir—that *Tirpitz* and *Scharnhorst* have sailed from Altenfjord."

Mid-forenoon in the Admiralty building in London. The news from Norway, a very unusual daytime transmission, had compelled the man at the table to switch his mind from the Italian surrender—news of which hadn't been generally released yet—and the imminent landings at Salerno, codenamed "Avalanche," to events in the cold north.

"PQ 19 is now—where, precisely?"

"Here, sir. Best estimate—not precise."

An arm with a mere three stripes on it had stretched to tap the chart with a pencil. The position of convoy PQ 19 was marked, and so was another to the west of it. This was only an updating brief before the man sitting at the table joined the team on duty in the Operations Room; before he got in there he wanted to be au fait, have his own perspective as clear as his subordinates' would be.

Clearer. Because the picture he'd have in mind would be much broader.

The commander cleared his throat. "That's if the convoy's up to schedule, sir. And this is the position—again, only estimated—of the fighting escort. They'll be altering course from north to north-east about now, to overhaul the convoy before dark."

"We had reason to discount the possibility of any surface attack on this convoy on its way north, did we not?"

"That's so, sir."

It had been a very convincing intelligence appreciation, asserting that there'd been a decision at the highest level—meaning Adolf Hitler and Admiral Dönitz—that the German surface units based in northern Norway would only be used against southbound convoys—meaning against Arctic convoys on their way back to Iceland and the United Kingdom.

"So the escort's somewhat light. And those cruisers are too far away to be any use to us if *Tirpitz* is steering directly to intercept. It would be rather too much of a coincidence that she'd have sailed at this juncture for any other purpose, so—well, I suppose we have to expect the worst . . ." Impassive: like a man studying a chess-board. "Battle squadron still in Akureyri, of course."

"They're raising steam, sir. C-in-C Home Fleet's signal—"

"But screened only by Hunts."

To provide a fighting escort of fleet destroyers, at the same time as a climactic battle on the North Atlantic convoy routes was drawing every small ship that could be whipped in—as well as all available escort carriers—the Home Fleet's battle squadron at Akureyri in north Iceland had been robbed of its escort of fleet destroyers and provided with a temporary screen of the smaller, short-range Hunt class. This imposed drastic limitations on the movements of the big ships: effectively they could only operate to the west of Jan Mayen Island, which meant that in support of the Archangel-bound convoy they could hardly be seen as anything but a very long-range bluff.

On the other hand if this was subterfuge, if the enemy were only using PQ 19 as an excuse for putting to sea, with the real intention of making a dash out into the Atlantic and joining in the convoy battle—well, the British battle squadron would be well-placed west of Jan Mayen.

"We've had no sighting reports at all—from aircraft, submarines, anyone. We haven't any clues at all, no idea what they're up to."

It had sounded like a statement, but the upward flicker of the man's blue eyes made it a question.

"No clues at all, sir," the commander added, "and visibility up there is bad. Sleet-showers, and fog on the ice-barrier."

That last piece of information would have come from the Norwegian weather station on Spitzbergen, relayed via the W/T station at Seidisfjord in Iceland. Wireless links were far from reliable in those latitudes ... The man at the table was silent, deep in thought as he leant over the chart. He asked, finally, "Has Admiral Barry been told his birds have flown?"

"Indeed he has, sir."

Rear-Admiral Barry was Flag Officer, Submarines. His target date for an attack on the *Tirpitz* by midget submarines was 20 September. One might guess that the enemy ships would be back in Altenfjord by then, but until their return could be positively confirmed Operation Source and almost a year's training and preparation were in the balance.

But here and now, that was a side issue. The immediate concern had to be for the convoy.

"Would you consider turning them back, sir?"

PQ 19 was already 250 miles north-northeast of Iceland. So any German ships looking for it could just as easily be to the south of it as anywhere else. Turning it back, therefore, might amount to turning it into danger. It was only a small convoy, northbound, the main object of the operation being to bring back merchantmen who'd been marooned up there all through the summer; the "empties" were badly needed, in view of a general shortage of shipping as well as Churchill's promise to Stalin of regular Murmansk runs during the winter months. In fact there was a slight complication just at this moment—a Churchill-Stalin row brewing; and the nights weren't yet long enough for operations in those northern waters. The go-ahead had been given despite these factors, and the timing was planned so that the southbound convoy would sail from North Russia after the X-craft operation should have eliminated *Tirpitz* as a danger to it.

Further considerations in the mind of the man at the table were one, that the First Sea Lord, Admiral Sir Dudley Pound, attending the "Quadrant" conference in Quebec at which Churchill and Roosevelt were approving outline plans for an invasion of the European mainland next year, had suffered a stroke and was returning to England as an invalid. You had a feeling of vacuum at the top, a sense of flying blind . . . And two, that convoy PQ 17, which had been thought to be under threat of surface attack very much as PQ 19 seemed to be now, had been thrown to the wolves as the result of a panic decision here in London. One of the lessons of that tragic episode was that tactical decisions should be taken by the commander on the spot, not by "chair-borne warriors" hundreds of miles away.

"Who's commanding this fighting escort?"

"Captain Sir Nicholas Everard, sir. In . . ."

"*Calliope.* Yes, of course . . ."

Motionless, gazing at the chart, like a clairvoyant staring into a crystal ball.

Calliope, at twenty-two knots, plunged and swayed over the long following swell. A string of flags at her yardarm whipped multicoloured in grey, cold air over a sea that was grey-green slashed with white where the ships' hulls carved and split it. Nick Everard, on his high seat in the starboard for'ard corner of the bridge, had a pipe in his mouth and binoculars intermittently at his eyes, examining the surrounding wilderness of grey Norwegian Sea enclosed by an horizon that was hazy at best and in the north obscured by what looked like cotton-wool. At this moment, though, his attention was on the screening destroyers, ahead and on both bows—low, thrashing hulls with white bow-waves curling, mounds of foam boiling under their pitching sterns. At each of the five destroyers' yards now a blue and white Answering Pendant had been hauled close-up, indicating that *Calliope*'s flag signal had been read and understood.

Moloch dead ahead, *Laureate* and *Legend* to starboard, *Leopard* and *Lyric* on the other bow. *Moloch*'s captain, the senior destroyer officer, was Tommy Trench; he'd been Nick's first lieutenant in *Intent* in 1940, when they'd survived a fairly hair-raising adventure in the Norwegian fjords and wound up by taking a hand in the second battle of Narvik. Trench was now a commander, with a DSO as well as the DSC he'd won in *Intent*.

"Captain, sir?"

The short, pink-faced character at Nick's elbow was Instructor Lieutenant "Happy" Bliss. A sheet of signal-pad—it was about the shade of pink to match the schoolmaster's complexion, thus indicating secrecy, a cypher as opposed to an ordinary, unclassified signal—flapped in his hand, and he seemed to be flapping too. But whatever was so exciting would have to wait a minute: Nick swung round to tell the navigator, Bruce Christie, "Executive."

"Haul down!"

The signals yeoman of the watch yelled the order to his minions on the flag deck, the hoist bellied outward on the wind as it came tumbling down, and at the same time the officer of the watch ordered *Calliope*'s wheel over to starboard. The hauling-down of the flags signalled the order to act on their message, and destroyers were racing—one ahead and two to port, while the other two cut their speed and angled outward—to take up positions that would leave them in proper station when the squadron steadied on its new course.

Calliope heeled to the turn as her rudder gripped the sea and hauled her round. Nick turned to the schoolmaster. "Now, then."

"Secret Immediate, sir, from Admiralty!"

Bliss's excitement was slightly irritating. Behind him the officer of the watch—Halcrow—ordered, "Midships . . ."

SECRET IMMEDIATE

FROM: Admiralty

TO: AIG311

SBNO N. Russia

Tirpitz and *Scharnhorst* reported to have sailed from Altenfjord with 10 destroyers approximately midnight. No indications of intentions or present position yet available.

Glancing at a three-quarter profile of *Laureate* sheeted in foam as she raced to adjust her station, the first reaction in his thoughts was, We're for it, then . . . Then eyes down again, rereading, and noticing from the signal's time-of-origin that it had been drafted nearly two hours ago. The next reaction was to ask, What help can I count on?—and the quick and easy answer was, None at all—you're on your own. Because surface attack had been virtually ruled out of the likely contingencies, and consequently the battle squadron temporarily based on Akureyri wouldn't be able to play any part at all in whatever was about to happen. The German force—according to this signal—had been at sea since last night, and Akureyri was nearly 300 miles astern; in any case those Home Fleet battle-wagons' range was strictly limited by their lack of a fleet destroyer screen. The distance-and-time factor also applied to Rear-Admiral Kidd's close-support cruiser squadron. It was a safe bet that C-in-C Home Fleet, from his flagship in Scapa Flow, would be ordering Kidd out of Akureyri at about this moment; and as the cruisers would already have had steam up, they wouldn't take long to put to sea. But they wouldn't be of much use either, if the *Tirpitz* and *Scharnhorst* were steaming directly to intercept the convoy.

Turn the convoy back?

He nodded to Bliss—who with Marcus Plumb, the chaplain, had the job of cyphering and decyphering all secret signals.

"Don't tell us much, do they." He was talking to himself as much as to the schoolmaster. "Ask the commander to join me in the chartroom, will you?"

"Aye aye, sir!"

But Bliss, poor fellow, seemed disappointed—no doubt at his captain's impassive acceptance of the dramatic news. It was dramatic, too: *Tirpitz,* sister to the late and unlamented *Bismarck,* was the most powerful fighting ship afloat in the Atlantic Ocean, and at close quarters with a lightly defended convoy she'd be like a great white shark in a school of mackerel. Bliss would be looking for a more electric reaction now from Commander Treseder . . . Nick, on his way to the rear end of the forebridge, saw that his ship had been steadied on her new course—064 degrees, up the convoy's track so as to overtake it from astern—and that all five destroyers were in station. Trench had a well-drilled team, there. He told Bruce Christie, his navigator, "I'll need you too, pilot." He rattled down the port-side ladder: one level down, he slid back the chartroom door. There was a chart-table at the back of the bridge too, but with no chance of sighting land for several days now they weren't using it.

Christie had followed him down. Nick passed him the signal.

"*Tirpitz* and *Scharnhorst* putting in some sea-time."

He saw the navigator's slow blink. Christie was a tall man, long-chinned and with deep-set, pale eyes. A Scot, and a mad-keen fisherman. Studying the message with one bushy eyebrow cocked, and no doubt resisting, Nick guessed—he was doing the same himself—an initial impression that massacre might be imminent. Taking this report at face value, assuming the worst . . . But as far as Nick had been able to assess his navigating lieutenant in a comparatively short acquaintance, he had him down for one who was as quick-thinking as he was calm and slow-moving. Thumb-nail sketch of the perfect dry-fly man?

Nick's pierhead jump into this command had landed him among a host of strangers. He thought he knew Christie reasonably well by this time, and a few others, but the great majority of his officers and ship's company were only faces to which one had constantly to make the effort to pin names.

"Want me, sir?"

Jim Treseder, *Calliope's* second-in-command, wasn't tall, but he was broad enough to have to turn sideways to pass through the narrow door-way. Duffle-coated, and with his legs straddled for balance against the ship's pitch and roll, short arms akimbo and his eyes on the pink sheet of signal-pad . . . "Something about *Tirpitz* being out?"

Christie handed him the signal. Nick bent over the chart, reaching for dividers and parallel rule. With no hard facts or even indications, the only way to approach this was to accept possibilities at their worst—assume the German battle group was informed of the convoy's position and steaming to intercept, that it had been steaming to intercept ever since putting out of Altenfjord.

In which case the prospects were—well, inauspicious . . .

Plotting it. Hearing Treseder mutter to Christie that after months of harbour time, with any luck the Huns would be as sick as dogs . . . Nick said, seeing one result in advance, "They could get to the convoy before we do."

Conceivably the two battleships and their powerful escort could inter-cept PQ 19—approaching it from ESE, its starboard bow—by about 1800 this evening. The convoy had its own close escort with it, of course, but that consisted only of two rather old destroyers, four minesweepers, an AA ship and a pair of trawlers. *Calliope* and her six fleet destroyers weren't ex-pecting to overhaul the convoy until about the same time. This of course could be adjusted easily enough by an increase in speed . . . He worked it out: increasing from twenty-two knots to twenty-eight would advance the rendezvous time by three hours.

Bruce Christie's mind was operating on the same wavelength. He sug-gested, "Come up to about thirty knots, sir?"

"Something like that. But wait a minute."

You had to think beyond it, first. For instance, whether to change the convoy's route now, signal the close-escort commander to swing the whole circus northward, steer them closer to the ice. Or even to reverse the convoy's course, bringing them back into the protection of this stronger escort more quickly. But doing either of these things would involve break-ing wireless silence—which would give away this squadron's position and perhaps also provide an indication of the convoy's, which might not yet be known to the enemy.

Guesswork was about all one had to go by: the Germans could only intercept PQ 19 this evening if (a) they already knew the convoy's position, course and speed, and (b) had steered the appropriate interception course directly and all the way from Altenfjord at no less than thirty knots. On several counts this seemed unlikely. First, there'd been no sign of the convoy's having been reported either by U-boat or long-range aircraft. PQ 19 had sailed from Loch Ewe in northwest Scotland, instead of from Seidisfjord on the east coast of Iceland which was the more usual assembly point, primarily to reduce the chances of being spotted early on—enemy reconnaissance had been concentrated on the Icelandic east coast area. *Calliope* and Trench's destroyers had set out later from Akureyri, in north Iceland, steering to pass west and north of Jan Mayen Island—which now lay about forty miles to starboard as the force pushed northeastward to catch up with the convoy . . . But second, one might question the German squadron's ability to maintain high speed for such a length of time. *Tirpitz* would be capable of thirty knots, according to latest information, but the 26,000-ton *Scharnhorst's* best speed had been estimated as twenty-eight. Another part of the equation was the known fact that German surface ships were hamstrung by an acute shortage of oil-fuel, and this cast doubt on whether those two monsters, with their huge consumption of fuel, would be allowed to burn up so much of it.

Particularly when one saw—as Nick did now, startled by the simplicity of it and annoyed with himself for not having seen it before—that they didn't need to!

Because if they knew the convoy's position, course and speed they'd also know it could only be making for North Russia. So by steaming north from Altenfjord at economical revs they'd only have to cover about half the distance in order to intercept it east of Bear Island, inside the Barents Sea, a day later. Saving fuel, and staying much closer to their base. It was so obvious—and as good as certain they wouldn't have come steaming out northwestward. So there was no need to break W/T silence, or slow the convoy's progress by diverting it. Not at this stage, anyway. In the longer term, by the time the surface threat could be close at hand, Admiral Kidd and his cruisers could be close, too.

Nick straightened from the chart.

"Revs for twenty-eight knots, pilot. Go up and see to it. It should bring us up to the convoy at about 1700. Before that we'll shift to line-abreast and . . ." he shrugged . . . "trust to luck."

Slight frown on Christie's hawkish face. Navigators didn't believe in trusting to luck—or at least, to admitting they sometimes had to. In point of fact there'd be a considerable element of chance in making this rendez-vous, however well he'd done his sums. There'd been a spell of foul weather further south, and no opportunities for sextant fixes, starsights or sunsights. Nor had there been any position reports exchanged, because of the need for strict W/T silence and the hope of slipping through undetected. On top of these factors was the overriding one that navigation in these northern reaches was never as accurate as you'd have liked it to be.

The door slid shut behind Christie. Nick looked at Treseder.

"Something bothering you?"

"Well, sir," a snort of humour, "*Tirpitz's* fifteen-inch guns do bother me, a little. And *Scharnhorst's*—what, eleven-inch?"

Nick thought, looking at him, that Treseder knew damn well what calibre of gun the *Scharnhorst* sported. The commander added, "And ten destroyers, with five point nines? Even they out-gun us!"

He was right. The Narvik-class destroyers were more like light cruisers in terms of armament. *Calliope's* guns were 5.25s.

"So what's your conclusion?"

"Well, sir," Treseder looked uncomfortable, "if they're out looking for us, and we hold on as we are . . ."

Nick sighed, turned away. He said quietly, "*Tirpitz* isn't within 300 miles of us, Jim."

"H'm . . ."

Puzzled; and hoping for an explanation. Nick let it ride. He believed totally in his assessment, and Treseder hadn't bothered to work it out. So—leave it at that, be proved right, and next time one might hope for this man's trust.

Trickery? Perhaps it was. But expertise in any field might be described as an amalgam of tricks, and leadership didn't have to be any exception. Nick was aware of his newness to this job, and that it was in the ship's best interests as much as his own that her officers and men should have confidence in him.

"But incidentally . . . You're right—if those destroyers are Narvik-class, they out-gun us. And compared to *Scharnhorst*, let alone *Tirpitz*, we're a sprat . . . But off Sirte in March last year—just bear this in mind, as a point of reference—Philip Vian had three ships of the same class as this one to defend a Malta convoy, and he drove off the battleship *Littorio*, three heavy cruisers and eight destroyers!"

"Yes." Treseder nodded. "Italians, though."

He had a point. But Germans, too, tended not to put their big ships at risk if it was possible to avoid doing so. And half the value of actions like that one of Admiral Vian's was that it demonstrated to others what could be achieved by the resolute handling of a small force against less resolute larger ones.

Whistling in the dark?

On his way back to the forebridge, a new thought kindled. It was a question: if his analysis of enemy movements was correct, why should they have sailed from Altenfjord thirty hours earlier than they need have? When (a) they were safer in those heavily-protected anchorages, (b) all the time they were at sea they were burning oil, and (c) by putting out so early they were giving advance notice of intention to attack?

It didn't make sense.

Able Seaman Tomblin, Nick's servant, asked him, "Be taking your dinner up 'ere, sir, will you?"

"Yes, please. But I only want a snack. Tell Parker, will you."

"Corned dog an' beans, sir?"

Parker was his PO steward, and Tomblin was a three-badger, a seaman with three chevrons on his arm indicating that he'd completed at least twelve years' service. He was a man of about Nick's own height, with a seamed, weathered face and slitted grey eyes. One of a particular species, quite distinct from the type who rose to Petty Officer and then Chief PO and eventually Warrant Officer. The Tomblins of the Royal Navy were unpromotable because they'd have regarded any suggestion of promotion as insulting.

"I'll have coffee with it, please."

The watch had changed. It was Ferrimore at the binnacle now instead of Halcrow. Ferrimore was an RN sub-lieutenant: tall, fair and in the process of growing a beard. Crossing the bridge towards his high chair, Nick thought it must be about ten days since the boy had requested "permission to grow." If the fuzz didn't shape up pretty soon, he'd be told to shave it off. He got up on the seat and put the strap of the binoculars over his head. There was one logical answer to that question of the premature sailing of the enemy battle group: that they'd put to sea for some purpose that had nothing at all to do with this convoy operation. Only one such purpose came to mind—a break-out into the Atlantic.

"Captain, sir. Another signal."

Bliss seemed to have control of his excitement this time.

"Let's have a look."

Again the prefix was SECRET IMMEDIATE. But it was from CS 39, to the same addressees as the previous one. CS 39 meant 39th Cruiser Squadron, which consisted of *Nottingham*—flying the flag of Rear-Admiral Kidd—*Rhodesia* and *Minotaur.* Kidd was informing all concerned that his squadron had cleared Akureyri and was steering 055 degrees at thirty-two knots.

"Cavalry to the rescue, Schooly."

"Sir?"

Bliss was a rather humourless young man, Nick thought. He reread the signal. It had been originated only twenty-eight minutes earlier, and he guessed it would have been transmitted from the shore W/T station at Akureyri after the cruisers had sailed. Kidd wouldn't have broken radio silence from sea. In present circumstances none of the participants in this game of hide-and-seek would let out a single peep unless an enemy was already in contact—air, surface or subsurface—in which case there'd be nothing to lose, with the cat out of the bag already. When it happened, you'd transmit all the signals you'd been holding back.

"Pilot." Christie approached, and Nick gave him the signal. "CS thirty-nine's cutting the corner to the south of us. Put it on the chart, will you."

He could visualise it—courses, relative bearings and distances—roughly, but well enough. If the cruiser admiral stuck to his present course and speed he'd most likely be something like a hundred miles south of the convoy by breakfast time tomorrow. A "close-support" cruiser force, in this kind of set-up, wasn't supposed to stay in sight of the convoy it was protecting; convoys attracted air and submarine attack, and the cruisers' function was to ward off surface interference, not to get themselves bombed or torpedoed. Kidd's aim would be to put himself between the convoy and the attackers, but with nothing yet to tell him which direction an attack might come from he'd be keeping his options open. And meanwhile—this new truth struck suddenly—if he held on as he was steering now he'd be taking his ships well into the range of bomber-strikes from the enemy airfields in north Norway.

So, he wouldn't. He'd make as much distance east as he could by dusk tonight, then turn up northwards to put himself nearer the convoy. Astern of it or on the quarter, perhaps thirty or forty miles away, to shadow until the enemy showed their hand.

You could bet on it. But would the German admiral have the nous to bet on it too? One guess you could hope he might make was that the British battle squadron would not be far behind the cruisers.

The air threat was a very real one, as previous Arctic convoy experience had proved. Passing around that high shoulder of the world and entering the Barents Sea—where PQ 17 had been torn to shreds—convoys and escorts had to run the gauntlet of all those airfields. Nick wished, sadly, that he'd been given an escort carrier on this jaunt; some fighter cover would have made all the difference in the world. One carrier had in fact been allocated, but then turned out to be not available; there'd been no replacement. There was a make-or-break battle raging at this moment on the Atlantic convoy routes, to which the U-boats had returned in strength after their heavy defeat in May and a few months of licking their wounds and some redeployment; also there were large-scale operations in progress in the

Mediterranean, in support of the battle for Italy. Against that background of high employment for all available ships, this operation had been mounted at short notice and provided with only as much as could be spared.

Rear-Admiral Kidd had told Nick, on board the cruiser-flagship in Akureyri: "There's a steaming row between Winston and Stalin. Mostly because Winston's very properly reading him the riot act over the bloody awful way they treat us up at Murmansk and Archangel, all their damned restrictions and red tape—and lack of any decent medical facilities. He's proposed sending a hospital unit of our own up to Vaenga—as opposed to a couple of doctors in a wooden hut—and the buggers won't allow it! So we're to fetch these empty ships back now, but Winston's not promising any more convoys until his points are satisfied."

The Russians certainly were inhospitable. Particularly so to men who risked their lives to bring them the material they needed. Perhaps the convoys weren't quite as vital to them now as they had been earlier, but late in 1941 when the Germans had got to within thirty miles of Moscow, this flow of war supplies had almost certainly tipped the scales and saved Russia from defeat. Which admittedly had been in the British interest too, but might still have inspired some gratitude—especially in a country which, until it had itself been attacked, had been quite happy to see Britain and all Europe ravaged by the Nazis.

Tomblin, with a covered lunch-tray and an odour of rum—natural enough at this time of day . . . He whipped the covering napkin off, revealing corned beef, baked beans, beetroot, a slice of buttered bread and a cup of coffee.

"Splendid. Thank you, Tomblin."

"We in for a dust-up, sir?"

"Your guess is as good as mine."

But one of the perks of Tomblin's job as Captain's Servant was to acquire snippets of information. To be in the know enhanced his status vis à vis the rest of the ship's company. Respecting this, Nick added, "My guess is that if we run into them it'll be by chance. We know they're at sea, but I don't believe they know we are. Not yet, anyway."

"Any 'elp near if we do fetch up with 'em?"

"Yes. Thirty-ninth Cruiser Squadron's chasing up astern now at thirty-two knots. They'll be in shouting distance by first light tomorrow."

Tomblin nodded approvingly.

"It's all in 'and then, sir."

Alone again, forking corned beef into his mouth, he marvelled at Percy Tomblin's bland acceptance of cruisers as a shield against two of the most powerful warships afloat. Tomblin's confidence contrasted with his own self-doubt, the disturbing question, What if I've got it wrong?

Chewing, glancing round and noticing Jim Treseder's preoccupied expression as he listened with contrived patience to a monologue from Fountain, the diminutive Captain of Marines; Treseder plainly did have doubts. He could be right, too. If—a new theory now—if enemy Intelligence had learnt that PQ 19 was on the way, and Admiral Dönitz—Hitler had sacked his former Commander-in-Chief and appointed the U-boat admiral in his place—had been really well informed, suppose Dönitz had decided to strike at the convoy before the fighting escort joined it?

At 1400 he ordered the destroyers into line abreast at 6000-yard intervals. The move had been prearranged, a minor item in Nick's briefing of Trench and the other destroyer captains back in Iceland. As the flag-hoist dropped from *Calliope's* yardarm all the destroyers' helms went over; his own destroyer-man's heart warmed to the sight of them fanning out at high speed to their new stations. Trench was putting three of them on *Calliope's* starboard beam and two to port, he himself in *Moloch* taking the centre starboard billet. The total spread of ships as they advanced, zigzagging, in search of the convoy which should now have been about fifty miles ahead but might easily be closer, was fifteen miles—plus the range of the wing ships' radar.

Half an hour later Nick increased the speed from twenty-eight to thirty-two knots. It was a measure of his anxiety—unrecognised, he hoped, by others. It was extremely important to link up with the convoy before dusk. Even if he'd been only half-wrong—or half-right . . .

He lit a pipe. Two of *Calliope's* three radar sets were in operation: the 281 air warning set with its aerial at the foremasthead, and the Type 273 surface warning set on the leading edge of the gunnery director tower. Also, up on the tripod foremast, a seaman lookout in the barrel-shaped crow's nest had binoculars constantly sweeping. Swaying in great arcs against grey sky as the cruiser rolled and pitched: to tolerate that motion demanded a cast-iron stomach.

Visibility was still variable. Not bad in some sectors, worse in others.

1440: Another Secret Immediate . . . This was from C-in-C Home Fleet, to the effect that the battle squadron had sailed from Akureyri and was steering 076 at twenty-eight knots. Bruce Christie took it down to the chartroom and came back to confirm what Nick had already guessed: that course would point straight across the Norwegian Sea at Altenfjord, and would be intended to make the enemy believe the battle squadron was aiming to cut them off from their base. But with only Hunts to screen them, the big ships wouldn't cover even half that distance.

1500 . . . Treseder, back on the bridge after lunching down below, was smoking a post-prandial cigarette and adding his binocular effort to the search. During the past hour the gap should have closed by eighteen miles. If all estimates were correct, there'd be at least an hour to go before you'd expect to make contact. Nick had shifted to the line-abreast formation early because the convoy was as likely to be astern of station as ahead of it. More so, in fact.

Treseder moved over to Nick's corner.

"Too bad we don't have an escort carrier with us, sir."

"Yes. The point was made, in Akureyri."

The carrier that had been included in the original orders had suffered either machinery breakdown or action damage. They'd said, in Iceland, "Forecast is you'll slip through to Archangel without much trouble, anyway. The U-boats are concentrating in mid-Atlantic and between Gib and the Azores, and we hear a lot of the northern bomber strength has been sent south too. Italy, you see. Then southbound, your main worry would have been *Tirpitz* and co, but we've reason to believe they'll be—well, taken care of."

"What does that mean?"

"It's not entirely clear, actually . . . But—apparently—inshore mining of some sort, backed up by a strong picket of submarines. We have no details, but that's the inference. You can take it that surface attack is—unlikely."

There'd been no U-boats piping up yet, either. But a patrol line some-where in the area of Bear Island wouldn't come as any surprise. Even if most of their strength was deployed in the mid-Atlantic air gap in a last gasp struggle for supremacy over the convoys. After the beating they'd taken earlier, if they lost this battle, you could reckon the U-boat threat was on the wane.

Calliope rocked across the swell, dipping her graceful bow to toss white sea streaming on the wind. From this viewpoint Nick was looking down over the tier of three forward turrets—three twins, two guns to each turret, and with two more aft she had an armament of ten 5.25-inch. They were dual-purpose guns, with a high elevation that suited them to anti-aircraft use—ideal for convoy protection when the main threat was expected to be from the air. Beyond the three turrets with their jutting barrels only a small triangle of foc's'l was visible from this angle—foam-washed, plunging . . .

Air attack would come, for sure. Whatever else might happen, you could count on bombers and torpedo-bombers east and south of Bear Island.

Treseder muttered as he moved away to the other corner, "Long as we find 'em before dark."

At 4:00 p.m. when the watch changed for the First Dog there was still no sighting, and nothing on any radar screen. Not that this should have been surprising: after days at sea and the bad weather they'd been through you couldn't expect pinpoint accuracy. Even if Christie the perfectionist did aim for it. He'd brought a chart up to the bridge table—it was at the back of this forebridge, close to the asdic cabinet and the entrance to Nick's sea cabin—and he was fiddling around, checking one theory after another. Christie was a professional as well as a perfectionist, Nick appreciated; only the amateur believed in his own infallibility.

1700: Tomblin brought tea and biscuits. He asked, "Mislaid 'em, sir, 'ave we?"

"What?"

"Convoy give us the slip, 'as it?"

Harvey-Smith had the watch now. He was senior watchkeeper and also *Calliope's* first lieutenant, which in a cruiser gave him responsibility for anchors and cables, seaboats and other upper-deck gear. He looked old for his two and a half stripes—and he was. He'd been passed-over for promotion a few years before the war, and retired, but he'd come back for war service—complete with a drink problem, on which Treseder was keeping a baleful eye.

One might have hoped for some more information by this time. Some damn thing . . .

Something did come in just after 1800: another Secret Immediate from Admiralty, announcing: Air reconnaissance this afternoon confirms only *Lützow* is now in Altenfjord and no heavy units are in Narvik or Trondheim.

All one learnt from that was that the two heavy-weights were definitely at sea, hadn't just moved to one of their other Norwegian bases.

Christie murmured a few minutes later, "I suppose we could have gone past them, sir, just out of radar range. In which case . . ."

"It's possible."

Christie was talking about the convoy, of course. But the German battle group could be just as close. There were still a couple of hours of daylight left, anyway. A month or two ago there'd have been no darkness at all: and in two months' time, in November, darkness would last round the clock, the sun never lifting itself above the horizon. That was the best time for running convoys north, from the point of view of cover from the bombers; the snag then was the weather, the constant gales and above all the ice— ships deep-laden with it, spray freezing as it came aboard, and the constant hard work of getting rid of it—chipping, shovelling, steam-hosing . . .

Haselden, Engineer Commander, came up—ostensibly for a smoke and a chat, but Nick allowed a silence to grow until he was obliged to come out with it.

"Bit worried about fuel consumption, sir, at these revs several hours now."

"So am I," Nick pointed at *Lyric,* a low, racing profile three miles on the beam. She was turning at this moment, as *Calliope* was too, to a new leg of the zigzag. "Particularly for them. But we have two oilers with the convoy, so they can all top up tomorrow."

Haselden seemed a pleasant-enough fellow, and he'd been quite right to raise the matter, but at that moment, with other things on his mind, Nick could have done without him.

If the convoy was as little as thirty miles to the north or south of its prescribed track, Christie was right and they could have passed it already, overhauled without making contact. On the other hand it could be thirty miles ahead, still: so if you turned now to try a sweep to the north or south, you might miss it, lose it completely... It would be best to hold on, he decided. At least, as good a bet as any... When the light went, of course, it would be real needle-in-haystack stuff...

A decision he'd have to make soon was the question of a night cruising formation. Enemy ships were at sea, and night encounters tended to be sudden, their outcome decided by speed of reaction; and this was no fighting formation he had his ships in at present. On the other hand he was reluctant to reduce the width of the line-of-search before he had to.

"Captain, sir?"

The chief telegraphist—CPO Tarrant—was offering him a clipboard. The plain white signal-pad sheets on it told him that whatever this was, it wasn't classified.

"If it's bad news, Chief, I don't want it."

"I'd guess you'd enjoy this lot, sir."

"Well," he nodded, "I'll buy it, then. What is it?"

"BBC bulletin, sir. Eyeties've jagged in. Armistice signed, the lot!"

Italy—surrendered?

After—how long? Putting memory to work ... June of 1940—when Mussolini had felt sure he was joining the winning side. Russia hadn't been in it at that stage, because Hitler hadn't yet ratted on his Soviet ally. When the Nazis had invaded Norway, and Nick and Tommy Trench had been trapped in a fjord in a broken-down destroyer, Molotov, the Soviet foreign minister, had broadcast: "We wish Germany complete success in her defensive measures." As when France fell, the Nazi ambassador in Moscow was offered the Soviet government's warmest congratulations on the Wehrmacht's "splendid success." The Italian jackal and the Russian bear had been eager for whatever pieces of the carcase they might snatch.

The dark age seemed more like thirty years ago now, than three.

"Sir," Tarrant pointed: "Flashing, sir—"

A port-side lookout was also reporting it. An Aldis clashed as a signal-man jumped to answer the winking light. Nick swung round to read the message for himself: it was *Laureate* reporting surface radar contact on bearing 358, seventeen miles.

"Yeoman—twenty-inch, port and starboard—*Six Blue*."

"*Six Blue*—aye aye, sir!"

Yeoman of the watch PO McLoughlin bawled to that signalman as he acknowledged *Laureate*'s report. "Shift to the twenty-inch, 'Arris. Make to *Laureate* and *Legend, Six Blue!*"

Leading Signalman Merry was taking the other side. The twenty-inch lamps were powerful, signal searchlights more than lamps, and the most distant of the destroyers would see them easily, with no need for the intermediate ships to relay the message down the line. The order "Six Blue" would turn all ships simultaneously sixty degrees to port, leaving them in a slightly staggered line-ahead formation but steering more or less directly at that radar contact.

It was probably a wing ship of the convoy's close escort. In which case it had been a lucky chance they'd picked it up, at long range from their own wing ship. If it had been just a few miles farther north, you'd have scraped by without knowing it.

On the other hand, this could be an enemy. The only safe way to play it was to assume exactly that.

"Message passed, sir!"

"Executive." He told the officer of the watch, "Bring her round to oh-oh-four." The big lamps' shutters clashed again, passing the executive order to carry out the turn. *Calliope*'s wheel was over now. It was the quickest way to get the whole force pointing in the right direction: now he'd adjust the course as might be necessary and also reorganise his ships into an attacking formation, on lines which he'd explained to the destroyer captains at the conference in Akureyri.

"By light to *Moloch*, Yeoman. 'My speed twenty knots. Destroyers form line astern six thousand yards on my port beam. Executive.'"

"Twenty knots, sir?"

"Yes, please." The reduction in revs was to allow the destroyers to gain bearing on *Calliope,* in the process of forming the squadron into two divisions, the five destroyers in their primary role as a torpedo force and the cruiser on her own as gunship. As they moved in closer to the enemy, Trench would have the option of keeping his flotilla together for a combined attack of the classic kind, or splitting it into two subdivisions; his decision would depend on the number of enemy ships and their formation. On the way in, Trench or his subdivision leader would also act as flank-markers for *Calliope*'s gunnery, reporting their observations of fall-of-shot over the talk-between-ships telephone.

Calliope was steadying on the ordered course, vibration and fan-noise lessening as engine revs decreased. Destroyers racing out to port: a sight of sheer beauty, if you'd had time to watch it . . . He told Treseder, "Get the hands up, please."

"Aye aye, sir." Treseder swung to face aft. "Bugler!"

Action stations . . .

CHAPTER THREE

· · ·

The Italian surrender announcement had been received in "Port HHZ"—codename for Loch Cairnbawn—as an excuse for a party. Broadcast the night before, it had been followed that morning by news of landings around some place called Salerno, and a glance at a map had been enough to show this had to be aimed at capturing Naples. As for the surrender, everyone realised that the German armies in Italy wouldn't be laying down their arms. The tide had turned, with a vengeance—North Africa had finally been cleared in May, the landings on Sicily in July had resulted in the island's capture last month and now Anglo-American armies were advancing in Italy while Russian forces progressed westward and, in New Guinea, American and Australian troops had just re-taken the Huon Gulf ports. But there'd still be long, hard roads to travel, and lakes of blood would flow before the end of it.

In fact it was likely to get tougher, as the beasts were cornered.

This morning the X-craft men's party spirit had been dissipated in drizzle and also anxiety over the whereabouts of the *Tirpitz* and *Scharnhorst*. RAF recce flights from North Russia had confirmed that only the tiddler of the group—*Lützow*, so-called "pocket battleship," 10,000 tons and eleven-inch guns—still lurked in her berth in Altenfjord. All three of those ships were listed as targets for the X-craft.

"Ace up, king towards." Spinning the dice to decide who would start . . .

Not that anyone was all that keen to play; but there was time to kill and a few of them were hanging around, waiting for news. Soft drinks on the table: this was mid-forenoon, "standeasy" time in the wardroom of the depot ship *Bonaventure*. Paul Everard, Dan Vicary, Johnny McKie and Tom Messinger . . . McKie won it with a jack, and scooped the dice into their leather pot. Vicary, a South African, growled, "Trouble is, man, the bastards might pitch up in some hole we never heard of. Some new anchorage, nets and stuff we don't know about?"

From the trots of X-craft alongside floated the rumble of Gardner diesels charging batteries.

"I wouldn't think it's likely," Tom Messinger mumbled, "RAF'll have been flying recces all over those fjords, won't they. At least—"

"Three nines, in two . . . Surprised the Russkis allow it. Seeing they wouldn't let the RAF use those same airfields for bombing attacks on *Tirpitz*."

"Wonder why the hell . . ."

"Bloody-minded, aren't they . . . *Tirpitz* might have gone south d'you reckon?"

"Then she'd be in bomber range from this end, and the RAF could look after the whole issue!"

"God forbid." Paul shook the cup. The thought of bombers doing the job—after all this training and preparation and with all of them now keyed-up and ready . . . A voice behind him suggested, "Someone shove up, so I can honour you with my company?"

"Hello, Louis." McKie asked him, "Nice outing?"

"Except I'm developing a chronic dislike of towing."

Louis Gimber had been out in X-12 on a night exercise, and he'd missed the party. His brown eyes rested on Paul as he slid in behind the table. Gimber had regular features and gleaming black hair that seemed always to have just been combed. He was the "tall, dark and handsome" kind that girls were supposed to like; but not all of them found him as irresistibly attractive as he thought. Paul had reason to know this, and to feel guilty—as well as some quite different emotions—when he thought about himself and Jane. Which he did, a lot. But he was probably the only man in Loch Cairnbawn who did not suffer from the delusion that Louis Gimber was every woman's dream.

Gimber asked him, "If they'd let us decide it between ourselves, would you take the passage job and let me have the fjord end?"

"Hypothetical question."

"Would you?"

"Would I hell."

Messinger's nines were still the highest throw. Paul threw two pairs and failed to make it a full house. Gimber persisted, "Think of the happy ending you'd be in line for. Coming back to my girl, with a clear field?"

"That's a bloody silly remark, Louis."

Vicary, the Springbok, had a reddish face pitted with old scars, either smallpox or acne. His rough-hewn features were in total contrast to the decidedly film-starish Louis Gimber's. He shook his head. "Stow it, would you mind?"

It wasn't the taunt about Jane he minded, which was Paul's business and Gimber's, and at that probably intended to be mildly humorous, since Gimber had no idea how far things had gone. What annoyed Vicary was the assumption that operational crews were unlikely to get back. He was right, too.

Gimber suggested evenly, with his attention on the dice, "I think you might consider minding your own business, Dan."

They didn't like each other. Resentment from Vicary's side was the primary cause. It emerged as contempt, from a rough diamond to a smoothly polished one. He envied those good looks and disliked Gimber's awareness of them, and was jealous of his reputation as a Don Juan. Gimber's family was rich, too. On the subject of the alleged success with girls, Paul knew he could have delighted Vicary and doubtless softened his attitude considerably, by imparting certain private truths; but it was out of the question, obviously.

He'd first met Jane when a group of X-craft men on weekend leave from Fort Blockhouse at Gosport—where the initial training had started—had got together in London to celebrate someone's twenty-first. It had been a long, hectic evening, culminating in a wild party in the Bag o' Nails. Louis had let them all know that he was serious about this girl, really serious, so although Paul had been strongly attracted to her he'd behaved himself, even tried to discount the encouragement she'd seemed to be giving him whenever Louis wasn't in close attendance.

Gimber was a romantic. He lived up to his own appearance. He was also sure of himself, of his own appeal to women in general and to Jane in particular. So much so that he'd actually asked Paul to telephone her and ask her out for a meal, a few weeks later: little knowing that by this time the stable door was already wide open.

"How about it, Paul? Seriously? Passage CO?"

"You're nuts. Anyway, what d'you think Jane is—one of your harem, to be handed over as a quid pro quo?"

"You misunderstand me, old boy. I'm not making you an offer, I'm simply pointing out that if you took the passage-crew job it would be a natural result—whatever view of it Dan here may care to take."

Vicary suggested, "Why don't the pair of you go down to a cabin flat and bash each others' heads in?"

"Nothing to fight about. She's Louis' girl. I've taken her out a couple of times, that's all." He jerked a thumb towards Gimber, "At his instigation."

"Nice cosy arrangement . . . Whose turn is it?"

"Mine." Gimber rattled the pot. Nobody was taking much interest in the game, though. Certainly not Paul, who was thinking about Jane.

She was flattered—or comforted—by Gimber's adoration. He was a very useful escort, too, when he happened to be in London. Plenty of money—family house in Oxfordshire and another one in Town. Recalling some of those early conversations, Paul could hear her now, telling him, "And he's so nice looking: and he knows his way around . . ."

"Aren't you in love with him—or supposed to be?"

She'd shaken her head. "I've never said I was, either. He just assumes that whatever he feels must . . ." He'd had to wait again, until she said "Really, it's like being with a brother. Someone one likes, but—"

"Honey—the way you dance together . . ."

"You mean like I dance with you?"

"Not in front of him, you didn't."

"Well, what d'you expect? I don't set out to hurt him, for God's sake! Paul, he's sweet to me!"

"So?"

"Well, for instance, where do I come in?"

"You know darn well where you come in! Here!"

He'd laughed. She was fairly outrageous: unless it only seemed that way to him, from his own rather limited experience . . . By this time he was too deeply involved with her to be sure of his own clarity of vision, or wisdom. He was in no doubt she lied about some things—perhaps they all did, to their boyfriends—and he thought she was probably a good actress. She was certainly two-timing Louis Gimber—who loved her, or thought he did; so you had to be aware that two-timing was perhaps to be expected.

Rather extraordinary, really. In his own case it wasn't love. Infatuation was the other thing, the other word people used: so, infatuation, and diffi-culty keeping his hands off her. Hands or mind. He thought this amounted to infatuation. It couldn't be love, he guessed, because he could see through some of her tricks too clearly and detachedly. Could you look at anyone that analytically and love them?

His father had asked him, when Kate had been away in the ladies' room at the end of that lunch, "How's your love-life?"

He'd hesitated; then admitted, "Exciting."

"Lucky man. One or more?"

"Just one, right now."

The first one who'd ever meant anything much to him. Until he'd met Jane he'd thought he might be different from the other Everards—including his own father—in that respect. Now he knew he wasn't. He was hooked. Just as a girl called Fiona had had first his father and then Jack Everard hooked: Jack who'd been a prisoner of war in Germany and had been reported "shot while attempting to escape." The news had come through last Christmas.

Rough luck on Fiona. One dead, the other married . . .

But Jane had been married—for a matter of months only, to a fighter pilot who'd been shot down over Dieppe. She cried quite often, especially in bed.

"Hey! Four kings!"

Paul came out of his thoughts—with Jane's sexy, tear-stained face in his memory and, right across from him, her would-be fiancé pointing accusingly at Johnny McKie. "Did I not hear the click of a finger turning up the fourth?"

"No, you bloody didn't!"

"Hi, Don . . ."

Donald Cameron had just walked in. Cameron, skipper of X-6 and the senior sea-going X-craft officer, had been the original of the species, the first recruit. He'd carried out the trials with the prototype, X-3, in the Hamble River, before any of the rest of them had even heard of X-craft. Don was twenty-six, married, and he had a four-month-old son.

"Anyone know where Godfrey might be?"

"*Ja.*" Dan Vicary jerked a thumb. "Over in *Titania,* man. Was, anyway . . . Hear anything yet, Don?"

"Not a whisper."

"We were . . . speculating. Suppose the buggers have shifted to some other fjord—some new place could've been got ready for them?"

"Wouldn't think it's likely." Cameron paused. "But I did get one buzz. Seems there's a Russian convoy operation in progress. That character from London mentioned it. The plan is we tie in with it, in a way. They're expecting that by the time the home-run gets under way we'll have nobbled the opposition. How's that for supreme confidence in us?"

"So it's still on, anyway."

"Of course it is, you silly bastard!"

"Glad to hear it." Vicary shrugged his heavy shoulders. "Just the timing seemed so bad. As if the Bosch knew —"

"Forget it." Cameron shook his head. "It'll be the convoy that's drawn them out, and in a day or two they'll be tucked up in that fjord again. Meanwhile I'm told crew lists will be going up today, and X-11 and 12 will be getting their side-cargoes tomorrow forenoon—right, Paul?" Paul nodded. Cameron put a hand on Vicary's shoulder. "Any other reassurance you want?"

"Well. I take it someone's told the bloody Germans to be back there in time to welcome us?"

Cameron turned away. "Anyone wants to know, I'll be over in *Titania.* If

I can get a boat over." *Titania*, first in service in 1915 and still going strong, was the depot ship for the towing submarines—for *Thrasher, Truculent, Syrtis, Sea Nymph, Stubborn, Sceptre, Scourge* and *Setter*. Cameron asked from the doorway, "Towing exercise satisfactory, Louis?"

"Except I'm not wild about the Manilla tow-ropes." Gimber frowned. "I had balsa-wood floats on mine today, and even then the damn thing's far too heavy. Care to swap?"

"Likely . . ."

He'd gone. Don Cameron had one of the three existing nylon tows. Not, of course, that he'd be passage-crew. He was operational CO of X-6, just as Godfrey Place, the man he was looking for now, had X-7. Place was the only RN officer in the seagoing X-craft force; he was twenty-two, an experienced submariner, and he was married to a Second Officer in the Wrens. During the months in which he'd helped Cameron in training the other crews, Place had lived through some nasty moments. He'd lost one diver, a sub-lieutenant, during a net-cutting exercise, and had another man washed off the casing and drowned. On that occasion the fore hatch had been open and the wave that swept the lad away had also flooded the W and D compartment, leaving the boat bobbing vertically with her artificer isolated in the fore end and Place himself shut in the engine-room. Houdini himself might have been proud to have got out of that one.

"You've a heap of ideas for swaps, Louis. Girls, jobs, ropes . . ." McKie said it. He was Dan Vicary's first lieutenant in X-11, almost certainly her operational crew. Vicary muttered facetiously, "Give him enough rope, he'll hang himself." He pushed his chair back. "Don't know about you bums, I've work to do."

Setter, last of the eight towing ships, entered the loch soon after noon and secured alongside *Titania* with the others. Cameron told Paul at lunch in *Bonaventure*, "*Setter*'ll be your towing ship, I gather."

Paul knew *Setter*'s officers reasonably well. She'd made several training visits to the loch at earlier stages, joining temporarily for exercises of one kind and another. The dress-rehearsal exercise had involved the midgets attacking the battleship *Malaya*: with a submerged tow first, then a solo approach, a long, fjord-like loch to negotiate and nets to cut through, and finally success, surfacing right alongside the old battleship inside her box of nets, having simulated a drop of side-cargoes on the sea-bed under her. The side-cargoes were the X-craft's only weapon, carried like contoured blisters on the sides and fitting from bow to stern. Each had two tons of Torpex high-explosive in it, and could be released from inside the boat after timefuses had been set.

Paul asked Cameron, "Crews been detailed yet?"

A nod ... "Lists will be up any minute now." The Scotsman added, "Can't be any doubt you'll have X-12 for the attack."

"I'm hoping, Don."

"You can count on it."

Finishing lunch, he got his coffee from the urn and went through to the anteroom. He was about to sit down beside Brazier when Claverhouse, Surgeon Lieutenant-Commander RNVR, touched his elbow and asked whether he could spare a few minutes.

"Brief chat? Would you mind, Everard?"

Cursing inwardly, Paul allowed himself to be led aside. In recent weeks he'd managed to steer clear of this character.

"Let's sit here. I shan't keep you long. A matter of completing the final records, you know. I'm supposed to—er—take soundings, from time to time?" He sipped at his coffee. "Well. How's life?"

"Not bad, sir." The "sir" acknowledged that extra half-stripe, but one use of it would now have to see the conversation through. Claverhouse was a psychiatrist, and a comparative newcomer to the medical staff. The others were all right, but there was something leech-like about this one. Paul added, "Except our birds have flown."

"Ah. Yes ... And I suppose you'd be very disappointed if the operation had to be cancelled?"

"Of course. We all would."

"But—why, Everard?"

This was really silly. At such a late stage, and with nerves already on edge through the disappearance of the targets. It would have to be Claverhouse's private initiative—none of the other medicoes would have been so ham-fisted. Paul told him, patiently but with effort, "We've been training for a long time. We're ready for it."

"Do you look forward to the attack itself? To the—er—action?"

"Yes." He did, too. Despite natural qualms.

"I find that curious."

Paul stared at him. The only thing that seemed curious, to him, was to have to put up with this nonsense. He explained patiently again, "We're ready, we know we can do it, and it happens to be a job well worth doing. I can't understand your even questioning it, frankly."

"You aren't worried—at all?"

"If you mean do I get butterflies in the stomach at times—yes, of course I do. You'd have to be bone-headed not to. But as I said—we know we can do it, we're trained right up to the eyeballs, so why shouldn't—"

"Rather begging the question, surely." The smile was irritatingly donnish. "You're trained because you offered to be so trained. Eh?"

In a much earlier session, part of the selection process down in the south, another head-shrinker had tried to suggest that Paul's motivation might be a desire to emulate his distinguished father. It wasn't so—except in so far as any leader set a standard, and Nick Everard was no exception to that generality. Paul had come to the conclusion since then that it wouldn't have mattered a damn if this had been his motivation

"I only wondered"—Claverhouse's tone was ingratiating, now—"entirely for my own interest as a psychologist, how you'd feel about it now, as it were on the eve."

"It's only the eve if those bloody ships reappear."

McKie, passing, had just winked at him. Claverhouse was frowning, brushing that off as an irrelevance.

"They'll have to reappear somewhere . . . But a point of interest in your case, Everard, is you surely have nothing to prove. I'm aware of your background, naturally, and as I recall it you were in a destroyer that was sunk at Narvik? Ordinary Seaman at that time, and a Mention in Despatches for saving lives? Then more latterly you won a DSC," he nodded at the ribbon on Paul's battledress jacket, "in the Malta submarine flotilla?"

"Place has a DSC, too. D'you hold that against him?"

"By no means against him or you—I only . . ."

"I've never tried to prove anything at all. At sea in wartime you can find yourself in certain kinds of situation, and—" he heard his own voice rising—"well, for Christ's sake—"

"Everard—please . . ." Claverhouse embarrassed now . . . "You seem to be—if I may say this without further offending you—well, wound up, rather. Under some degree of stress?"

"Wouldn't you be?"

"You're conscious of stress?"

"If I am, it's because our targets have vanished. That makes me anxious, sure. But . . ."

"What about dreams?"

He'd been reaching to put down his coffee cup. A muscle tensed: he'd fumbled, cup and saucer rattling as he just managed to lodge them on the table. Claverhouse's interest was sharp: "You have been worried by bad dreams, have you?"

There'd been nightmares, all right. And he had been worried by them, was worried by them. They were none of this clown's business, though. They were his, Paul Everard's, to live with, deal with as best he could. He had an urge to use one short, four-letter word, then get up and walk away: then out of the blue—or desperation—a better way out of this occurred to him. He told the psychiatrist confidentially, "Wet dreams." The man's expression changed dramatically: he was blinking, stupid-looking, like a parrot being poked off its perch. Shocked? Could a trick-cyclist be a prude? Paul added in that same confiding tone, "If you call wet dreams bad ones?"

Actually he did quite often dream about Jane. Deliberately, sometimes: in the process of dropping off to sleep he'd concentrate his mind on her, try to dream about her instead of about being suffocated or falling over cliffs, crushed under heavy rocks . . .

But something was happening, beyond the double doorway. Crew lists? He asked Claverhouse, "Excuse me now, please?"

"Well, if we could just . . ."

"I'm sorry. There's really no point, you know."

It was a stir of movement, a general flocking towards the notice board. Crew lists, for sure . . . He remembered, as he went to join the gathering crowd, briefings they'd been given on how to cope with German interrogation techniques, and wondered if this might have played a part, helped him to block that dream question despite its having thrown him for a moment. Then he forgot Claverhouse. He was edging into the scrum, getting close enough to the board to see it was a list of X-craft crews. Then reading it—over Louis Gimber's shoulder . . .

His eyes skimmed down to the lower section of the type.

X-11, towing ship *Scourge* (Commanding Officer Lt M. S. Vallance)
Passage:

Commanding Officer	T. F. Messinger
Crew	J. W. Hillcrest
	C. E. J. Amor

Operation:

Commanding Officer	D. V. Vicary
Crew	J. McKie
	T. N. P. Maguire
	T. Brind

X-12, towing ship *Setter* (Commanding Officer Lt E. A. MacGregor)
Passage:

Commanding Officer	L. W. Gimber
Crew	O. T. Steep
	A. L. Towne

Operation:

Commanding Officer	P. H. Everard
Crew	R. S. Eaton
	H. A. J. Brazier
	J. Lanchberry

Louis Gimber swung round, tight-lipped with disappointment; although he must have known this was how it would be. He brought up short, finding Paul—of all people—right there in front of him. Paul said, quite genuinely sympathetic and knowing how he'd have felt, "Sorry, Louis. We couldn't both have got it." His eyes went back to the list. It had been inevitable, anyway; it was only because he'd wanted the job so much that he'd had any doubts of getting it, whereas Gimber had been trained primarily as a passage CO.

Gimber smiled. "You know the saying, old boy. Lucky in war, unlucky in the only thing that really matters?"

"Well," emerging together from the throng, "perhaps you have a point."

And perhaps I'm a bastard . . .

But not necessarily. Wasn't it more that Louis had the wrong end of the stick, about Jane?

"Louis, the passage command's the toughest. The fact they picked you for it shouldn't make you feel done-down."

"Balls."

"We don't know how they decided, do we. Maybe they spun coins. But now look—we have work to do. Quite a lot, and not too much time. For starters, since she has to be hoisted out at sparrow-fart . . ."

"Lighten ship, etcetera." Gimber nodded wearily. "Ozzie has the preliminaries in hand."

X-12's tanks had to be pumped out, every moveable weight taken out of her, so that the depot ship's crane could swing her up on to the well-deck for side-cargoes to be fitted. The other six boats had already been fixed up; there wouldn't have been space for the two late-comers on that deck as well, and in any case their side-cargoes hadn't arrived on the fifth, when the others had had theirs fitted. But there were other things to see to as well, and this afternoon there was to be a briefing on the subject of an overland escape route, then a COs' meeting to recapitulate on the alternative target-area plans, those for Narvik and Trondheim.

Dan Vicary, who was one of two South African X-craft COs, slammed a meaty hand down on Paul's shoulder. "Just the job, man, ay?"

Gimber, throwing the Springbok a frigid look as he departed, clearly disagreed. Then Dick Eaton joined them—diffident, as always, but more cheerful, like everyone else who'd had his billet in an operational crew confirmed. Brazier too—looming like a man-mountain through the thinning crowd . . . "Arf, arf!"

It was a Popeye expression, which he used to express pleasure or enthusiasm. He added, "But we've lost the sods, haven't we?"

"They'll turn up, Bomber."

"Hope you're right." Brazier snapped his fingers. "Had a message for you, skipper. SDO sent it down, while ago. RPC drinks on board *Setter,* eighteen hundred, operational and passage crew—OK?"

"Fine." Paul nodded. "Tell the others, Louis's gone down to the boat and Steep's down there too, I think."

"Right. Poor old Louis, eh?"

"Yes. We're lucky."

To an outsider it might have sounded crazy—and it would to Claverhouse—to think of yourselves as lucky, in being picked to transport four tons of high-explosive through miles of narrow, defended waters—and minefields—and get it through nets designed to be impenetrable, then deposit it precisely under the belly of the most vital naval target in the world; and to do it in some expectation—hope, anyway—of remaining alive, even getting home again!

The overland escape briefing was at 1430 in the recreation hall down aft.

The briefing officer, a Norwegian expert sent up from London, told the assembled submariners, "An overland trek might prove to be the only escape route available to you. I say might . . . Obviously it's hoped you'll do the job successfully and then get out to sea, make the planned rendezvous with your parent submarine and come home in triumph. Or say, in comfort . . . But since many factors are not predictable, we can't count on it. So this overland exit is just an extra string to your bow, and despite the very limited stowage space in your X-craft you'll be taking certain escape gear with you. But first, before we discuss the equipment—here, on this map, bare as it is, what you see is as much as anyone can tell you about the terrain you'd be crossing."

A blackboard easel supported a map that was, indeed, unusually featureless.

"First, right from the shore of Altenfjord, you'd have these mountains to climb. Definitely a climb, not a steep walk. Then if you made it that far, you'd find you were facing several hundred miles of plateau—which I can't describe in any detail because it's never been properly mapped. The simple fact is that to reach the Swedish border, which would have to be your destination, you'd have no option but to cross this expanse of—nothing . . . And you see—well, we're in autumn now, early autumn; but that area might with a little poetic licence be called the roof of the world, and it won't be long before it's deep in snow. There'll be snow up on the tops there already. Once the winter sets in, it'll become more desolate, more hostile, than ever. In fact—I'm being straight with you fellows—it'll get to be bloody horrible.

"There are some features, and some of them are shown on the maps we're giving you—maps printed on parachute silk, very pretty, your girls'll love 'em and I dare say that could be the best use for them, because I wouldn't swear they're accurate or show enough to be worth having. Once the land's under snow, mark you, this won't matter in the least—you wouldn't find any of those topographical features anyway. Even without snow covering them, you'll find it very difficult to identify any one—er—landmark positively. The features, those that exist, tend to be repetitive and very much alike. The only people capable of navigating by them, effectively, are the Lapps. And this, please note, is very important to you—by far your best chance would be to make contact with Lapps and have them guide you. They're nomads, as you may know, and they know this territory like you know Piccadilly. They migrate right across it twice a year, driving bloody great herds of reindeer, so they have to know it pretty well; and they'd be perfectly capable of steering you over the Swedish border—which otherwise you probably wouldn't see even if you were standing on it. Just a stone marker here and there—buried in snow, of course . . . Yes?"

"Excuse me, sir." The questioner was Toby Maguire, X-11's diver. "Would the Lapps be likely to co-operate?"

"I was coming to that. And—well, you'll find them reasonably well-disposed. Not hostile, anyway. But in any event you'll have the where-withall, in your kit, to bribe them. No—let's say reward them. You'll have Norwegian and Swedish cash, and blocks of chewing tobacco—most Lapps'd sell their mothers for it . . . Apart from that, you'll have to rely on your natural diplomacy, charm and bullshit."

Maguire muttered, "I'll be all right, then."

He got a laugh. The lecturer warned, "Don't be too sure of it. I'm giving you a rough idea of the terrain, but remember there's a hell of a lot of it—and it tends to be swept by snowstorms, sometimes for weeks without a break. All right, so you'd be starting around September twenty-first, twenty-second—and you're thinking that's early in the year, you'd make it before the really heavy snows? But listen—you won't climb those mountains and then get yourselves over hundreds of miles of the hardest going in the world in just a week or two. You'll be into winter, sure as eggs. I have to emphasize this—you'd be crossing a frozen wilderness, temperatures way below zero, storms that last weeks and snow continuous for days. You'd have to contend with frostbite, snow-blindness, hunger, crevasses to fall into and sheer cliffs you won't have the strength to climb, nights when you daren't sleep because if you do you can't be sure of waking up again . . . Now, why am I painting this in somewhat stark colours?" He pointed. "Let me check your agile brain. Sub-lieutenant . . . ?"

"Hillcrest, sir." He was first lieutenant of X-11's passage crew, and known as "Bony" because of an alleged resemblance to Napoleon. "I'd imagine you were advising us not to attempt it."

"You'd imagine right. Except that it might, in some circumstances, be your only way out. You'd have the choice then, but obviously you have to know what you'd be taking on. The hope—as I said—is you'll do your stuff, extricate your boat from the fjords and make the prearranged rendezvous with your towing ship, and Bob's your uncle. But we have to accept that it may be easier said than done. An alternative, which has been discussed before, of course, is to surrender; scuttle your boat, first destroying anything inside it that could help enemy intelligence if they got at it later, and turn yourself in. This may simply happen to you, without any question of choice. But in case you can't get out and you're in a position to choose between the alternatives, we're providing you with certain basic equipment that would allow you to try the overland route home . . . Point taken?"

He went on, "Don't imagine that because you're in peak condition now, those physical difficulties won't bother you. Try to imagine how you may be after a couple of weeks. Those conditions, iron rations, no certainty of survival, and starting right after a spell of action that's liable to drain a lot of the stuffing out of you . . . But all right, you've been warned. Now I'll tell you about the gear we're giving you. First, the obvious things—protective clothing, boots suitable for climbing as well as walking, ropes for the climb, compasses and the silk maps. Plus the other things I mentioned—pack-rations, money, tobacco. But also first-aid kits, which include small surgical saws for amputating frozen toes or fingers. That item may help to underline some of the points I've been trying to make. And in addition—this is as important as anything, because you could have Hun patrols chasing you—you'll have Luger pistols."

He moved over to the table.

"Gather round, now. I'll show you this stuff and how it works. I dare say you've been wondering where you'll find room to stow it, but in fact it packs into a very small kit, as you see here . . ."

Later in the afternoon, Paul and the other COs and flotilla staff conferred again over the alternative target plans. Whatever *Tirpitz* and *Scharnhorst* were doing now, they might well turn up in Narvik or Trondheim, where they'd spent certain periods before.

"If there's still no news by the day after tomorrow, all things being equal you'll be sailed on schedule and you'll get your orders later by W/T. As you know, moon and tides are right for 20 September and for a few days after, but if we're forced to miss this chance—well, with short days, winter darkness and iced-up fjords coming shortly, there'd have to be another long postponement. To next spring, in fact."

Groans. They were ready to go now.

"No word of attack on the PQ convoy, sir?"

"None. No sighting, no sound."

By 1800, when X-12's operational and passage crews went alone for drinks on board their towing ship *Setter* alongside *Titania,* a fresh RAF reconnaissance report had been signalled from the Admiralty. There'd been no change: *Lützow* was still in Altenfjord, and the other berths were still empty.

There were seven X-craft guests. Passage crews consisted of only three men, since there was no job for a diver en route. About a dozen submariners packed the tiny wardroom, with some overflow to and from the artificers' mess where Messrs Lanchberry and Towne were being entertained.

MacGregor, *Setter's* lieutenant-in-command, raised his glass.

"Welcome. Glad to have you aboard." He glanced at Louis Gimber. "Or as the case may be, on the string back there."

Paul said, "I'm afraid we'll crowd you. But if I may, sir, I'd like to stand a watch."

Eaton said he'd like to, too. Brazier had no watchkeeping experience, and offered to stand watches as a lookout. Towing ships would be on the surface for the first few days of the passage.

Brazier said at one stage, "Beats me how there can be a convoy on its way, and those battle-wagons out hunting for it, and not a sound out of anyone!"

"It's a big area. This time of year the ice barrier's as far north as it ever gets." MacGregor stubbed out a cigarette. "And visibility's often zero. Plus the fact all parties will be maintaining wireless silence."

Massingbird, *Setter's* red-bearded engineer lieutenant, reached for the gin bottle. "My guess is the bastards have sneaked down south, to some German port. Into the Baltic, very likely."

MacGregor said, "Rubbish, Chief." Crawshaw, the first lieutenant, shook his head at the engineer. "Bloody old Jeremiah."

The beard jutted: "Want to bet?"

"Certainly. Five bob that we'll sail with X-12 in tow day after tomorrow."

11 September, that would be. Eight days on passage would lead to arrival off the fjords on the nineteenth. Attack, 20 September.

CHAPTER FOUR

. . .

Before noon on the same day, the German battle squadron, having demonstrated their destructive power, had been turning their sterns on Isfjord, in Spitzbergen. *Tirpitz* increased to twenty-eight knots and *Scharnhorst* took station astern of the flagship, while the escort of ten powerful destroyers disposed themselves into an arrowhead screening formation across the big ships' bows. Astern, smoke rose thickly and widely enough to fill half the sky, billowing from the shattered and still burning weather-station and wireless shack, accommodation huts, stores, other collapsed, smouldering structures. Nothing has been left standing or intact, and there were dead Norwegians sprawled among the ruins, as well as live prisoners in the ships. But no word of this had got out, yet. The squadron had made its approach at dawn, the ships growing like huge phantoms out of the mist and skirting the loose ice which, despite the Gulf Stream's northerly flow along this west coast of the island, cluttered the offshore approach. At first sight of the enemy, the operator on duty in the W/T station above Barentsburg had begun tapping out an urgent message, but *Tirpitz*'s radiomen had been ready for it and they'd jammed the transmission. Then the monster's guns had made that wireless station their first target, reducing it to a blazing wreck in one devastating salvo.

The destruction and rounding-up of defenders had continued for five hours. Then the destroyers had re-embarked their landing parties and transferred Norwegian prisoners to the battleships. Well pleased by the easy triumph—although *Scharnhorst*'s captain, Hoffmeier, was critical of his own ship's gunnery performance—the battle group under Admiral Kummetz was now on its 500-mile journey south, steering to pass about twenty miles west of Bear Island.

. . .

"Green one hundred—angle of sight five!"

Bruce Christie—as well as the lookout who was yelling his report of it—had picked up the approaching aircraft in his glasses. It had been on the 281 air-warning screen for several minutes, and several pairs of eyes and binoculars had been concentrating on that hazy southern horizon. It would almost certainly be a snooper, and Nick was hoping it might swing away before it sighted them, might decide it had come far enough north: against the murky northern background, it didn't have to have seen the convoy, at this range . . . But—sadly—it would close in now, close enough to see all it wanted while still keeping outside gun-range; its crew would count the ships and note their shapes and sizes, the strength and dispositions of the escorts, and one of the airmen's priorities would be to check whether there was an escort carrier here. The Luftwaffe commanders would be tickled pink to hear there wasn't. The snooper's report would of course start with the convoy's position, course and speed; the zigzag wouldn't fool him, because he'd hang around long enough to see the pattern of it. In fact, mean course was 065 degrees, speed twelve knots—making good about ten, since zigzagging reduced the actual rate of advance—and at this moment Bear Island was about 145 miles due east. Time—1820. The report which that snooper would send out would be the first intimation to Luftwaffe bases on the Norwegian coast that this very worthwhile target was now entering the radius of bomber strikes.

"Send that signal, sir?"

Calliope's ready-coded signal to Admiralty, Christie meant. Among the recipients of it would be Admiral Kidd, whose cruisers couldn't be far away. Kidd would be glad to know exactly where the convoy was—although it would be less good news that the enemy had the same information.

"No. Not yet."

A minute or two wouldn't make much difference, and it would be as well to make sure this was a snooper. There'd be another decision to make, too. If for the time being one stayed silent, and if the German flyer waited too, didn't send his sighting report out while he was making his full assessment and meanwhile came into reasonable close range, it might be worth using this convoy's one and only catapult-launched Hurricane, to shoot the intruder down, if by doing so you could be sure of gaining a few more hours' privacy. It would be dark soon, so you'd be starting tomorrow still undetected, a hell of a lot better than having the bombers swarming over at first light . . .

But with only one shot in your locker, you didn't want to waste it. If you launched that fighter too soon, and the German was about to send out his report at just that moment—well, there'd be very small dividends from shooting him down after he'd sent it.

Nick had the approaching aircraft centred in his own glasses now: like a very small mosquito stuck on a dirty window. It was the visibility, the surroundings, not the lenses . . . He still hesitated: not from indecision, but from a stirring of doubt.

"It's a seaplane, sir."

Exactly. He was sure of it now, as the image hardened. A float plane, and a small one: certainly no Focke-Wulf or Blohm and Voss long-range reconnaissance . . . *Tirpitz* carried four seaplanes, and so did *Scharnhorst*. But he didn't think this was one of them. If he had thought so, that Hurricane would be belting off by now. The seaplane was flying directly towards the convoy, coming from the south; *Calliope*'s helm over at this moment as she, along with the solid block of ships surrounding her and the perimeter screen of escorts too, swung to a starboard leg of the zigzag—which put the unidentified aircraft on the bow instead of the beam. The convoy was in five columns of three ships, with *Calliope* in the centre of the front rank leading column three, and the anti-aircraft ship *Berkeley* astern of her. To port and starboard of the AA ship were the two oilers—*Bayleaf* as centre ship in column two, and the Russian *Sovyetskaya Slava* in column four. Tommy Trench's five destroyers were spread across the convoy's van with his own ship *Moloch* as its spearhead and the two older destroyers, *Harpy* and *Foremost*—who'd brought the merchantmen up from Loch Ewe—integrated with that screen. All destroyers had fuelled during the day, Trench's ship from *Bayleaf* and the other pair from the Russian—which had taken much longer, because the Soviets were new to the refuelling drill, and clumsy at it . . . Then on each flank were two minesweepers—*Redcar* and *Radstock* port side, *Rochdale* and *Rattray* starboard—and astern the two trawlers, *Arctic*

Prince and *Northern Glow.* It wasn't too bad an escort for just ten freighters, two oilers and a rescue ship—except for that serious omission of an escort carrier—but the return convoy of empty ships would be a lot bigger.

Examining that slowly-growing but still miniature aircraft image, Nick had become fairly sure he was recognising an almost domestically familiar shape.

"Swanwick!"

"Sir?" Swanwick, an RNVR lieutenant, was ADO, Air Defence Officer. Nick asked him, "Are we certain there's no IFF?"

"Operators say not, sir."

IFF was a radar device: "Identification Friend or Foe."

"Then this fellow's isn't working, or it isn't switched on." He was sure he was right. He looked round, for Christie, and found the commander, Treseder, beside him. "What d'you make of it?"

"Beginning to look rather like a Walrus, sir."

"That's exactly what it is!"

At the same time a spark of light appeared on it, grew into needle-point focus and began to flash short-long, short-long . . .

"Aircraft signalling!"

And no doubt at all now—it was a Walrus from the cruiser squadron. From Kidd's flagship, probably—which might not be far over that hazy southern horizon. The flying-boat—its shape was entirely clear now as it turned—was flying parallel to the convoy's course, its rather slowly winking light drawing acknowledgement word by word from an Aldis clacking sporadically in *Calliope's* bridge. Nick turned away to sweep all round, checking on the other side where visibility was worse; turning again, he saw the signing-off group, and PO Ironside, yeoman of the watch, scrawling a time-of-origin on his pad as he came for'ard.

"From CS 39, sir. I intend holding my present position forty miles south of you until 0600/10. Thereafter I shall cover your approach to Archangel from the south and west, if enemy air permits. Walrus reconnaissance this afternoon drew blank between your present position and Bear Island." Ironside looked up. "Message ends, sir."

"Make to him, 'Many thanks. So far so good.'"

Really, very good. The signal he'd had cyphered-up and ready for transmission wouldn't be sent, after all; wireless silence could be maintained. It
meant at least another twelve hours' immunity. To have reached eight degrees east longitude without being detected wasn't a bad start at all: and
it was very satisfactory to know where Kidd's ships were and to know he
knew where the convoy was.

And still no U-boat reports . . .

He glanced up at the sky. In about a quarter of an hour the hands would
be called to action stations, the routine sunset precaution, and at the same
time he'd take *Calliope* and Trench's five destroyers out ahead, leaving the
convoy in the hands of the other escorts. His own ships would then have
freedom of movement and be in a position to engage any enemy encountered during the dark hours. For enemy, read *Tirpitz, Scharnhorst,* ten
destroyers . . .

Where the hell were they?

The Walrus dwindled, vanished southward; after a few minutes it was off
the radar screen as well. The convoy was turning back to its mean course,
Calliope heeling to starboard, graceful as a dancer as she swung, her slim
length dipping to the swell. On her beams as she steadied were the *Tacora*—
the commodore's ship, to starboard—and the *Carrickmore*, the CAM-ship,
with its Hurricane perched on the catapult gear on her foc'sl. Beyond her,
leading column one, was the *Plainsman,* whose American master was vice-
commodore. Four of the ten freighters were Americans, and on the decks
and in the holds of the ten were 1600 trucks or other military vehicles,
200 battle tanks, 50 fighter aircraft and 70 bombers, 18,500 tons of avia-
tion spirit and about 75,000 tons of ammunition and other war material.
This was probably the smallest convoy, Nick thought, that had ever been
brought to North Russian ports, but the Soviets should still be glad enough
to take delivery.

As glad as the Germans would be to stop it.

The commodore was signalling, How nice to know we have company.

He'd have read that message from the Walrus, of course. He was a former
Royal Navy captain by name of Insole; Nick had never met him or heard

of him before this trip. Politeness demanded some kind of answer; he told the yeoman, "Reply, 'We may yet have need of it.'"

Kidd's report of clear seas ahead at some time in the afternoon was no guarantee for the coming hours of darkness. *Tirpitz* and company might well have been lurking somewhere to the east of Bear Island—having sailed from Altenfjord much sooner than they'd needed, and decided to lie in wait?

Night, now—and cold, as the convoy and its escort drew closer to the ice. Radar aerials circling, binoculars probing darkness that was thickened by the mist like flour in clear soup. *Calliope,* plunging rhythmically across the swell, was eight miles ahead of the convoy, with *Moloch* ahead of her and two others on each bow. All of them with asdics pinging, pinging . . . The convoy had ceased zigzagging at dusk, largely because for the merchantmen in close formation the dark made it too dangerous; a small error of judge-ment or a quartermaster putting his wheel the wrong way near the end of a tiring, boring watch, could easily lead to collision. But the fighting escort still wove to and fro, with slightly increased revs to allow for the convoy's greater speed of advance. *Calliope's* 271 radar kept its eye on the ships astern—primarily on *Foremost* and *Harpy* in the van of the close escort.

Calliope was at the second degree of readiness: all quarters closed up, but some gun, torpedo and director crews sleeping at their stations. The ship could be brought to instant readiness within seconds.

Nick dozed under an oilskin in a deckchair behind his high seat. It would take only about one second for him to be up and on his toes, but meanwhile it was in the ship's interest as well as his own that he should get some rest while things were quiet. You could hope they'd stay quiet, but certainly not count on it. The staff officer who'd said in Akureyri, "You'll slip through without any trouble, if my guess is right," had never himself been up here with a PQ convoy; he was the kind of theorist who'd read an intelligence summary stating that the enemy's bomber squadrons had all been moved south, and believe it . . .

By dawn, they'd be well inside the bombing zone. This quite apart from the chance that just east of Bear Island might be where *Tirpitz* and *Scharnhorst* were patrolling. At slow revs, conserving fuel, one might guess.

He reminded himself, Remember Vian.

"Captain, sir?"

"Yes, pilot."

Christie told him, "Coming up for one o'clock, sir, and Bear Island will be abeam. We should alter to oh-nine-oh."

"Go ahead."

He'd use TBS—talk-between-ships—to pass the course alteration to the destroyers. The VHF telephone system wasn't detectable over any great distance—over more than the radius covered now by the type 271 radar, for instance—and it was by far the best way of communicating quickly with a number of ships at once.

"Rabble, this is Thief. Course, zero-nine-zero. I say again—course, zero-nine-zero. Over . . ."

Christie was using the set himself. Rabble was the collective call-sign for the destroyer force, the five here and the pair fifteen thousand yards astern. *Foremost,* back there in the darkness and identifiable only as a blip on the 271 screen, would pass the order to the commodore, who'd promulgate it to the other merchantmen by fixed signal-lights at his masthead. Meanwhile the Rabble had a routine sequence in which to respond. *Moloch* first, with her call-sign Tinker: then *Laureate, Legend, Leopard, Lyric, Foremost* and *Harpy,* identifying themselves as Tailor, Soldier, Sailor, Richman, Poorman and Beggarman.

Nick went aft to the chart-table, to light his pipe under the cover of its hood. He heard the acknowledgements coming in; and he could visualise Tommy Trench—six foot four in his socks and broad in proportion, looming over *Moloch*'s jolting, swaying bridge as he listened to the same sequence of replies. Trench who in Akureyri had wrung Nick's hand, beaming in delight at their reunion . . . "Heard you got spliced, sir. In Australia?"

He'd nodded. "Yes, Tommy. Kate's in England now, though. And we have a son, getting on for a year."

"Well, that's splendid!" Trench's broad, infectious grin ... "Bit late for congratulations, sir, but all the same—"

"Thanks, Tommy. And how's your family?"

"Two sprogs now—boy and a girl!"

"Don't you ever put in any sea-time?"

He had the pipe going: he ducked out from the chart-table cabouche. Christie reported, "They've all acknowledged, sir. Executive?"

"Yes, please."

Course would become due east now, rounding Bear Island and leaving it about fifty miles to starboard. That course, with the edge of the ice roughly thirty to forty miles north of their track, would be held until dark tomorrow evening. Then there'd be a turn southwards for the run down to the White Sea.

Barring prior interference, of course.

Kate had begged him, the last night they'd been together, "Please, be careful?"

He'd kissed her. "I always am."

"Like hell you are!"

"Nowadays. I have a wife and child, you see."

"Just keep us in mind, huh?"

He'd had no answer to such an unnecessary instruction. But she'd burst out again—later when he'd been dozing and woken abruptly with her voice in his ear—"I'm scared, Nick! I hate it, I'm not used to being this way!"

"What?" Half asleep still, having to struggle to make sense of it—not only with waking, the blurred mind and sense of alarm, but with Kate's panic, startlingly out of character ... "Darling, what are you talking about?"

"All I can say is it's real, and I'm frightened, and . . ."

"I don't know what you're telling me." Drawing her closer, tight against him. By this time she'd woken fully and so had he. She was crying—wet-faced, his shoulder damp from it. "Kate, darling what's this nonsense?"

Some dream she'd had? Intuition?

He'd told her, "You must have been dreaming. Forget it, now. Everything's all right, my darling . . ."

Calliope was under helm, carving a bright curve of white in black, ice-cold sea.

Dawn: radar screens still empty.

He'd slept and dozed, hearing the watches change, the murmur of night-watch routines, the roar of the ship's fans and the slamming and creaking of her motion as she zigzagged eastward. Now, with her company at action stations as the light grew and no enemy showed up, he was about to turn her back to the convoy to resume the day cruising formation, which was designed for countering air attack.

To port, at some indefinable distance, fog lay like a rolled blanket along what would be the beginning of the ice, the loose litter of its fringes perhaps twenty miles away. Fog was to be expected, where air warmed by its passage over the long northerly drift of the Gulf Stream suddenly found itself on ice, and reacted in white vapour. It might hang there all day, or you might come to an edge where it abruptly ended. Or you could run into and through patches a hundred miles deep, slowly drifting.

It looked fairly clear ahead and to the south. Daylight entrenched now, and in *Calliope's* bridge wind-whipped, stubbled faces were clearly visible to each other. Nick slid off his seat, and stretched. Glancing round, seeing bridge staff at their action stations—Treseder with his glasses up, feet straddled against the roll, Swanwick the ADO farther aft near the port target-indicator sight and his panel of communications to the close-range weapons. Harvey-Smith was at the binnacle: an unhappy man, ambitions disappointed years ago. Pennifold the torpedo lieutenant—roundfaced and double-chinned despite the fact he wasn't thirty yet. The tin hat on his head made him look even rounder: and Pennifold might be persuaded to take some exercise, Nick thought. Not that he was going to be able to do much with this crowd, as a new arrival and expecting to stay no more than a month or two . . . Bruce Christie had binoculars up and sweeping the blind side, the fog-bank to the north: close to his elbow was the chief yeoman, CPO Ellinghouse, squat and frog-like with that wide, heavy jaw.

Nick told Treseder, "Fall out action stations. Better send them to breakfast right away."

So as to get the meal over quickly, while things were quiet. This peace couldn't last much longer. If it lasted the whole day, so that tonight PQ 19 would be starting the southward run still without having been detected, that simpleton of a staff officer in Akureyri would have been proved right—which seemed, to say the least, unlikely.

At 0740 there was an "Immediate" from CS 39 . . .

> Am being shadowed by Focke Wulf. My position 74° 12′ North 18° 40′ East, course 060 speed 15. Convoy is approximately 60 miles to the north. Intend turning south and west if air attacks develop.

That "if" was somewhat superfluous, Nick thought. If Kidd was being shadowed, it wouldn't be long before he came under attack. The message ended with a weather report and was addressed to Admiralty, repeated AIG 311—meaning all ships and authorities concerned with PQ 19—and to SBNO, North Russia.

"I'm going down for a shave. Who's PCO?"

"I am, sir."

Spalding, the gunnery officer. "PCO" stood for Principal Control Officer: he, Treseder and Christie shared the job, when Nick himself was off the bridge.

The cruiser squadron's position was twenty miles southeast of Bear Island. Kidd's present course of 060, northeasterly, was bringing him up closer to the convoy's track. He must have passed well south of Bear Island during the night, but his intention as indicated in this signal was to turn away from the convoy rather than draw attackers up towards it.

The wild card was still the *Tirpitz*.

"Ready for your breakfast sir?"

Percy Tomblin, back again. The ship's company had already fed, but Nick hadn't wanted it, earlier; he'd been conning her back into the convoy formation when Tomblin had last suggested it.

"Yes, please." Wiping foam from the razor. "Up here, right away."

But he needn't have rushed it. It was an hour and a half before CS 39's next signal came in . . .

> Under attack by Ju 88s. My position 30 miles SE of Bear Island, course 130.

Evidently Kidd had changed his mind about altering to south and west; he must have decided that the battle group was still potentially a threat to the convoy. He was increasing his distance from PQ 19, but in fact only cutting the corner of the convoy's planned route, so he was keeping his squadron in the general area where he could hope to take a hand in any surface action that did develop.

Nick thought about it, and arrived at two conclusions. One, the Admiralty was unlikely to sanction CS 39's continued presence in such extremely dangerous waters, not for much longer or unless there was some solid expectation of a meeting with the battle group. Two, the air activity down there would surely extend itself northwards soon, at least in terms of reconnaissance initially; the Germans weren't all stupid, they'd realise that a cruiser force wasn't subjecting itself to air attack for no purpose. He told McLoughlin, yeoman of the watch, "By lamp to the commodore—'In view of enemy air activity in the south, propose altering mean course to north for about two hours.'"

Use of the word "propose" was a courtesy to the commodore. "Intend" would have been more accurate. As escort commander he, not the commodore, was responsible for PQ 19's defence, and whether Insole liked the idea or not he was going to get closer to that fog, close enough to make use of it if he needed to.

Insole concurred.

"Right. Yeoman—by TBS to Rabble . . ."

Time, 0920.

At 1019, CS 39 signalled:

> Large formation of He 111 torpedo bombers and Ju 88s approaching from south. My course 290 speed 18.

Kidd shouldn't have been allowed east of Bear Island, Nick thought. Hindsight, of course; but that message reminded him of Crete in 1941, when such alarms had been commonplace and as often as not the pre-liminaries to much worse news. Ships operating without air cover close to enemy air bases—it was an old, old story. That signal said it all: and having been there oneself, on occasion, no description of what it would be like for those ships was necessary.

Treseder murmured, "Afraid they're in for it."

At least the convoy was ten miles farther from the bombing than it had been an hour ago. Pretty soon they'd catch a sight of the ice: then he'd turn, head east again. He asked Treseder, "You were in the Crete thing, weren't you?"

"I was sunk in *Fiji* sir." The commander nodded. "Picked up by *Kandahar*. At least we had a warmish sea to swim in." He nodded again, catching Nick's meaning. "Yes. There's a familiar ring."

It rang worse at 1034.

Minotaur hit on "B" turret. Attacks continuing, mostly high-level Ju 88s. Two He 111s and one Ju 88 destroyed.

Ice was visible ahead at 1050. A blue-green, fiery shimmer under low-lying haze; but the fog had rolled back, piled and driven by a freshening southwest wind. The ice-edge was farther south than one might have ex-pected at this time of year. It meant the fog wasn't going to be quite the ally he'd been looking for—except as an obscuring background against which these ships would be less easily visible from the south.

"Yeoman—make to the commodore, 'Propose resuming mean course 090.' And by TBS to Rabble, 'Stand by to resume mean course east.'"

The Aldis began to stammer out the message, while Clark, signal yeoman in this forenoon watch, passed the stand-by order over the radio-telephone. Nick asked Christie, "What's our distance from the cruisers?"

"Plot makes it ninety miles, sir."

Better than he'd thought. And as Kidd was now steering west, convoy course of due east would widen the gap fast. And then of course, if you ran into the *Tirpitz* you'd be sorry . . . But PQ 19 might stay lucky, for a while . . . The W/T office bell rang: Christie answered the voicepipe, and listened grimly.

"Very good. Send it up."

He came over to Nick's corner. "Signal from CS 39, sir. Simultaneous bombing and torpedo attacks in progress. Four more aircraft destroyed and further minor damage sustained by *Minotaur.* Then he gives a position, course still two-nine-oh and speed eighteen."

PO Clark suggested, "Executive, sir?"

"Yes, please."

The executive order was being passed, and that signal was arriving in the bridge; destroyers were racing to adjust their stations. Swanwick the ADO called from the after end of the bridge, "Bogey on one-six-oh, range fourteen, closing!"

"One single aircraft?"

In other words, a single reconnaissance plane, or an attack on its way? For just a snooper, he wouldn't call the ship's company to action stations . . . "Yeoman—hoist 'aircraft bearing'—whatever it is . . . Pilot, have the W/T office stand by with a position and 'am being shadowed by aircraft.'"

Christie kept Bliss and the padre—who did their cyphering job in the plot—supplied with regularly updated position, course and speed data. It was to the plot he was talking now, through its voicepipe. And that flag-hoist was whisking up—the aeroplane flag, a red diamond on white background, surmounting the bearing pendant and three numerals—one, six, zero.

Swanwick had confirmed this was a single aircraft approaching. You'd know when the pilot sighted the convoy, because the right-to-left movement—which he'd also just reported—would cease as he turned towards.

A new range now, new bearing. The ADO's communications were to the radar offices, the director tower, guns and close-range weapons; and his target-bearing indicators, one each side of the bridge, could put either the director or the guns on to a target first spotted from the bridge. It was a very flexible system.

The convoy was steadying on its course of east. Nick moved from one side of the bridge to the other, checking around and astern to see whether any of the ships might be letting out enough smoke to catch a German observer's eye. There was a slight leak from *Papeete,* the long, low-built freighter leading column five, on the commodore's starboard beam. But the *Papeete* was about a cable's length astern of station, with the *Galilee Dawn* treading on her heels, and very likely the reason for that smoke would have been a terse order to her engine-room to speed up. Astern of the *Galilee Dawn* was the American *Caribou Queen,* her upperworks visible over the Soviet oiler's tank-tops. No tell-tale smoke-trails there, anyway; even the *Papeete*'s had cleared now. On the other side the *Carrickmore* and the *Plainsman* beyond her were both angling outwards, adjusting for having closed in too far during the turn. The oiler *Bayleaf* steamed in the *Carrickmore*'s wake, and the rescue ship *Winston* trailed the oiler. A whisp of greyish smog swirled from the *Earl Granville*'s tall stack—she was next-astern of the *Plainsman*—and he focussed his glasses on it, but again it was hardly enough to make a fuss about. Astern of the *Granville,* the third ship in column one was the American *Ewart S. Dukes*—with the minesweeper *Radstock* veering out across her stern . . . Nick leant out, turning his glasses back to where the AA ship *Berkeley* had finished the turn very neatly astern of *Calliope;* astern of her the *Republican,* another of the US contingent, was nosing into station.

"Nine miles, sir, true bearing one-five-five!"

Still closing, and still moving slightly from right to left. He went back to his tall chair. Treseder, Christie and the yeoman were all on the starboard side with their glasses up. *Calliope*'s motion was a combination of pitch and roll, with the long swells lifting under her quarter.

"Range eight miles!"

"Aircraft in sight." Treseder had got it. "Green six-oh, angle of sight—zero. It's a Dornier two-one-seven, sir."

Nick was on it too. Very low to the horizon—and even with that slight degree of profile it was easily recognisable, the "flying-pencil" shape of the long-range Dornier . . . Swanwick called from his ADO position, "Turned towards, sir!"

No element of profile at all now. The Dornier was a darkly hostile intruder lifting very slowly against pearl-grey sky.

"Two-eight-one continue all-round sweep. See the lookouts do the same."

Otherwise they'd be watching the approaching recce plane instead of looking out for newcomers. Who would undoubtedly be along, by and by. Perhaps not quite immediately—since they already had one target closer to them and already damaged—but they'd be coming.

"Tell them to get that cypher away, pilot."

The Dornier spent about fifteen minutes limping around the convoy in its characteristic nose-down position, the posture of a wounded dragonfly. It stayed carefully out of range while it completed its inventory of merchantmen and escorts and then turned south, dwindled, finally vanished from the radar screen.

Treseder said grimly, "Matter of time now, sir."

But it always had been. Nobody could have believed in that prediction of getting through unscathed.

At 1144 there was a new and worrying signal from CS 39.

> *Nottingham* damaged by near-miss. Speed temporarily reduced
> to 14 knots. Large formation of Ju 88s closing from southeast.
> My position . . .

The position was twenty miles south of Bear Island, and Kidd was still steering 290. He was obviously in bad trouble, and the Luftwaffe's interest in the cruiser squadron explained why they hadn't yet moved against this convoy. Having hit *Minotaur* and now damaged the flagship, you could guess they'd be encouraged to keep up that effort.

In the interim he'd altered the convoy's mean course again, slanting up thirty degrees to port. Two hours on this northeasterly course would bring them as close to the ice as might be reasonably safe at present speed. It would add a few miles to the distance between the convoy and the Luftwaffe, and put them closer to the area of uncertain visibility; there was even a chance of fog spreading southward, providing real cover.

"Cooks to the galley" and then "Hands to dinner" were piped earlier than usual, on the heels of "Up spirits," in the hope of getting another meal over before the bombers came. Nick had his own lunch tray on his knees when at about 1215 the chaplain, the Reverend Marcus Plumb, came up with a freshly decyphered signal from the Admiralty.

Plumb's appearance didn't match his name. Far from "plummy," he was quick-eyed, brisk and muscular—a Welshman, and a rugger player of renown.

"This'll remove one of your headaches, sir."

SECRET IMMEDIATE
FROM: Admiralty
TO: CS 39
REPEATED TO: AIG 311 and SBNO North Russia
Tirpitz and *Scharnhorst* are reported to have returned to Altenfjord. Withdraw to the west at your best speed.

Astonished: reading it over twice . . . "I'll be damned." Glancing round— "Here, pilot . . ." Then, "Thank you, padre. If you haven't lunched yet, I suggest you tuck in while the going's good."

"I shall indeed, sir. Soon as my oppo's back from his repast."

By "oppo" he meant Happy Bliss. Nick wondered where the German battleships had been. Up in this area, searching ineffectually for the convoy? Given up, sneaked home again, running out of fuel? Whatever the answers, for the moment you could forget them: and it did simplify the tactical problem. The snag was that as Kidd's cruisers pulled out westward now, increasing their distance from the enemy airfields, the bombers would feel free to switch their attentions to this convoy.

He asked Bruce Christie, "How far has CS 39 to go before he's out of their range?"

"On his present course, about eighty miles, sir."

At fourteen knots, six hours. But *Nottingham's* engineers might improve on that, of course.

A luminous streak underlying the northern haze was a reflection from the ice. Nearly 1230 now. He decided he'd hold this course for about

another hour or an hour and a half. Loose ice couldn't do anyone much
damage, and if there was a chance of getting into fog up there it might
be a lifesaver.

The watch had changed at noon, and now with the midday meal finished various individuals came up to the bridge, hung around for a while,
wandered off again. Pitcairn, the paymaster commander, came to talk to
Treseder about new arrangements for action messing, and the gunnery
officer, Keith Spalding, came to confer with Swanwick. At one stage the
PMO—Francomb, surgeon commander—brought Nick some quandary
about medical stores they were carrying for the so-called "hospital" at
Vaenga, the base settlement in the Kola Inlet, the approach to Murmansk.

As this convoy was destined for Archangel, not Kola, the stores would
have to be trans-shipped, and Francomb's concern was that the Russians
shouldn't get any chance to steal them. The obvious solution, Nick suggested, was to transfer the stuff to one of the four minesweepers, who'd
be staying in North Russia, relieving others who'd be returning with the
convoy of empties; sooner or later the sweepers would call at Vaenga and
be able to slip the stores ashore—surreptitiously, perhaps, to avoid entanglement in Soviet red tape.

At 1345 Christie suggested they'd come far enough to the north and
should alter back to 090. Nick agreed, and a few minutes later the six-mile-
wide block of merchantmen and escorts swung back to point east. It was
getting on for three hours since the Dornier had fingered them.

A lookout's yell came just after the convoy had settled on the new
course . . .

"Aircraft, green one hundred, angle of sight ten, closing!"

He'd beaten the radar to it . . . All around the bridge binoculars sought
and found the oncoming attackers—midge-like objects, a scattering of
them approaching from the south.

They were Ju 88s: nine of them, flying in and out of cloud now, at about
7000 feet. Swinging left, cloud swallowing them . . .

Radar and the director control tower were on target—had been, but
now only radar held the contact. The tower, above and abaft the bridge with

its rangefinder behind it, pivotting this way and that as its crew strained to pick up a fresh sight of the bombers, resembled some seamonster's stiffly raised head with eyes out on stalks. When it found the target, the guns would follow, pointers in electronic receivers lining-up, with additional calculations thrown into the circuits by the TS, transmitting station, deep in the ship's bowels where Royal Marine bandsmen and others laboured, locked in a cavern of armoured steel. All guns elevated, ready, and all personnel in this bridge and other exposed positions were in tin hats and anti-flash gear. Close-range weapons—Oerlikons, pompoms and multiple point-five machineguns—manned, sky-searching . . . An answer from Tommy Trench crackled over TBS: Roger, Thief. Out. Then Trench was calling Tailor and Sailor—meaning *Laureate* and *Leopard*—ordering them to take up new stations in the convoy's rear while *Foremost* and *Harpy* spread outward to cover the sectors they'd vacated.

Nothing to do but wait and watch now. Eyes on the clouds, fingers on triggers, ships plunging, ploughing white furrows in grey-green sea.

"Bogeys closing from astern, sir!"

That was a report from the 281, "bogeys" being radar talk for hostile radar contacts. The Junkers would attack by diving from astern. Some might drop a bomb or two through cloudholes overhead, but the main weight of the attack would come from aircraft diving over the convoy's wakes. *Laureate* and *Leopard* had wheeled and were racing back between the outer columns of merchantmen with guns cocked up, bow-waves high, ensigns whipping, the two sleek-looking ships sheeted in foam as they rushed to their new stations. Without them, there'd only have been the two trawlers astern, where most of the action was bound to start. Unfortunately their armament of four-point-sevens wouldn't be as effective as one would like, since they were low-angle guns and couldn't elevate enough for overhead attackers. *Moloch,* one destroyer class later, had dual-purpose guns, as did *Calliope* with her 5.25s. Those L-class destroyers did have one high-angle four-inch, in fact, and of course their close-range weapons could fire vertically, like everyone else's.

Astern, someone had opened fire . . .

Three Ju 88s, emerging from cloud and in shallow dives aimed at the convoy's heart. Almost certainly they'd be going for the oilers—for *Bayleaf* and the *Sovyetskaya Slava*. Nick had already passed the order to open fire when ready. Tracer was rising from several of the merchantmen: and now *Leopard*, almost on her beam-ends in a high-speed turn as she fell into station astern of column two, opened up with her four-inch. *Laureate* too. *Calliope's* two stern turrets joined in, the ship's steel ringing to the crashes, the entire convoy at it now like a great percussion band with ship after ship coming into it, sound thickening from individual explosions into a solid roar, and the sky around the diving Junkers—two other sections of three in sight now all nose-down and on their attacking runs—pock-marked with brown and black shellbursts, streaked with the garish tracer that seemed to curve as it rose ahead of them then bend sharply to whip away astern. Noise deafening, composed not only of the large-calibre guns but also the Oerlikons' harsh snarl, pompoms' thudding, the Bofors' distinctive barking too, and the metallic clangour of point-fives. Bombs separating, slow-looking, from the first group of planes as they swept over—one with an engine trailing smoke; the trio splitting now their bombs had gone, two banking left and the smoker pulling out southward—the smoke was darkening and the machine looked as if it was having trouble staying up. Bucketing upwards . . . Gunners' aim shifting to others, two threesomes merging into one rough echelon of six roaring over the columns at about 2000 feet, everyone deaf by this time, bomb-splashes lifting here and there, destroyers under helm dodging bombs while their guns blared. The merchantmen's close-range weapons were lacing the sky overhead so thickly that it was amazing any of the attackers could fly through it and not be hit. He saw a near-miss on the *Bayleaf*. The sight of it—a column of sea leaping right on her quarter, too close not to have done some damage—was frightening: *Bayleaf* being the one ship you couldn't afford to lose. The second bomb of the same stick raised a spout on *Calliope's* beam, midway between her and the *Carrickmore*, and two others splashed in ahead, in the space between the convoy and the destroyer screen. Noise diminishing as the last of the attackers droned over; a voice over the wires from the director tower was intoning "Check, check, check . . ."

A bomber had nose-dived into the sea ahead; *Legend* was going out in search of survivors.

"The *Bayleaf*'s in trouble, sir."

As he'd guessed she would be—but still hoped ... He went to the other side and looked astern. The oiler was falling back, and the rescue ship, *Winston,* had put her helm over to pass clear. The trawler *Arctic Prince* was standing by the *Bayleaf.* There was a lot of smoke right astern, out of his sight from here, and he guessed at a ship on fire on the other quarter.

"Chief," talking to the chief yeoman, Ellinghouse, "to *Laureate* by TBS— report on damage to the *Bayleaf.*"

Swanwick told him, "That's the *Springfield* on fire astern, sir."

The *Springfield* was next-astern to the *Sovyetskaya Slava.* One of the bigger ships in this assembly, she had a deck cargo of tanks and trucks, and a between-decks load of explosives.

But it was the *Bayleaf* he was most concerned for. She was indispensible—not so much for now, because at a pinch the Russian oiler could serve the destroyers' bunkering needs, but for the return trip when she'd be the one and only source of replenishment.

He was waiting for a reply from *Laureate.* About half a mile astern, she was closing in towards the damaged oiler. Her captain would confer with the *Bayleaf*'s master by loud-hailer.

Time now—1417.

The *Springfield* had also dropped astern, gushing smoke more thickly than before. The other trawler, *Northern Glow,* was forging across the convoy's rear towards her, and *Leopard* was also there.

"Rigging hoses ..."

Commentary by Treseder, with his glasses up and muttering to himself. That activity on the destroyer's foc's'l was hidden as she turned sternto, following the *Springfield* round. She'd be turning head to wind, Nick realised, because the fire was on or in her after-part and this would make it less likely to spread forward. The *Northern Glow* was turning to catch up with the convoy. He heard *Laureate*'s report coming in over TBS: there'd been something, garbled by atmospherics, about a fractured oil-feed and repairs in hand, then the voice broke through the static and he heard clearly, Maximum of five knots for at least half an hour. Over.

It sounded less bad than it might have been.

"Tell *Laureate* to stay with her."

Dense smoke drifting from the *Springfield* hid whatever was happening there. *Leopard*'s captain would have his hands full with the attempt at fire-fighting, though, and there was no point bothering him with questions. Except perhaps whether he wanted help: and the idea of detaching another escort, when a new attack might develop at any moment, was unattractive. If he wanted help, he could ask for it. Every pair of glasses in *Calliope*'s bridge was sky-searching: the air-search radar hadn't been any help last time.

"Swanwick—what happened to the 281?"

Legend was reporting she'd picked up two German airmen, one wounded.

The ADO came over. In the summer of 1939 he'd been starting a career as an actor in repertory at Bexhill-on-Sea; he was a good-looking young man in his mid twenties, but the tin hat with its stencilled letters "ADO" looked too big for his rather narrow head—like the top of a mushroom. He said apologetically, "They tell me the set's all right now, sir, but—"

The *Springfield* blew up. A muffled roar built into a thunderclap: flame shot vertically, snuffing itself out in black smoke through which a second explosion lobbed a fireball—crimson, disintegrating in its turn into oily-looking smoke. Swanwick with his mouth still open, goggling; Nick focussing his glasses on what was now a foggy mess extending for several hundred yards across the convoy's wakes. He couldn't see *Leopard:* but she'd have been right in there, close enough to have been reaching the freighter's deck with her hoses. A glance to the side showed the *Bayleaf* well clear and *Laureate* leaving her heading for the new disaster area. The *Arctic Prince* was still with the oiler. Then, where the *Springfield* had been, he found *Leopard* lying stopped and shrouded in thinning smoke which was coming from the destroyer herself, from a fire on her port side. A seaboat—a whaler in its davits—was blazing, and there were other burning areas, while that side of her bridge superstructure had been blackened by scorching.

"Chief—general signal, 'Speed five knots.'"

Still no bombers. Everyone expecting them, surprised by every minute that passed with the sky still empty.

· · ·

By three o'clock the *Bayleaf* was back in station astern of the *Carrickmore*
and speed had been worked up to twelve knots. Allowing for the zigzag
this gave a true rate of advance of a fraction over ten. Five badly burnt
survivors of the *Springfield* had been picked up and they and eleven
wounded from *Leopard* had been transferred to the *Winston*—which had
a doctor, wards and even an operating theatre. *Leopard*'s wounded included
her captain, and the first lieutenant had assumed command. Her damage
was superficial; that whaler and some other upper-deck gear had been
destroyed, but very little else. The casualties, suffering from burns and blast
concussion, had all been in her bridge and for'ard guns' crews.

Column four had only two ships in it now instead of three. The empty
billet, which had been the *Springfield*'s, was astern of the *Sovyetskaya Slava*
and between two Americans, the *Republican* and the *Caribou Queen*.

Worsening visibility on the port side suggested fog might be extending
southward. If so, it would be welcome. Binoculars caught the glint of ice
as they swept over that sector: but only a suggestion, a gleam underlining
the soupy haze.

The *Bayleaf* seemed to be all right now. During the half-hour wait
when he'd had only her engineer's relayed promise—therefore no guarantee at all—he'd considered what might be done if they failed to improve
on her five-knot speed. One possibility would have been to send her to
Spitzbergen, perhaps into Bell Sund in the island's ice-free west coast where
she could have holed-up to work on the repairs and then been picked up
again somewhere north of Bear Island in about ten days' time. An alternative might have been to start her back towards Iceland and request support
that would have needed to include another oiler with a destroyer escort.
But this would have been tantamount to asking for the moon: Spitzbergen
would have been the best answer. Even though you'd have had to leave a
destroyer with her . . . One had to think ahead, be ready with solutions,
alternatives . . .

He'd put out a signal to the Admiralty—wireless silence being unim-
portant for a while, with the Luftwaffe knowing all it needed to—reporting
the attack, damage to the oiler and the loss of the *Springfield*. There'd been

nothing new from CS 39, and he guessed Kidd's squadron would be out of range of bombing by this time. Touch wood . . . But the corollary was that here, soon, one might expect the enemy's full weight.

"Cup o' char, sir?"

Tomblin had brought tea and biscuits.

"We're still at action stations, Tomblin. Where's your tin hat?"

"Ah." A surprised look suggested this was a completely novel idea. "That's a point, sir."

"Fetch it, and don't appear on this bridge again without it. And anti-flash gear, for God's—"

"Bogeys, one-seven-five, fourteen miles, large formation!"

"All quarters alert!"

Voicepipes and telephones were suddenly busy again. A flag-hoist ran up to the yardarm, drawing other ships' attention to that bearing. Two minutes later, radar reported a second wave of attackers coming in behind the first. Bearings were unchanging, indicating a direct, purposeful approach. Treseder said, "At least the two-eight-one seems to have pulled itself together."

Count your blessings . . .

But sparing a thought, another one, for the idiot in Akureyri who'd been so sure PQ 19 would get through unopposed—by way of a let-out, of course, for failure to lay on an escort carrier. Nick would have liked to have had that man here now, to watch—as they all did, a few minutes later—the first group of bombers sliding round astern, high enough to be flying in and out of the lower extremities of cloud, and dividing into three sections of respectively four, four and five aircraft—these were Ju 88s again, thirteen of them.

"Large formation green eight-oh, angle of sight five, flying right to left!"

That was the second bunch . . .

One quartet of Junkers had turned, to start their approach from astern. The group of five still circled on towards the port quarter. The third section had climbed into cloud and were out of sight.

"These are Heinkel 111s, sir!"

Torpedo bombers . . . Swanwick had his glasses on them. He added, "I make it two batches of nine Heinkels in each, sir." They were circling from right to left, out there to starboard, and they'd be likely to attack from the bow either in two waves or all together. Simultaneous attack would be preferable from the convoy's point of view, and with any luck it was what the Germans would put their money on. But there'd be the Junkers to contend with at the same time, of course.

The first group of them was droning in now. Looking like bloodthirsty black bats. Not quite as poisonous as Stukas, the Ju 87s, but still foul enough. Quite a distance astern, as yet, and high.

Nick spoke to Trench over TBS.

"Tommy—with your armament, *Moloch* would do better astern. Put the other two up front to frighten the Heinkels?"

"Aye aye, sir!" Trench added, "Out . . ." Then he was calling the two astern. He might have thought of this himself: there was barely time now to make the switch before the attack came in. *Laureate* and *Leopard,* with low-angle four-sevens, were equipped to counter the low-level torpedo bombers, while *Moloch's* high-elevating guns could be used against the 88s. *Moloch* was already under helm, and before Trench had finished passing his orders the other two were beginning to move up, cracking on full power to pass up between the columns; they'd have been prepared for it by hearing Nick's call to Trench.

Leopard seemed to be handled well enough by the first lieutenant who'd assumed command.

Waiting again. Gun barrels lifted, ready. Eyes at binoculars or over sights watching the enemy deploy for an assault in which they must have known some of them would die. The group of Junkers that had crossed astern was circling back, to swing in behind four that were already on their way in. And there was another group up there somewhere, above the clouds. While out on the bow the two parties of Heinkels had joined up to form a single line-ahead; when they turned to start their attack, there'd be eighteen of them in line-abreast, so you'd have an echelon of thirty-six torpedoes raking in on that bow. But the long straggle of them was still in profile, snaking up . . . *Moloch* swept past at about thirty-four knots, all her guns jutting skyward, tin-hatted seamen clustered at each mounting. There was an exchange of waves—and the large bulk of Tommy Trench, towering in the front of that bucking swaying bridge, lifted a hand in salute. Astern, the *Berkeley's* high-angle four-inch opened fire, and the "ting" of *Calliope's* fire-gongs was just audible before her after guns came in on the act. Her three for'ard turrets and the two after ones could be used and controlled as two separate batteries, when targets proliferated so that a division of her fire-power was needed. Now the racing *Moloch's* for'ard turrets opened up. *Leopard* and *Laureate* still lancing up to the convoy's van, one each side, each in a welter of flying foam, and the first black-brown shellbursts opening like puffballs under the diving Junkers' noses. Oerlikons in action, and pompoms—at an 88 roaring over on a slanting course, diving, coming from the direction of the port bow and bombs already in the air—two, three, four—and another on the tail of that one, two others a few hundred feet higher and coming from right ahead. *Calliope's* five turrets thundering: firing, recoiling, firing, smoke belching away and the reek of cordite heavy in the wind. Bedlam as guns of many calibres and types engaged both the attackers from astern and these ambushers, queue jumpers, whom nobody had seen as they'd broken cover, diving out of the cloud-layer more like 87s than 88s—and thank God Swanwick had caught on to it just in time. A bomb whacked in fifty yards off *Calliope's* port bow, a second between her and the *Sovyetskaya Slava,* and the next one hit the *Galilee Dawn* amidships. Other bomb-splashes leaping: the rescue ship had been near-missed—Nick saw the mushroom of sea dumping itself across her quarter. Every ship in the convoy was using every gun it had: the *Galilee Dawn* included, on fire but holding on.

Then the noise-level was falling. The change came suddenly, as the last two 88s swung southward, climbing out of shellbursts. Nick had seen one go into the sea, and he thought a second, just before that hit on the *Galilee Dawn,* and at least one German had been trailing smoke as he departed. But there were still four to come, this last section already boring down from astern: there'd been a lull, a good half minute with no guns in action, time for gunners to clear away some of the litter of empty shell-cases and for ammunition-supply parties to build up stocks and refill the ready-use lockers, Oerlikons to change ammo drums, pompoms to fit new belts. *Moloch* had opened up again. The *Galilee Dawn* was still burning, a squad of fire-fighters visible in her for'ard well-deck, hoses gushing, and the mine-sweeper *Rochdale* was nosing in to help. The *Berkeley* opened fire, and *Calliope,* the whole deafening orchestra at full blast again. Shellbursts opened all around the leading bomber: bombs falling away only seconds before it was hit, flinging over as a wing buckled, bits flying off and the machine vertically nose-down streaming smoke. Numbers two and three coming in together, the fourth a long way astern. The *Winston,* rescue ship, was listing to port and falling back, alone, losing way—result of that near-miss . . . He had his glasses on her and on the *Arctic Prince* who'd turned to stay with her, the trawler part-hidden under a haze of smoke from her own close-range weapons which had only that moment ceased firing, when Treseder—unable to make himself heard—touched Nick's arm, pointing out on the bow to where the eighteen torpedo-bombers had swung into line-abreast, low to the sea and racing in.

CHAPTER FIVE

· · ·

The Heinkels were about sixty yards apart and thirty feet above the water and the destroyers were deploying to meet them in a line slanting across the convoy's van—*Lyric, Leopard, Foremost, Harpy, Laureate, Legend* . . . Nick would have taken *Calliope* out to join them, but there were still two 88s to come—from astern, where *Moloch* had just started banging away again. With those six destroyers out of the close AA defence, *Calliope*'s guns were needed here, for the moment.

One Junkers was turning away—banking to port, exposing loaded bomb-racks as it tilted. No reason clear, so far . . . *Berkeley*'s guns had opened up, after the briefest of breathers. Now he heard *Calliope*'s fire-gong, and her after turrets thundered, the vibration rattling her hull. There was no close-range in it yet; that 88 was still high, and its turn had taken it out to the convoy's quarter.

Another coming over now . . .

The one who'd swung away had done so in order to go for the *Winston*—the rescue ship, well astern and alone except for that trawler standing by her. Listing hard to port: that near-miss must have holed her, or opened a seam, or seams. *Arctic Prince* opening up with all her close-range weapons—and *Moloch* shifting target, throwing up a defensive barrage under the bomber's nose.

Bombs slammed in between the *Berkeley* and the Russian oiler. The *Galilee Dawn*'s upper-deck fire was out, but she was still leaking smoke, and there might be fire below decks. The second bomb of that stick fell close to the *Tacora*'s stern, and a third just over her bow on the other side. Some of the destroyers ahead opening fire; and as if he'd taken that as a reminder of the torpedo threat, the commodore's siren blared for an emergency turn to starboard.

Time for *Calliope* to move out . . .

"Full ahead together. Starboard fifteen."

AA fire from the merchantmen died away. The action was astern now: and ahead, all six destroyers were engaging the Heinkels. The emergency turn—the convoy's helms all over to starboard as *Calliope* also turned but speeded, drawing ahead—would leave the ships' sterns pointing straight at the attackers. Harvey-Smith reporting from the binnacle, "Fifteen of starboard wheel on, sir, both engines full ahead."

"GCO" into the director telephone, "I'm moving up between *Foremost* and *Harpy*. When your range is clear, use the for'ard turrets against those Heinkels." Over the wire, as he pushed the telephone back on to its hook, he heard the control officer shifting target and ordering red barrage—red meaning long-range fuses, as opposed to white and blue for medium or short.

"Midships, and meet her."

"The *Winston's* sunk, sir. Direct hit from that . . ."

"Steady as you go!"

"Steady, sir . . ."

Steering her into that gap. All the destroyers' for'ard guns in action, the whole wide front of the torpedo attack plastered in shellbursts. But it wasn't stopping them: they were dodging, bucketing up and down, but still coming. *Calliope's* three for'ard turrets about to join in: just for the next few seconds as she lunged forward, thrusting across the swell, her range was still obstructed by *Foremost*. He saw a Heinkel hit—flung on its side, cartwheeling into the sea. Calling over his shoulder, "Two hundred revolutions!" She was in the gap now: he heard the tinny clang just before her 5.25s crashed out—brown haze rushing over, with the reek of cordite—and rapid fire, barraging: left barrels fired, recoiled, right barrels fired, recoiled. Noise, flash, smoke, and the jarring concussions ringing in her steel, through your feet and bones. In his memory's ear, under the racket, was an echo of a report from Christie—the rescue ship, sunk. With those survivors in her. Her loss was serious, for now and also for later, in Russia and on the way home with the bigger convoy. The *Winston* hadn't been just a ship detailed to act as rescuer, she was specially fitted and equipped to look after survivors . . .

A Heinkel climbed, pulling up steeply and banking away: two others followed suit. They'd have fired, their torpedoes would be on the way, and all the others would be dropping their fish about now.

You could see them, splashing in. But others were holding on: getting in close to make more certain of their shots. It would take some nerve, he thought, to hold on into that barrage.

"One-sixty revolutions."

Leopard and *Lyric* diverging to starboard—countering a diversion by a group of Heinkels at that end of the line ... Another one hit—the third he'd seen—on fire before it hit the water in an eruption like a shallow depthcharge. Torpedo exploded there, he realised. The attack was breaking up—two still coming, but the others splitting away right and left, some climbing as they turned, others at sea-level ...

"Torpedo tracks port side!"

But the torpedoes themselves would already have passed: the tracks rose to the surface astern of them. Some would be getting to the convoy any moment now: and not a damn thing anyone here could do, except hope.

"... starboard, sir!"

It was all he'd heard of a strident yell. An open mouth, pointing arm—and a single white track ruler-straight, converging: and too late, too bloody ...

A clanging impact, from somewhere aft on the starboard side.

Nothing else. He'd felt that jar as well as heard it. Faces tense, breath held ...

No explosion, though. *Calliope* dipping her shoulder into greenish sea and digging out white foam. That torpedo's warhead had not exploded. Treseder shouted, "Glanced off us, sir!" Arms spread—and a guffaw of a laugh picked up and echoed by others—"Bounced off her!"

An explosion farther astern, though, wasn't anything to rejoice in. It was the semi-smothered but hard, knocking thump one had heard all too often. Christie shouted with his glasses trained back on the convoy, "I think that was the *Papeete* ..."

A second hit came like a duplicate of the first.

Guns falling silent, seeping smoke. A telephone buzzed, and the chief yeoman was there answering it—listening ... He reported, "Engineer

Commander says something walloped the ship's side abreast the after boiler room, sir, but no damage." And that would be *Calliope*'s full ration of luck for this trip, Nick thought. It was the glancing angle of the impact that had saved them. The quiet, as gun-fire ceased altogether, was startling: you'd been living in noise, encased in it. The sound of yet a third torpedo finding a target was shocking—like a dirty punch after the bell had rung to end a round.

No aircraft targets now. Two Heinkels had flown down the convoy's starboard side but they'd been circling away, getting out of it.

TBS calling: and it was Tommy Trench's voice . . . Thief, this is Tinker. Minesweeper *Redcar*'s gone, sir. Blown to bits. *Arctic Prince* is looking for survivors. I'm standing by the *Caribou Queen:* doubt if she'll float much longer. *Papeete*'s crew is abandoning her: *Northern Glow*'s with her. I have fourteen survivors from the *Winston*. Over . . .

1710. The *Caribou Queen* and the *Papeete* had both gone down. Survivors from them and from the *Winston* were on board *Moloch* and the two trawlers. When time permitted he'd get some transferred into *Calliope,* who had more room for them. There'd been no survivors from the minesweeper.

In the past forty minutes, in this lull which was still lasting, Nick had conferred with the commodore and then re-formed the convoy into four columns. *Calliope* was leading now, on her own between the block of merchantmen and the destroyer screen, which as usual was spread across from bow to bow in an arrow-head formation. He'd put two of the minesweepers into vacant billets at the rear of columns one and four, while the third, *Rattray,* was astern between the two trawlers guarding the assembly's rear. The two oilers were in the middle, well surrounded and with the AA ship right astern of them.

Fog a few miles to the north looked dense, but there'd be ice there too. His prayer was for the fog to spread south. But to be of any value it would need to happen quickly: the Luftwaffe would be as aware as he was himself that there were only a few hours of daylight left, and they'd be keen to take advantage of the light and of these calm conditions while they lasted.

Some sort of mix-up developing astern. He swung round, with his glasses lifting . . .

Bayleaf, in trouble again?

Focussing on the oiler's stubby, rather old-fashioned shape—bridge superstructure separate from and some distance for'ard of the upright, solid-looking funnel—which at this moment was leaking black smoke. The *Bayleaf* was no juvenile: she'd been launched in 1917, with triple-expansion engines to give her fourteen knots—which was more than most currently available oilers could claim, and would explain her inclusion in this convoy. He remembered that bomb bursting within a few feet of her side: and plainly the repair job hadn't lasted, so here was a major problem back again . . . Swanwick the ADO chose this moment to present him with another one as well.

"Radar has bogeys on bearing one-eight-four, sir, nineteen miles, closing!"

"Flag-hoist, Chief."

"Large formation, sir—fifty to sixty aircraft!"

He murmured, "Better and better." Watching the *Bayleaf* still dropping back, smoke coming out of that funnel in black gushes that would be visible for miles.

Flags rushed bright and fluttering to the yardarm.

"Chief yeoman—make to the *Bayleaf,* 'What speed can you maintain?' And to the commodore, 'Request speed reduction to five knots to keep *Bayleaf* with us. Large formation of aircraft approaching from south.'"

That number of bombers against so small a convoy would be hard to cope with. He was also aware that a lot of ammunition had already been expended. With about two hours of daylight left, and then from dawn tomorrow something like 400 miles to cover—forty hours if you could make-good ten knots, but twice that long on the *Bayleaf*'s present showing.

"From *Bayleaf,* sir, 'About seven knots. Regret funnel-smoke temporarily uncontrollable.'"

"Range sixteen miles!"

"By light to the *Bayleaf*—'Convoy speed five knots. Resume station before arrival of bomber formation now fifteen miles south.' Then TBS to Rabble: 'Speed five for *Bayleaf* to catch up. Radar indicates incoming bomber strength fifty to sixty.'"

Convoy speed was already falling, and there was some bunching in the columns. The last thing one wanted was confusion just as an attack came in. *Calliope's* guns were cocked up to starboard and inching round as they followed the radar bearing. Treseder grumbled, with his glasses up, under the rim of a tin hat which had three short gold stripes on it, "One escort carrier. Fighters'd be scrambling now. All the difference in the world."

He was right—although it wasn't much use moaning about it. If they'd had a carrier with them, her fighters would be airborne and winging out to break up that attack before it came anywhere near the convoy.

"Bearing one-nine-five. Range fourteen . . ."

Bayleaf, shepherded by *Arctic Prince,* was creeping up past the AA ship while the *Earl Granville* edged over to port to give her more room. If she was making seven knots to the convoy's five, the 400 yards she had still to cover would take—mental arithmetic—six minutes . . . Anyway she was pretty well in the fold, close under the umbrella of the *Berkeley's* guns and with the sweeper *Radstock* on her port quarter. The minesweepers each had two four-inch AA guns, as well as Oerlikons.

He thought, Five minutes: then we can increase by two knots . . .

"Captain, sir."

Swanwick: looking puzzled. "Range has begun to open, sir!"

Nick thought, Impossible. Radar's getting it wrong again . . . Then he saw a possible explanation. "Probably circling away to come up astern." Treseder was staring critically at Swanwick. Nick guessed the attackers might be making a wider sweep now because they might not be sure of the convoy's exact position. But once they caught sight of the *Bayleaf's* smoke-signals . . .

"Range sixteen miles, sir!"

"Bearing?"

"Two-oh-three, sir . . ."

So they'd be flying northwestward, roughly. Circling clockwise, they'd come to the ice and then turn east, ending by coming up astern. One factor was they'd be at the limits of their fuel-range; they wouldn't have much margin in hand for hanging around, up here.

Treseder said, "*Bayleaf's* almost in station, sir."

Things were better than they might have been. But in the back of his mind was a sharp awareness of losses incurred already, depleted ammo stocks, distance still to cover, possible fuelling problems if *Bayleaf*'s troubles got any worse.

"Bearing two-oh-oh, range eighteen, opening!"

Bruce Christie said, quietly but with an air of certainty, "They're pushing off, sir."

A bit too soon, he thought, to jump to that happy conclusion. He told Ellinghouse, "Ask the *Bayleaf,* 'Can you maintain seven knots now?'"

Leading Signalman Merry jumped to the ten-inch lamp and began to call the oiler.

"Bearing one-nine-four, sir, twenty miles!"

They might still turn back: might realise their mistake and make a cast in this direction. He guessed they'd decided they'd been heading too far east: but whatever the reason, it seemed to be the second miracle of the day.

"Radar lost target, sir . . ."

So—all right. For the moment, count your blessings. But he couldn't imagine the Germans not having another try, while daylight lasted. Three quarters of an hour later, when he was in the chartroom and Treseder came to tell him that radar had picked up a new incoming bogey, he was only surprised they'd been so slow about it. Drawing at a newly-filled pipe, he went up the ladder to the forebridge. He'd been studying the chart, working out how the convoy route might be altered to cope with the speed-reduction *Bayleaf*'s problems had forced on him; her master had said he could maintain the seven knots, with any luck, but he needed a few days with the machinery shut down, to make a proper job of it.

Seven knots meant a thirty per cent longer exposure to bombing between here and Archangel.

"Where are they?"

"It's a single aircraft this time, sir. Bearing one-seven-three, range nineteen miles."

He got up on his seat. One fast all-round look showed convoy and escorts all in station. He'd come up here expecting an attack to be coming in, and it seemed this must be a recce flight, a scout sent to check on how that last expedition had gone wrong.

"Radar confirms one single aircraft, sir. Bearing one-seven-four, range seventeen."

An idea kindling . . . With the chart in his mind's eye, and this convoy's position on it, and the rough line of the ice and this snooper nosing up towards them from the south . . . Time now being 1807: about an hour of daylight left, say. Hardly time, therefore, for a new bomber strike to be launched—unless one was already on its way this snooper out ahead of it as guide.

"Bearing one-seven-eight, fifteen miles!"

He thought the recce flight would have been sent north—this one and perhaps others too—because that large strike had failed to locate its target. They'd hardly have sent off another full-scale strike without first locating the convoy. Fifty bombers burnt a lot of gas. This reconnaissance, he guessed, would be aimed at pinpointing the target so that new attacks could be launched at dawn.

He had his glasses on what looked more like cloud than fog. Sea-hugging murk with the ice somewhere inside it.

"One-seven-five, range thirteen!"

Drawing slightly left, but near-enough steady to be sure that unless the snooper gave up and turned for home in the next few minutes, he was bound to find this convoy. So—make it worth his while? Make use of him?

There wasn't time to sit and think about it. You either did it or you didn't. And the passive line—waiting, and accepting punishment—never got anybody anywhere worthwhile.

"Chief yeoman—make to the commodore. 'Request immediate emergency turn starboard.'"

He saw Treseder trying to fathom it. He was a direct, rather simple man, and his thoughts—puzzlement, now—showed in his face. Ellinghouse had put his leading signalman on that job: Nick told him, "Now to the *Carrickmore*. Tell him, 'Hurricane stand by. Target a snooper closing on bearing one-seven-oh range twelve. Do not launch until further order.'"

The *Tacora's* siren wailed, ordering the turn. Nick told Harvey-Smith, "Bring her round." Then to the chief yeoman, "TBS to Tinker. Captain to captain." Ellinghouse called *Moloch* and got Trench on the line, then handed Nick the microphone.

"Tommy, and Rabble, listen to this. This emergency turn starboard is for the benefit of a snooper coming in on bearing one-seven-oh. I want him to think our mean course is southeast. So move *Laureate* and *Legend* from the port wing to the starboard wing—now, passing astern of the convoy . . . Second point: this snooper is not to be fired on. I want him to get his report out, before I set our tame bird-man on him. D'you understand? Over."

Shifting those two to the other wing of the screen would help to make the course look like southeast. The emergency turn wasn't as good as wheeling would have been; it was simply the quick way to get them round. It had to be done quickly because otherwise the recce plane's pilot might see the bend in the convoy's wakes, and decline to be bamboozled.

Bruce Christie was wearing an enigmatic highland smile as the convoy steadied on the course of 130 degrees. Treseder reported, with his glasses on the *Carrickmore,* "Pilot's in his Hurricane, sir."

"Good." The commodore was flying the signal for "Commence zigzag." A lookout shouted, "Aircraft—green four-oh, angle of sight ten!"

Zigzag recommencing now: the first leg would be to starboard, putting the convoy on a course of 170. The pattern of ships would be confusing to the airmen, but they'd be sure to settle for a south-easterly mean course. Nick watched the Dornier as it came in closer: it might have been the same one that had visited them this morning.

"Swanwick—tell radar to watch for any new formations."

Because this might be a scout heralding the arrival of an attacking force . . .

He'd be transmitting now, anyway. Circling up towards the bow. Could they recognise a CAM-ship when they saw one, Nick wondered? The fighter on its launching gear was very noticeable—from here. Perhaps less so from the air than in this low profile view.

Treseder asked diffidently, "Might have sent his message out by now, sir?"

"Yes. But I want him astern, where he won't see the launch."

He wondered how the Hurricane pilot would be feeling. Sitting there waiting, knowing his flight could only end with a swim in ice-cold sea. It wasn't usual, to send CAM-ships with Arctic convoys.

"Pilot's got out. He's going aft to the bridge."

"Chief yeoman. Make to the *Carrickmore*, 'Dornier now bears—whatever true bearing is—circling anti-clockwise. I will order launch when target is astern. Following destruction of enemy, Hurricane should ditch close to starboard wing destroyer, who will be ready for pick-up.'"

Ellinghouse scribbling it down on his pad, one shoulder braced against the ship's side for support against the roll . . . "Give me the microphone, will you. What's *Lyric*'s codename?"

"Richman, sir."

Zigzag bell again, for a swing back to port. Over TBS to *Lyric*'s captain, Nick suggested warm blankets and hot whisky should be ready for the Fleet Air Arm pilot. He watched the Dornier limping round the bow, thinking that with any luck they'd be in for a much longer swim.

Long, icy-looking swells sliding in on the beam rolled *Calliope* heavily as they ran under her. All ships in convoy were feeling it—masts swaying like metronomes, and deck-cargoes would be straining at chocks and lashings.

"Message passed, sir."

The Dornier was flying from the port bow round towards the beam. And the convoy was now steering 130 degrees. The next leg of the zigzag would be to port, bringing the German back from the quarter to the beam again; but the turn after that, to starboard, would put him right astern. With six minutes on each leg, say in twelve minutes.

He checked the time . . .

"Call the *Carrickmore* again. Make, 'I expect to order launch in about ten minutes. Good luck.'"

The pilot would be on her bridge to take in that message, and watching his target as it circled. Target so far unaware that it was a target—or victim . . . The Hurricane's engine would be ticking over, warming up. Leading Signalman Merry had begun to pass that signal, and Nick ran over the plan in his mind, looking for flaws in it . . . First, the Dornier had to be shot down, having already reported the convoy as being on course for Archangel or Kola: so at first light the Luftwaffe would be out hunting for it a long way south, perhaps only about 200 miles from its destination. When they didn't find it, that would be the general area they'd search. In fact, PQ 19 would have turned north—into the ice and its attendant fog. The southern area of the ice should be navigable, loose and patchy after the comparative warmth of the summer months. Up there he'd detach the *Bayleaf,* with a trawler as escort and if necessary ice-breaker, destination Hope Island, to anchor in the island's lee and make those repairs she needed, while the trawler kept her from getting iced-in. The convoy would mean-while push on eastward at twelve knots, just clear of the ice until daylight and then in it—in fog too, please God—through the daylight hours. Then at dusk tomorrow, right turn, for Archangel. If it all worked out, the enemy would have mislaid their target for something like thirty-six hours.

He explained these intentions, briefly, to Treseder, with Bruce Christie bending an ear to the explanation.

"What about the *Bayleaf,* sir?"

"We'll rendezvous with her north of Bear Island on our way west with the return convoy."

Treseder nodded. "And fuelling the destroyers?"

"Tomorrow. Under cover of fog, I hope. The Russians'll have to improve on their performance quite a lot—we might put a few stokers on board her to speed them up."

Christie coughed. "Might not get 'em back, sir. Half that Russian crew's female."

Nick had his glasses on the CAM-ship; he'd seen the pilot walk for'ard and climb into his machine, and now the convoy had completed its turn to port. Christie was asking, "One thing, sir—what if the ice is too thick for the *Bayleaf* to make Hope Island?"

"She could simply lie-up. Stop engines. Weather and fog permitting. The trawler would have to keep on the move, circling her. Alternative would be to make for Bell Sund, in Spitzbergen." With an eye on the Dornier, which was now limping round to the convoy's quarter, he checked the time . . .

Zigzag bell. Helms would be going over to starboard now.

"Chief—make to the *Carrickmore*—'Launch.'"

He'd trained his binoculars on the CAM-ship's foc's'l again. *Calliope* rolling fiercely as she turned: and the Dornier would be astern now. He could hear the clack of the Aldis, identify each letter by the sound. Last letter, and now the signing-off group . . . He saw a lick of flame, bright in the fading light, as the launcher fired: the Hurricane shot forward, and was airborne. Banking to starboard, but still low, using the ships as cover as he picked up speed, throttle wide open and flying at wavetop height across the convoy's van: only seconds after the launch the fighter sped past astern of *Calliope*. The pilot wouldn't have seen those caps being waved at him: he'd have his mind on other things entirely, mainly the Dornier—still there, completing its circuit of the convoy. Out of gun-range, of course, feeling safe, doing its best to ensure the destruction of these ships and the deaths of the men who sailed them. That Dornier crew would have no legitimate grounds for complaint, Nick thought. The Hurricane pilot would want to get as close as possible before the Germans spotted him: he'd catch them easily enough, but he wouldn't want a longer chase than necessary. He'd swung around the *Galilee Dawn* and he was hard to see now, with other ships in the way. A glimpse, just for a second, as he flew across the space between the *Galilee* and the *Republican:* then after a moment he was in sight again—climbing, and heading westward. The Dornier was several miles out on that same quarter: it was turning, evidently preparing to fly up parallel to the convoy's course at a discreet distance off to starboard.

"They've seen him!"

Treseder was right . . .

The Dornier had rolled to starboard, swinging violently away. A panic reaction—but the Germans didn't have a hope. One young Fleet Air Arm man had them at his mercy—which in the next half-minute might not be exactly brimming . . . The Dornier was trying to run for it—low to the sea, but with the Hurricane already there, going down on his tail in a shallow, killing dive.

No sound. It was happening too far away, and the background sound was the roar of *Calliope*'s fans, the slamming of sea as she rolled. There was a flash, out there: the Dornier's nose came up in a convulsive effort to remain alive before it nose-dived into the sea. A leap of spray caught the dying light as the Hurricane swept over its kill; then it was turning, banking steeply round, perhaps looking to see if there might be survivors on the wreckage. But by the time a destroyer could have got there, any swimmer would have died of cold. A few minutes was all it took: you either pulled them out instantly, or you found Tussaud-like dummies with open, staring eyes, stiff in their life jackets, bobbing to the waves. He'd seen it, more than once: and he was thinking about the Fleet Air Arm boy now, who'd be the same age more or less as his own son, Paul.

Who was doing God-knew-what, to be so close-mouthed about it . . . His thoughts returned to the pilot as the Hurricane steadied on a course to fly back up the convoy's starboard side.

Nick reached for the microphone.

"Richman, this is Thief. Your guest is about to drop in. Get him out double quick, now. Over."

He switched to "receive," and waited. It was only seconds before the answer came.

"Thief—this is Richman. Lieutenant-Commander Clegg speaking, sir. We're ready for him, and the whisky's warm. Out."

You couldn't see it from here—*Lyric* being about four miles away—but she'd have a whaler manned and low on its falls, ready to slip, a scrambling-net rigged and her doctor waiting with the rescue party.

"Chief." Nick was looking for the Hurricane, but it was out of sight, down at sea-level and hidden behind the ships of the starboard columns. "Make to the commodore, 'Request alteration of course to zero-two-zero.'"

He'd explain it all to Insole later, over the loud-hailer.

The Hurricane was in sight for about two seconds before it bounced into the sea close to *Lyric*. On the far side of her. A sheet of foam flung up, travelled with the skidding fighter and then vanished. All you could see then was *Lyric's* length shortening as she swung to starboard, losing way.

"They'll have him all right." Treseder talking to himself, with glasses at his eyes. "Can't see a bloody thing . . ."

TBS hummed into life.

"Thief—this is Richman." It was Clegg's voice again. "Sub-lieutenant Jones is in good shape and tucking-in to the refreshment. Barely got his toes wet, I'm glad to say. Over."

Nick laughed. Out of relief, more than amusement. He thumbed the switch to "transmit."

"Richman, this is Thief. Well done. Give Sub-lieutenant Jones my congratulations. Out."

And now—the ice . . .

CHAPTER SIX

• • •

From the railed Oerlikon deck at the back of *Setter's* bridge, Paul watched X-12 as the Manilla rope took the strain, hauling the midget's bow around. Tow beginning now—and a thousand miles to go . . . Dusk was spreading over the lower slopes of the surrounding hills, shadowing the water of the loch, and the last glow of cloud-filtered sunshine was highlighting the depot ship's silhouette; from *Setter's* bridge a bosun's call squealed in salute, and *Bonaventure's* bugle—a nobler, rounder note—acknowledged the tin whistle . . . MacGregor, the submarine's captain, was at the salute, all hands in her bridge and on the casing at attention, *Bonaventure's* high decks crowded with sailors. The bugle sang out again, signalling "Carry on," and the pipe shrilled; then for the fourth time on this Saturday afternoon that crowd of men were cheering, waving their caps, shouting final "good lucks."

It was quite a moment, Paul thought. Conceivably, historic.

Jazz Lanchberry took a plainer view. He growled, "We really gone an' done it, now."

"Unless anyone wants to jump off and swim." Brazier pointed astern, at Louis Gimber erect on X-12's casing with an arm hooked round the induction trunk. "I wouldn't blame that poor sod if he did."

Nobody envied the passage crews. *Setter* was quite a small submarine and her wardroom was going to be uncomfortably crowded, but it would be like living in the Ritz, compared to the eight days' close confinement facing Messrs Gimber, Steep and Towne in that tin sardine-can two hundred yards astern.

At least the weather forecasts had been good. At this time of year it was a toss-up whether you'd have fair weather or force ten gales, and the prospect of a tow across the Norwegian Sea at its worst, or even half-worst, was not a happy one. But for the next few days the outlook wasn't at all bad.

They were about to pass the other depot ship, *Titania*. It still wasn't quite sunset, so the piping ritual was starting all over again. After sundown, you didn't have to do it: but now—salutes, followed by more cheers, a sea of waving caps . . . That small, dark object astern—Gimber saluting with his free right hand as he faced the old depot ship's upperworks looming above him—looked ridiculously small, even in the confines of the loch. In open sea it would look and feel like a toy.

As lethal as it was miniature. But not necessarily lethal only to the enemy. Brazier murmured, as the "Carry on" sounded for the second time, "D'you think we're all nuts?"

Dick Eaton nodded. Beside Brazier he was like a whippet in company with a Great Dane. Paul said, "Think how good it'll feel when we've done it." He waved his cap for the last time, settled it back on his head; Lanchberry observed, "Like banging your Swede on a wall so it'll be nicer when it stops?"

Setter and X-12 were the third team to sail. First out had been Don Cameron's X-6, in tow of *Truculent*. Willy Wilson had the passage command. Then Kearon's X-9, behind *Syrtis*. Now X-12; and later—with the last of them not leaving until tomorrow, Sunday—would be X-5, whose operational CO was Henty-Creer and towing ship *Thrasher*, X-8 towed by *Sea Nymph*; Godfrey Place's X-7, passage crew commanded by the South African Peter Philip, towing ship *Stubborn*; Hudspeth's X-10 with *Sceptre*, and X-11—Dan Vicary's boat—towed by *Scourge*.

Eaton said, "You could shut your eyes and believe this was just another bloody exercise."

Paul had the same feeling—difficulty in grasping that this was it, the real thing at last. After so long, the long period of training first at Blockhouse and then in the Firth of Clyde at Port Bannatyne and Loch Striven, and then finally up here in Sutherland . . . It had seemed at times like interminable preparation for something that might never happen.

Even until yesterday there'd been no certainty. Then the news had broken like a clap of thunder—*Tirpitz* and *Scharnhorst* back in their anchorages.

A preliminary report of it had come early in the forenoon, from some intelligence source, and later it had been confirmed by Spitfire reconnaissance from North Russia. The Spits' photographs were being flown down from Russia by Catalina flying-boat, but in advance of their arrival the decision had been taken immediately by Flag Officer Submarines: Operation Source was to go ahead, on schedule and with departures commencing next day—today, Saturday 11 September. The admiral himself had flown up to Port HHZ to see them off.

Sunset now: from astern, bugles sounded as ensigns were ceremoniously lowered. *Setter* was passing various other Twelfth Flotilla craft now, and astern of her X-12 was towing easily in the sheltered, darkening water. There was some more waving and shouting: if you allowed yourself to feel it, there was a touch of emotion in this farewell—but not much to be heard over the rumble of the submarine's diesels. One last contact with the shoreside lay ahead, where Admiral Barry, accompanied by the two flotilla captains, had put out in the *Bonaventure*'s motorboat to bestow a final blessing on his children as they left home. He'd given a dinner party for them last night, on board *Titania:* it had been a lively evening, with a lot of shop-talk but good food and drink as well, and the admiral on top of his form, clearly delighted by the cheerful confidence around him. The party had continued later—for some—back on board *Bonaventure.*

A fly in the ointment was the non-arrival of those reconnaissance photos. They were needed for a final check on the positions of the targets and of the nets enclosing them. Without those pictures the final attack plan— choice of certain alternatives, but including the allocation of the various X-craft to this or that target—couldn't be decided. Barry had ordained they'd sail without them, with final details to be settled later by signal to the towing ships.

Crawshaw, *Setter*'s first lieutenant, called a warning from the forepart of the bridge: "Here's FOSM—port side, chaps . . ."

Flag Officer Submarines, Claude himself, waving his brass hat and shouting goodbye, good luck . . . MacGregor saluting, and the X-craft men on the Oerlikon platform responding too. The motorboat was nosing in close to the tow, to within hailing distance of Louis Gimber—who in this fading light could have been a scarecrow perched on a half-tide rock. The admiral would be well aware that the passage-crew assignment was going to be at least as hazardous as the attack itself.

Voices carried across the water, over the rumble of diesel exhaust; motor-boat and X-craft were practically alongside each other, with a lot of talk in progress. Brazier asked Paul, "Louis somewhat pissed last night, was he?"

"He wasn't the only one."

Eaton smiled. "Say that again. Old Dan, for one."

Lanchberry said, "You're a bunch of alcoholics. Opened my eyes, this lark has, to wardroom antics."

"Never saw you exactly abstaining, Jazz."

"Well. When in Rome . . ."

After dinner last night Paul had gone to his cabin in the depot ship to finish a batch of letters he'd started earlier—one to his mother in Connecticut, one to his father, and the longest to Jane—when Louis Gimber had sloped in, distinctly under the weather.

"Writing letters, eh."

He'd thought of answering no, feeling trees. But he had an inclination to be kind to Gimber. Because of Jane—which was at least partly a sense of guilt—and for the bad luck of drawing the passage-crew job. It certainly wouldn't have been a good idea to have Louis know he was at this moment writing to his girl—or the girl he thought of as his. When Jane wrote to Paul she used a typewriter and plain white paper instead of the violet-coloured stationery she used to Gimber. She was so good at this kind of thing, seemed to take it so naturally, that Paul sometimes wondered how much practice she'd had in the arts of two-timing. She'd certainly had some: for instance, talking about her dead fighter-pilot husband, she'd mentioned quite freely that the squadron's CO had "had a thing" for her, that he'd more than once taken advantage of Tom's absence from the station to take her out dining and dancing. There'd been some bits of the narrative miss-ing, non-cohesive, suggesting more to it than she'd cared to divulge: and whether her volunteering that much, so unashamedly, was an indication of amorality or innocence was hard to say. But she could tell that story, and still weep for Tom . . . One aspect Paul saw and understood was that since he had no thoughts of any permanent relationship with her, while Louis Gimber did at times propose marriage, she felt she could afford to share her secrets—or some of them—with him, but not with Louis; which might suggest she was taking a raincheck on the marriage idea?

"I've done all my letters." Gimber leant against the bulkhead—white-enamelled steel, and exposed piping, angle-irons; this was just a steel hutch for a man to sleep in and stow his gear. He added, slurring slightly, "Left hers open so's to add a few famous last words. Give her your love, shall I?"

Paul turned the envelope which he'd already addressed to Jane over on its face, and left his hand on it.

"Jane?" He nodded. "Please do."

"Smoke?"

"No, thanks."

"D'you have a few popsies to write to Paul?"

"A dozen or so regulars. Plus a few reserves." He folded the letter to his father and slid it into its envelope, addressed to HMS *Calliope,* c/o GPO London. "But that's to my old man."

"Where's he now?"

Paul shrugged. "Not the faintest."

"Sent him your Last Will and Testicles?"

He shook his head. "That's silly, Louis. We're going to pull this job off, and survive." He saw cynicism in Gimber's dark-skinned face. "I'm sure of it. And the others all feel the same. We know what we're up against, we've sorted out the problems—what the hell."

"You're still writing letters."

"I often do. Particularly when I know I'm going to be away on patrol or something for a while. A letter doesn't have to be a suicide note, you know."

"Qui' a few of the others have made wills."

"They must be concerned for their worldly goods, more than I am." He pointed. "Some dirty shirts in that drawer, and odds and ends, is all. They send that kind of stuff to your next-of-kin automatically . . . Anyway—I want to finish this letter, Louis, then get some sleep."

"I'll give her your love, eh?"

"Thank you. Fine."

"If you come back and I don't, Paul—"

"Oh, stuff that!"

"—would you see she's all right?"

"Certainly." He shrugged. "Although I imagine she'd survive pretty well without my help. But—sure, you can count on it."

He thought it was much more likely to be Gimber who got back, if it had to be one or the other of them, and that Jane would survive the loss of either or both of them very well, even stylishly. He had no idea at this time, of course, how absolutely right he was.

"But," Gimber pointed at him with a waving finger, "what I'm saying is—look after her. Really look after . . ."

"Message received, Louis. Loud and clear. Wilco, out—because it's getting bloody late and we need to be fit tomorrow, and you're shall we say slightly—"

"Paul."

He sighed. "Yes, Louis."

"You're a real bastard, aren't you?"

He smiled at him. Not really wanting to go into anything like that too deeply, here and now. He said, "I suppose I could be. But you're as pissed as a coot, old horse."

"So I am." Nodding, as at a declaration of profound truth. "So I am. But you hear this. If I get back, I'm going to marry her. Hear me? Marry her!"

"Delighted for you both. Marvellous. I'll be your best man, if you like. But now for God's sake, Louis, go to bed."

"Bastard!"

"Louis—fuck off?"

You wouldn't have mistaken that object astern for a prospective bridegroom. In these last shreds of daylight it looked more like a palm-stump on a sand-spit. *Setter* and X-12 were emerging from the loch, pushing out into the loppy water of the bay. The light might last just about long enough for a sight of the midget when she slipped under, Paul thought.

The "thing" between himself and Jane—"thing" being her word for an affair possibly deriving from the currently popular song *Just One of Those Things*—had started in the first instant they'd set eyes on each other. Right at the start of the party, to which he'd taken a girl he'd met the day before. Jane of course had been with Louis. Later—it was a dinner-dance at the Dorchester in aid of some "good cause"—he'd asked her to dance, and she'd moved into his arms as if she'd been wondering when he'd suggest it. Dancing together again much later, at the Bag o' Nails, he'd dated her for the following weekend. She was a WAAF, Women's Auxiliary Air Force, and was stationed at some secret establishment in Buckinghamshire where most of the personnel were Wrens; this in some indirect way was how she'd met Louis Gimber. Paul had proposed that she might come up to London next weekend: she'd told him with her head back, looking at him under those long brown eyelashes, "One condition. Not a word to Louis."

"You got it."

"Sometimes you sound quite American."

"My mother married one. After she and my father split up, when I was a kid. She lives in Connecticut, with her millionaire, and—well, I was at college over there."

"What fun!"

"My father's more so. He's terrific. He has a new wife too now, an Australian army nurse. She was in a hospital unit in Crete and he snatched her from some beach under the noses of the Germans. How's that for romance?"

"You're an interesting bunch, you Everards." She'd moved closer: not for long enough for Gimber to have seen it but long enough for Paul to know it and for the glow to brighten. "Tell me all about them next Saturday?"

Then on the Tuesday of that week, at lunch-time, he was coming in through the hall of the wardroom block—at Fort Blockhouse, the submarine headquarters at Gosport—just as Gimber emerged from the glass-walled telephone kiosk. Gimber looked unhappy.

"What's up, Louis?"

"You can buy me a beer, if you like." They went into the mess. Gimber told him, "I just rang Jane. But she's on duty this weekend, can't get away. So—" he shook his head; he seemed surprised as well as disappointed. "Too bad. I won't bother to go up, there's no point. But she never had weekend duties before—she told me, the WAAFs don't have to because the poor bloody Wrens do it all, for some reason."

"Well, you better find yourself another girl."

"There isn't another girl!"

"How about Betty?"

Betty lived in Southsea, on the other side of the harbour, and at one time Gimber had been more or less shacked up with her. At one time or another, quite a few submariners had been—more or less . . . Gimber muttered, as if that once familiar name hadn't been mentioned, "Now I know Jane, there never will be."

"Bad as that, Louis?"

"Don't you think she's a smasher?"

"Well." He'd looked away. Feeling more like a heel than he'd have liked. But nodding: "Since you mention it. She's really something."

That Saturday he took her to the Gay Nineties, then dinner at the United Hunts Club in Upper Grosvenor Street; much later, it was her idea that they should go to the Bag o' Nails. For old times' sake, she suggested—"old times" meaning the previous weekend. It was already foggy at midnight, but when they left the nightclub that Sunday morning London had been gripped in a really thick, traditional pea-souper, unnavigable without radar and a compass. It was also bitterly cold, and Jane was audibly whimpering, cat-like sounds emanating from the bundle of fur coat stumbling beside him, fur arms hugging one of his while they blundered in a mile-wide circle and twice asked directions from the same policeman who loomed up, at about one yard's visibility and after a half-hour interval, on the same street corner. The policeman was an elderly reservist, a "special," and his attitude on the second occasion was paternal as well as humorous. He advised them to give up trying to get to where Paul had had hopes of finding a taxi; he directed them instead to a hotel only about one block away. There was a night-clerk on duty, and a room available—which was providential, because there were never any rooms to be had in London at weekends. From there on memory was confused but interspersed with moments of graphic recollection: then he'd been waking up in grey morning light, Jane's eyes slowly opening—those huge, thick eyelashes, eyes greenish in her pale, oval face with its surrounding heap of very soft, dark-brown hair. She'd been puzzled, trying to remember, the tip of her tongue testing sore lips. The green eyes wider then, fixed on his.

"Paul?"

He kissed her. "Well done. Clever girl!"

Meaning she'd got his name right. She'd protested: "I must've been plastered. All that hooch! You shouldn't've—"

"If you were stinko, how d'you know we did?"

"I—" she'd shut her eyes—"I do know."

"You were frozen. It was an act of charity."

The green eyes slid open: surprise gave way to laughter which had to be smothered in the bedclothes because of people in the rooms on both sides; then they'd begun to make love again, conscious of each other and their isolation, the silence of London all around them—London fogbound, gagged and blindfolded.

Six weeks later, after the training programme had been transferred to Scotland, he'd been planning a weekend in London. In fact he'd had to spend the following week at Vickers Armstrong at Barrow, where X-12 was being completed, and the duty trip was giving him the chance of a few days off which he'd spend with Jane. Before he'd left Gosport they'd met whenever it had been possible; she'd come down to a pub in Petersfield one weekend, and for another they'd met in Midhurst. But there wasn't much leave being granted from Port Bannatyne at this stage. Then Louis Gimber had astonished him by suggesting, "Care to give Jane a ring? Take her out for a meal, or something? I'd like to hear how she really is—and you could explain why I can't get away for a month or so?"

"Well—I'd really planned to spend most of the weekend with Sally, but I suppose . . ."

Lying came easily, which it never had before. In fancy he wondered whether he could have been possessed by the spirit of the late Jack Everard, his half-uncle, to whom the ends—personal inclinations—had always justified the means . . . But another aspect was Gimber's own embarrassment, and recognition that what he was after was a check on Jane, on what other involvements she might have now Louis himself was so far away.

Paul had nodded. "OK. Where can I get hold of her?"

Setter's casing party were climbing up into the bridge and dropping down into the hatch. Last to come was Bob Henning, the ship's gunnery and torpedo officer. He reported to MacGregor, "Casing secured, sir."

"Very good." MacGregor raised his voice: "Everard, want to talk to your pal, ask him if he's ready to dive?"

"Aye aye, sir." He lowered himself on to the ladder and climbed down into the submarine's control room. The helmsman looked round, then turned back to his gyro repeater ribbon, and the PO of the watch—it was the coxswain, CPO Bird—growled, "Evenin', sir. All right, are they?"

"Just about to check."

This end of the tow-line telephone was in the wireless office, a cupboard-sized box between the control room and the engine-room. Paul edged in, nodding to the two operators, one of whom was reading *Picture Post*.

"I want a word with X-12."

"Be our guest, sir."

He pointed at a nude pin-up on a grey metal case of radio gear. "Rather be hers."

"Ah, well . . ."

"Hello, X-12?" He wound the handle again. "X-12, d'you hear me?"

Ozzie Steep's voice came through thinly, under a lot of extraneous noise. "Steep here. Hello?"

"Hello, Ozzie. Everard . . . All well there?"

"All fine so far, sir. Want the skipper?"

"Yes, please." There was a loud thrumming, a fluctuating roar, and most of it would be the noise from the induction pipe, sea and wind. Gimber would be climbing down inside now; Steep could have passed the telephone up to him but over that racket at sea-level you wouldn't have heard much.

"You there, Paul?"

"How goes it?"

"No problems—yet. Time to dive now?"

"We're ready when you are."

"OK. As soon as she slows, I'll pull the plug."

"Communications check at twenty-two hundred, then every two hours. And you'll surface for a guff-through at oh-two-double-oh, right?"

He went back up to the bridge. The telegraphist on watch would answer any emergency calls from the X-craft. *Setter* would reduce speed for the actual dive, then work up to ten knots again. X-12 would tow at about sixty or one hundred feet—Gimber's option—depending on sea conditions, comfort and stability, and every six hours he'd surface for fifteen minutes to ventilate the boat.

He told MacGregor, "They're ready to dive, sir."

Setter's captain ducked to the voicepipe: "One hundred revolutions!"

Back there astern you could see the white flare that was the midget's bow-wave, but not much else, even with binoculars. He wondered—as presently that white patch faded, disappeared, the sea mending itself over the tiny craft which would now be at the mercy of every tug and strain imparted via the heavy Manilla rope—wondered what Jane would think of it: her "earnest" boyfriend on the submerged end of 200 yards of rope and her "charitable" one—that adjective had stuck in her mind, since his "act of charity" in the hotel—here at this end of it, with a thousand miles to cover, and then God only knew what outcome . . .

Gimber's chances depended on that rope and on the weather holding up. Paul's rested on a dozen or more factors, and the most important element might be luck.

"Nip down to the telephone, Dick, and let us know when Louis's ready for ten knots."

The towing submarines would stay on the surface until they were nearer the target area, because the rate of progress dived would have been too slow. Nearer the Norwegian coast they'd be dived for reasons of security—which was primarily why the midgets were to keep out of sight right from the start. One chance sighting by some recce aircraft or U-boat could abort the whole operation: the bases in Norway would be alerted, anti-submarine forces concentrated, quite likely the target ships moved elsewhere.

On his way to the wardroom for supper, Paul stopped for a look at the chart. The first few days' courses were already pencilled in. From Cape Wrath, course for all the towing submarines would take them through a point seventy-five miles west of the Shetlands, and from there they'd diverge, fanning out on to parallel tracks twenty miles apart for the long haul northeastward.

Soames, *Setter's* navigator, paused beside him.

"Make sense?"

"More or less." Turning his back on the chart, he was in the gangway but to all intents and purposes also in the small space known as the wardroom. "What bothers me is how we're all going to fit in here."

In fact there were five bunks; but one was always empty, its owner on watch, so one extra man could be accommodated by "working hot bunks"—i.e. when you came off watch you got into the bunk someone else had just left. There'd be space for another body under the wardroom table—his head and legs would stick out at each end, so he'd be trodden on sometimes—and a hammock was to be slung in the gangway for a third. Jazz Lanchberry was being accommodated in the ERAs' mess, so that would do it.

Brazier pointed out, "You'll be better off when we make the changeover. Only three in the passage crew, instead of the four of us."

"But we've got to put up with you for a whole week, first?"

"Eight days, Chief."

Massingbird, the engineer, shook his head. "Bloody hell . . ."

MacGregor glanced at him. "Hospitable little ray of sunshine, isn't he?"

Paul turned in early, using Soames' bunk, Soames having gone up on watch. He was taking the midnight-to-two watch himself, so he left it to Eaton to make the 2200 communications check, and made another himself when the control room messenger shook him at ten minutes to midnight. It was Ozzie Steep who answered: Gimber was off-watch, he said, asleep in the fore end. That bow compartment was the only place in the X-craft where a man could stretch out full length, on top of the wooden cover of the battery. Steep said everything was all right: plenty to do, but no problems. From the background "Trigger" Towne shouted, "No problems yet, chum!" Paul said, "Give Trigger my regards and tell him he should have more confidence in his own machinery."

Steep repeated it. Then, "I won't tell you what his answer is."

"I can guess. Tell him to get stuffed too. Listen, I'm going on watch now, I'll contact you again just after two. You'll be due for a surfacing then, but tell Louis to wait for my call first, will you?"

The routines wouldn't have to be spelt out, after a day or two. But Towne was right, you did have to expect problems, defects, sooner or later. None of the X-craft had been run for a solid week, for instance, until now. Also, the passage crews were going to be kept busy—checking machinery performance, carrying out constant maintenance and keeping the boat dry. Condensation would be a problem, and damp would be a threat to insulation, and thus all the electrical equipment. There'd be a lot to do, all round the clock, for the two men on watch, and as well as maintenance and mopping up there'd be meals to prepare. The food was all tinned stuff and concentrates, and the cooking equipment consisted of one gluepot for heating things in, and a kettle. But the maintenance, of course, would have one vitally important purpose—to have the boat in tiptop condition when they reached the Norwegian coast and switched crews.

Keeping his watch in *Setter*'s bridge, alone except for the two lookouts behind him while the submarine drove northward at a steady ten knots, Paul was constantly aware of Gimber down there at the end of the towrope. Of the fact that they were friends—on the face of it—and also relied on each other for their lives ... Feet braced apart against the submarine's jolting, wave-bashing motion: binoculars at his eyes in a constant lookout for enemies, searching the surrounding darkness, black sea and an horizon that was no sharp division, only a vague merging of sea and sky ... One of the discomforting aspects of his involvement with Jane was that it would really devastate Louis Gimber if he ever found out about it. To start with it hadn't seemed so serious: there'd been the phrase "all's fair in love and war" in mind, and the fact that wartime relationships had tended to be—well, transient; girls like Betty, for instance: nothing so very serious or long-term. But Paul knew he was hooked now, he couldn't have given her up, despite the fact that if Louis got to know about it, it would kill him.

He stooped to the voicepipe.

"Control room ... Tell the W/T office to call X-12 and ask if they're OK."

It was an hour since he'd spoken to Ozzie Steep. No harm in an extra check.

He'd asked Jane, a few months ago, why she didn't break it off with Gimber. Why not tell him she didn't love him, so there could be an end to pretence. Jane's answer had been, "Because I'm really fond of him. Don't you see? I don't want to hurt him, Paul, why should I?"

"But aren't you deceiving him? You've told me he wants to marry—if you let him believe it's on the cards—when it isn't, is it? So he has to find out some time, you can't string him along for ever!"

"I can't just brush him off, either—when he's so kind, and . . ."

"But when it gets to a point when he's actually pressing you to marry him?"

"That's just him, it's not my fault. He knows very well that as far as I'm concerned marriage is out of the question. I've told him so—oh, fifty times . . . I've been married—and you know what happened."

"Wouldn't it be less hurtful in the long run to let him know he doesn't stand a chance?"

"But why should I hurt him like that? When he knows I don't intend marrying anyone while this bloody war's still going?"

Round and round. Leading nowhere.

"Bridge!" He bent to the pipe. The helmsman told him, "Lieutenant Gimber says all's well, sir!"

"Very good."

Straightening, resuming the careful all-round search. Behind him the two lookouts, one each side of the bridge, pivotted slowly, each man sweeping from bow to stern and across the stern and then back again. Diesels rumbling through submerged exhausts while the sea rushed and boomed over the curve of the pressure-hull a dozen feet below the perforated platform that he stood on, and white foam seething, leaping, all along the submarine's slim, plunging length.

All Jane knew about Paul's job or Gimber's was that they were submariners and in the same flotilla. When they'd been down in Hampshire, and as often as not free for weekends in London, she'd asked him why none of them ever seemed to go away to sea. She'd said, "You're like a fighter squadron. A crowd of you all part of the same outfit and—well, always around!"

His mind hadn't been on the question—war, fighter squadrons, X-craft, anything like that.

"You're sensational. Really absolutely . . ."

"So what's the answer?"

She'd been on top, looking down at him, her face in darkness because of the brilliance of the chandelier in the middle of the room behind her. They'd booked into the Savoy, that weekend. Jane's idea—the Savoy being one of a handful of places where you could be just about sure of not running into any of your friends.

"If you don't tell me, I'll just sit here, I shan't move!"

"That's all right. I like the view."

"Please, tell me?"

"I'll do the moving."

"About time . . ."

"Submarine patrols can be quite short. And some people are what's called spare crew, not permanently in any one boat . . . Did I mention you're the most beautiful thing I ever saw?"

"Bridge!"

He leant down. "Bridge."

"Relieve lookout, sir?"

"Yes, please." So it was now fifteen minutes to the hour. Lookouts and OOWS changed over at staggered times so there'd always be some eyes up here that were already tuned to the dark.

At ten past the hour he was in the W/T office and had Gimber on the telephone. X-12 was due to come up now, to "guff-through"—meaning to get the stale air out and fresh air in.

"How's it going, Louis?"

"Like always—stuffy and damp. We're porpoising a bit, but not too badly. Any new met forecasts?"

"Not that I know of. Keep your fingers crossed, we might get this weather the whole way over. But stand by, now—we're slowing down."

Engine noise, and the rush of cold air past the wireless office, lessened as diesel revs decreased. Gimber's voice distantly over the line, "Stand by to surface," then the click as he hung up and the wire went dead. This was to be the routine for the eight days of towing: four times a day, so thirty-two surfacings and a total of eight hours up top during the whole period. The last surfacing would be for the changeover of crews, close to the entrance to the fjords. Thinking of that as he put the telephone down, Paul was looking forward to the moment, probably as much as Gimber would be: he wanted to get there, get it over.

"Excuse me, sir."

The telegraphist was holding back an earphone, uncovering the ear on this side. "Asking about weather forecasts, was he?"

"Yes. Why?"

"On the log, sir. Be on the chart-table now, most likely."

"Thanks."

He edged out, slid the door shut and moved for'ard. MacGregor was coming the other way, dressed for the bridge, and the helmsman was shouting up the pipe to Crawshaw, "Captain coming up, sir!" MacGregor asked Paul, "Been talking to them?"

He nodded. "Surfacing now, sir."

The signal log was on the chart, and the new meteorological report was the top sheet in the clip. At first glance, the first words he saw were bad enough: he began again, getting the detail, wanting that first impression to have been wrong. It had not, though. What this promised was a new weather-pattern approaching from west-southwest and reaching the Norwegian Sea by tomorrow night or the day after—a deep depression accompanied by south-westerly gale-force winds.

CHAPTER SEVEN

· · ·

Light from a new day's dawn glinted on the crests of a lively, rising sea. Wind on the beam, and *Calliope* rolling hard; with his glasses moving slowly across the convoy's bows Nick heard Treseder's gruff report, "Ship's at action stations, sir."

He'd only just come out of his sea-cabin, having enjoyed a few hours' sleep. And how good or foul a day this might turn out to be would depend very largely on how soon the Luftwaffe located them. This was the main consideration, at the moment. The amount and height of cloud would be a factor in it and would reveal itself more clearly in the next half hour; but the rising wind might well break it up, however promising it might look to start with, so the wind was to the enemy's advantage.

Another factor was simply luck. And perhaps—recalling his own words of yesterday—no, day before yesterday—it might be unwise to count on more of that, when they'd had so much already. Torpedoes that didn't explode, for instance; and fog in the right place at the right time; and Kidd's cruisers taking the brunt of the Luftwaffe's ire ...

Until dusk last evening the convoy had still been in pack-ice and its accompanying fog. In air like frozen soup, sea blotched white, a black-and-white surface rising and falling as regularly as if the ocean were taking long, deep breaths; a great ice-bound lung expanding and contracting, surviving in deep sleep, hibernation, blind to the double column of ships forging eastward through it from dawn to dusk, ghost-ships gliding through a mysterious, silent wasteland. *Calliope* had led the starboard column, with the commodore's *Tacora* abeam and the rest of the merchantmen and the AA ship in double file astern. Up ahead the trawler *Northern Glow* had cleared the way where necessary, her strong hull and stem being better suited to occasional arguments with floating ice than a destroyer's thin plating would have been.

From dawn onwards Nick had mentally kept his fingers crossed, dreading an end to the fog-bank where the convoy could, at very short notice, have found itself steaming out into clear, bright day. In fact it had thickened, if anything; then the night was coming and finally they'd finished with it, having taken maximum advantage of its shelter. With the darkness, PQ 19 had re-formed, and steered south.

Now, inevitably, the holiday was over. Or very soon would be.

Northern Glow was the only trawler with them now. *Arctic Prince* was escorting the *Bayleaf* to—or towards—Hope Island. Before they'd diverted, *Bayleaf* had fuelled three of the destroyers, while the *Arctic Prince* had gone scrounging around the convoy to collect as much white paint as could be begged from close-fisted bosuns. Nick had suggested that either at Hope Island or on the way there, or wherever they might have to heave-to, both ships should paint their upperworks white. Then if, or when, the fog lifted they wouldn't so easily be spotted.

The other four destroyers had fuelled during the day from the Russian. Practice had improved the performance of the *Sovyetskaya Slava*'s part-female crew, and it hadn't gone too badly. The *Slava* was back in the middle now, in the centre billet of three columns each of three ships; she had the *Tacora* ahead of her and the AA ship astern, and Americans—the *Plainsman* and the *Republican*—on both sides. *Calliope* was on her own, 400 yards ahead of the commodore, with *Moloch* another 1000 yards ahead and *Harpy* and *Foremost* almost abeam, on the convoy's bows. *Laureate* and *Legend* were close to port of the block of merchantmen, *Leopard* and *Lyric* to starboard, while the rear was covered by the minesweepers and *Northern Glow.* Course 170, speed twelve: Cape Kanin, guarding the entrance to the White Sea, was now about 350 miles ahead.

Improving light allowed him to see *Moloch*'s dark superstructure rolling crazily above the white froth surrounding her, while to port that very familiar H-class silhouette was *Harpy,* clearly outlined against the rising dawn. Nick's glasses swept past *Foremost,* and on round to the starboard quarter.

That was the *Galilee Dawn* leading column three; beyond her, only just visible from here, was *Leopard*. That was the dark side and the dangerous one, where an enemy would be hard to see but would have any of these ships clearly in his sights. Although the only enemy one would have expected here would have been a U-boat, and there'd been no sight or sound of any. All busy down south. To that extent the intelligence appreciation seemed to have been right. Much less so when it came to the shifting south of air-strength: German airmen would be watching this dawn, too—impatiently, with search planes ready for take-off, eager to seek out this target for the bomber squadrons.

The last news they'd have had of PQ 19 would have been thirty hours ago, when that Dornier would have reported it as 200 miles west of here and steering south. Since then they'd have realised it could only be hiding in the northern fog, but not necessarily that it had been pushing east. If they'd been fooled by that southerly course they might even be panicking now, imagining their target might have eluded yesterday's searchers and practically reached its port or ports of destination. Which they might assume to be Murmansk, the Kola Inlet.

"Anything on the screen, Swanwick?"

The ADO said no, the 281 screen was clear. Not that one could rely on that set entirely.

In London, admirals would be worrying, wondering where PQ 19 had got to. The last they'd have heard would have been when the convoy was under attack and losing ships.

"Pilot." Christie moved up closer. Nick told him, "Draft a signal to SBNO North Russia, repeated to Admiralty and AIG 311. Give him an estimated position for dawn tomorrow, and request rendezvous with local escorts, ditto fighter cover. Let me see it before you give it to Bliss to code."

He'd hesitated over this one. Mostly because to predict where they'd be by this time tomorrow seemed like a twisting of the devil's tail. But chances of getting some help from Soviet destroyers and some fighter cover might be improved by putting the request in early. Also it would be as well to get everything off your chest at the first contact with an enemy, get it out when you had the opportunity and if necessary amend it later if things went badly.

Tomblin brought breakfast to the sea-cabin. While he ate it he thought of the day ahead, his dispositions, orders to the escorts and arrangements with the commodore. Whether there might be anything he'd overlooked or that could be improved. By this time he'd already shifted *Moloch* to the convoy's rear . . . He'd finished eating and was lighting the first pipe of the day when Tomblin came to collect the tray.

"More coffee, sir?"

"No, nothing else."

"Is it right we're for Archangel this time, sir, not Kola?"

He nodded. "Because that's where the empty ships are, that we're collecting. Moved there to be further from the German airfields."

The anchorage at Vaenga in the Kola Inlet was a frequent target for bombers.

"So now it's bring on the dancing girls, sir, eh?"

"Except they have to find us first." He added, "When they do, don't let me see you without a tin hat on."

It would have been a shorter trip to Kola, the Murmansk approach. Better therefore from the fuelling angle too—which was partly why it had been essential to have the *Bayleaf* available up there—but in any case a shorter period of exposure to the bombers as the convoy ran south. But Archangel was where the empties had congregated, and bringing them home was the main purpose of this operation. Archangel being ice-free still, which in a month's time it probably would not be.

Radar picked up its first contact just after five in the morning. The bearing was 224, range eighteen miles.

"One aircraft, or more?"

"Single bogey, sir."

It was too early in the day to be found—with fourteen hours of daylight yet to come, and the enemy only about 300 miles away, flying-time lessening every minute.

"Drawing left. Bearing two-two-one, range sixteen."

A minute later the bearing steadied. Indicating a direct approach. Then it began to draw right. Christie murmured with his hands together as if in prayer, "Turned for home. Please God."

"Tempt not the Lord thy God." Treseder growled it, with his glasses up on that bearing. Swanwick reported, "Bearing two-two-five—bearing steady—range fourteen!"

Treseder said, "Warned you, pilot."

A minute passed. Two minutes. The German was still coming straight for them.

"Aircraft—green five-oh, angle of sight ten!"

It was Merry, the leading signalman, who'd made the sighting, but suddenly everyone else could see it too. Treseder looked round at Nick. "Seems to be flying left to right now, sir."

"Yes, I'm on it." It was a Blohm and Voss this time. And no Hurricane left to deal with it. Very shortly it would be delighting the Luftwaffe commanders with the information they'd been waiting for: and there wasn't a damn thing you could do about it.

He saw the thing's profile shortening, as it swung towards the convoy.

"He's spotted us."

"Yeoman—flags—aircraft on that true bearing."

You could only sit and wait now. With a fair idea of the likely pattern of the next fourteen hours. It would start quite soon, he guessed; the bomber squadrons would almost certainly be lined up and ready, they'd only need to get the snooper's signal and take off, fly 300 miles ... One thing you could do now was get that signal away.

The first attackers appeared at 0728, and the red air-warning flag, which had been bent-on and ready, rushed to *Calliope's* yardarm. Radar tracked bogeys coming in dead straight from the southwest, obviously knowing exactly where they were going, this time. By the time they came in sight the bearing was shifting to the right; it was a force of a dozen Ju 88s and it was deploying to attack from astern, as usual.

Cloud-cover was patchy, wind-driven at about 6000 feet. The ships were rolling heavily, bedded in foam, the destroyers in particular finding the going hard. Bombers like black insects against the patchwork of grey and blue; they were flying in and out of cloud, which was widespread enough to provide them with cover but not so thick as to impede their frequent viewings of the convoy.

They'd be chatting among themselves. Schultz and Muller go for the cruiser, Schmidt and Braun take the oiler . . . Guns like pointing fingers following them round, gunners' eyes slitted through the white cotton antiflash masks under the rims of tin hats.

Nick used his telephone to the control officer in the tower, to remind him not to waste ammunition. "Shoot at incoming aircraft only. This is likely to be a very long day." He hung up. Glancing round astern, checking that all ships were in station: and they were, Commodore Insole had his mob well disciplined. The view had some of the quality of a panorama in oils: the bright colours of the day, the warships' slim lines, plunging hulls and waiting guns, and the stolidly advancing merchantmen. There was a look of doggedness about them: they were ignoring the approaching enemies, simply getting on with the job that mattered, the delivery of their cargoes.

The leading pair of Ju 88s were turning to come up astern.

"Attacking, sir . . ."

"Tell radar to keep all-round watch."

There'd be more coming behind these. Probably some already on their way. The best you could hope for would be reasonably good intervals between assaults—time to draw breath and tidy up. Off Crete, he remembered, there'd sometimes been no intervals at all; the enemy bases had been so close that the Stukas had run a shuttle service—some attacking, others flying back for new bomb-loads, the fresh waves always coming in. Day-round bombing: Crete had been about as bad as it could get.

Except, as Treseder had said the other day, the water had been warm enough to stay alive in.

Moloch opened fire, at two 88s coming in at about 2000 feet with their snouts down. Two more behind them, doubtless attempting to slip in un-opposed while those front-runners drew the flak. Another pair, higher and farther back, banking round to tag on to the queue . . . All the rear part of the convoy was in action by this time, the sky dirtying rapidly with shell-bursts and the haze from disintegrated bursts, tracer soaring red and yellow through it. A lot of that was the sweepers and the trawler, who were very close to the rearmost ships—*Moloch* crossing astern of them, weaving and with her four-sevens cocked up and spitting. The *Berkeley* had opened up: she'd be barraging over the Russian oiler. Now *Lyric* and *Legend* from the beams—with the Junkers down at about 1500 feet, one slightly astern of the other and both going for the centre, straight into the defensive barrage over the *Sovyetskaya Slava*.

Bombs starting, in slow-motion . . .

The one astern flared like a match being struck. Pieces flew off: then it was a black nucleus plunging seaward, trailing smoke and flame: the sea on the *Berkeley*'s port side received it in a sheet of foam. Bombs were going in astern of the Russian and off her bow and abeam of the *Galilee Dawn*. First brush, and so far the only blood spilt was some of their own. Second pair coming and a whole day of it stretching ahead, about as forbidding as a day could be.

"Captain, sir . . ."

Bridge messenger: red-faced, about eighteen, the look of a farm-boy, tin hat seemingly resting on his ears. "Yes?"

"From the ADO, sir—new formation two-three-oh, sixteen miles!"

He was looking up at two Junkers flattening from their dives over the rear of columns one and two: they were wing-tip to wing-tip, and their bombs were falling away together, twisting slowly as if suspended on elastic but then accelerating so you quickly lost sight of them; two more attack-ers were in their shallow-dive approach paths. A bomb smacked in within yards of the stem of the *Earl Granville*—so close that she was steaming on into its splash, a shower of white rain sprinkling her deck cargo. The second exploded on the *Plainsman*'s stern: he saw the flash, flame and smoke in the split second before another went in amidships and she blew up—splitting open, gushing skyward, flame and smoke and a thunderous roar from the explosives that had been packed into that midships hold. The *Earl Granville* vanished into the wide mess of it and came out again on this side: she'd have had no room even to put her wheel over, she must have scraped past as much of the American as was left—no more than wreckage, burning still, while the sweeper *Radstock* nosed in to look for survivors. Not that you'd expect any. *Legend* tearing in, barraging with her close-range weapons in the face of another German slanting over from the quarter.

"Aircraft green six-oh, angle of sight ten, closing!"

This would be the second wave. The Luftwaffe would be determined to make a job of it now, make up for the day they'd lost while PQ 19 had been hiding in the ice. And there was to be no pause this time. The fellow coming over now was, like his recent predecessors, going for the Russian oiler. Oilers were always priority targets, coming second only to escort carriers ... *Calliope*'s guns thundering as she rolled from beam to beam under a sky plastered black and brown and that 88 banking away, baulking at it, nose coming up and the pilot getting the hell out, funking—but the bombs coming, too—less aimed than ditched. Nick was wanting to turn away to look at the new formation coming in, see what they were and how many. But with those bombs in the air and every ship in the convoy shifting target to greet the next comer—from astern again, this one straight and purposeful ...

The first of the stick of four randomly sprayed bombs went into the sea abeam of the *Tacora,* a second farther out, a third off *Calliope*'s port quarter, and the last—*Harpy.*

It hit amidships. Seeing it was like feeling it: a kick in your gut, or brain. He saw a flash, a gout of smoke breaking out with things flying in it: as she rolled back to starboard he thought the hit had been in her engine-room. But—she'd broken in half. The urge to get over there was countered by the need to stay exactly where he was, where *Calliope*'s guns in combination with the *Berkeley*'s were of the greatest use, barraging above the merchantmen. *Harpy* was hidden in what looked like smoke but was more likely steam: the bomb-burst had been in her belly and it would have been a boiler exploding that had torn her apart, he guessed. *Calliope* barraging over the *Tacora* and the *Sovyetskaya Slava* as this 88 levelled at about 1200 feet and its bombs began to fall away in a straight line right over the middle of the convoy. Looking back at *Harpy* again he saw the bow section on its own and the *Carrickmore* swinging inward to pass this side of it; beyond was *Laureate,* like everyone else ceasing fire as that last enemy swept over, roaring over astern of *Calliope* and banking right, beginning to climb but with smoke coming out of its starboard engine. He was aware of a fleeting prayer in his heart for the damage to worsen, flames to spread, engulf, fry . . .Astern of *Carrickmore* the bow section of the wrecked destroyer was ver- tical in a blossoming of white foam: he could see figures still clinging but others leaping off, and *Laureate's* whaler in the water, *Laureate* herself within yards and stopped, *Legend* passing on her far side—and the *Earl Granville,* rolling ponderously and with a large area of empty sea ahead of her where until about eight minutes ago the *Plainsman* would have been. *Moloch* was moving fast across the *Earl Granville's* stern and engaging another bomber: a bomb-splash went up to starboard of the commodore, and that attacker was removing itself, now, climbing, *Calliope* therefore shifting target—*Berkeley* too, at an 88 peeling to starboard to go for *Laureate. Moloch* coming to help, Tommy Trench having seen this danger, his ship under full rudder, on her beam ends as she turned at flat-out revs, all her guns blazing . . .

Time: 0804.

In the second wave there were only seven aircraft—Ju 88s again—and they'd gone by 0830, leaving one of their number in the sea. There was a lull then, and by 0900 there was still nothing on the radar screen. Nick had taken the chance of relaxing his ship's company from action stations; it was a chance that might not come again all day, and therefore worth taking. Not that "relaxing" was quite the word: you watched the minutes crawl by, knowing that the enemy would be back, and soon. Every minute that passed meanwhile was of value, not only recuperative, but a fractional erosion of the long hours of strain that lay ahead.

Five survivors of the *Plainsman* had been picked up by *Radstock,* and

Laureate had fifty-three on board from *Harpy*. There was too much of a sea running now for wounded men to be transferred from ship to ship and all those five in *Radstock* were in bad shape, so *Legend* had put her doctor into the minesweeper by seaboat. *Laureate* had taken *Harpy's* position on the convoy's bow, *Legend* had moved up and *Radstock* had joined her on that port side.

A signal had gone out to Admiralty, repeated to AIG 311 and to the rear-admiral in North Russia, reporting the new losses. It would also alert the rear-admiral to the possibility of delay in making the proposed dawn rendezvous with locally-based escort forces.

The *Plainsman's* master had been vice-commodore, the man who'd have taken over as commodore if Insole in the *Tacora* had come to grief. Insole had appointed Captain Hewson of the *Carrickmore* to replace the American, who'd been lost with his ship.

0910 now. It felt more like noon. Nick wished to God it had been noon.

Visitors, taking advantage of the lull, came up to the bridge for various purposes. Surgeon Commander Francomb, the PMO, was one of them, reporting on the state of the wounded men among the survivors who'd been transferred into *Calliope* two nights ago from the trawlers and from *Moloch;* they were survivors in fact from the *Winston,* the *Papeete* and the *Caribou Queen*. Francomb had had to operate on one American, a radio operator from the *Caribou Queen,* to remove a piece of metal from his ribcage, and the patient was apparently in good shape.

Next came Mr Wrottesley, Commissioned Gunner.

"Ammo state, sir."

He accepted the piece of paper. "Thank you, Mr Wrottesley."

"Not much to give thanks for, sir."

Studying the figures for ammunition expended and remaining, and knowing these levels would apply equivalently in the other ships, was like considering a list of unavoidable expenses for which you didn't have the cash in hand. If attacks continued at this rate, by dawn tomorrow there'd be very little to fight back with.

He passed the list to Treseder, and told the gunner, "We'll last out, I expect."

"I expect we better, sir!"

Pink, smooth face, freshly shaved. Small, bright eyes, and a nose like a dab of putty. Mr Wrottesley was president of the warrant officers' mess, and he was always dapper, brushed and polished. Nick guessed he'd have shaved specially for this visit to the bridge. Asking now, "Four of 'em downed, was it, sir?"

"Three and—"

"Bogeys bearing two-four-oh, eight miles, sir!"

"—and a probable, Mr Wrottesley."

Eight miles was very close for the radar to have picked up a new attack. He glanced at Treseder: "Action stations."

"Radar lost contact, sir!"

Treseder, with his mouth opening to pass that order and one hand simultaneously reaching to the alarm push-button, hesitated, looking back at him; Nick nodded, and the commander shouted "Action stations!" That was for the Marine bugler, whose station was at the back of the bridge near the tannoy broadcast system; the buzzer duplicated the urgent message and also specified the nature of the emergency by sounding repeatedly the morse letter A, standing for air attack. Nick meanwhile guessing at the reason for close-range detection and then immediate loss of contact—they'd be low-flying aircraft, most likely torpedo bombers, approaching under the radar loop, with one or more of them climbing for a better view when they'd known they were somewhere near their target. Having spotted the ships, dipping down again—and the next contact, as likely as not, would be visual.

All hands were rushing to their stations, putting on anti-flash gear and tin hats as they ran, climbed or flung themselves down ladders, the ship's rolling adding to the hazards. The red warning flag was hoisted, and an Aldis lamp was clashing, to flash a message to the commodore: a loudspeaker boomed over the general racket of the process of closing-up, "Director target! Torpedo bombers, true bearing two-six-oh, range seven miles, angle of sight zero, flying right to left!"

He picked up the telephone. That broadcast system was an emergency way of overriding the routine communications links, which tended to be cluttered at moments such as this one, to alert all quarters to a new threat.

"What are they?"

"Heinkel seaplanes, sir—one-one-fives. About fifteen of them."

"Right." Decision took about two seconds. "When they start to turn in, I'll take her out to meet them." He hung up. He'd try to break up the attack before it got in close. "Pilot, give me the TBS." He told Treseder, "Fifteen Heinkel one-one-fives, this time." Then: "Tinker, this is Thief. Captain to captain. Over."

Moloch piped up: Trench here, sir. Over.

"Tommy, these are Heinkel one-one-fives—now green sixty-five, range about five miles. When they show which way they're coming from, I'm going out to head them off. Whatever birds get past me will be yours. You'd better come up this way now. Out."

"Ship is at action stations, sir."

"Aircraft green six-oh, seaplanes, angle of sight zero!"

That had been a lookout's yell, and Nick had his first sight of them at about the same moment. Studying them, he realised that unlike yesterday's 111s these would have only one fish each. They were slower too, and should be easier to hit.

The loudspeaker warned, "Enemy turning towards! Bearing green five-eight!"

Time to move out, then . . . "Three hundred revolutions. Starboard ten." He'd scrape out under *Foremost*'s stern.

"Ten of starboard wheel on, sir. Three hundred revolutions passed."

Moloch was pounding up between columns two and three, passing in a welter of suds between the *Republican* and the *Sovyetskaya Slava* as *Calliope* swung to starboard, heeling as she pitched bowdown, her foc'sl buried in the sea, for'ard turrets lashed by the flying spray: then her bow was rocking upwards and her four propellers, gripping in deeper water, thrust her forward. He shouted back to Harvey-Smith, "Midships—steady her on two-three-oh!"

The sad-looking, greyish face dipped to the voicepipe: "Midships . . ."

From the Heinkels' cockpits *Calliope* would be just one grey fragment of a jumbled crowd of ships. In these sea conditions she wouldn't easily be distinguishable from a destroyer, at that distance and to a flyer's untutored eye, so until she'd passed astern of *Foremost* and pulled herself right away from the convoy they wouldn't know what was being prepared for them.

"Course two-three-oh, sir!"

She'd cut through *Foremast's* wake about thirty yards astern of her. Christie had checked that the destroyer's bearing was changing, drawing left, so the anxious look on Harvey-Smith's face was hardly justified. He wasn't a destroyer man, of course—and Nick was handling *Calliope* like a destroyer now. Not getting much of a view of the seaplanes at this moment because of the sheets of spray that she was flinging up . . . Cutting astern of *Foremost* now: the destroyer's X and Y guns' crews and depthcharge team huddled in shelter, watching the cruiser race by: she'd be quite a sight, too. He put his glasses up again. Not wanting to open fire too soon and waste shells, nor leave it too late either. Thinking of the ships lost in that first torpedo attack, the sense of defeat he'd suffered from then, and also remembering the experience of the previous convoy, PQ 18, in similar circumstances: in one assault by Heinkel 111s, out of seven ships in the two starboard columns six had been hit—and sunk—and another two in the centre of the convoy as well. It wasn't a form of attack to be treated lightly. His tactic now was to leave the convoy well defended by its destroyers and at the same time carry the attack to the enemy at some distance from it.

He'd adjusted the course to 225. The convoy was well astern now, and the Heinkels in plain sight ahead. Low, wave-hopping, looking like clumsy birds with legs down ready for a landing. Torpedoes ready between those legs . . .

"Open fire, sir?"

"Yes. Open fire."

The gongs chimed: and the for'ard turrets roared, *Calliope* quivering from it as she plunged. Rising—and another salvo, smoke and cordite fumes rushing over. With his glasses on the attackers and the three turrets falling into a rhythm of steady barraging he saw the bursts opening, sea-planes bucking as if to bounce over the stuff exploding in their faces. Guns in faster rhythm and in triplicate—fire, recoil, fire, recoil—alternately left and right barrels in each turret. It was having its effect too: he saw two bombers collide and a third in the sea on its nose, tail up and somersaulting over. Some were turning away and another, pouring smoke, light glinting on its torpedo dropping askew, before the seaplane burst into flames and went into the sea. About seven were still coming—three of them circling away to their left. The guns were still concentrating on the larger group: of which another had gone down . . .

"One-four-oh revolutions!"

Sea flying, wind whipping, familiar stench of battle acrid in eyes and nos-trils. High speed was no longer necessary or desirable; slowing down would reduce the pitching and make the gunners' job easier. There were four at-tackers still coming, that he could see. One of them turning—another's wings slanting as it banked to follow. Three had split away earlier on their own, but Trench would be taking care of them. Nick was deaf, by now, from the guns' noise: Treseder's shout came so faintly that it might have been from fifty yards away instead of six feet: "Convoy's altering to starboard, sir!"

To comb the tracks of an attack by that trio, he guessed. A quick glance astern showed destroyers in action. Turning again, focussing his glasses on the last two Heinkels—which were close, now, slanting over from the port bow like droning, jinking moths—they must have swung right and then left, he realised, manoeuvring for an attack not on the convoy now but on this ship herself—he saw one fish splash down: then the other . . .

"Port fifteen!"

"Port fifteen, sir . . ."

No problem—it was just a matter of turning her head-on to the torpedo tracks, to let them pass harmlessly each side of her. Oerlikons and pompoms were in loud action: he thought suddenly, Wasting ammunition—imagining they'd be shooting at the pair whose torpedoes he was now avoiding. He hadn't realised, at that point, that there'd been a third Heinkel coming in at *Calliope* from the other quarter.

Explosion, right aft . . .

It had been a crash so unexpected that for a second you couldn't believe in it. Then you were hearing its echo deep in the ship's bowels, a jolt that shook her hull and frames: pure shock, under the roar of a seaplane banking away to starboard, turning and climbing for safety.

"Torpedo track starboard side, sir!"

He'd centred the wheel. But engine vibration had ceased—engines stopping. Guns silent: the only enemies were tail-on, departing. Gunfire from the direction of the convoy was also petering out. About thirty seconds might have passed since he'd given that helm order. She was still swinging, but with her screws stopped the swing was slowing. Wind and sea were on the port quarter: looking aft, where seas were breaking over, his mind registered that fact that she was down by the stern and taking a list to starboard.

0925. A fine time and a fine place to have been crippled.

CHAPTER EIGHT

. . .

Calliope, with no power of her own to resist the forces of wind and sea, rolled helplessly from beam to beam, slowly turning. Treseder had gone down to take charge of damage-control; Nick told Christie, "Ask Trench whether he has anything to report." He had his glasses focussed on the convoy, where Insole was in the process of turning his ships back to the mean course of 170: they'd have been fully occupied with the Heinkels who'd got through to them, and probably wouldn't have seen what had been happening here. Nick's primary requirement was a report from *Calliope's* engineer commander, but knowing what things would be like below decks he was restraining himself from asking for one: when Haselden had time to pick up a telephone, he'd do so. Nick raised his voice over the sounds of wind, sea and the battering of his ship: "Swanwick, what's on the two-eight-one screen?"

"Screen's clear, sir!"

That was something. And something else that the set was even working, had power on it. He picked up the director tower telephone to ask whether the stern turrets were functioning—this telephone was working, too—and the answer was affirmative: communications and circuits had been tested and found correct, ditto magazines, shell-rooms and ammo hoists. So there was a bright side . . . He heard Tommy Trench's voice over TBS informing Christie that there'd been no torpedo hits in either convoy or escort, and one He 115 had been shot down by *Leopard.* The message ended, Do you require assistance? Over.

He took the microphone.

"Tommy, I've been torpedoed, on the starboard side aft. No assessment of damage yet. Send one destroyer to stand by me, then push on and I'll catch up later. Out."

The damage-control telephone was buzzing, its pinpoint of blue light flashing. Ellinghouse answered it, and passed it on to Nick as he left the TBS. You needed at least one hand free for holding on, with this savage roll . . . "Yes?"

"Treseder here, sir. All the damage is right aft. It's a big hole and we have extensive flooding on the hold and platform decks, and either both the starboard shafts are bent or the screws are damaged—or A brackets—or the lot . . . Heselden's about ready to try again now with port screws only— he stopped everything because she was shaking herself to death. They're checking the shafts first. The flooding's contained well enough, I'd say, and we're strengthening those bulkheads."

"All right. Keep me informed. Tell Haselden the priority's to get her moving."

Christie told him as he put the phone down, "*Lyric's* on her way to us sir."

He wondered about the rudder. Stopping on his way aft across the bridge—he'd been going to the tannoy to let the ship's company know what was happening—he joined Harvey-Smith at the binnacle. Clinging to the binnacle—to the compensating spheres—because dead in the water as she was now, she wasn't just rolling so much as performing acrobatics. Recalling that the tiller flat was well abaft the screws, which were set on her flanks—so there was a chance the steering could be intact.

"Check the steering." Shouting, above the wind. "Every five degrees all the way to full starboard rudder, then same the other way, wheelhouse checking against the rudder-indicator—all right?" Harvey-Smith nodded dumbly, lowering his face to the voicepipe, while Nick began to think about what he'd do if she was unsteerable. With the starboard screws out of action, you'd need to carry port wheel: if you couldn't do that, there'd be no way on her own of steering a straight course. One of the mine-sweepers, perhaps, with a wire to *Calliope's* stern—if necessary another at the bow—the two of them holding her straight, or when necessary turning her. Hand-held flags from this bridge to tell them what was wanted . . .

When the bombers attacked again, she'd be an easy mark for them . . .

Harvey-Smith said into the voicepipe, "Midships . . . Seems to be answering normally, quartermaster?"

"Nothing wrong far's we can tell, sir."

Harvey-Smith shouted, straightening, "Seems to be answering, sir!"

He nodded. Reminding himself that he'd brought ships out of worse predicaments. "They'll be getting the port screws turning, in a minute. Then we'll see." Because the gear could be working normally—conceivably— even if the rudder had gone . . . He reached the tannoy now, switched it on, began, "D'you hear me—Captain speaking . . ." Men trapped below decks and sticking to their jobs now as they had to do—if the ship was to survive or have any chance of surviving—were entitled to know what the situation was, and primarily that she wasn't in any danger of sinking, that the damage had been contained and that it was hoped she'd soon be on the move again. Christie was taking a call from for'ard engine-room at the same time. Both engine-rooms would have to be in use, since one drove the inner screws and the other the outer ones. Nick felt it start while he was still speaking—vibration first, its quality changing as revs built up, and the change in her motion as the screws began to take effect: it allowed him to finish with "There—as you can feel now—we're under way . . ."

By 1015, when the next incoming air attack was picked up on radar, they'd got her moving at a steady ten knots. Vibration was excessive, but this had to be accepted. Repairs would have to be made in Archangel—or dockyard facilities might be better in the Kola Inlet . . . She seemed to be carrying about eight degrees of wheel: steering would be affected not only by the fact the starboard screws weren't useable, but also by her list to starboard and sterndown posture in the sea.

A cyphered signal to Admiralty, repeated to others including SBNO North Russia, was being transmitted at this moment: *Calliope reduced to 10 knots by torpedo hit aft. Maintaining convoy course and speed. New bomber formation approaching from southwest.*

"Bearing two-three-two, range seventeen—large formation . . ."

Calliope was steering the convoy's mean course of 170 but she wasn't zigzagging. He'd brought her into the position astern of column two which had been *Moloch's*. If mechanical problems worsened, or her clumsy steering put her off-course, she'd be in no other ship's way here. *Moloch* had transferred to *Calliope's* former station, in the van with *Foremost* to starboard of her and *Laureate* to port. *Calliope* was on her own, much of the time, as the convoy zigzagged ahead of her, but *Northern Glow* and the sweeper *Rochdale,* making independent zigzags, stayed fairly close.

"Bearing two-three-oh, fourteen miles . . . Second formation on two-three-five nineteen!"

He told himself, There've been worse times. Plenty . . .

And a drubbing today had been inevitable. Put yourself in the Luftwaffe chiefs' shoes—an easy target only about 250 miles away, and their ears ringing with the Fuhrer's insistence that Allied convoys to North Russia must be stopped . . . He thought, We should have had an escort carrier with us. We really should . . . Glancing aside, he found himself under the somewhat hawkish scrutiny of Bruce Christie. Not for the first time, in recent days. Christie's expression was less questioning than analytical—no questions to ask, but his own mind to be made up, through observation of how his new commanding officer was reacting or would react to this heightening of the risks . . .

He told Ellinghouse, "Chief yeoman—TBS to Rabble. 'Second bomber formation is approaching five miles behind the first. *Moloch* inform commodore.'"

Moloch was close ahead of the *Tacora,* but from here, depending on which way the zigzag was going, there were always others in the line of sight— usually the *Berkeley* and the *Sovyetskaya Slava* in the middle column.

"Coffee, sir?"

Percy Tomblin: properly dressed in a tin hat.

"Good idea. Thank you, Tomblin."

"Left these in your cabin, sir."

Matches—Swan Vestas . . . He took them, slid them into a pocket. Life's trivia—in present circumstances faintly ridiculous. So much in the balance— lives, ships and a war cargo worth risking them for: but essentially men's lives—and in the middle of it they brought you cups of coffee, boxes of matches . . .

Treseder, back from another inspection of the damaged area aft, appeared behind Tomblin. He was trailed at a respectful (or wary) distance by his "Doggie," an ordinary seaman by the name of Wilson. Nick said, playing the game of trivialities, "The commander might appreciate a cup of your coffee, Tomblin."

"Aye aye, sir." Tomblin eyed Wilson, obviously thinking he might have been sent for whatever sustenance his master wanted. Treseder murmured, "Most kind, sir." He added, with a glance at Tomblin, "Coffee that tastes like coffee being as rare as it is on this bridge." Tomblin, mollified by the compliment, glanced again at Wilson as he left them. Nick told Treseder, "We have a second attack coming in behind the first bunch."

Treseder nodded, pursing his lips as he turned his eyes south-westward. Swanwick's communications number called, "Bogeys on two-three-oh, ten miles, and two-three-one, sixteen miles, both formations closing, bearings steady!"

Treseder said, "The old one-two again, perhaps, eighty-eights and bloody Heinkels."

Binoculars were all trained on and around that bearing. *Calliope* plunging, soaring, rolling. The violence of her motion worried the damage-control people, of course, because there was added danger of bulkheads splitting under the constantly shifting, uneven strains.

1019. Minutes crawling by so slowly that clocks and watches might have had treacle in their works.

"Bearing two-two-nine, eight miles, sir!"

But no sighting yet?

"Above the cloud." Treseder muttering to himself. Lowering his glasses, cleaning their front lenses but with his eyes still on the sky. Christie pointed out, "Cloud is lower than it was, sir. If it'd thicken up a bit, now . . ."

Looking for another miracle?

"Aircraft—green six-oh—angle of sight—"

"Where?"

It had appeared and gone again: flown into cloud ... Swanwick questioning that lookout—which way had it been flying, what height, what type ... Christie was right about the cloud-layer being lower, Nick realised. If it hadn't been for the wind that was tearing holes in it for bombers to see through, it could have been an ally.

Pray for the wind to drop, he thought. Wind drop, cloud thicken. Better still, ask Marcus Plumb to do the praying, since he presumably would have a direct connection ...

"Aircraft in formation green eight-oh, angle of sight one-five—eighty-eights, sir!"

In the open, suddenly. Strung out in groups of six to eight: but more cloud there again now, so appearing and disappearing. Flying from left to right: ships' guns elevated and following them round although they weren't in range yet. *Calliope* rolling as hard as ever, ensign whipping in bright colour against grey sky; the black, twin-engined bombers were below the cloud now and coming round astern. Treseder announced, "I count thirty-six." Back into cloud—but before they were swallowed in it one group had been separating from the mainstream, turning right, this way. The whole lot were hidden in cloud again.

"Second formation bears two-three-oh, nine miles ..."

DCT telephone: "We have a group of them coming in on the quarter, sir. Permission to engage when ..."

"Open fire when you're ready."

In effect, this meant immediately. Before he put the phone down he saw them coming in—nose-down, already in their dives—and heard the ritual war-cries from the team up there in the tower: "Green one-four-oh, angle of sight three-five!"

"Cut!"

"Have height, have plot!"

"Range oh-two-six!"

"Ready!"

"Range oh-two-four!"

"Open fire!"

Fire-gong's clang, and the turrets' ringing thunder. The *Berkeley* joined in, and *Rochdale* . . . *Calliope's* ten 5.25s plus the *Berkeley's* six four-inch amounted to a lot of barrage when it was all directed at the same piece of sky, a barrier of explosive no pilot in his senses would choose to fly through if he had any option. The noise of gunfire combined with the ship's erratic motion made for an impression of confusion, bedlam: if you came through this you'd work out afterwards what had happened, how you'd performed, but while it lasted it was a matter of second-by-second action and reaction and a fast-moving picture buried in noise—as if vision were indistinct and understanding fogged as well as hearing deadened. Bomb splashes lifted between *Calliope* and *Northern Glow:* they hadn't come from the 88s that were attacking from the quarter, but from others overhead at higher level, releasing bombs through cloud-gaps and out of sight in cloud again immediately. Another splash, on the *Berkeley's* quarter: he looked astern, at those four coming in steeply, ranged back at intervals but aiming themselves directly at this ship, shellbursts opening under them and in front and all around them, close-range weapons in it too—and one of them hit, pulling upwards after the explosion, smoke like black blood streaming: then it was spinning, falling, but bombs slanting from the front-runner now . . .

The killed one had raised a tower of blackish sea. Second bomb-stick releasing and the first well on its way. He shouted at Harvey-Smith, "Hard-a-starboard!"

The first lot had begun slanting away to port before he'd lost sight of them, hadn't looked like hitting or even like falling close, but the second batch had appeared to be dead right for line. He wouldn't have taken this avoiding action if it hadn't seemed essential since it would take an age, in *Calliope's* wounded state, to get her back in station: the convoy needed the protection of these guns and *Calliope* needed to be close to the collectively defensive barrage as opposed to being stuck out on her own. But he'd had to do it. She was turning fast: a starboard turn was easy, with the port screws to drive her round. Two bombs thumped in just off the bow: he shouted, "Midships, and meet her!" His own voice was barely audible to him: he'd never been able to wear ear-plugs in action, and consequently was quite used to ending up five-sixths deaf. In old age he'd regret it, but this wasn't old age yet. Another thought there, but there wasn't time for thought. Harvey-Smith had heard the order, anyway. Two splashes astern of the *Berkeley*—and others in a line right up the centre of the alley between columns one and two. There'd have been a lot one hadn't seen, of course: those two that had gone in close to her bow would have been hits if he hadn't put the wheel over, there wasn't any doubt of it. The swing had been checked now: he ordered, "Port thirty."

The third and fourth members of that Junkers group had refused to be put off when *Calliope* had turned, they'd held on as they'd been going, only saving their bombs for the *Sovyetskaya Slava*. She was answering the full port helm, but slowly, and she'd lost several hundred yards of distance on the convoy. The gap was still opening as she dragged herself around: it would have been quicker, he realised now—too late, of course—to have let her complete the circle to starboard the way she'd been fairly whizzing round. There were Ju 88s in all directions and at all levels now, like a swirl of mammoth crows. Two more coming at *Calliope* at this moment, and bombs in the air over the middle of the convoy—then a near-miss on the *Ewart S. Dukes,* rear ship in column three. This was a painfully slow turn— the ship's wounds handicapping her, wind and sea not helping either. He saw an 88 belly-flop into the sea over beyond the *Rochdale,* skidding in a sheet of spray for a hundred yards or so before it turned up on its nose and sank. *Northern Glow* was off *Calliope*'s bow to port, her close-range spouting tracer at the pair attacking now, *Calliope* blazing at them too: every time her steel shuddered to the crashes of her guns the damage-control men down below would be expecting seams to open, bulkheads to collapse. By dropping back they'd lost the protection of the AA ship: the *Berkeley* was busy enough half a mile away, barraging over the Soviet oiler.

Treseder shouted, something like "Take cover"—pointing, a stab of one of his short arms towards a Ju 88 approaching at what looked like mast-head height—probably twice that height—but pulling out of its shallow dive now, and bombs leaving it, black eggs turning in the air: he didn't see how they could miss. But the pilot now paid the price of having pressed in so close: his port engine exploded, the wing flew apart, bombs smacking into the sea close to *Calliope*'s port side—one abreast her second funnel, the other close to her foc'sl—the twin explosions as close and jolting as if she'd been hit by some giant sledgehammer. It was probably the swing still on her that had spared her from direct hits. Nick shouted to Harvey-Smith to steady her on 170: acknowledgement was a mouth that opened and shut but emitted no sound. Nothing audible, over the total enclosure in noise. Two more splashes went up ahead. Another attack coming from the quarter—this one also low—Swanwick getting the pompoms and Oerlikons on to it, a cone of multi-coloured fire with its apex on the German's snout, *Calliope* back on course, aiming up the convoy's wakes. Close-range guns racketing in that attacker's face while the three for'ard turrets added their quota to the barrage above the convoy's rear. And that 88 was suddenly one of the good ones—meaning harmless, dead, a carcass in a mass of smoke and upside-down, on its back as it hit the sea.

Bomb splashes to starboard, and Treseder bawling in Nick's ear having been aft to talk to Swanwick during some flurry of alarm there—"The second wave is another lot of eighty-eights, sir!" Pitching his voice high at a range of two inches and at the same time pointing at the procession of small groups, a total of something like twenty aircraft approaching from ahead. A lull in the action at this juncture was giving an illusion of respite; Nick had his glasses on the convoy, to check on what was or had been happening there, and the guns up ahead were already increasing the density and rate of fire, engaging some Junkers approaching at about 1200 feet from the beam, *Radstock*'s Oerlikons hosing tracer that curled in coloured streamers past the bombers' noses as they swept over ahead of her—going for the *Earl Granville* perhaps—one lot of bombs starting down, but the *Berkeley*'s guns concentrating on them now and the second German banking away out of it—to starboard, this way, across the convoy's rear towards *Calliope. Northern Glow* acting as if she felt this was her bird—but the *Earl Granville* had been hit, amidships, smoke and a fire there—and the second one had survived the trawler's attempts to stop it, had swept on over and was aiming at *Calliope,* close now, nose-down. A wing-tip sparked, became a flaring trail of smoke with glowing objects in it but the bomber extraordinarily holding on dead straight, the dive steepening a little and bombs appearing now . . .

He knew they'd hit. He was seeing it about to happen, and nothing he could do could prevent it. Too close, too late, too every bloody thing, the 88 smoking and diving, a long incline towards the sea, towards certain death for its crew, while the bombs had started then blurred into the background of pockmarked, smokestained sky. He was aware of the bomber hitting the water close to his ship's stem but also that those bombs were going to hit. Guns deafening, and a roar of aircraft engines thickening the sound like new instruments joining in the orchestral thunder: it was an 88 flying down the starboard side so low that from this bridge you saw the white crosses on the tops of its wings as it blasted past. Then *Calliope's* for'ard funnel split, flamed, blew to pieces, the starboard strut of the foremast tripod kinked, and the launch in its davits on that side was fuelling a fire whose flames shot up the after part of the bridge superstructure. Those had been the visible and immediate effects of one bomb: another—Haselden the engineer commander was telling him about it a few minutes afterwards, over a sound-powered telephone from damage control headquarters on the main deck aft—had burst against the ship's side below the waterline and abreast the after boiler-room. All he'd known of it from up here had been the crash of the impact booming through her, a jarring thump powerful enough to send men flying and stop her engines—and, just about, your heart.

"It's very bad generally, I'm afraid, sir. After boiler-room's filling, and there's been a lot of casualties—concussion, and steam—"

"The for'ard boiler-room's still intact?"

But he recognised the sum of it before the engineer had finished his catalogue of damage. Other telephones were buzzing, reports arriving from all quarters while Haselden explained that the flooding aft, result of earlier damage, couldn't now be controlled for long; and with that boiler-room gone—it was a very large compartment . . . "Even if we got her going, sir—one boiler-room, one engine-room and probably the port outer shaft—you'd get two or three knots, no more—and not for long, because . . ."

"All right." He was right, of course. If you didn't accept it, all you'd be doing would be throwing away good men's lives. There were men wounded down there, the survivors of other ships, and you had to work for what could be saved, namely those lives and the convoy . . .

The broadcast boomed, "Main armament in director control!"

So they'd got those circuits working. The guns hadn't ceased firing so they must have been temporarily in local control. He told Haselden, "Prepare to abandon ship. Is Treseder there with you?"

"Yes, sir, he's . . ."

"Give him that order. And tell the PMO I want his patients brought up right away. Under the foc'sl deck port side, and the launch's davits can be used for lowering them in Neill Robertsons. But we'll take this step by step: we can't abandon yet, and the guns have to be kept working until we're ready."

Bombs were separating from that Junkers. And from the other, too. *Calliope's* three for'ard turrets pounding at them. What he'd meant in that message to Treseder via Haselden, a point Treseder would take immediately, was that as long as there were living men on board this ship she'd have to be defended against the bombing, and to use her main armament involved the manning of the complete turrets. What was often referred to as a turret was in fact only the gunhouse, the turret as a whole extended deeply into the ship, through upper and lower decks, platform deck and hold deck, with magazine and cordite-handling room in its base, shell-room above that, then the ammunition hoist feeding projectiles and charges straight up into each gunhouse. But when you cleared lower deck in order to abandon ship, all those positions would be evacuated and the guns would be starved of ammunition . . . The ship was still swinging, wind acting on her superstructure as on a sail. Splashes to port—that Bosch had held on to his bomb too long. He didn't see where the second load went: Christie was shouting in his ear, "Commander Trench asks do you require assistance, sir!"

The sky over the convoy was heavy with shellbursts and the dirt of battle. The *Earl Granville* was on fire but seemed to be maintaining her station. The convoy's tail end—where *Northern Glow* and *Rochdale* were barraging over the *Ewart S. Dukes,* which was putting up a bright canopy of tracer of her own—seemed a long, long way off.

"Tommy. When you can spare her, I'd like one destroyer to stand by me, and if possible a second when things ease off a bit. I intend abandoning ship, then one of them can put a fish in her. Meanwhile the convoy's in your hands. Good luck, and out."

Four 88s, one trio and one plane on its own, were boring in on widely separated bearings. Swanwick leaning over from the starboard-side lookout bay and yelling to the Oerlikon gunners down there to engage the enemy coming from that quarter. His telephone links with the close-range had failed, presumably. A voice on TBS now: "Richman, this is Tinker. Stand by *Calliope,* prepare to take off her ship's company and then sink her. Over." It came in the same tone of voice that had passed a thousand other messages: and now *Lyric* was acknowledging in the same flat tone, as if this were no more than routine or perhaps an exercise. It heightened the sense of unreality, while Nick dealt with dozens of points of detail—just as if these proceedings were real, were actually in progress. Points such as the ship having no motive power or steerage way, so the steering position could be evacuated. The job of OOW had also ceased to exist in practical terms, so Harvey-Smith could be sent down to organise the preparation of Carley floats for launching, also any boats that might be intact, and the davits of destroyed boats to be made ready for lowering wounded men. There was a signal to be coded and transmitted, and Christie was to put his "Tanky" and another couple of spare hands on to the job of destroying all CBs—confidential books—and classified documents. The TS—transmitting station—was to be evacuated too. The kind of gunnery that was called for now was barrage work, and the intricacies of the HA control table were superfluous, so the Marine bandsmen could now be brought up from the steel cell in which for some hours they'd have been listening to the sounds of battle. An 88 roared over, passing it seemed only yards above the bridge, and behind it an explosion and a shoot of flame told of a hit somewhere on her starboard side, somewhere amidships. An object—a ready-use ammunition locker, something that size and shape—rose spinning to more than masthead height. A second bomb splashed in twenty yards clear of the bow to port, and there were three more 88s approaching from ahead; the chief yeoman's voice bawling in Nick's ear, "There's four men 'urt on the flagdeck, sir."

"Get a stretcher party if you need it, but get 'em down to the foc'sl break port side quick as you can. You'll find other wounded there. You plus one signalman will be enough to leave up here, so send all the rest down too. Rig the loud-hailer, will you?"

For talking to *Lyric*—who was on her way, ploughing northward up the convoy's starboard side, her guns lifted and in action as she came. There was some distance still to cover: the gap between *Calliope* and the convoy was wide, now. A line of splashes—from high-level bombing, he guessed, since no enemies were in sight there at the moment—fell near that starboard column, but not near enough to worry anyone. Here, gunfire mounting in intensity again as those three droned in, in echelon'd line-astern and diving . . . Treseder appeared: "I've started the hands coming up, sir, mustering 'em under cover both sides. I've put officers and POs in charge of various parts of ship and routes to the assembly areas. All the sick and wounded are up already—and I know exactly which parties are still below, so . . ."

A bomb burst on the roof of number three turret, which was about thirty feet for'ard of the bridge and slightly below it. Wind deflectors on the bridge's leading edge deflected the blow-torch flame from the explosion too, but it blistered paintwork on the front of the director tower. *Calliope* bow-down, rolling to port, but more sluggish now with the huge weight of water in her. A second bomb hit somewhere aft, and splashes went up to starboard. Christie, just back from clearing out the safe for the destruction of CBs, pointed and yelled, "Heinkels, sir!"

Heinkel 115s. And their target was going to be *Calliope*. They were in loose formation on her bow, spreading themselves outward as they flew in. Slow-looking, moth-like—and tracer was lobbing out to meet them. *Calliope's* for'ard turrets shifting target, gun-barrels lowering swiftly as they swung. *Lyric* had put her helm over; obviously she'd spotted them and decided to meet them head-on, putting herself between them and *Calliope*, which had been his own earlier tactic and was basically sound enough—to take the offensive, carry the attack against the attackers and possibly even stop them attacking effectively at all—but not such a good idea in present circumstances because in a minute she'd foul the range and *Calliope's* own heavier armament would be silenced, for fear of hitting her. *Lyric* on her beam ends as she turned at high speed under full rudder, half-buried in foam, sea streaming over and away from her on the wind, pendants of clear white against green background. *Calliope's* guns were making themselves felt: with any luck *Lyric* might wake up and see it and scram out of the light. Two Heinkels had swung away, to fly up the convoy's wake, and one of the others had been hit, trailing smoke. *Lyric* had put her wheel over the other way—having caught on to the facts of life. Two Heinkels still threatened: and a torpedo dropped, down-slanted, gleaming, splashing in . . .

Nothing you could do about it, in a ship that couldn't move. If it ran true, it would hit.

Now the other. A splash, the Heinkel's wing-tip almost touching the water as it banked to get away. The guns were shifting again—swinging round and lifting swiftly—to meet an 88 coming from the quarter at about a thousand feet, flying straight and level. *Lyric's* pompoms and Oerlikons had drawn attention to it—a bit late, with bombs already spilling from the racks—two, three, four . . .

Moloch's guns were still at maximum elevation but silent, lacking a target as the last of those attackers climbed away southwestward. She was forging up between columns one and two, overhauling the *Tacora,* who'd had some of her deck cargo blown overboard. Trench was aiming to pass within half a cable of her; he had his loud-hailer rigged, and a group of tin-hatted men were waiting in the wing of the *Tacora's* bridge, watching the destroyer plunging up from astern. Trench talking meanwhile to Poorman, *Foremost,* telling her captain, Batty Crockford, to join *Lyric* in standing by *Calliope.*

From as much as Trench had been able to see, in glimpses during recent minutes and with a lot of other action in all directions, *Calliope* with *Lyric's* support had beaten off an attack by Heinkels, two of which had turned away to make a pass at the *Berkeley, Rochdale, Northern Glow* and *Radstock* had blocked this, destroying one of the pair and driving the other away. Only minutes earlier *Radstock* had been trying unsuccessfully to get in close enough to the *Earl Granville* to help fight the freighter's upper-deck fires. The *Earl Granville's* crewmen had been losing the battle, by the looks of it; her master couldn't turn his ship to minimise the effect of the wind without isolating himself from the convoy and its escort—which would have guaranteed the bombers concentrating on him. *Moloch* had been in the centre of the convoy at the time, practically alongside the *Sovyetskaya Slava*. Trench using his loud-hailer to talk to the English-speaking woman radio operator. The oiler had had a hole punched in her side by a technical near-miss; she was leaking oil and her speed was down to eight knots, but her captain had been adamant he'd keep going. His ship's upperworks were filthy from an earlier fire which they'd fought for a long time and finally put out; at that time there'd been comparatively little wind.

Now he had to tell the commodore that the speed reduction was to be permanent. He lifted the loud-hailer: "*Tacora,* ahoy ... commodore, sir!" *Moloch* pitching violently, Trench swaying on his high seat, long legs wrapped around its struts. Looking astern, seeing *Calliope* as a grey smudge in whitened sea: binoculars showed that she was down by the stern and listing heavily. She'd lost most of her for'ard funnel, one of her foremast struts had gone and the mast itself seemed to be swaying independently of the ship's rolling. A single Ju 88 beyond her, flying south, was momentarily in sight between a gap in the clouds.

Insole's voice came on the wind: "What can I do for you, commander?"

Lifting the loud-hailer again, facing to starboard where the *Tacora* butted stolidly through the waves, but at the same time throwing a quick glance back to see what might be happening around *Calliope*—and not wanting to plague Everard with questions over TBS ... Attack might be resumed at any moment, the loss of *Calliope's* guns and now of two destroyers as well was a serious reduction of the defensive strength: it wasn't a situation you'd want to prolong if you could help it ... He began to tell the commodore about the Soviet oiler's damage, the need to accept a four-knot cut in speed. This in itself was a serious handicap, increasing by one third the convoy's period of exposure to attack. It was Everard's business as escort commander to make this kind of decision, but in the first place there wasn't much option and in the second it wasn't practicable to consult him; in any case he'd said, "Meanwhile the convoy's yours." The only alternative to slowing the convoy would be to abandon the oiler and sink her: discussing this—Insole agreed that the Russians would most likely refuse to accept that decision anyway—Trench looked back towards *Calliope* again just as a Heinkel's torpedo struck her, a pillar of sea shooting vertically on her farther side; in the next blink she was hidden in a rain of bombs.

She'd been hit by three of them while the geyser of upthrown sea from that torpedo had still been hanging in the air, the cruiser making a slow roll to starboard, her stem lifting, and sea flooding across her quarterdeck. Sam Clegg, captain of *Lyric,* had had his eyes on the foremast as it carried away completely, crashing down in a tangle of wreckage on the other side. He'd thought she was going, there and then; then the bombs fell in a tight pattern—one in the sea, one on the flooding quarterdeck, one (he thought) down the second funnel, but possibly into the boiler-room with a subsequent explosion up through the funnel, and the fourth on her starboard side abreast "B" turret. Clegg ordered, "Away seaboat's crew. Slow ahead together. Starboard five." To nose in closer. *Lyric* already had scrambling nets down, Carley floats ready to be dropped, and parties mustering for rescue work; also medical and other preparations—piles of blankets and hammocks warming on the engine-room gratings, and hot soup in preparation—all of which could help to save men's lives, if you got any alive out of that freezing water. He'd ordered the whaler to be manned because *Calliope's* suddenly worsened predicament had impelled him to do something: but how much use the boat could be, in this sea and with the large number of men there'd be to cope with, was questionable. But *Calliope* herself could have no boats: you could see at a glance that her upper deck was a shambles.

"Stop together. Midships the wheel."

Smoke hung over her, thickest where she was on fire amidships. Her bridge was a scorched mess, but men were moving in it, including one in its forefront who, Clegg guessed, must have been Everard. Stench of burning . . . He'd brought his ship up in the cruiser's lee, thirty to forty yards of tumbling sea between them, close enough for survivors to have a chance . . . Some Carley floats—*Calliope*'s—were already in the water, and stretchers were being lowered on boats' falls at the two pairs of davits on this side; men in the floats waiting, handling lines dangling from the stretchers—Neill Robertson stretchers, the kind that strapped around a man's body, converting him into an object that could be slung around like a stoutly wrapped parcel. There'd been an attempt five minutes ago to use the crane, but electric power must have failed because they'd abandoned it, transferred to the falls. The floats alongside were tossing and crashing about, despite being in the cruiser's lee: and her side was stripped completely bare of paint all along the waterline, where ice had scraped.

There'd be more wounded than they'd have stretchers for, now—or floats for.

"*Foremast*'s joining us, sir."

Clegg had made his mind up that despite the sea, and the fact *Calliope* might turn turtle at any moment, he was going to risk getting right in alongside her. It was the only way, now, to save those people's lives.

"The whaler's manned, sir!"

"Get 'em out of it. I'm taking her alongside. Starboard side-to . . ." He called down, "Slow ahead port, slow astern starboard." He'd had her lying broadside-on, so he had to turn her where she lay before he could move her in closer . . . "Is Cramphorn ready?"

"Yessir." Cramphorn was *Lyric*'s doctor. "Your day cabin and the wardroom—"

"Stop starboard. Starboard twenty-five."

"She's going!"

Clegg saw it himself, at that same moment. She'd resumed the roll to starboard which had checked at about the same time as the bombs had struck. There might have been some counter-flooding at that time. Now the resumption was at first slow, but by the time you'd seen it happening the momentum was increasing, becoming swift, unstoppable . . .

"Stop port. Midships. Slow astern together."

Wash and suction from the roll were capsizing the floats, turning them on end, spinning them like leaves in a whirlpool. Most of them empty now, some with men clinging: but bodies in Neill Robertsons couldn't cling . . . *Foremost*—Clegg had seen her moving up but had not had time to take her movements into consideration—was backing off, too: she'd been approaching gingerly, stem to stem with the cruiser, her captain—Batty Crockford—aiming to put his bow alongside *Calliope*'s foc's'l, and there'd been a crowd of men gathering there, ready for the chance to jump over.

Gunfire beginning again, swelling from the direction of the convoy . . .

"I'll need the whaler, after all."

"Aye aye, sir!"

"Stop together . . ."

Roar of aircraft engines mingled with gun noise. *Lyric*'s after four-sevens were engaging some attacker, and now her pompoms and Oerlikons had joined in. Clegg had to leave all that to his control officer in the tower: his concern was *Calliope,* and the darkening that wasn't dusk or doomsday but the cruiser's forepart lifting to shadow the space of sea between them: she was on her side and the roll seemed to have stopped again, stern buried and the long foc's'l lifting completely out of the water now, rising towards the vertical and displaying her scarred body naked to the day for these last agonising moments. *Lyric* and *Foremost* both in action; *Calliope*'s raised forepart alive with men—some holding on, some jumping into the seething foam. Bomb splashes shot up on her other side, then one off *Foremast*'s port bow as she drew away, and a fourth exploded in the sea between *Lyric* and the dying cruiser. A scream of fury from a sailor on "B" gundeck, harsh as a seabird's shriek, cut through the petering-out of gunfire: "Christ, lay off, you bastards!" Guns had ceased fire: a new sound was the rush of escaping air as *Calliope,* vertical now, slid stern-first into littered, convulsing sea.

Trench said into the TBS microphone, "All right, Sam. Resume your previous station. Out."

Tone as flat as he felt. Clegg had just reported that seventeen of the bodies who'd been dragged on board *Lyric* might be kept alive: but none of them was Nick Everard. Before that, Crockford of *Foremost* had reported having picked up fifty-three men of whom twenty-two had died or had been dead before they'd arrived on board—leaving thirty-one, many of them in very poor shape. Here again, no news of Everard.

"The *Earl Granville's* in trouble, sir."

He swung round on his high seat. McAllister, his navigator, had binoculars aimed through the space between the *Tacora* and the *Carrickmore*. The *Earl Granville* had been on fire for the last couple of hours. She was down by the bow, after an explosion in her for'ard hold which her master had claimed would not prevent him maintaining the present eight knots—and now she was turning out to port and seemed to be losing way.

In fact she'd stopped her engines. There was no bow-wave at all.

Radstock was closing her, and *Northern Glow* was only about six hundred yards astern. There were no bombers overhead, and nothing on the radar screen either, at this moment: Trench suspected there might not be many other moments like it, between now and sunset. The idea of putting the *Earl Granville* in tow—perhaps of the *Berkeley*—entered his mind; but it would slow the whole convoy by several knots, prolong the exposure to attack still further, as likely as not cause further losses. Better, he thought, to cut those losses—especially as she looked burnt-out, had flooding for'ard and fires in 'tween-deck areas elsewhere, was hardly worth risking other ships and lives for.

He reached for the TBS again, and called *Legend,* told John Ready to close the *Earl Granville* and talk to her master. If she couldn't keep up she was to be abandoned and sunk. He slid off his seat. "Hold the fort, pilot. I'll be in the chartroom."

One of the things he'd learnt from Nick Everard was that as long as options were open, a wise man kept them all in mind. The most dangerous thing was to act like a tram on tracks, unable to re-think a plan or intention when changing circumstances demanded a new approach. Everard had taught a lot of people a lot of things simply by demonstrating that objectives which might seem unattainable could often be reached by varying the route to them. This was exactly what he was thinking about now—and he was motivated not only by the natural and proper desire to get as much of these cargoes into North Russia as could possibly be fought through, but also by what felt like a personal obligation to Nick Everard to do so. In Trench's mind it was still Nick's convoy, his own position that of caretaker.

Everard had been Trench's CO at Narvik, where their performance in the destroyer *Intent* had—well, had been highly productive, after a thoroughly forbidding start. Nick had subsequently given Trench a boost in his own career with a glowing personal recommendation. It was one of the characteristics of the man that he'd always stood by the people who'd served under him.

Trench leant over the chart-table. He was escort commander now, and he didn't want to be off *Moloch's* bridge a moment longer than necessary. But the plain fact was that the distance between here and Archangel—he set dividers against the latitude scale—was, say 350 miles to get to the White Sea, then another 160 or so through to Archangelsk, as the Russians called it. Roughly 500 miles. A hell of a long haul at eight knots and under this intensity of attack.

Suppose PQ 19 diverted to Kola. From dusk this evening. Hold this present course for five or six hours, then at sundown alter course for Kola. That would be a run of only two hundred miles.

It was probably the only way to get most of the remaining cargoes through. It was also—Trench thought—most likely what Nick Everard would have done. In fact the more he looked at it, the more obvious it became. He pulled a pad towards him, and began to rough out a signal which could be put into a more complete form presently . . .

To SBNO North Russia, repeated to Admiralty and AIG 311, from *Moloch* . . . *Calliope* sunk by torpedo and bomb attacks in position—?—as—?. 48 survivors including wounded picked by *Lyric* and *Foremost,* but commanding officer is missing.

He poised the pencil over that word "missing." Then he decided, scowling, that it was as good as any other word for it. He wrote, *Earl Granville,* and left a space for a mention of this new loss, which surely was imminent. McAllister could fill in all the blanks—positions, times etcetera. Trench scrawled swiftly.

> Oiler *Sovyetskaya Slava* holed by near-miss and reduced to 8 knots maximum. This and continuing air attacks make diversion to Kola Inlet essential. Course will be altered at dusk to 220 degrees. Request fighter cover and early rendezvous with local escort. Estimated position of PQ 19 dawn 13th—?

McAllister could fill in the missing bits. You didn't keep a dog and do your own barking. He left the signal on the chart, and ran up to the bridge.

"Slow together."

McAllister passed the order down. Trench's intention was to drop astern for a loud-hailer chat with the commodore, tell him about diverting to Kola. McAllister told him as he straightened from the voicepipe, "The *Earl Granville*'s abandoning, sir."

Cramphorn took the stethoscope from his ears and told Sick Berth Attendant Bowles, "Don't bother."

Bowles had been wrapping a pre-warmed blanket around a lanky, ginger-haired body, the ninth of eleven hypothermia cases and the second to die after being brought down here. This was the captain's day cabin, interconnecting with sleeping cabin and bathroom. Officers' cabins which led off the flat outside had also been commandeered. *Lyric* rolled suddenly and powerfully to starboard, sending camp-beds and stretchers sliding . . . Cramphorn said, "Get him up to the lobby." He was checking the list. "No identification?"

"Got 'im on this one, sir." Bowles had it. "Name of Keeble—torpedo-man. No identity disc, but that Killick knew 'im—bloke with the duff left 'and."

Cramphorn had been operating on a leading seaman—he'd finished the job only a few minutes ago—an amputation at the wrist of a hand that looked as if it had been chewed by a shark but in fact had been caught in the block of a boat's falls and crushed. Cramphorn had been using the officers' bathroom as an operating theatre, an advantage of the cramped space being that he could jam himself in between his patient and the bulkhead and thus avoid being flung off his feet during the course of the operation. While he'd been doing that and another job, Leading SBA Murchison with Bowles and two wardroom stewards as assistants had continued the treatment of hypothermia cases, a production-line system devised by Cramphorn and involving immersion for ten minutes in water at a temperature of 45 degrees—sea water, in the skipper's bathroom, which connected with the adjoining sleeping cabin—then a rubbing-down with warm towels, and finally enclosure in blankets, also pre-warmed. Cramphorn had studied the experiences of others, mainly of doctors in small ships on Arctic convoys, and he'd trained this team, making the best use he could of limited facilities. He'd impressed on them that too much warmth would be as fatal as too little: but he'd still been worried, having to leave them at it on their own while he was operating, that their enthusiasm and anxiety for the patients might run away with them, so they'd overheat the bath-water ... But what really determined success or failure—meaning life or death—given reasonably good treatment and men who hadn't been in the sea more than a few minutes, was the individual's physique. They were all unconscious now, of course, knocked out by the cold, and the questions were firstly, whether consciousness would be regained in time, and secondly, whether there might be brain damage, which could be either temporary or permanent.

Only two to go, now. Murchison and the others had put three men through the defreezing process while Cramphorn had been performing his two operations. They were the only surgical cases he had, although he'd expected dozens. The reason, of course, was the cold water: badly wounded men had simply not survived. And this was the best time of the year: in January, one minute in that sea would be as effective as a bullet in the brain.

"This lad's for an 'ammock, sir. Carry on, shall we?"

"Hang on." Cramphorn went over, with his stethoscope. All bunks were now occupied, and this next patient, and then one other, would go into warmed (body-temperature) hammocks slung in the wardroom flat. The two stewards were carrying the red-headed torpedoman through there now, and up the ladder to the quarterdeck lobby; Bowles had gone next-door to give the last man his towelling. Staggering like a drunk as *Lyric,* under helm and heeling, pitched to a head-on sea.

"Be better off in an 'ammock, I'd say."

Less likely to be thrown out, he meant. But all the bunks had lee-boards on them, and bedding strapping the patients in tight. Cramphorn asked, applying his stethoscope, "Got this one's name and rate?"

There was a heartbeat, thank God. Faint enough, and breathing so shallow you'd only detect it by vapour on a glass, but there was life—despite an appearance of death, dead-pale complexion which emphasized a puckered scar running from the left eye to the corner of the mouth. No beauty now, this fellow—but largeboned, deepchested, and Cramphorn had no doubt he owed his life to that powerful constitution. His life so far— and to have survived even this long, after at least several minutes in that sea, was fairly miraculous. Wonders never ceased; and David Cramphorn, who'd been a medical student when the war had started four years ago, marvelled at them all.

Murchison had answered that he didn't know this patient's name or rate.

"Weren't no disc on 'im, nothing." Checking his own list again. "Yeah, I'm right. We 'ad to cut the suit off of him. It 'ad a label sort of thing saying *Everard* . . . 'ere, flaming 'ell!"

Reeling—he'd been squatting on his heels—and grabbing as he fell at the camp-bed, to stop its slide across the deck. On the new course the motion was worse than it had been. Cramphorn checked his own notes. "You did say *Everard?*"

"Yeah, but didn't seem to be 'is name, like, more just . . ."

"On a suit, you said?"

"Sort of—well, flying suit, might've been. Zipfastener, an' all. Couldn't shift it, so Lofty Smith pulls out 'is pusser's dirk an' . . ."

A pusser's dirk was a seaman's knife. Cramphorn had looked round as the stewards came back in. One of them came over to help with this patient, the nameless man who'd worn a flying suit, and the other went through to help Bowles. Mention of a flying suit had confused Cramphorn for a moment; he'd thought of Jones, the young Fleet Air Arm pilot they'd picked up and who was still on board—how anyone in *Calliope* could have been in his suit . . . But there was no connection—except Jones had also been in the drink, for about ten seconds . . .

He'd found that name in his notes now.

"Parrot." Addressing the steward. "I'll lend a hand here. You nip up to the bridge, give the skipper a message. Tell him we have an unconscious hypothermia case down here who I believe may be Captain Sir Nicholas Everard."

"Cor, stone the crows!"

Staring down at the pallid, lifeless-looking features . . .

Cramphorn added, "Be bloody careful how you go." He'd jerked his head, drawing the steward's attention to the pounding of heavy seas across the deck above their heads.

Trench had been talking to the commodore by loud-hailer, explaining his intention of diverting to the Kola Inlet. He finished, "Then we can collect the homebound lot from Archangel—or they might sail with a local escort and we'd meet them at sea. How does it strike you, sir?"

He lowered the hailer. On the far side of the strip of lively sea that separated them, Insole raised his.

"I agree—it's the best thing, in the circumstances. Mind you, Trench, the Russkis won't like it."

Trench said, not into his loud-hailer, "Bugger the bloody Russkis!"

"Hear, hear." A grin from Willy Henderson, *Moloch's* first lieutenant. Trench had the hailer up again: "Have to like it or lump it, won't they?"

There'd been a call on the radar voicepipe, and McAllister had answered it. Trench told Henderson, "Two-eight-oh revs, Number One." McAllister reported, "Radar has aircraft formation closing on two-five-three range seventeen miles, sir."

"Red flag, yeoman."

"Red air warning flag—hoist!"

Moloch was surging forward . . . Trench's thumb on the alarm buzzer to bring his ship's company back to their action stations. The respite—he checked his watch—had lasted three quarters of an hour. Focussing his glasses now on the smoking hulk of the *Earl Granville:* she was a long way astern, and *Legend* was still there with her. They should have got all her crew out of her by this time, and with a new wave of bombers coming in they'd better be told to get a move on. He looked round, to tell his yeoman, Halliday, to call *Legend* on TBS, but someone else piped up on the radio-telephone at that moment. It was *Lyric* calling, Sam Clegg, her skipper, wanting to speak to Commander Trench.

CHAPTER NINE

· · ·

"So where is he now? I mean, where's Calliope?"

Setter was plugging through a choppy sea, this evening, in a rising wind that promised badly for tomorrow. The weather forecast had been right, it seemed. Up to now the going hadn't been at all bad, but at this half-way point it looked as if Messrs Gimber, Steep and Towne were in line for some discomfort.

Paul told Crawshaw, "I've no idea. Last time I saw him was in London, and his ship was at Chatham. In dock, bottom-scraping or something. By this time she could be anywhere."

"They might have sent her down to the Med." Massingbird, the engineer, eased the lid off a tin of fifty Players. He was a graduate of the Royal Navy's engineering college at Keyham—Devonport—but after these few days at sea he looked more like a recent escaper from Devil's Island. He added, "Salerno, all that malarkey."

MacGregor brought the conversation back to where he'd started it in the first place—the Everard family.

"What about Admiral Sir Hugh Everard? I know he'd retired before the war and went back to sea as a convoy commodore—but is he still do-ing that?"

"No. On the beach again, much to his annoyance. Arthritis—he can hardly move. He's my great-uncle; nice old guy."

"He's more than that. What about his part in the Battle of Jutland—when he commanded the battleship *Nile*, right?" Paul nodded. MacGregor told the others, "He turned her out of the line—positively Nelsonian, and what a sight it must have been! Poor old *Warspite* was getting really bol-locked by the entire Hun battlefleet, and he turns *Nile* straight towards

them and draws their fire!" MacGregor wagged his head. "Not a doubt he
saved *Warspite*."

"My father was at Jutland too. He was in a destroyer. He'd been in a
battleship's gunroom in Scapa Flow, in the Grand Fleet. Hated it—he was
'under report,' supposed to be a failure. Then he got this break—I think his
uncle Hugh pulled a string and got him the draft-chit to this destroyer—
Lanyard, her name was . . . Anyway, she was in the thick of it, and he finished
up as the only officer left alive—he was a sub-lieutenant then, not quite
twenty-one—and he brought her back, three-quarters wrecked, having torpedoed a Hun destroyer en route." Paul smiled. "Then promptly got into
hot water over something else. I forget what—but he was never what anyone would call orthodox."

"Your mother's a White Russian?"

"Well, she's American now. But yes—he married her in the Black Sea
in 1919, when we were trying to help the Whites against the Bolsheviks.
But they split up when I was still a child. He has a new wife now—a real
honey."

"Might say he has it made, then." Crawshaw could have been envious.
"Terrific reputation, a honey of a wife, you say, a title, medals by the yard,
big house, land in—Yorkshire, you said?"

"West Riding." Paul accepted one of Massingbird's cigarettes. "Thanks,
Chief."

Henning, the navigator, was on watch, and Dick Eaton was up there with
him. Brazier was sitting next to Paul, but he hadn't contributed a word to
the conversation. He'd never been exactly talkative. Crawshaw asked. "Mind
a personal question, on the subject of your family?"

"No, I don't mind."

"Are you in line for the baronetcy? I mean, are there any other Everards
ahead of you?"

"No, there aren't. So if I survived my father—yes, I am. But that's a toss-
up, really, in present circumstances." He lit the cigarette, in a general silence.
No-one wanting to agree with him, when that would imply that chances of
survival from the X-craft operation were slim. Which they were, of course—

and knowing it was good enough reason not to mention it. Paul added, "My stepmother's had a baby son, a year ago. Named Hugh, after the great-uncle. So if my father was knocked off and I was too, that's who'd inherit."

"I'm sure we all hope that neither your father nor you will get *knocked off,* as you call it!"

"Thank you, sir." Paul glanced up at the electric clock. "But if you'd excuse me now, I have to go and make a phone call."

X-12 and the three men in her were never out of his mind. Particularly now, with the weather turning bad. He went aft through the control room, through the cold rush of air which the pounding diesels drew in from the hatch; he slid back the wireless office door, pulled it shut again behind him to keep out the noise and cold.

"Evening, Colbey."

The telegraphist moved over. He was grey-headed, unusually old-looking for a submariner. Paul sat down in the spare chair, pulled the telephone closer and cranked its handle. All he got was static: he waited, anxious, remembering a dream he'd had last night. He'd been doing this, trying to get through—but no sound at all, the wire had gone dead, tow-rope parted, X-12 lost . . . Then Gimber's face and staring eyes seen through a film of water, Gimber's body floating on its back—inside the craft, and the realisation suddenly that he, Paul, was also inside it with the corpse and trapped, water-level rising swiftly, roaring as it always did when it jetted in under pressure . . . He remembered too the psychiatrist, Claverhouse, asking him "What about dreams?" A truthful answer would have been, I have them quite often, and they're terrifying . . . He'd cranked the handle again, and now Gimber's voice came through loud and clear: "What's for supper in the Grand Hotel, then?"

"You sound cheerful, Louis."

Gimber adopted the voice of Mona Lott, a character in Tommy Handley's ITMA programme: he whined, "It's being so cheerful keeps me going . . . Actually I have an unpleasant feeling that things are becoming bumpy. Any worse than this, we'll have to trim her heavy for'ard. What's the forecast now?"

He could visualise them, in that cramped space a hundred feet under the sea, the other two with their eyes and ears on Gimber, dreading the answer to that question. Paul told him, "It's not too good, I'm sorry to say."

"So what is it?"

"Force four, southwesterly."

Actually the forecast had been for winds force four and five, sea rough to very rough. There didn't seem any point in laying it on thicker than you had to. It would happen anyway, you couldn't do anything to stop it . . . Paul added, "We've coped with a lot more than force four on exercises, Louis."

"Exercises lasting a few hours, not whole bloody days on end . . . Anyway, don't wet your pants, we'll make out . . . Any news from FOSM?"

"Not yet."

The news they were waiting for would be the reconnaissance photos of Altenfjord, the details of the targets' positions and net protection. When the photo–intelligence experts had completed their analysis of the pictures there'd be a signal from Admiral Barry spelling it all out and ordering one or other of the alternative attack plans.

Gimber grumbled, "I thought we'd've had it cut and dried by now."

"Maybe the Catalina developed more pigeon problems."

They'd been flying the pictures down from Russia by Catalina flying-boat; and this was a reference to Soviet red tape. The Catalinas up there had carrier pigeons in them for life-saving purposes, to carry SOS messages back to base in emergency. Soviet customs officials had impounded the birds, on the grounds it was illegal to import livestock. There were jokes now about the pigeons having to be Party members to get in.

"How's the routine going, Louis?"

"OK. Except if you take Benzedrine to stay awake it's bloody impossible to sleep when you come off watch. Also your mouth tastes like a garbage pail . . . What's the news from Italy, if any?"

"The Bosch are said to be pulling back, above Salerno, and the Eighth Army's linked up with the Fifth. Us and the Yanks, that means, I suppose."

"Of course that's what it means, and Eaton told me the same thing two hours ago."

"It's good news, anyway."

"Tell you what I'd call good. A hot bath, some big eats, a night in clean sheets, a first-class warrant down to London, Jane there to meet me."

"She will be, Louis. In due course."

"I wonder."

"What's that mean?"

"Would you give a damn, anyway?"

"I'm not quite with you, Louis."

"Say that again, old boy . . . But now listen. If the weather gets worse—when it does—might be sensible to check communications every half-hour instead of hourly. Can do?"

The air stank inside the midget. It was one of the things you just had to live with. "Trigger" Towne asked Gimber as he replaced the telephone, "What's that weather news?"

"Force four's expected." Gimber looked at Steep. "I'll take over, Ozzie. Get some rest."

"But it's your turn." Steep looked harassed as well as ill. "I'm OK, honestly."

Pale, dull-eyed; sweat gleamed on his face and forehead. In the last twelve hours he'd developed chronic seasickness; he was very far from "OK" and he didn't seem to be getting any better. X-12 was porpoising on her tow-rope, depth varying all the time between about seventy and ninety feet in more or less regular undulations; she'd been doing it for two days, except for the six-hourly breathers on the surface. Steep was on his seat at the after end of the control room, with a bucket beside him which he'd been using since last night; it did nothing to improve the atmosphere, despite his emptying it into the heads—the lavatory, in the W and D compartment—at frequent intervals.

Gimber told him, "That wasn't a suggestion, Ozzie. It's an order. Go for'ard, get your head down."

X-12 launching herself downward now. A fifty-foot steel cylinder weaving up and down like a kite on a string. Towne winked sympathetically at Steep as the sub-lieutenant climbed out of his seat and went for'ard, squeezing past Gimber under the dome, pausing in the W and D for his own purposes and then crawling through into the fore-end, on to the wooden pallet that covered the top of the boat's battery. All Gimber could see from this end now, looking for'ard through the openings in the two transverse bulkheads of the W and D, were the soles of his tennis shoes. He was lying on his face, head pillowed on crossed arms: he'd just crawled into that position and stopped moving. He'd left the bucket in the W and D.

Gimber said quietly, "Trigger—be a good bloke, put a lashing on that bucket?"

"Eh?" Then he caught on. Before the bucket started flying around, Gimber had meant. Towne slid off his seat and crept into the W and D. Gimber was settling himself at the controls, on the first lieutenant's seat. Before the telephone conversation with Everard he'd been doing some mopping-up, a chore which Trigger Towne would now continue when he'd secured the pail. It was one of a number of routine chores that had to be done for several hours each day, to keep the dampness under some kind of control.

Gimber murmured, as Towne came back, "Poor sod."

"Wouldn't have thought it." Towne wrung out a swab. "We had worse than this, training, and I never saw him puke."

"It never went on this long. It's either that or it's the Benzedrine affecting him, some sort of reaction to it." Gimber was moving the hydroplane control very cautiously, aiming to reduce the amount of porpoising but careful not to overdo it. A little too much plane angle could make this worse instead of better; and if you had her fighting the drag of the tow, you could easily snap it. He shook his head: "He'll get over it. By tomorrow, I'd guess."

"You didn't think to tell Everard."

Gimber shrugged. "Wouldn't be much point."

"Except if it goes on—or he gets worse—"

"Odds are he'll have his sealegs by tomorrow."

"Bloody hope so." Towne scowling: he was on his side with his legs drawn up and his bearded face against the casing of the trim-pump, one arm reaching down into the bilge and the other doubled out of the way behind him . . . "How long before the next guff-through?"

Gimber checked the time. "About an hour." He'd found the optimum angle for a permanent setting on the hydroplanes: she still porpoised, but slightly less, in slightly flattened curves. By "permanent" he meant of course in terms of present sea conditions: wind and sea were getting so it wouldn't last for long. By morning, in fact, life might be distinctly less than comfortable. Still, he had his hands free now, so he could keep an eye on the depthgauge and the bubble but at the same time do some drying-out maintenance, wiping moisture off the inside surface of the hull, off pipelines and machinery and exposed wiring. Most of the dampness—and actual water, gathering finally in the bilges—came from condensation, and its main threat was to equipment, particularly electrics. The prime symptom would be reduction in insulation values, but electrical gear generally was at risk. The creeping damp also affected human beings—wet clothes, wet skin inside them, hair that remained wringing wet as if you'd been swimming . . .

Well, nobody had been expecting a joyride.

Towne was wriggling backwards, as a preliminary to getting himself into an upright or partially upright position. You couldn't just sit up or lie down or turn around: you had to look first to see what was where and how best to fit around it. With the whole bag of tricks swooping up and down all the time. Towne swearing softly to himself as he extricated his long legs, then folded them the other way; he muttered, "I better take a shufti at the compressor. Right?"

They'd thought it was noisy when it had last been running. It was driven by the main engine, the Gardner, and its function was to compress air into steel bottles from which main ballast tanks were blown, for surfacing. High-pressure air was a precious commodity, since it was basically your ticket to the surface, and the machine that provided it was therefore a vital item of equipment. Not that any single item was superfluous: if any had been, the designers would hardly have wasted valuable space by including it. And as every single piece of gear had to be in the best possible running order when the operational crew took over in a few days' time, maintenance was a very important part of the passage crew's duties.

Only two of them to do it all, if Ozzie was going to be kaput for long.

Gimber frowned, remembering the end of his conversation with Paul Everard. It had just slipped out: result of the strains of the recent days, he supposed, but no less unfortunate for that. He'd have liked to have wiped it out of his own memory and Paul's: and it was a reminder that, under pressure as they were, you needed to watch out: he hadn't realised that the rot had already set in, to that extent . . .

Trigger Towne, having extricated himself from his recent Houdini-like entanglement, broke into Gimber's thoughts.

"Compressor, then—OK? Got an hour, you said?"

He nodded, waking up. He'd been staring at the depthgauge in a sort of daze. You could get hypnotised, gazing at its shine for hours literally. Seeing nothing, or seeing—everything. Jane, for instance, and Everard's relationship with her. If any. Her sweetness and her ambivalence, his own patience out of consideration for the dreadful hurt she'd suffered. Jane as one of the walking wounded of this war . . . He transferred his eyes from the bubble to Trigger Towne. "Say fifty minutes."

"I'll do it in more like thirty."

Towne began to squirm aft. The compressor was in the engine compartment, the after-end. To run it—when you were on the surface or at least had the induction trunk up, because the diesel couldn't run without air—you clutched it in at a point between the engine-clutch and the for'ard end of the main motor. It was a hell of a spot to get at; the designers didn't have to.

By daylight it was blowing force four, as promised. *Setter* pitching hard with the blow on her port quarter, and Paul was scared about conditions down there in the midget. Gimber wasn't saying much on the telephone; only that it was "much as you'd expect." Then: "For God's sake, do I have to describe it to you?"

"Not if you don't want to, Louis. But keep your wool on."

"Yeah . . . And if you want to know, I'll tell you—it's fairly bloody!"

"Anyone seasick?"

"Of course we're seasick!"

"All of you?"

"Trigger's all right. He's got no more belly on him than an eel has, he doesn't know how to be sick."

Paul heard some muttering in the background. Towne's voice. He said, "I didn't know you did, Louis."

"Well, this motion is somewhat exceptional."

MacGregor commented, when Paul told him, "I can't imagine much worse. Seasickness on its own is bad enough—but in that tin can . . ."

On the surface during her last ventilation period, X-12 had hardly been visible in the waves sweeping over her. But the change of air would have more than compensated for such a minor discomfort as getting soaked. From what Gimber had said, their clothes were permanently sodden anyway, just from condensation.

Paul had been wondering about Gimber's cryptic but hostile remark over the telephone the previous evening. It might have meant very little—a very minor undercurrent of jealousy or suspicion exacerbated by conditions. Gimber might have been having some problem with Jane and imagining she'd have discussed it with Paul. But it had sounded like more than that—like smoke indicating fire. Ordinarily Paul might have shrugged it off, thought *All right, so he's caught on, we can play it in the open now.* He'd have been glad of that—ordinarily. But this was no time for emotional complications.

They were having breakfast in *Setter's* wardroom when FOSM's signal arrived. Part of the table was cleared, and Brazier and Eaton did the decyphering. Jazz Lanchberry, who'd got the buzz that the all-important message had come in, shuffled aft from the ERAs' mess and sipped at a mug of wardroom coffee, leaning against the bulkhead door while he waited for answers. Brazier muttered, as they started work, "Could be they've taken off again. Fjords empty, no bloody targets—turn round, come home . . ."

Massingbird said from his bunk, "Then you'd be lucky."

They ignored him. Eaton said, "First word is 'reconnaissance.'"

The aerial photographs had been analysed. *Tirpitz* was in her protective box at the end of Kafjord, and *Scharnhorst* was similarly penned nearby. *Lützow* was in Langfjord, in her own private enclosure; the system of nets and barriers was as it had been before. FOSM's order to the X-craft flotilla now was "Target Plan 4."

MacGregor was standing on one leg in the gangway, pushing the other into waterproof trousers in preparation for a visit to the bridge. Hopping on the one leg as she rolled, Lanchberry backing out of his way. MacGregor asked Paul, "What does that mean for you, Everard?"

"We go after the tiddler."

"Lützow?"

He nodded. It was disappointing. All right, to destroy a 10,000-ton "pocket battleship" would be a good day's work, but one had hoped to get a crack at the big one, *Tirpitz*. Under Plan 4, *Tirpitz* would be attacked by X-5, X-6 and X-7, *Scharnhorst* was allocated to X-9, X-10 and X-11, and Paul would share *Lützow* with X-8.

MacGregor said, reading Paul's mind, "Hardly a tiddler. I'd call that a very worthwhile target." He added, into a silence—Brazier and Eaton were looking glum too—"I wouldn't mind." Meaning he'd be glad to get *Lützow* in his sights from *Setter*. It was a point well made: and at least the thing was fixed now, they could get on with it. Paul got out his chart and large-scale diagrams, and settled down with the others to check over the approach route, distances and timing. X-12 and X-8 would be the last to go in, as their target was the closest and the entire attack needed to be synchronised. Otherwise if you were in the fjord when someone else's charges went up, you could be blown to kingdom come: or a premature attack could spoil all the others' chances. Routes for different craft were varied, but there was a minefield to be crossed to start with and for most of them the last part of the approach to Altenfjord would be through a narrow channel called Stjernsund. But X-12 was to use Rognsund—a narrower passage somewhat trickier.

It would be an extraordinary moment, getting there. Being there inside, with those enormous enemy ships in reach. Other enemies too, no doubt. He couldn't guess, now, how he'd feel—mainly excited or mainly terrified. And in any case you had to get there first.

Eaton murmured, "I'd have liked a shot at the Beast."

"The Beast" was said to be Winston Churchill's name for the *Tirpitz*. Churchill was personally very keen to see her put out of action. The Germans, taking a different view, had nicknamed her "the Queen of the North."

Nobody had ever given *Lützow* a pet name. She'd been laid-down in 1931 as the *Deutschland*. "Pocket battleship" was a meaningless term: effectively she was an exceptionally powerful heavy cruiser.

"I'll be back." Paul slid out from behind the table. "Have to tell Louis."

Gimber said, "So you're the third eleven."

"Thanks. How's the boat, Louis?"

"Christ. What a question."

"I mean electrics and mechanics—defects, if any."

"One or two little things. Had a leak on the periscope gland, was the latest. We took it down, and I've just put it together again. Seems OK, at the moment, but I'll watch it. Trigger did a job on the compressor—but I told you about that. Most of the little things have been electrical, caused by the damp. Which is the worst—no, belay that, second worst thing's the damp."

"Seasick, still?"

"Ozzie is. He's really bad."

"Well." Paul hesitated. "I suppose one of us might take over—if he's really sick, and we could make a transfer. I'd ask MacGregor, if . . ."

"Wait. I'll ask Ozzie."

He heard Gimber and Steep talking—thin, distant voices. Then Gimber was back on the line.

"Ozzie says he'll stick it out, thanks all the same. Says he's getting over it. He doesn't look like it, and every few minutes he doesn't sound like it, either. Tries to puke, but all he can do is make revolting noises . . . But we'd better accept his word for it—the aim is for you lot to be all bright-eyed and bushy-tailed when the day dawns, isn't it."

"Meanwhile you and Trigger are sharing all the work?"

"Most of it. But we can handle it."

"All right. But let me know if . . ."

"Yeah, yeah. Paul, what I would ask for is a call from you every fifteen minutes. Possible?"

"Well, of course it's possible, but . . ." He thought, Must be worse than he's admitted. He asked, "You mean, in case the tow parts?"

"Or in case Trigger and I both pass out. But we've parted tows before this, haven't we, I mean it can happen, and being trimmed heavy for'ard as we do have to be now."

"Yes, I'm with you."

"It might be nice for you to know we were still with you. Every quarter-hour?"

"All right. I'll set it up."

"Very kind."

"Is that sarcasm?"

"Could've been . . . Question now, though—where are we? How far to the target area?"

"We're a hundred and twenty miles west of the Lofotens. About three hundred and twenty miles to go."

"So we've covered about seven hundred already . . . Afford to slow down a bit, couldn't we?"

"Not really, Louis."

If he'd been in better shape he wouldn't have suggested it, Paul thought. You had to remember how desperately uncomfortable—and unnerving, at times—it must be, down there. He heard Gimber argue, "But three hundred miles at ten knots—"

"Louis, it won't be ten knots for more than another day or so—day and a half, say. Towing ships are to make the last part of the passage dived, remember?"

Dived, *Setter* would make-good three or four knots, not ten. The lapse of memory was extraordinary, and it showed how right the planners had been to decide on having separate crews for passage and for action. The passage men would be mentally and physically exhausted by the time they reached the Norwegian coast. Paul reminded Gimber—appreciating the enormous strain he was under at this moment, and that his mind was already clouded to some extent—"Besides which, old horse, we can't risk falling astern of schedule. The last-quarter moon's on the twentieth, which is the day we start in, and if we didn't take advantage of that waning moon—"

"Paul."

"Huh?"

"Teach your grandmother?"

They'd need some moonlight for the passage of the outer fjords, after getting across the minefield, and also a high tide to take them safely over the moored mines. Those were the basic essentials for the kick-off, and such conditions would prevail in the few days starting on 20 September.

Gimber had hung up the telephone, muttering angrily to himself. Trigger Towne asked him, "Problems, skipper?"

X-12 bouncing, jerking, her porpoising movement three-dimensional and with sharp, sudden angles in it now.

"They'll make contact every fifteen minutes. Bit of a bloody nuisance, but—well . . ." He knew Towne hadn't heard him. You got sick of asking for repetitions, when someone didn't shout loud enough over the constant noise. He yelled, "I'll take her now."

"If you want." Towne hadn't moved, didn't seem to be about to move.

"You've been on at least three hours, Trigger."

"So what?"

Gimber tapped him on the shoulder. "Change round. Get your fat head down."

"Nah." There was no point trying to sleep, when you knew the Benzedrine wouldn't let you. You needed the pills in order to stay awake, and sleeplessness was the price of it. In any case, there was plenty of work to be done, and only the two of them to do it. He shouted, easing himself off the first lieutenant's seat, "Job or two first." Turning, coming face to face with Louis Gimber: Towne's face bearded, sunken-eyed, the eyes inside there bright and glaring, crazy-looking. He kept one hand on the hydroplane control wheel until Gimber had reached to it: then they were sliding around and past each other, each needing a spare hand for steadying himself against the bucking motion of the craft. Trim would have gone to pot, with two men's weights shifting around like this and no immediate adjustment, but the trim was all to hell anyway, bow-heavy and entirely dependent on the tow's drag. Towne bawled, "You're looking better, skipper. Like a corpse half warmed-up. Hour ago you looked like one on the slab."

"Charmed!"

"It's me old-world courtesy got me where I am . . . Take a shufti at the Sub, should I?"

"No. Let him sleep it off."

Rest was probably the best medicine for Ozzie. Until he'd passed out he'd been as bad as he had yesterday—retching, groaning . . . He'd slept, finally, because the effects of the Benzedrine had worn off; Gimber had suspected the pills might have been making his sickness worse, and he'd told him to stop using them. The drawback was that he and Towne were now entirely reliant on them, since they had all the watch-keeping and maintenance chores to share between them.

"W and D pump motor," Towne was crouching behind Gimber, yelling into his ear, "claims me attention, like. Want to compensate?"

To work on that pump in the wet-and-dry compartment meant a big shift of weight, one that would make her even heavier for'ard than she was already. As things were now, you had not only extra ballast in the bow trim-tank, but also Ozzie Steep in the fore-end. Some heaviness for'ard was necessary, to reduce the boat's tendency to dance like a cork in a waterfall, but if you overdid it you'd be increasing the strain on the Manilla rope to such an extent that it was almost bound to break. Then the weighted bow would drag her down—plummeting, as likely as not very difficult to stop in time. There was a vicious circle in this hydrostatic problem, too: the deeper a submarine dives the heavier she becomes, and even in normal circumstances you had to be alert to this, ready to pump ballast out as depth increased. With the bow-heavy trim, circumstances were a long way from normal and a lot more dangerous.

Gimber had two other things in mind, when he thought about it. One, that his own reactions and Towne's might not be as fast as they should have been, now, and two, that X-12 had something like ten thousand feet of water between her and the ocean floor—which would make for a long, long dive.

He nodded to the ERA "Right!"

Left hand on the pump lever. Glancing round, seeing Towne move to wait amidships, under the dome. Gimber pulled the lever aft: visualising the valves opening and then the pump motor starting; then he was counting, with his eyes on the bubble in the fore-and-aft spirit-level, while seawater flowed through the trimline from the bow tank to the stern one.

Enough . . . He pushed the lever back to its central position, neutral. This movement would first have stopped the pump, then shut the valves. They had to be shut, obviously, or water would be sloshing through from one tank to the other as the midget plunged around. Then you'd have had no control over her at all. Gimber turned his head, saw Towne already crawling into the W and D, dragging a bag of tools.

X-11, in tow of HM Submarine *Scourge,* surfaced at noon for her routine period of ventilation. The sea was rough: standing on the midget's casing was like riding a surf-board. But Tom Messinger, X-11's passage-crew skipper, was enjoying the fresh air too much to give a damn about getting soaking wet in freezing Norwegian Sea. (Not quite freezing: but bloody cold.) The hatch was shut, of course—if it hadn't been the boat would have filled and sunk within about two minutes—and the induction trunk raised, Messinger with a rope's end securing himself to it and his arms wrapped round it too: there was an enormous expanse of wildly tossing sea around

him, and if you were washed off you knew you'd have no hope of being
seen alive again. The pounding Gardner diesel was sucking air throatily
down the pipe and through the boat, filling her with fresh, clean air in place
of the putrid fog they'd been breathing for the last few hours.

Two hundred yards ahead, *Scourge* had reduced speed to five knots: she
was still towing, because the diesel was running at its lowest revs, entirely
for air-change purposes. Messinger's watery view of *Scourge* was end-on—
swaying bridge and periscope standards, two lookouts in black silhouette,
sea heaping white, the submarine's after casing alternately engulfed in the
white mound of it then rising shiny-black as her forepart plunged. That
after casing was a lot higher out of the water than this midget's casing: the
seas sweeping over X-11 were waist-high, at times. He shouted aloud—
addressing only himself, sea, sky and the cutting wind—"This is a hell of a
way to get around!" Then laughed—crazy, happy, which left no doubt you
had to be pretty far gone—filling his lungs with the air, revelling in daylight and the brilliant seascape under scudding grey. Enjoying too the fact
of being part of this truly extraordinary adventure—three men in a boat
and the boat a tiny, highly-explosive one at that, and seven other identical
rigs out there, each as solitary-feeling as this one. To starboard and ten miles
away there'd be X-12 with *Setter,* while to port the line-up was *Sceptre* with
X-10, *Thrasher* with X-5, *Stubborn* and X-7, *Sea Nymph* and X-8, *Syrtis* and
X-9, *Truculent* and X-6. Spread like chariots in a race, in distant line-abreast
advancing east-northeastward . . .

But it was time to go down now, so that *Scourge* could increase to ten
knots again. Joy faded at the prospect of return to cramped confinement,
the continuous banging around and the steadily deteriorating air. Messinger
shouted down the induction pipe, "Stop the Gardner. Tell *Scourge* we're
about to dive. Shut off for diving."

A last look round: and another at *Scourge,* where Dan Vicary, Johnny
McKie, Toby Maguire and Tommo Brind were lolling in the lap of luxury.
Comparatively speaking . . . Messinger had got the rope off the induction
pipe and was holding on with one arm locked round it; he was giving Hillcrest time to pass that message by telephone and Charlie Amor a

moment to shut the induction pipe's hull-valve. It was only the action of a moment—a lever-operated valve on the port side at shoulder-level to the helmsman, he had only to stretch out and yank it shut. He'd have done it by this time. Messinger lowered the pipe on its hinged base, crouching and holding to the casing itself with one hand while he forced it right down, horizontal. The pipe's top end was sealed by a flap-valve which tripped shut when the pipe was fully lowered—as it was now, flat to the deck. And the diesel had stopped. Crouching, still hanging on with one hand, using the other to open the hatch at a time when she'd risen to a wave and was well clear of the water: Messinger slid in feet-first and fast, pulled the lid shut again over his wet head and forced the central hand-wheel round so that the securing dogs engaged under steel lips around the rim.

"Sixty feet."

Water running off him puddled on the deck boards. Bony Hillcrest, on the first lieutenant's seat, repeated the order and swung the hydroplane control wheel to "dive"; Amor had opened the main vents and she was already going down. He'd been as sick as a dog, day before yesterday, but he was all right now; they'd all been under the weather for a time.

Forty-five feet. Fifty . . .

Hillcrest was holding the dive-angle on her. Messinger would have been easing it by now, starting to level her. But he didn't want to seem to be breathing over the shoulder of a number one who knew his job as well as Bony did.

He'd begun to take the angle off now, anyway.

Messinger noticed that the bubble was still well aft. In other words, his boat still had a pronounced bow-down angle on her. Of course, Hillcrest would have put some extra weight in her bow, but—

Telephone. Messinger reached for it.

"Yup? That you, Dan?"

The Springbok's voice assured him, "It's not Adolf Hitler. Might be, if you didn't have an unlisted number . . . You all happy there?"

"Could be happier. Say if we'd brought some bints along."

He meant girls. Mediterranean service had injected a lot of Arabic into the language. Vicary said, "I'll make that point to FOSM, man, suggestion for the next op . . . Call you in an hour, ay?"

"Don't you mean half an hour?"

"Oh, ya, half—"

"Dan, I meant so they'd cook hot meals for us."

He hung up. He'd been watching the depthgauge all the time, and she was at seventy feet now with a three-degree bow-down angle. He said, "Let's have her at sixty, Bony."

They called Hillcrest "Bony" because he was supposed to look like Napoleon. Messinger saw him ease the trim-pump lever aft, to suck some weight out of the bow tank. Just as he was doing it the tow-rope snatched upwards so violently that it felt as if she'd hit a rock. Her bow shot up: if Messinger hadn't been holding on he'd have gone flying. Everything happening in one second, as if in one movement, connected parts of the same event: Hillcrest falling sideways against the lever, pushing it forward—he was on top of it, Messinger frantic in the effort to pull him up, only too well aware that ballast was flowing into that bow tank now. Bow-down, diving. Seventy-five feet—eighty, angle and rate of dive increasing. Hillcrest had got himself off the pump lever: he pulled it to neutral and then aft, to the pump-from-for'ard position. Messinger shouted, "Blow number one main ballast!" He should have ordered this before, but he'd been preoccupied with Bony's predicament. The needle was swinging past the one hundred mark: she was steeply bow-down and accelerating in her dive. One-twenty; one-forty . . .

Blowing. Charlie Amor had wrenched open the high-pressure blow to number one main ballast. But it wasn't making any difference—yet. One hundred and sixty feet. One-seventy-five. Hillcrest shouted at Amor, "Blow one and three!" Amor agleam with sweat, teeth bared in a snarl as he twisted open the other HP blow. You couldn't blow the midships main ballast tank, number two; it didn't have an HP airline to it. One and three were blowing all the stored air gushing to them from the bottles, but—incredibly—it was having no effect at all. Two hundred feet: she was nose-down, diving very fast indeed. Hillcrest turning to stare at Messinger, face contorted: "Christ, skipper . . ."

Messinger saw it. He flung himself towards the half-dazed ERA's blowing-panel. He screamed, "Main vents!"

Too bloody late. Knowing it, there and then, in those seconds before perdition. Main vents were still open from the act of diving and all that air had been blowing straight out into the sea.

A bunch of *Setter* and X-12 officers were playing poker dice, the variety of the game known as Double Cameroon, that evening, when Brazier took his turn to go along and make the routine telephone-call. When he came back, squeezing his large frame on to the bench, he said, "Louis's complaining he can't get any work done when we interrupt him every few minutes. He wants to make it half-hourly again."

"Fine. But that was his own idea ... Now there's the high straight I needed ..."

Gimber must be feeling better about things, he concluded. Seasickness on top of all the other discomforts would be fairly shattering to morale. He wished the weather would ease a little.

After supper, a signal from *Stubborn* was picked up and decoded. She was reporting having come across X-8 loose and wandering, having parted her tow from *Sea Nymph* earlier in the day. *Stubborn* gave the midget's position, course and speed, so that FOSM could arrange for *Sea Nymph* to rendez-vous with her and re-establish the tow.

"Darned lucky finding her." MacGregor was turning in. "Odds against must've been in thousands."

"And I wouldn't like to be in Jack Smart's wet socks." Paul scooped up the dice. Smart was X-8's passage-crew CO. "A whole night on the surface, in this sea?"

At midnight there was another urgent signal. X-11's tow had parted, and *Scourge* had reversed course in the hope of finding her.

Nobody made any comment. But you couldn't rest easily, either, after that. It was all too obvious that X-11 might not have had X-8's luck. Luck, or skill, or whatever combination of the two you'd need, in whatever the circumstances might have been ... Paul went to the wireless office to call

X-12, and it was a relief to hear Gimber's voice over the wire, even though the tone of it was peevish.

"I had Eaton on this thing only about twenty minutes ago!"

"So, I've warmed the ball a bit . . . But you're OK, are you?"

"You might say so, at a pinch. Ozzie's still out for the count."

"Oh, is he . . . Well, d'you want someone to . . ."

"No, I don't!"

Paul waited a moment. Then he tried again. "I was about to ask—"

"I know, I'm sorry, I don't want any bloody thing at all. Ozzie'll soon snap out of it, and meanwhile we're coping all right." There was some distant mumbling: Gimber talking aside to Towne, he guessed. Then the voice came back: "Trigger agrees, we're all right as we are. Benzedrine's the answer . . . Any news?"

There was no point telling him about X-8 and X-11. Paul said, "Nothing worth repeating. You'll be up for a guff-through at two, right?"

"If our luck holds out, we will."

He certainly wasn't his normal self. Perhaps one shouldn't have expected it. Paul told him, "I'm turning in, now. Talk again later."

"Ha. Sleep tight. Pleasant dreams."

"In four days' time, Louis, you'll be doing the sleeping-tight routine."

"D'you ever dream about her, Paul?"

Hanging up, Gimber stared grimly at Towne. He muttered, "Four days . . ."

CHAPTER TEN

· · ·

Trench leant over the bunk, staring down at him. Looking for something he didn't find. Outside, the sounds of work in progress were loud and constant—from the deck above, and from the jetty and from *Foremost* who was secured on the other side—while in this semi-dark cabin the tranquillity was an illusion, a phoney quiet in which Trench's deep concern for Nick Everard's life was at odds with his need to be elsewhere—in about half a dozen other places, at this very moment. He asked *Lyric's* doctor, Cramphorn, "Is there really a chance he can take in what's said to him?"

"It's quite possible, sir. And probably best to assume he can. I mean, for his sake."

Trench didn't know what he'd meant by that. *Foremost's* doctor—also an RNVR two-striper—saw the frown, and explained quietly, "Sort of to keep him in touch, sir. By engaging his attention, getting the brain back into gear, as it were. Could make a lot of difference."

Trench's eyes rested for a moment on this other doctor. He didn't look much more than twenty years old, but of course he had to be more than that. He nodded. "I see." Turning back to the man in the bunk: wondering what it would be like to hear things that were said to you but not be able to answer or even signal that you'd heard.

"Are you hearing me, sir?"

To be asked a question would be even more frustrating. But it might be like hearing a voice in a dream, he guessed. He was still looking for reaction—for the movement of an eyelid, the twitch of a muscle—and not seeing any at all. Trench wasn't enjoying this—either the situation itself or the charade of addressing someone who was so deeply unconscious that it felt like talking to a corpse. He had no confidence in being heard, or of doing any good at all: it was simply a matter of taking these quacks' word for it, accepting that they'd have to know more about it than he did himself . . . "It's Trench here, sir. I expect you feel bloody awful, but the doctors say you're doing well, so there's nothing for you to worry about. Just prove them right, get better—and I'll handle the trip home, you've nothing to worry about at all."

Rubbish. He told himself, If he's hearing me, he's thinking, "What a load of codswallop!" He'd glanced round again, at the two doctors. Feeling idiotic . . . This cabin belonged to *Lyric's* first lieutenant, or had done until it had been commandeered to become Nick Everard's sickroom.

Trench forced himself to start yacking again . . . "Everything's under control, sir. We're at Vaenga, in the Kola Inlet. I diverted because if we'd stuck to the Archangel plan there might not have been much left of us by the time we got there. You're on board *Lyric*—they picked you up when *Calliope* went down. You're in what the doc calls a coma, as a result of hypothermia—that's a technical term for too long in cold water. It's like a bang on the head, apparently—knocks you out . . . But you're in good hands, sir, and they tell me you'll be sitting up and taking notice before much longer."

Lyric was alongside Vaenga pier, and *Foremost* was berthed outside her. Some of the survivors had been moved into the AA ship, the *Berkeley,* while fit men or those only lightly wounded were being distributed among the destroyers. Only men who were considered unlikely to survive the journey home were being left ashore, but whether they'd survive here was something of a toss-up; the hospital was little more than a shack, with inadequate lighting, heat or sanitation and only the most basic equipment: the medical stores which had been on board *Calliope* were now at the bottom of the Barents Sea.

Trench had brought the remnants of PQ 19 into the Kola Inlet soon after dawn this morning. The last hundred and fifty miles had taken twice as long as he'd expected, mostly because the *Sovyetskaya Slava* had been hit again, on the afternoon of the day of *Calliope's* loss, and her speed reduced from eight knots to four and a half. Then the *Carrickmore* had also been

hit and a fire started in one of her holds; she'd still been smouldering internally when the merchantmen had gone to their berths for discharging
cargo. But yesterday there'd been only one attack, high-level and ineffectual.
They'd owed this mercy to the wind having dropped overnight and the
cloud thickening, pressing down towards the sea, providing cover which
must have been infuriating to the Luftwaffe. So this morning Trench had
delivered the *Tacora,* the *Sovyetskaya Slava, Carrickmore, Republican, Ewart
S. Dukes* and *Galilee Dawn* and their more or less intact cargoes of war
material. The Soviet tanker, as she'd plugged slowly on up the inlet with a
tug to help her, had gone so far as to signal a "thank you," which in Trench's
experience was unprecedented.

He described these events to the unresponsive patient. There was some
coming and going behind him while he was talking, and when he paused
and looked round he found Sam Clegg, *Lyric*'s captain, at his elbow.

"Crockford's waiting in my day cabin, sir. D'you want him in here?"

"No—we'll go through."

Crockford was captain of *Foremost,* and Trench had sent for him to
come over. Saving time, while he was here—two birds with one stone . . .
Cramphorn was telling Clegg he'd stay with the patient; Trench asked him
whether Nick would need to have someone with him all the time.

The doctor nodded. "Within sight and sound, anyway. When he comes-
to," he added more quietly, "or if he does . . . It could happen soon, or
not for days . . . When he does, he probably won't have any memory—
for events or people, may not even know his own name, for some time
. . . We'll be keeping him here in *Lyric,* will we, sir? Home to the UK?"

"Home to the UK, but I think not in *Lyric*. Although it might be an
idea for you, Cramphorn, to stay with him."

Clegg asked, "Stay where with him?"

"In *Foremost*. If these chaps will agree he can be moved. But I'd also suggest Cramphorn here might move over with him. Change places with your
own doctor." He'd glanced at Kingdon. "Simply for continuity. Cramphorn
started with him, might as well carry on?" Trench beckoned to the two
doctors. "Couple of minutes, he won't come to any harm." He asked them

outside, out of earshot of the patient who might or might not have heard, "You do agree he shouldn't be left ashore?"

"Yes," Cramphorn said, "same with all the hypothermia cases. There simply aren't the facilities."

"But you think," he nodded to Crockford as they filed into Clegg's day cabin "you're confident he can survive the trip home?"

"No, sir." Cramphorn shook his head. "At this stage, it's a toss-up. But he'll have a better chance coming home with us than he would have if we left him here. If we have a reasonably quiet passage."

"Nobody can promise that." Trench lowered himself into an armchair. He told *Foremost*'s captain, "I'm arranging for him to be moved over to you, Crockford, because being close escort you're less likely to be dashing around, and the ride shouldn't be as bumpy. Also—we've just been talking about this—I think it would be as well if Surgeon Lieutenant Cramphorn moved over to you with him, having looked after him up to now, d'you see. Sam here could have the loan of your doctor, a temporary swap?"

Crockford asked, "D'you mind, Kingdon?"

Cramphorn excused himself, to return to the patient. Kingdon left, to also put in hand arrangements for Everard's reception on board *Foremost*. Trench talked to the two destroyer captains now. He was glad the doctors had agreed to change places. It had been his own instinctive preference, a choice of Cramphorn as the man most likely to keep Nick Everard alive. Trench was to admit, later, that it had been no more than a hunch. He'd simply wanted to give Nick Everard the best possible chance of survival that could be provided, and Cramphorn had seemed the best bet.

He told Clegg and Crockford, "I can't tell you exactly how soon we'll be sailing from here, but I want to be ready to go as soon as we get the word. Fuel and fresh water's laid on. You'll have had that signal, I suppose?"

They had. Clegg put in, "But no answer yet about four-seven ammo, sir."

"That's being taken care of, don't worry. And tomorrow forenoon I want all commanding officers on board *Moloch* for conference at 1130 sharp. I've no idea why we have to wait for permission to sail: the thing is to have everything on the top line so we can get cracking as soon as possible. In principle it's been agreed that QP 16 can be sailed from Archangel with an escort of Soviet destroyers plus minesweepers who'll be coming all the way with us. The ones we brought will be staying here as their reliefs, of course. But there'll also be a small Russian oiler with the convoy—she'll turn back to Archangel with their destroyers after we've fuelled from her. That'll see us through until we meet the *Bayleaf* somewhere near Bear Island—thanks to the good sense of that man in there." He jerked a thumb towards the sickroom. "But as I say, we may have to wait a day or two, or even several days. SBNO doesn't know the reason—or isn't divulging it, anyway."

Crockford asked him as they got up, "What's made the Russkis so co-operative?"

"I suspect they've been persuaded that until we get these empties home we won't be bringing them any full ones." Trench said, "While I'm here, I'm going to take another look at him. No need for anyone else to hang around, though."

Cramphorn was beside the bunk: he'd been talking quietly. Trench shut the door. "Any sign he might be receiving you?"

"There couldn't really, at this stage, sir." The doctor got up, and pulled his chair out of the way. "But it's worth trying."

"He could stay like this for days, you said."

"Yes." The doctor opened his mouth to add something: then shut it. Trench crouched at the head of the bunk: the size he was, it was the only way he could get down to that level, without breaking his back.

"It's Trench here, sir. We'll be moving you over into *Foremost* before long. You should have a more comfortable passage in her, and I've arranged that you'll keep this same sawbones with you. His name's Cramphorn—poor fellow . . . He'll take good care of you until we get you home. Then you'll be surrounded by all the experts and specialists, and I shouldn't be surprised if one of the nurses was Australian . . . So just hang on, sir, take it easy, and don't worry. You can leave all the worrying to the rest of us, for a change."

Cramphorn came with him to the doorway. Trench thoughtful as he looked at him. The doctor was a smallish man with steady eyes and a direct, take-it-or-leave-it manner. Scrawny little bastard, and he looked as if he could have used about twenty-four hours' sleep. But then, who couldn't have . . . Anyway, Trench had a good impression of him. He warned, "This man's worth his weight in diamonds. Believe me, he's one we can't afford to lose."

Cramphorn said, "They all are."

Paul said into the telephone, "OK, Louis. We'll reduce to five knots now. I'm due on watch, I'll be up there when you surface."

"Wow." Gimber's voice was thin over the line. "The very thought makes my heart go pit-a-pat."

He'd got over his own seasickness, he'd said, although Ozzie Steep was still out of action. You couldn't blame a man for getting sick, but Paul was still glad he hadn't taken Ozzie for operational first lieutenant in Eaton's place, which at one stage he'd considered. He went into the control room and addressed the helmsman: "Relieve officer of the watch, please." Henning replied "Yes, please," and Paul climbed up through the wind-tunnel of a conning-tower into the dark, swaying bridge.

The weather hadn't eased at all. *Setter* was making eight and a half knots, lurching clumsily through a whitened sea, rollers sweeping up from her port quarter. Spray burst in bathfuls across the bridge, flung up by her butting, slogging progress. He told Henning—ducking spray as he yelled it—"Revs for X-12's surfacing routine, please?"

Straightening, he got a faceful. Henning calling down for two hundred revolutions: then shouting as he turned to Paul, "I wouldn't like to be surfacing that little object in this lot!"

"You would if you'd been under for the last six hours with one of your crew puking every five minutes. I'll take over, if you're ready?"

There wasn't much to hand over. The course, the revs, when he'd last "blown round," the captain's night orders—which in any case were in the night-order book on the chart-table, and no different from last night's or the night before. The main difference on this jaunt was that if you ran into an enemy—a U-boat being the most likely variety—the orders were not to attack, but to evade and remain unseen. It was obvious, however, to anyone with experience of night encounters on the surface that the odds were you'd see each other at roughly the same moment, so secrecy could best be preserved only by the quick destruction of the U-boat.

But it would depend on the range and bearing of an enemy when you sighted him. The X-craft had all been warned of the possibility of sudden dives by their towing ships.

X-12 duly surfaced, spent fifteen minutes impersonating a half-tide rock while she "guffed through," then slid under again. Five minutes after she'd disappeared Paul told the W/T office watchkeeper to call through and check that all was well; confirmation of this came up the voicepipe at 0228, and he increased to revs for eight and a half knots again.

He wished he'd been able to tell his father about this business. On the face of it, it was silly that he hadn't. As if Nick Everard, of all living men, would have gone around talking about it! But the security angle had been stressed so hard, had been dinned into all participants so vehemently and regularly all through the training period, that you'd have hesitated to have whispered about it even to yourself. There'd been fatuous gags about security—like, "These orders are to be burnt before being read."

He swung the binoculars slowly across the bow, intently following the indefinite curve of dark horizon. Mountains of sea, white flashes like bow-waves everywhere you looked: the only comfort was that a real bow-wave would look different. When you saw it, you'd know it . . . His father would hear all about this Operation Source eventually, of course, and he'd under-stand the need there'd been for secrecy. Despite this, Paul still wished they'd been able to talk about it together.

Gimber had been doing his first lieutenant's job, taking her down to ninety feet and—in a manner of speaking—levelling her there. If you could use the word "levelling" when she was being flung around like an old boot in a mill-race.

Ozzie Steep yelled, "Take over, shall I?"

Gimber looked round at him. He also noticed an expression of alarm on Trigger Towne's now fully-bearded face. Towne had that blue-black, silky-looking growth that made the brightness of his eyes seem like a madman's. Ozzie Steep's eyes, in contrast, were as dull as if he was looking at you through dirty water. He looked weak, and—despite that offer—unsure of himself.

"You're not fit yet, Ozzie. Maybe tomorrow, if the weather eases—or when *Setter* dives."

"But I'm fine now, skipper!"

"So you can do some wiping-up." Gimber pointed. "There, to start with."

Towne had got out of his seat; he put a hand on Steep's shoulder as he squeezed past. The other hand latching on to an overhead pipe for support. He shouted to Gimber, "After end. Tail-clutch."

Wherever you looked, condensation gleamed, trickled. Keeping her almost dry was a full-time job, and there was plenty of other maintenance as well, so if Steep could lend a hand now it would make life a lot easier.

Every time *Setter*'s stern rose, X-12's bow was wrenched upward. But *Setter* was rolling as well as pitching, so the imparted motion was lateral as well as vertical. As it continued hour after hour, day and night after day and night, it caused a degree of strain and discomfort that made you hate that thing up there—to a point where for an interval of peace you could have crawled for'ard and wound the handle that would slip the tow . . .

Ozzie Steep's conflicting feelings showed in his pale, ginger-stubbled face. He wanted to be doing his job, and it shamed him that he was not, but he also knew Gimber was right. Gimber guessing, meanwhile, at how anyone would be after such a period of chronic sickness: you'd feel hollow inside, weak and shaky . . . He shouted, with his eyes on the depthgauge and the bubble, "She'll be diving tomorrow. It'll be smooth-going, then, and you'll be stronger, too. It's not your fault, Ozzie, nobody's blaming you."

It would be a lot easier and far less uncomfortable once *Setter* was dived for the approach to the Norwegian coast. But Gimber doubted whether he'd let Steep have charge of the boat even then. Not unless he got himself together very rapidly. This was no job for a man operating at half-strength. In the immediate situation, this crew's lives depended on the man in the first lieutenant's seat, and in the longer term one eighth of the operation's chances of success rested in the same pair of hands. Just as much as in the boat's commanding officer's.

Gimber didn't know about the loss of X-11 yet, of course, or about X-8 being motherless.

Steep was mopping wet surfaces on the starboard side, behind Trigger's vacated seat. Trigger, back there in the after end, was in the midget's narrowest, tightest space while he lubricated the tail-clutch mechanism. It would be like lying in a pipe that had uncomfortable projections in it, and so constricting that you'd have problems with your elbows as you worked. When she turned her snout up—which she was doing now, a surging bow-up swoop—he'd be head-down, as good as stuck until she levelled again. But she'd been dragged up and then pulled hard to port—a solid jar right through her as the tow-rope stretched bar-taut. You could visualise the movement out there in the black water: it didn't exactly soothe the mind to do so, but imagination tended to operate on its own, didn't ask permission, the pictures simply flashed in there, matching the gyrations . . . Bow falling now. There'd been a compensating jerk to haul her back on course; Gimber had seen Steep's apprehensive glance for'ard at the same time as in his mind's eye the Manilla tow had slackened and then sprung rigid again: the downward swing of the bow had checked, but then continued. *Setter* was tormenting the midget like a child dragging a puppy on a string. The tow-rope came up all-standing for a second time: mentally he saw it quivering-taut, stretching ruler-straight through black turbulence. That jerk had been powerful enough to have wrenched her stem off. Gimber had felt it in his own body, like the hideous jar a man might get from the rope as he drops feet-first through the trap.

Christ, imagination . . .

Quiet, suddenly. He was waiting for the next upward drag, the cycle of violence to recommence.

But it didn't. Hadn't. She was bow-down, and the needle was beginning to swing slowly around the face of the depthgauge. Ninety-three
feet—ninety-five . . . Three degrees bow-down: ninety-eight feet. He felt
it, then—a sensation of drift, of idling in the water without steerage-way
or any grip from the hydroplanes.

Gimber leant sideways, reached for the telephone.

Nothing. No jerking from the tow-rope either. X-12 was in a smooth
glide: and the telephone line was dead. A hundred and four feet on the
gauge, bubble six degrees aft of centre. Downward movement accelerating:
a hundred and ten feet. Gimber snapped, "Blow one main ballast!" Steep
throwing himself into Towne's seat and reaching to the HP air valve. The
hollowness in your gut might have been fright but there wasn't time to
take notice of it, and another precious moment passed while he reminded
himself, No use using the screw until she's got her bow up . . . A hundred
and twenty feet. Gimber had seen Ozzie check that the vent-levers were in
their shut position before he'd wrenched that valve open. One-twenty-five
feet. Air was scorching through the pipe to the for'ard main ballast tank.
One-thirty feet, bow-down angle eight degrees, a minute object sinking
through a vast surrounding mass of sea. In spite of the bow-down angle
Trigger Towne was appearing feet-first, wriggling backwards out of the
engine-space, panting like a dog.

Levelling. Gauge showing one hundred and thirty-nine feet, Gimber's
left hand had pulled the trim-pump lever aft, and now with his right he
closed the main motor field switch—to start the motor—and then span a
twelve-inch hand-wheel through the positions for slow, half and full ahead
grouped down, on through slow and half to full ahead grouped up: this
was maximum forward power, the two battery sections linked in parallel
to put full power on the motor. As he'd begun to throw the speed-control
wheel round he'd ordered "Blow number three main ballast!" Steep had
opened the valve, and now he and Towne were changing places. Gimber
knew he'd have to take a chance on Steep now—let him take over here
at the controls so that he, Gimber, could be in the CO's position for surfacing, opening the hatch and then getting out on to the casing. But first

things first . . . He beckoned to Steep, and he'd stopped the trim-pump. He shouted to Towne, "Stop blowing one!" She'd been taking too much of a bow-up angle. The midships tank was still blowing, though, to give her overall bodily buoyancy: it wasn't a time for halfmeasures, and he'd be wanting her well up, when she surfaced, as high in the waves as she'd ride. He was getting out of the seat, to let Ozzie in. Telling him—because he was already out of reach of the rheostat control—"Half ahead grouped up." Then he tapped Trigger on the shoulder: "Stop blowing three!"

Theoretically he should have stopped her at periscope depth, not taken her straight up. He should have held her there while he took a look to make sure he wasn't surfacing her right under *Setter's* bows—*Setter* perhaps having guessed the tow had gone, and turned back to search. But (a) this wasn't likely, (b) even at periscope depth—nine feet, or even less in this sea, *Setter* would still have run her down if she'd been there to do it, (c) you wouldn't see much anyway, in this weather, and (d) at eight feet she'd be unmanageable. So you could forget the drill book.

Ozzie was doing all right. Something rather odd about him, but he wasn't making any mistakes.

The next telephone check was to have been at 0300. In sixteen minutes. They wouldn't know the tow had parted until they found the phone was dead. In sixteen minutes at eight and a half knots *Setter* would have covered just over two miles: two sea miles—well, 4250 yards. It would take her about the same time again to get back to where the rope had snapped: or a bit longer, if MacGregor reduced speed, which he probably would do, because spotting the X-craft with her low freeboard in this wild sea wouldn't be at all easy. All they'd know in *Setter* was that the tow had parted at some time between 0230 and 0300, and they wouldn't know with any certainty that X-12 hadn't done a nose-dive to the bottom.

Gimber told Steep, "Soon as I'm up there and the induction's open, start the donkey, half ahead."

"Aye, aye, sir!"

Fifteen feet. Twelve . . . At nine she was rolling like a barrel.

·   ·   ·

"Officer of the watch, sir!"

Paul swung round. The lookout told him, "Tow may have gone, sir. Saw an end washing loose. Least, I think . . ."

He'd dipped to the voicepipe, "Control room—tell the W/T office, check communications with X-12—quick!"

"Aye aye sir!"

"Time?"

"Oh-two-four-nine, sir."

May Louis Gimber have been wide awake and on his toes . . .

"Bridge—telephone line's dead, sir!"

He'd expected it, and was ready for it. "Stop port. Port twenty-five. Shake the captain, tell him the tow's parted. Shake the X-craft officers too." It was up to MacGregor who else got shaken.

The casing officer—Henning—and the second coxswain, surely; but that was his business. *Setter* was swinging, taking green seas over as she turned across the wind.

They won't see us . . .

Teeth clenched, eyes slitted against wind and salt water, muttering to himself, desperate . . . X-12 battling through waves more than over them. Not even the sharpest-eyed lookout would spot her, except by pure chance.

All right, he told himself. All right. Calm down. It's up to me to do the spotting!

And in fact—getting used to it now—the motion wasn't as bad as he'd expected. Waves were crashing over her but she was riding it well, forging ahead at about three knots; it was a quartering sea and she was rolling, naturally. He spoke to her, told her that she was doing marvellously, that he was pleased with her. He had no rope lashing, but both arms wrapped around the induction pipe. At this stage he could spare both hands for his own safety.

He was reckoning on an interval of twenty to thirty minutes before he'd have much chance of seeing *Setter,* but he still searched for her, straining his eyes through the flying spray in case his calculations were wrong. He was doing this, and going over the figures again in his mind, when he did see her. He couldn't believe it, at first, thought he'd imagined it—but that was her, all right! To port—a white flurry of broken water, and in the next blink the black loom of her conning-tower above it. Two or three more blinks, to make certain it wasn't his imagination playing tricks. It hadn't been. He estimated that she was between two and three cables' lengths away.

"Aldis! Quick, now!"

He'd warned Ozzie to have it ready under the dome. The price of getting it up on to the casing was a few bucketfuls of salt water sloshed down into the boat. Then he had the lamp out and the hatch shut again, he was rising to his feet with both arms round the induction pipe and the Aldis in both hands.

During that gymnastic feat, he'd lost sight of her.

Fright was sharp, breath-stopping. He knew that if they passed each other without contact, it might never be regained. This was no sheltered loch or bay X-12 was floundering in. The effort now was to steady his mind as well as his body and the lamp; hugging the pipe while the craft under him bucked, rolled and pitched . . . He had the lamp's pistol-grip in his right hand, its weight on his left forearm: he pressed the trigger, swung the beam slowly left, scything horizontally across the wavetops.

And—he bellowed it into wind and sea—"There!"

So pleased that he told X-12 again, "Good girl!" Although she was still trying to fling him off. Like talking to a crazy horse, trying to placate it . . . *Setter* was on the beam to port. They'd seen Gimber's light, obviously. He watched her, saw the turn she was making—slowing, and turning about forty degrees to port, putting herself beam-on to the sea. It was an invitation to him to bring X-12 up into that lee, into the small amount of shelter to be found there. MacGregor had swung her into that position, and he'd be working his motors as necessary to hold her there: motors, not diesels now, because diesels couldn't be put astern, either in *Setter* or in the midget.

Setter must have reversed course quite soon after the tow parted, he realised. Paul Everard was, on the whole, fairly clued-up. Gimber was turning X–12, to get her up close and in *Setter*'s lee: *Setter*'s own Aldis on him like a searchlight. Throwing herself every which way as she turned: and he was passing the lamp down, Ozzie snatching it from him and the hatch banging shut, after some more sea had burst in. Rising, clinging to the pipe, relief still enormous but subsiding somewhat in facing up now to the business of passing a new tow. It was an exercise that had been practised often enough, and it would be done without any exchange of signals—nobody needed to explain to anyone else what to do.

When he had her in *Setter*'s lee and bow-on to her, about fifty yards clear of her port side, he called down the pipe to Steep to stop the Gardner, take out the engine clutch and put the electric motor to slow ahead. This gave him the manoeuvrability he needed. *Setter,* broadside-on to the weather, was rolling like a cow. It wasn't much of a weather break, for all that. Better than nothing. Lying bow-on to her, X–12 was both stemming the sea and in the best position to accept the new tow. *Setter*'s Aldis lit activity down on her sea-swept fore-casing, near her gun: men in waterproof clothes and lifebelts were inflating the rubber boat and coiling down the Manilla rope. Two men moving aft now with its inboard end—clambering cautiously around the catwalk, clinging one-handed to the rail surrounding the tower. That inflatable boat would be used again in a few days' time for the change-round of passage and action crews.

Slow-ahead speed on the motor was just about keeping her where he wanted her, countering the sea's drift and providing enough steerage-way for Trigger Towne, as helmsman, to hold her head on the ordered bearing. Ozzie Steep, meanwhile, ready for orders to reach him through the pipe—slow down, speed up . . . Steep seemed to be functioning, more or less. Give it a day or so, Gimber thought—watching the work on *Setter*'s casing, waiting for the new tow to be floated down to him—and Trigger and I might get some rest. Have to cut out the Benzedrine intake first. You couldn't keep going for ever on bloody pills, anyway . . . The rubber boat was being launched over *Setter*'s side. A cluster of men on the casing there, some standing and some kneeling: one of them was climbing down into the boat while others held it alongside. The one climbing down—he recognised that man-mountain easily enough. They were passing the end of the Manilla down to him: the whole evolution floodlit by an Aldis from *Setter*'s bridge, and going exactly as they'd rehearsed it, in Eddrachillis Bay. It hadn't seemed real, there, more like a game, an exercise to keep them all busy: but it was real now, and he was very glad indeed they had rehearsed it. The tricky part—which would be coming during the next few minutes—was beginning to look more dangerous and difficult than it ever had before. Because he could only hang on here, watch the thing develop: he wasn't going to leave the induction pipe until he had to. When the time came, he'd be flat on his face on the midget's bow, with the sea washing right over him: and he'd need both his hands to work with, with no spare for holding on.

The only sense in which he was eager for it was to get it over.

The boat was clear of *Setter*'s bulging saddle-tanks. Men behind her gun—they had a small degree of shelter there as well as a curve of guard-rail for security—were paying out a light line attached to the boat, and also the Manilla. The man in the boat, rubber-suited and—when the Aldis flickered over him—larger than life, was Bomber Brazier.

X-12's bow was drifting off to port. Quite a long way off. Now, of all times . . . Gimber shouted down the pipe, "Watch your steering! Half ahead, main motor!"

It was all right. She was coming back on course. Half a minute, and he was able to order slow speed again.

Brazier was such a mild, placid sort of individual that in the early stages of the training programme there'd been a tendency to pull his leg. The way he so seldom spoke—just listened, smiling . . . Then one evening in a pub an RAF character made one taunt too many, and Brazier, as usual, laughed: but he did a double-take, then, and knocked the flight lieutenant across the bar and through a door which had looked quite solid until he hit it and went through it. It had been generally agreed afterwards that any of the Bomber's friends could have made the same remark and got away with it: from a stranger Brazier had considered it de trop.

Time to move. The boat was more than half-way over. Tossing about, with Brazier kneeling in the middle with the end of the Manilla in his big hands. From *Setter's* casing they were paying it out yard by yard, not feeding him more weight than they had to. In that fragile, cavorting boat, keel-less and extremely unsteady, having to keep his balance while keeping both hands free for handling the rope, it wasn't by any means an easy job. Not even for Bomber Brazier.

Gimber eased himself down to casing level. There was a low enclosure of rail to cling to here: it protected the night periscope, which was a fixed protuberance set in a stub above the casing. When you made use of it you'd have the boat only just covered, that stub like an eye just breaking surface. Gimber crawled forward over the well containing the fore hatch—the outlet from the W and D—and down a step to the narrowing section for'ard. There were holes in the casing for fingers to hook into. He was already soaked through to the skin, crawling not through foam but at times through solid water—having to hold his breath as she dipped, stopping, just hanging on while the sea dragged at him. He got a hand to the mooring cleat on her bow: this was fine, enabling him to haul himself right for'ard. Waves breaking in his face and right over. You had to enclose yourself in the immediacy of the task, never see yourself as it were from the outside or think of the risk or the forces involved, the performance—your own—as breathtaking as any high-wire artist's. If you'd let your imagination loose to that extent, you might easily discover that you were terrified. Then you'd fumble, hesitate, doubling the chances of failure—failure here being synonymous with disaster. Lifting his head and shoulders clear, he saw the boat with Brazier in it a dozen feet away, tilting on a crest. Brazier yelled something but he didn't hear it: he was holding on with one hand, reaching over the midget's snout with the other, groping for the towing-slip. The old tow should have dropped clear, since Trigger had released it from inside and then reset the gear to accept the new one. It was a simple-enough device: the towing pin was locked by an interrupted ring; by turning this until the gap in the ring coincided with the position of the pin, the pin hinged away and the tow was released. Gimber heaved himself for'ard until his head and shoulders projected well over the bow: as she lifted, exposing her whole stem, he could see as well as feel that the slip was clear. One step at a time . . . But lifting again now, and ready for Brazier: through a film of salt spray he had a bird's eye view of him while the rubber boat was in a trough. Still a yard too far to reach . . . Brazier with the end of the tow gripped under one arm, pointing this way and ready to be passed over. From *Setter's* casing they were inching out both the tow-rope and the boat's securing line, knowing he was almost in the right spot, that a bigger wave than usual could lift him and the rubber boat and dump them right on top of the X-craft—if they let out too much slack at this stage. But from their angle and in the dark it would be extremely difficult to judge the distance, despite *Setter's* Aldis being on the boat and on X-12, blinding in Gimber's salt-washed eyes. Reaching: the tow's shackle dangling . . . Brazier for some reason howling like a wolf as Gimber reached towards him. Brazier continued, not howling, but bellowing, a gale-beating volume of sound out of those huge lungs so that Gimber caught a few words of it—". . . for a life on . . ." The wind's howl and the waves' crashing drowned it, while Gimber's hand grasped the shackle: the rubber boat rocked sideways, spinning, Brazier nearly ejected but swaying his weight back in the nick of time, yelling the last words of what had evidently been a question: ". . . the ocean wave?"

Gimber had his boat's sharp stem under him, between his elbows, while his hands clawed at the end of the Manilla—most of its weight across Gimber's boat, but even this yard or two of it extremely heavy: he was forcing the shackle towards the towing slip. Choking, coughing out salt water, and blind . . .

Bow-down. Crashing down. A glimpse of Brazier silhouetted against the light's beam, tottering: Gimber holding on, but half over the side—drowning . . . Coming up, at last. Catching a lungful of air with sea in it: life itself consisting solely of the need to complete this—now . . .

Connecting!

Screw-threaded pin one-handed into the shackle. The two pins at right-angles but not much weight on them yet, so turning this was—was feasible, even with numbed fingers . . . Bomber Brazier's shout as the rubber boat shot upwards: "Not me for one!" Brazier howling with crazy laughter: a happy man, delighted, in his element and loving it, turning with an arm up and waving to the men in *Setter*'s bridge to tell them, "all fast—heave in . . ."

Gimber told the others, when X-12 was at sixty feet, on course and under tow at eight and a half knots again, porpoising as before, "Brazier's round the bend. I hadn't realised."

Thinking as he said it that he'd never seen the Bomber in such a state of exuberance. Towne nodded, crawling aft. "I reckon. He's a good hand, though."

Ozzie Steep nodded. Expressionless. He was functioning all right, but in the manner of a zombie. He was in his first lieutenant's seat, he'd handled her competently in the dive, caught a trim with just about the optimum weighting for'ard; now as Trigger Towne moved aft he moved the trim-pump lever again, sent a few gallons from stern to bow in compensation for the shift of one man's weight. But there was a goon-like quality about his movements and manner. Gimber thought it would be unsafe to trust his reactions in any new emergency: therefore, that he mustn't be left un-supervised. But since the principle was to have two men on watch and one man resting, a private word with Towne, a warning to him to keep his eyes open, might answer the problem.

Which might in any case be imaginary.

There weren't any more tow-ropes. *Setter* had been carrying one spare. And in submarine emergencies, reactions had to be immediate and right. Delayed action or the wrong kind . . .

He thought, I can't risk it . . .

Hang on until tomorrow, when *Setter* would be dived and the tow smooth, emergencies far less likely to arise?

Steep looked round at him. Gimber had been checking bilges. Steep said, reaching for his mug—Trigger had heated a can of soup after they'd dived, and as usual poured his own straight down his throat scalding hot— "Skipper, you ought to get your head down. I'm perfectly all right now."

"I doubt if I could." Gimber wondered if Ozzie had been reading his thoughts. He explained, "Up to here with bloody Benzedrine."

"Oh." Ozzie turned back to the depthgauge. Gimber slipped another tablet into his mouth. First one for several hours: he'd been thinking of cutting them out, so as to be able to get some sleep, but—glancing at Ozzie again, still unsure of him but also unsure of his own judgement ... Then he saw Trigger Towne—he'd turned his head like a man on guard, afraid of being caught out doing something illegal, like surreptitiously taking that pill, and there was Towne, this side of the after bulkhead, glaring at him. He had his hand on a canvas roll of tools he'd left there behind Ozzie's seat, and had now come back for. Crouched with his head half-turned, eyes burning out of dark holes in his head, he looked like some wild animal ready to dive back into its burrow. He shouted, lifting that hand to point at Gimber, "Oughter get in some zizz-time, skipper!"

"So ought you, chum."

The ERA gestured dismissively, as the midget's bow slammed down and brought up hard on the new tow-rope: Gimber heard, "Got jobs waiting, Christ's sake . . . " Gimber pointed at Ozzie's back—grimacing, waggling a hand palm-down to convey his doubts; Trigger watching the pantomime, frowning, working out what it was he was being told. Then he nodded, made a gesture of helplessness before he turned away and slithered back into the engine-space. Gimber crawled for'ard to the W and D to fetch a bucket and a cloth.

Brazier told Paul confidentially, "Louis G did a good job. He's not bad, when he gets his finger out."

That had been a long speech, for the Bomber. He'd have given it some thought before he made it, too. Paul reflected, looking at him across the wardroom table, that if Gimber had made a hash of it Brazier wouldn't have commented at all.

The quick recovery of X-12 underlined one's fears for X-11. The last news of her had been that *Scourge* had turned back to look for her. One whole day ago—and it felt like a week.

Crawshaw said at supper, "*Scourge* couldn't break W/T silence now, though, could she. Now we've got this close to the target, don't we have to go right up almost to the Pole if we want to transmit?"

"Where we are now, yes." MacGregor pointed out, "But *Scourge* turned back. She'll be a long way south still."

The restriction applied within a certain radius of the target: wireless silence inside this area was to be total. The last thing one could risk was for the enemy to be alerted to the presence of submarines on their battle squadron's doorstep. But *Scourge* would still be outside the restricted area: so if she'd found her baby, she'd have piped up.

Good news arrived just before Paul was due to talk to X–12 at ten o'clock: X–8 was back in tow of *Sea Nymph*. Paul told Gimber this, over the telephone: "X–8 did the same as you did, apparently. Tow parted, but she's back on the lead now."

"What happens when the second rope busts, with no spare?"

"Just make sure it doesn't, Louis . . . No, actually I've been talking to MacGregor about that, and we'd improvise with a two–and–a–half–inch wire. If we had to . . . How are you three now?"

"Ozzie's back in shape, more or less. Trigger and I are so stuffed with pills we're pretty well on automatic."

"Can't you lay off the Benzedrine, now he's fit?"

"Tomorrow. When you dive. To which event we're counting the minutes, believe me . . . No news of any of the others?"

Paul told him falsely, "Only that X–8's back in tow."

Lying to Louis Gimber was becoming a habit.

He wondered what Louis had meant by those remarks about Jane. He couldn't remember exactly what had been said, now, only that he'd sounded snide and that it had been unexpected and disturbing. But time itself was becoming confused, the days telescoping, and 20 September seeming constantly to recede. It would be worse still for the passage crew, he realised, especially under the influence of those pills.

A signal was coming through. Colbey, the grey–haired telegraphist was taking it down when Paul finished his chat to Gimber and hung up the phone. He left him at it, and went back to the wardroom.

"Signal coming in."

Heads lifted from books and magazines. Massingbird's eyes, from the recess of his bunk, gleaming like an old fox's before they shut again. Eaton with a copy of *Men Only* open at one of the famous "Ladies out of Uniform." He turned it face-down, and slid off the bench. "May as well get the book out."

The signal turned out to be from *Scourge*. Twenty-four hours' searching had yielded no trace of X-11, who had now to be presumed lost. *Scourge* was proceeding to her patrol billet off the target area.

Brazier muttered, "Bloody hell." Eaton scowling as he took the code book back to the control room safe. MacGregor muttered from his bunk, "I'm very sorry."

The picture had been developing in Paul's mind while the message had been taking shape on Dick Eaton's signal-pad. Three faces clearly defined: Tom Messinger's, Bony Hillcrest's, Charlie Amor's. There was also a vision of an X-craft interior split open and under 1600 fathoms of Norwegian Sea: it would be still, by now, at rest, those bodies sprawled ... The stuff that dreams were made of—and there were enough of those already, God knew. He wrenched his thoughts back to practical considerations—such as the fact that Dan Vicary's X-11 had been one of the three boats detailed to attack the *Scharnhorst,* and only X-9 and X-10 were now left for that job. He guessed there might be a switch now, that either he or X-8 might be redirected from the *Lützow* to the *Scharnhorst.*

He was in the process of turning in, on the camp-bed under the wardroom table, when the next instalment of bad news arrived. He lay still, listening to Henning and Massingbird decoding it, the engineer doing the looking-up while the torpedo officer read out the groups and wrote down the translation. It was from *Syrtis* to Flag Officer Submarines, repeated to all concerned in Operation Source: X-9's tow had parted, and *Syrtis's* captain had reason to be certain the midget had gone to the bottom.

X-9's passage crew had been Kearon, Harte and Hollis.

It was hard to accept as fact, at first. Right on the heels of the other one. But it had happened, it was real—and you had to accept that there might be other losses too, before the attack itself went in. Paul thought of

Gimber, Steep and Towne, whose chances were exactly the same as those other teams' had been ... Also, that with such a high incidence of loss on passage, FOSM probably would not order any variations to the attack plan until he knew for sure how many X-craft he had surviving.

CHAPTER ELEVEN

· · ·

As long as the bloody rope held . . .

Gimber prayed with his eyes shifting between the depthgauge and the bubble, Please don't let it part?

Setter was on the point of diving, so as to be down and out of sight before daylight exposed her to any wandering German aircraft. She'd dived for the first time yesterday, but come up again last evening to spend the night on the surface; this was necessary both to maintain the scheduled progress northward and to charge her batteries. So for X-12 there'd been another seven hours of acute physical discomfort exacerbated by the tension of knowing the tow-rope could snap at any moment.

Yesterday the hours with *Setter* dived had been marvellous. Hour after hour of smooth running. Gimber had slept for two hours, then taken over from Towne, who'd been unconscious for nearly four.

Towne muttered now, "Get on with it, get bloody under!"

Longing for a resumption of that peace and quiet. Also to get the act of diving over—and for MacGregor to handle it carefully, take his ship down gently, in slow time . . . X-12's bow jerking upwards and to port: then the strain was off the rope and she was hanging, drifting with her bow falling quite slowly. The two could have gone already, could have been broken by that last tug. But it hadn't—there was a yank to starboard, just as he'd been beginning to think she might be on her own . . . She still carried the slight list to port, oddly enough. Gimber looked at the transverse spirit-level, the one on the deckhead that showed angles over to port or starboard. She was in her gliding state again—the tow slack, no pull on her nose, but the bubble still showing the two-degree list to port.

There was no obvious reason for it. Towne was in his seat—which was

on the starboard side—and Steep was flat-out, asleep, in the fore end. The
battery and its wooden cover which served as the off-watch sleeping berth
was also, as it happened, on the starboard side. Nothing had been moved
from one side to the other, so far as Gimber could see or recall, and an
X-craft had no port and starboard trimming tanks. Most of the food and
drink was stored on the port side of the bow compartment, so as the cans
were emptied the tendency would be for her to be lightened on that
side—the opposite to what seemed to be happening.

The telephone buzzed; Towne stretched out a long left arm to pick
it up.

"Yeah?" He listened for a few moments. Then: "Roger." He was half-
turned on his seat, looking like a first cousin to Rasputin—gaunt, bearded,
with those deepset, gleaming eyes. He told Gimber as he hung up the
phone, "She's diving now. Brazier, that was."

Everard would have his head down, no doubt. *Setter* diving quietly on
the watch. Gimber would have preferred to have known Paul was awake
and looking after X-12's interests at a time like this. At this moment she
was on an upward swoop with the needle in the gauge swinging past the
sixty-five-feet mark. But no jerk: there'd been a long, steady pull angling to
starboard, and now it had ceased. She felt loose again, drifting, bow slowly
sinking as the forward motion slowed.

Adrift again?

About once every two minutes, that was how it felt. Imagination, of
course, yet another of the coward's thousand deaths. But there'd been no
jar, no sudden wrench. And in point of fact the imagining part wasn't so
much fear as the need to anticipate, to have a mental picture of what was
happening outside the hull so you could be ready to cope with an emergency when it struck. Like having worked out in advance that if this new
tow did part they'd replace it with the two-and-a-half-inch steel wire rope
which *Setter* was carrying lashed inside her casing. He'd discussed this again
with Everard; the wire's weight would make it a hell of a thing to handle,
from this end, but at least it existed—another accident wouldn't necessarily remove X-12 from the operation.

"I'm taking her to one hundred, Trigger."

"Aye aye . . ."

Setter would go to sixty. Gimber's intention was to be well below her, out of the wash from her screws. These were all new techniques, history in the making; despite the facts that his mouth tasted like the bottom of an old dustbin and that he'd rather have been in Wimbledon.

Autumn—first signs of it, the trees beginning to change colour . . . Except it would be pitch dark there at 0200 . . .

Going quiet now. The pull was steady, all in one direction. She'd already be under, he guessed, below the surface turbulence. The time being 0200 and the date—18 September. Concentrating harder still, Gimber concluded that it had to be a Saturday. With seventeen hours of tranquillity ahead, and his own turn to take a rest.

Except Eaton probably needed that sleep.

He had her levelled at a hundred feet when the telephone buzzed again. Brazier informed Towne that *Setter* was now in trim at sixty feet.

"How is it with you now?"

"Better 'n it was, chum, I'll say that . . . Might even get some shut-eye later." Towne was frowning, looking around like an animal suspecting danger while he listened to whatever Brazier was saying. He'd craned outward to see the depthgauge and the hydroplane indicator. Nodding: rasping into the telephone, "That soon?"

Brazier said something else. Towne nodded. "Yeah. Right," and hung up. Gimber said, "You've noticed it, have you."

"What is it—three degrees?" Towne got out of his seat and moved a few feet aft, to check on the position of the bubble in the transverse spirit-level. "Just under."

"So what's doing it?"

"I'll look around."

"Checked the bilges lately?"

"Yeah, course. But I will again. Mind you, I've a feeling . . ."

"Well?"

"Tell you in a mo' . . ." Rasputin jerked a stained thumb in the direction of their towing ship. "Tomorrow night," he said. "Crews change over. Big eats and all night in—what about that, then?"

"I'll believe it when I'm inboard ... Trigger, see if you can trace this list."

"Butterflies, Sub?"

Massingbird, stroking his red beard, grinned at Dick Eaton across the table. Eaton was refusing breakfast: he'd drunk some tea, but declined all offers of food. His voice was thin as he told the engineer, "If a sharp pain in the guts can be caused by butterflies—yes."

Massingbird's implication had been that Eaton's digestive problem might be connected with the imminence of action. Which wasn't either far-fetched or insulting. Paul was aware of the flutter of those abdominal insects, at times, and Jazz Lanchberry had admitted to it readily. Brazier muttered now, "You're lucky if it's only butterflies. I've got bloody great pterodactyls in my gut."

"Well," Crawshaw smiled, "you've got room for them, in there."

"Is it really bad, Dick?"

Eaton told Paul tightly, "Bad enough to hope it'll stop soon."

"When did it start?"

"In the night. I was OK on watch, so it must have started after I turned in."

MacGregor suggested, "Perhaps the cox'n had better take a squint at you."

Submarine coxswains did some kind of medical course as part of their training. *Setter's* CPO Bird would have a kit of drugs, and some implements, and a handbook of symptoms and treatments, but apart from first-aid it was likely to be rough-and-ready medicine. Eaton's glance at MacGregor made it plain he was well aware of this.

"I'll be all right, sir. I'll turn in, wait for it to wear off."

"Anyone else got stomach trouble?"

Nobody had, so you could say it hadn't been last night's canned pilchards. Whatever it was, Paul thought, it had certainly chosen its moment, with the changeover of crews scheduled for tomorrow evening.

MacGregor commented, "Your first lieutenants seem to be out of luck. First Steep, now Eaton."

"Steep's back on the job, Louis says."

"So will I be, skipper, by tomorrow."

"Well, let's hope."

"I'm sure of it. It's just a belly-ache, nothing serious."

But he was barely able to haul himself up into the bunk—the upper one, against the curve of the pressure-hull—which Crawshaw had recently vacated. The pain was probably worse than he'd admitted, Paul guessed. In fact if it hadn't been pretty bad, he wouldn't have mentioned it at all. One had now to face the fact that he might not get over it, whatever "it" was, in time to move over to X-12: there'd be no question of taking him along in this state.

Over the telephone at 0800, Gimber reported that the midget had a list of six degrees to port.

"It's the side-cargo, a slow leak on one of its buoyancy chambers. That's Trigger's assessment, and I agree with him. There's nothing else it could be."

The side-cargoes had buoyancy chambers so that their weight wouldn't throw the X-craft out of trim. All the banging around they'd be subjected to must have damaged this one.

"Is the list increasing?"

"Well, it was, but I'm not certain, it could have got to where we are now and stopped."

One thing after another . . . He said—thinking aloud—"We may have to ditch that one."

She'd still have one two-ton egg to lay underneath the *Lützow*. Gimber hadn't commented. He had enough on his plate with the passage job; what happened afterwards would be Paul's headache. Paul asked him, "How's Ozzie now?"

"Oh—he's OK. Sleeping it off." Gimber dropped his voice somewhat. "To be honest, he isn't really a hundred per cent yet. Be a bit much to expect he would be, after several days of all that." He'd paused . . . "Anyway, it's hard to judge, we all look like rats and feel like—" He checked the splurge of words. "Well. Every two hours from now on, right?"

"Yup. And you'll surface to ventilate at midday—so take the noon call first, will you? Tell Ozzie I'm glad he's better."

Because he might need him as a replacement for Dick Eaton. It wasn't a happy idea, to start with one member of the team already played-out; but maybe a dose or two of Benzedrine . . . There'd be no option, if Eaton didn't make a quick recovery: and it wouldn't be enough to have him claim to be all right, then maybe collapse at some crucial moment. The first lieutenant's job was a very complicated one, requiring a lot of experience and skill: you couldn't put just anyone on that seat. You couldn't do without him, either. Jazz Lanchberry would have his hands full, Brazier's task as diver was something else altogether, while Paul's business was at the periscope, conning the midget and her high-explosive cargo through whatever obstacles lay between her and the target. Under, over, or through the nets, and the man who did the trimming had to be one hundred per cent sure and right in every move he made.

Paul wondered whether he could possibly take the boat in with a heavy list—accepting some clumsiness in the boat's handling as the price of taking her in fully armed.

Gimber asked him, "What time tomorrow do we change round?"

"Soon as it's dark. Which would mean about nineteen-thirty . . . Is it nice and quiet for you now?"

"It's quiet. I wouldn't call it nice."

"What, because of the condensation?"

"Mostly."

Like water trickling down your face and neck as you hung up the telephone. They were too busy keeping the inside of the boat and her essential equipment dry to bother much about themselves. Human bodies, fortunately, didn't rust or get insulation problems. But clothing clung damply to cold skin: and Gimber's beard felt like a wet cloth around his jaw.

With *Setter* dived, it was almost too peaceful. Sitting and gazing at the depthgauge—which did have to be watched—it would have been easy to doze off, now one had less Benzedrine in the nerve system. The yellowish gleam from that circle of glass was mesmeric: and the constant thrum of water-noise was only background, the basic structure of the silence.

There was this list to watch, as well. Still six degrees. Just one buoyancy chamber flooded, he guessed, and the flooding now complete, so that this was as far over as she would lean, unless it began to affect another chamber too. If it did get worse, the boat might become awkward to handle, and it was going to be tricky enough inside those fjords without having a craft that wouldn't do what she was told. It would be for Everard to decide, anyway.

Gimber was humming—running through it for (he thought) about the second time, "A Life on the Ocean Wave." It was the Marine bandsmen's signature tune, but it was on his mind because that lunatic Brazier had been bawling it out when they'd been passing the new tow. But he was also humming to keep himself awake. Trigger Towne meanwhile checking hull-valves: one of his routines, crawling through the boat from stern to stem, stopping wherever his mental check-list told him to. In the control room now, he suggested mildly, "Mind changing the record, skips?"

Gimber looked round at him. Two long-term prisoners in a deep, damp dungeon, staring at each other like men about to come to blows.

"Have I regaled you with that ditty more than once?"

"You been bloody torturing me with it ever since we dived."

"I hadn't realised. Sorry. If it starts again, tell me."

"Yeah." Towne said, "Why not give us a renderin' of 'Eskimo Nell'?"

"Oh, I doubt I'd remember it well enough to—"

"Garn! I heard you do it, word perfect!"

Months ago. Some jaunt ashore when they'd been at Port Bannatyne. He remembered now: they'd been stuck in Gouroch and had to spend a night at the Bay Hotel. He began to run the verses through his mind, checking whether he could still manage it. Silence, meanwhile—except for Towne's heavy, dog-like panting as he crawled towards the W and D.

Ozzie Steep screamed in his sleep.

Gimber jumped, his gut tightening with the shock of it. Towne froze—like a pointer. The scream echoed in the steel enclosing them. As it died away, an echo only in your mind now, Ozzie began to snore. Regular, pig-like honks.

Towne said to Gimber, "Some lucky lass'll have that for life . . . Shake him, shall I?"

Steep choked: then yelled stridently, "Get her up! Christ's sake, up!" He screamed again. Gimber shouted—while the noise still reverberated and Towne was already crawling forward, furious-looking, virtually trotting on all fours—"Wake him up!"

Setter surfaced at seven-twenty that evening, by which time it was pretty well dark.

Eaton had only toyed with supper, sipped at a mug of soup and then turned in. He'd been dozing in his bunk. MacGregor had heard him groan, and sent for the coxswain.

Chief Petty Officer Bird seemed to be embarrassed at having to play the part of doctor. Theoretically he'd been taught how to deal with any more or less ordinary kind of injury or illness, but there was very rarely any opportunity to practise his art, beyond handing out a few asprins or bandaging a cut.

"Where's it 'urt, sir?"

"There."

Setter pitching, slamming through the waves, diesels hammering away and the boat full of cold Arctic air.

"I'll 'ave to—er—exert a slight pressure on that spot, sir. If you don't mind . . ."

"Oh, bloody hell!"

He'd twisted away, in agony.

"Sorry, sir." Bird glanced at MacGregor. "We won't do that again." His chuckle was entirely forced, as he edged out around the table; there was hardly space between it and the bunks for a solidly built CPO like Bird to slide through sideways. He shook his head, unhappily. "Well, I dunno. Proper turn-up, this is. Strike a light . . ."

MacGregor asked him, "Are you trying to tell us something, cox'n?"

Bird was in the gangway, with a hand on the latched-back watertight door for support.

"Rather not 'ave to say it, sir. Let alone bloody do it."

"Come on, let's hear."

"Captain, sir." This was Garner, the PO telegraphist, pushing past Bird. "Cypher, sir."

"Thank you, PO tel." MacGregor looked back at Bird. "Go on."

"I better check in the manual before I—er—confirm the diagnosis, sir."

"Appendix?"

Bird winced. "I'll just 'ave a little read, sir."

"All right. But make it quick." He passed the cypher to Massingbird. "Sort this one out in your book, Chief . . . Ellis, let's have some coffee in here!"

The wardroom flunky's head appeared round the bulkhead from the galley.

"Tea do, sir? I just wet some."

"All right."

Massingbird growled, "Can't tell the difference anyway." Brazier helped him with the decoding of the signal: they'd discovered, by the time the coxswain came back, that it was from *Sea Nymph* to Flag Officer Submarines, repeated to forces and authorities concerned in Operation Source. Decoding work ceased now: Bird was staring gloomily at Eaton, who was on his back with his eyes shut. Bird looked at MacGregor and raised his eyebrows, gesturing towards the control room. MacGregor got up, and they went aft together.

Sea Nymph's signal was to the effect that X-8 had been forced to jettison her side-cargoes, and had been badly damaged by the explosion of one of them at a range of several miles. She had now been abandoned and scuttled.

Brazier muttered, "Leaves us on our todd."

X-8 was to have been X-12's partner in the attack, each with a half-share in *Lützow*. Now X-12 would have that target to herself; just as X-10 would be the only boat attacking *Scharnhorst*. *Tirpitz* would still be honoured by the attentions of three boats—Cameron's X-6, Place's X-7 and Henty-Creer's X-5.

The messenger of the watch appeared in the gangway and asked Paul, "Step aft just a minute, sir?"

MacGregor and Bird were waiting for him, near the diving panel. MacGregor told him, "Bad news, Everard. Cox'n says there's no doubt at all, it's his appendix. Which of course means he must be operated on."

"When?"

CPO Bird suggested, "Sooner the better, sir. Playin' safe, like. Not that safe's the word for it."

"Don't under-estimate your own abilities, cox'n. Even more important, don't let Sub-Lieutenant Eaton think you're anything less than confident. But as to the timing—it can wait twenty-four hours, can't it?"

"Depends, sir. But I'd sooner . . ."

"After the crews change, we'll have one less body in the wardroom. We'll also have time on our hands. Will you do the job in the wardroom?"

"Well—if that's all right, sir."

"He'll be laid up for the rest of the patrol, won't he."

Bird nodded. "Best if he could be in your bunk, sir."

"Why the hell?"

"On its own, sir, no bunk above nor below it, so there's access like, and a light right over it. I could stand on the bench—that way I'd be right on top of the job, like."

MacGregor nodded. "All right. When the time comes, I'll take over the first lieutenant's bunk . . . But we'll do it tomorrow night, cox'n, after the transfer. I'll go deep, so it'll be quiet and steady for you."

"Aye aye, sir."

Paul was wishing it could have been done immediately: Bird was obviously worried. But this surface passage tonight was necessary, in order to keep up to schedule, and as long as *Setter* had the X-craft in tow, with the possibility of some emergency at any minute, you couldn't guarantee there'd be no interruptions . . . MacGregor asked Bird, "He isn't going to die on us before tomorrow, is he?"

"Well—if it turned what they call *acute,* sir, I reckon he'd let us know. I mean he'd sing out, like. Then we'd need to look lively, no matter what."

"All right. You'd better read-up your manual carefully, cox'n. I'll break the news to him, and I'll tell him you've taken out an appendix before and you say there's really nothing to it. Purely for morale." He turned to Paul. "What are you going to do about this?"

"I'll take Ozzie Steep, sir. There's really no option."

A highly unsatisfactory solution, none the less. Everything seemed to be going wrong, at this point. Three boats out of the running, X-12 with a duff side-cargo, and now she'd have a first lieutenant who'd be decidedly below par right from the start.

"Better warn your friend Gimber. Perhaps he could make sure Steep gets a lot of rest between now and change-over time . . . Make sense of that cypher, did they?"

Paul nodded. "X-8 abandoned and scuttled. Had to ditch her side-cargoes, and the explosion wrecked her, apparently. Leaves only five of us in it now."

On his way to the wireless office, he was wondering whether X-8 had had to ditch her charges for the same reason that his own boat might have to get rid of one of hers. But he'd hang on to it if he could—as long as the list didn't get completely out of hand. It was Ozzie Steep who'd be coping with whatever trimming problems might arise . . . In the W/T office, he called through to Gimber.

"How's that list now, Louis?"

"No worse than it was. Hard to tell, though, when you're being thrown all over the bloody shop!"

"Yes, I dare say. Second question—is Ozzie completely fit now?"

"Well," Gimber was shouting, over the noise surrounding him down there, "up to a point, yes."

"What does that mean?"

"Look—Trigger's got his head down—he and I have stopped taking pills—and Ozzie's on watch with me."

"So you can't talk about it."

"My God, you're quick, Paul!"

"Is he really on top of the job, is what I want to know."

"Well—I'm *on top* of it, so—"

"You mean you wouldn't trust it to him alone?"

"Right. I may be wrong, but . . ."

"Listen. Dick Eaton's out of it. Appendix. As soon as we've swapped over tomorrow evening *Setter*'s going deep while her cox'n operates. See? I need Ozzie. And you say you could be wrong, so . . ."

"Not that wrong. Not for the action job. Just making out until tomorrow evening's one thing, but . . ." There was a pause. Gimber finished, "No. Out of the question, Paul."

There was a longer silence. You couldn't argue with that degree of certainty. Paul asked him, "Is he still sick, or—"

"Washed-out. It was very bad for several days, you know. You can't imagine. It leaves a man—well, drained."

Paul said, "And that leaves you, Louis."

"I thought it might. About ten seconds ago, I thought—"

"There's no alternative."

Roar of the sea drumming around hollow steel . . . Then Gimber's voice grating through his teeth and over two hundred yards of wire, "Jesus Christ Almighty . . ."

He'd been dreaming—re-dreaming, that old one about being crushed under rocks. Every detail was the same, and no less frightening for being familiar. He'd woken, struggled to shake it out of his mind, and he'd succeeded, but only to have it replaced by nightmarish reality—Eaton's appendicitis, for a start. Remembering it, Paul got out of his bunk and took a look at him. Eaton was asleep, but twitching and murmuring to himself, the actual words indistinguishable under the hammering racket of the diesels and the noise of seas crashing against the casing and guntower overhead. *Setter* was inside the Arctic Circle now, and the air inside her had a bite to it; it would be knife-like on the bridge, but none of the X-craft men was standing a watch tonight.

Eaton had been appalled by the decision to put Gimber in his place. Disappointment had seemed as bad as the pain in his stomach. He drew plenty of sympathy: the others knew how they'd have felt—even without the prospect of being operated on by CPO Bird. As Jazz Lanchberry observed, out of Eaton's hearing, Bird would be deft enough with a marline-spike, but splicing rope and wire didn't make for a surgeon's hands. And Bird himself looked about ready to jump overboard.

Paul turned in again. The object was to get in a sound night's sleep, since once you'd embarked in X-12 there wouldn't be much, if any. Tomorrow, there might be some restful periods, of course . . . Thinking about the procedure for the change-over, the rubber boat and who'd go first in it, and so on, he dropped off to sleep. His father, glad to see him after so long a break, asked him, "What are you up to now, old chap? You're not going on this crazy attempt to nobble the *Tirpitz,* are you?"

Paul told him yes, he was. His father was wearing rear-admiral's stripes on his sleeves, he noticed. But Operation Source was supposed to be highly secret. He made this point—a little stiffly, considering it was his father he was talking to—and Jane burst out laughing.

"Secret, my foot!"

Tossing her hair back—a warmly familiar gesture . . .

But Jane—with Nick Everard? She was Paul's girl or Louis Gimber's, or both, but—his father's? She could see how shocked he was, and she was amused, enjoying it. He wondered where Kate was, and whether she knew about Jane. Jane telling him, with a hand squeezing his father's arm, "Even the Germans know all about it. They'll have the welcome mat down for you!"

He woke again, feeling as if it was her laughter that had woken him. It was an enormous relief, this time, to be awake, to know it hadn't been anything but a dream. He could see how Jane had got into it: he'd had Gimber in his mind a lot, naturally, and if you thought about him long enough you were bound to get round to Jane. As to his father, and the question he'd asked—well, he'd been thinking about him too, wishing he'd told him about this X-craft business.

MacGregor had said he'd be diving *Setter* on the watch, so the X-craft team's sleep wouldn't be interrupted. But Paul didn't feel like sleeping any more. He was lying there thinking about the attack plan, and the trimming of the boat with that list on her, when a new signal came in.

He checked the time while the control room messenger was shaking Massingbird, and saw it was just after 1:30 a.m.. So they'd be diving in not much more than half an hour. Massingbird was cursing softly as he climbed out and went to fetch the code book; when he came back and slumped down at the table, under the dim red light that was supposed to be good for bridge watchkeepers' eyesight, Paul slid out and joined him.

"I'll give you a hand."

Massingbird stared at him. "Thought you chaps were supposed to be getting your beauty sleep?"

"Ah, but I'm lovely enough already . . . You read out, I'll look up?"

The signal was from Admiralty, to practically everyone under the sun, and it conveyed an intelligence report to the effect that *Tirpitz*'s crew would be changing her gun-barrels and also dismantling her A/S detection gear for overhaul between 21 and 23 September.

Massingbird read the message over, combing his beard with his fingers. He asked Paul, "How in hell would we get to know a thing like that?"

"Haven't a clue. Unless we have spies in Norway. Which we do, of course." But the information could have been obtained from intercepted signals, too. "Doesn't really matter, long as it's reliable. If it is, it's good news—guarantees she'll be there and won't stir during those three days."

They decided not to wake MacGregor, as there was nothing urgent about it and in any case he was due for a shake at 0200. Massingbird put the signal in the clip and turned in again; he seemed to have an unlimited capacity for sleep. Paul went to the wireless office and buzzed X-12; he'd intended to give this news to Gimber, but Ozzie Steep answered and said the skipper had his head down.

"Resting up for stage two, sir. I wish you'd let me take Dick's place."

"You've been under the weather, Ozzie. That's the only reason. It's bad enough having to take Louis, after a week cooped up already, but what you've been through's something else again. I just can't take chances—not ones I don't have to take."

Steep said yes, Gimber had explained all that ... "But the fact is, I'm now as good as new. I mean, really."

"I know how you feel, Ozzie. Dick's fed up too. But the decision's been taken, so let's leave it ... How's the list, still the same?"

"Yes. Six degrees exactly, still. I've got used to it, now."

"No trimming problems?"

"Not since we lightened her to compensate for the flooded buoyancy chamber."

There was a copper strip between each side-cargo and the X-craft's hull. When you dropped them—by turning a wheel on each side—the strip was detached and this flooded the side-cargo's buoyancy chambers so that it lost its neutral buoyancy and sank to the bottom. This one must have lost some of its buoyancy already, and this was giving X-12 her list.

"D'you think she'll handle all right, in the fjords?"

"No indication that she won't. Apart from the problems you'll have there anyway."

The problems would be from variations in salinity and therefore water density, arising from freshwater patches where streams or mountain ice entered the salt-water fjords.

"What other defects d'you have?"

"Defects?"

Paul frowned at the telephone. "Yes, Ozzie. Defects."

"Oh. Sorry ..." As if he was waking up. Gimber had been right, Paul thought. Steep said, "We had that leak on the periscope again, but Trigger fixed it. Twice. He had some trouble with the heads hull-valve too—didn't you, Trigger, when I was ..."

"Ozzie, put Trigger on now, would you?"

"Right."

"*Setter*'ll be diving at about a quarter past. You'll get some comfort then."

"We'll be ready for it. Here's the mechanical genius."

"Hi, skipper!"

Defects, it turned out, had been only minor. The periscope-gland leak was a nuisance and would be likely to recur, and the list was something that one would have to cope with, one way or another. The head's outlet valve had been only a temporary problem, which had been cleared by a lot of blowing. Towne and Steep were now hard at work to get on top of the problems of condensation.

"We'll have her on the top line for you, don't worry."

"That's fine, Trigger. See you this evening."

Back in *Setter's* wardroom he found MacGregor at the table drinking kye. He asked, pointing at the signal log, "This makes no odds to you, of course."

"None, sir. Doesn't tell us anything about *Lützow* or *Scharnhorst.* Very nice for the three who've been given *Tirpitz,* of course."

It was quite a coincidence the main target of the operation was to have her teeth drawn, so to speak, right in the period chosen for the attack. Almost too much of a coincidence, that the enemy should have picked on that stage of moon and tide—and let the news out?

The dream—Jane, and her red carpet?

He told himself, Ridiculous . . .

Eaton groaned as he rolled over on the bunk. MacGregor, about to go up to the bridge for a look round before he dived her, stopped, staring at the blanket-wrapped figure. Paul could sense his anxiety. In the interests of Operation Source the decision to get the crew-change done with before anything else was surely right; but if the delay cost Eaton his life . . .

It wasn't a good day for CPO Bird, either.

Setter was in trim at sixty feet by 0230. And X-12 surfaced for her routine ventilation at six. The midget simply planed up against the pull of the tow, spent a quarter of an hour bouncing about on the surface, while the upward tugging at her stern affected *Setter's* trim making it hard work for the control room watchkeepers, and then planed down again.

At eleven in the forenoon, since this was Sunday, MacGregor conducted a short religious service in the control room. He included a special prayer for X-craft crews, for the success of the operation and a safe return; Paul, head bowed and eyes on the toes of his own plimsol shoes, with Brazier's on one side and Lanchberry's on the other, couldn't remember ever knowingly being prayed for before. He wondered how God would see it. After all, they were preparing to take four tons of high-explosive and plant it under a crowd of people who had no idea what was coming to them, and not all of whom could be entirely villainous. The strategic requirement was obvious, the Germans were not in Norway to help old ladies cross the streets, and equally plain was the inevitability of fighting this entirely defensive war; but if the Almighty was primarily concerned with the souls of men, might he take a different view? This occupied Paul's thoughts for the next minute or two; when he surfaced he was hearing the end of another special prayer, for Dick Eaton's recovery. In MacGregor's place, he thought, he'd have said one for the coxswain, too. But praying was done with: they were singing *Eternal Father Strong to Save.*

It was a restless day, more than restful.

Louis Gimber took X-12 up for another breather at noon. He told Paul after he'd dived her again that the weather was improving, wind and sea moderating; if this trend continued, tonight's change-over should present no problems.

X-12 was still carrying her list of six degrees to port.

"Will you guff-through again at six, Louis? Or stretch it for the extra hour or so?" Because they'd be surfacing for the crew-change soon after seven.

"Might as well stay down. The air's perfectly OK after six hours, now nobody's being sick. Condensation gets heavier, but what's one hour?"

"All right. When the time comes we'll do it in two boat-trips. Jazz and I in the first one, and the boat brings Ozzie and Trigger back here, then the Bomber can be wafted over on his own. You getting plenty of rest, I hope?"

"Hell, yes. It's bloody luxury, down here."

Old Louis was feeling sorry for himself . . . But the words and tone must have jarred in his own ears too. He added, "I've had as much sleep as I can take. Tell you the truth, quite looking forward to seeing your repulsive faces this evening . . . How's Eaton?"

Setter broke surface at 1920 and X–12 materialised 200 yards astern of her a few minutes later. It was about half to three-quarters dark. The rolling as *Setter* wallowed up had seemed to give the lie to Gimber's theory of improving sea conditions, but as she rose to full buoyancy one realised that wind and sea had eased. MacGregor manoeuvred his submarine to put her to wind-ward of the midget, both to provide a lee and so that the rubber boat could be floated down by wind-power.

Leading Seaman Hallet, second coxswain, and two sailors came up with the boat and a coil of hemp line, and climbed down on to the fore casing, to the gundeck where there'd be room to inflate the boat. MacGregor called down the voicepipe, "Ask Lieutenant Everard and his crew to come up."

Without binoculars, X–12 was only a black smudge in a patch of white: she wasn't in sight all the time, and as one's eyes adapted to the darkness the figure of Louis Gimber on her casing could be made out, apparently riding the waves.

Hallet called, "Boat's ready, sir!"

"Very good." MacGregor turned to Paul and the others. "It's been a pleasure having you on board. Good luck now, all of you."

"Thanks for your hospitality, sir." They shook hands. This wasn't quite a final farewell, as there'd be telephone contacts between now and slipping time tomorrow night. Paul and Lanchberry climbed down the rungs and cutaway footholds to the cat-walk, and around it to the gundeck. Hallet saw them coming: he and his assistants had already launched the boat and were holding it alongside.

"Trip round the 'arbour, sir, 'alf a tanner?"

"Worth every penny . . . Go on, Jazz."

Lanchberry climbed down. When the boat had steadied again, Paul followed, with a heaving-line coiled over his shoulder. The casing party wished them luck and began paying out the hemp securing line. All that was necessary was for the boat to drift along the lie of the tow-rope—which was where the wind would take it anyway. Within a few minutes the X-craft loomed up ahead—narrow, bow-on, sawing up and down on its tether. Gimber was standing, holding on to the induction pipe and now ready for Paul's line; he'd also have an infrared torch tied to his belt for signalling to MacGregor—for instance, to tell them to stop paying out any more hemp. Paul waited until only a few yards separated them before he tossed his line, lobbing its weighted Turk's Head high over that plunging, end-on black shape. He saw Gimber's arm reaching for it: then Lanchberry bawled, "Owzat?" A minute later Gimber was hauling them alongside—bumping, the boat tilting dangerously, Paul finally scrambling up and crouching in cold wave-tops to hold it alongside—Jazz out too, and steadying the boat's other end. Gimber had the hatch open and figures emerging—Towne first, slithering down into the boat with shouts of "Wotcher, Jazz!" and "Best of British, mates!" Ozzie, close behind him, contrastingly silent.

"All set?"

"Let her go!"

Gimber flashed his torch at *Setter*'s bridge, signalling for the boat to be hauled back. Lanchberry meanwhile sliding feet-first into the hatch, Paul close on top of him. A glimpse of Gimber's pale face and black beard, face screwed up against the weather, a face like a Halloween mask lit by the glow thrown up through the hatch. Inside now, in the small, yellowish-lit cavern that was X-12's belly. He'd forgotten how small: Jonah might have had more elbow-room. But at first sight it didn't look bad—considering this tub had been dragged through a thousand miles of rough sea, inhabited by three men for—however long it was . . . Jazz was on his helmsman's seat, checking over the controls surrounding it. Paul called up the pipe, "Louis, I'll look after the trim until you've dived her, OK?"

It seemed tactful, as well as practical. Gimber shouted down, "Make yourselves at home!"

Lanchberry got off his seat, crawled for'ard into the W and D. Looking around, checking the gear, inspecting this and that. Examining the hatch for seepage. X-12 was hurling herself around like an unbroken colt on a lunging-rein. Paul making his own inspection at this stage by eye; he needed to stay close under the hatch in case Gimber wanted help. He tried—since it was one of the things within reach—the starboardside viewing port. There was one each side, a thick glass window set in the pressure-hull at head-height, with external steel shutters that could be opened or closed from inside. He slid this one open as a first step in a preliminary check on moving parts; during the next twenty-four hours, before finally parting from *Setter,* he meant to test every single fitting and piece of equipment. Through the uncovered port there was nothing to be seen except breaking sea, white explosions and the rush of foam along her flank: he cranked the shutter closed again, and he was checking on the portside one when Gimber yelled down, "Boat's alongside *Setter.* I can see the Bomber getting in."

There'd be about five or ten minutes to wait, then. Despite the roll, the list to port was easily discernible: the transverse bubble centred itself on six degrees right of centre instead of on the centre mark. Paul decided that another job for tomorrow, the last day in tow, would be to work out what stores might now be superfluous and ditch them to lighten her. Most of the consumable stores, cans of food and drink, were carried on the port side, and every pound of weight removed from there would help.

"Boat's on its way. Looks like there's an elephant in it!"

Lanchberry smiling his sardonic smile as he passed, crouching double, on his way aft. Using the interval for a very quick inspection. Paul stayed where he was: the boat with Brazier in it had to be getting fairly close now, to explain that shout from Gimber, a wolf-cry into the wind. If there'd been an answer it wasn't audible. He had to squeeze aside to let Jazz get past again, the ERA returning to his helmsman's seat just as the dinghy thumped alongside and Brazier hauled his bulk aboard.

Colossal legs in wet trousers descended through the hatch, in a pattering shower of spray. "Hi, skipper. OK, are we?"

"No problems yet." Gimber dropped inside and pulled the hatch shut, reached up to wrench the handwheel round and secure it. Paul was moving to the first lieutenant's seat, to let him dive her before he himself assumed command, but Gimber grabbed his arm, pulling him back.

"That's my job. Thanks all the same."

X-12's bow soared, crashed down . . . Paul checking that Lanchberry had shut the valve on the induction pipe. Gimber confirmed, as he slid into what had been Ozzie's seat, "She's shut off for diving."

"Thank you." He had to wait for about two minutes, until the tow had got under way again, on course and battering through the waves. Looking round, seeing Gimber's back view—shaggy and spray-soaked but relaxed, waiting for the order to dive—and Jazz Lanchberry's crewcut head and square shoulders over the back of the helmsman's seat, Bomber Brazier peering from the W and D like some great St Bernard in a kennel . . . The telephone buzzed, and he answered it.

"Yes. Diving now." He hung it up. "Open main vents. Sixty feet."

CHAPTER TWELVE

. . .

I asked Tommy Trench, "How was it QP 16 set out from Russia before the X-craft boys had done their stuff? Wasn't the idea that *Tirpitz* and Co. would be knocked out before you sailed?"

He nodded. "That had been the intention. Not that I knew it at the time. We were supposed to wait for some damn thing—that's all—but not even Nick Everard had been told about X-craft. He didn't even know his own son was in it."

Now in his seventies, Trench was a stooped, gaunt man, with more bone to him than flesh. He still did a full day's work though—seven days a week, he'd told me—and his grey hair was thick, a lot bushier than he'd have worn it in his service days. This was Captain Thomas Trench, DSO and Bar, DSC, RN (Retd)—in corduroys and a patched tweed jacket, the left sleeve of it empty, pinned into a pocket. I'd run him to earth on his mink farm in Norfolk. It was the second time we'd met; the first had been in London about eight years before, when he'd helped me with detail of Nick Everard's adventures on the Norwegian coast in 1940. And I do have reason for going behind the scenes, as it were, at this stage. First because, approaching the end of a story in nine episodes covering more than a quarter of a century, I think a change of perspective may give a more realistic view of the climax and its aftermath; and more particularly because when I'd last consulted him, and we'd touched briefly on these later events, he'd offered, "When the time comes, look me up. I may be inclined by then to give you the real facts of it."

Over the years he'd kept his mouth shut whenever he'd been invited to comment on his action in defence of convoy QP 16. I doubt if anyone else had ever suspected there might be "real" facts behind the known ones, and I only knew of such a possibility myself because of that half-promise he'd made.

He'd been lighting a pipe—managing the job one-handed with a dexterity that had to be seen to be appreciated—but he had it going now and he continued with his answer to my question about the convoy's departure from North Russia.

"At the time, all I knew was they were keeping us waiting—which I didn't go much on, mostly because I wanted to get Nick Everard into a proper hospital as soon as possible—and then suddenly came this order to sail. 'With all dispatch'—meaning 'Get a bloody move on'—after what seemed to me a quite unnecessary delay. This was a signal from Admiralty, of course. Later it transpired that the reason behind it had been a Norwegian report of *Tirpitz* having her gun-barrels changed, and some other incapacitating thing. London assumed this meant she wouldn't leave Altenfjord whatever temptation might be offered. The change of gun-barrels, incidentally, was because she'd worn them out bombarding Spitzbergen a week or so before—the only time she ever used them in anger, as it happened. Net result was our lords and masters decided it behoved us to scram out of the Barents Sea while the going was good."

"Which in the event it was not."

I added that the report from the Norwegian resistance group, about *Tirpitz,* had been signalled to the X-craft force as well, as an indication to them that at least their major target would be there when they arrived.

Trench stared out of the window, puffing smoke. He mused, "I've often wondered who actually drafted those signals. I mean the ones with 'From Admiralty' in the address heading. I've asked myself how long such characters would have been left gibbering around that august building before people in white coats came for them."

I laughed, but he didn't crack a smile. He said, "Those Norwegians were extraordinary, you know." He glanced at me, and nodded. "Well, of course, you do know ... The really sad thing about it is one of 'em was caught, some weeks after the X-craft attack, by the Gestapo. Did you know that?"

I let him tell me, anyway.

"They tortured him, in Gestapo headquarters in Tromso. He jumped out of an upstairs window and killed himself, having told them bugger-all despite having had all his fingernails pulled out. I'd say chaps like that were the bravest of the brave, wouldn't you?"

I admitted I agreed entirely.

"Rasmussen, his name was. Karl Rasmussen." Trench shook his grey head. "If they haven't put up a statue to him by now, they ought to have their nails pulled out . . . What else d'you want to know about my convoy?"

The truth was that I knew most of it; I had the facts from the official history and from papers in the Naval Historical Branch of the Ministry of Defence and in the Public Record Office. But there was some new angle he'd hinted at.

I prompted, "When you joined up with the convoy off Cape Kanin, QP 16 consisted of twenty-six empty ships plus the AA ship you'd brought up with you, and the escort comprised your five fleets, plus *Foremost* and the trawler, whose name for the moment . . ."

"Northern Glow?"

"Yes. And two sweepers. *Barra,* and—*Duncansby?"*

"You've done your homework."

"And the commodore was Insole again."

Trench nodded. "He flew from Vaenga to Archangel in a Catalina and installed himself and his staff in a ship called the *Lord Charles.* She was one of the two we lost to U-boats, and he went down with her, poor old bugger. U-boats were my main concern, when we were heading north. I was worried for the *Bayleaf,* the oiler Nick Everard had salted away for us up in the ice. She was coming down to meet us in the vicinity of Bear Island, and we were getting reports of U-boats mustering to form a patrol-line there. She had only the trawler *Arctic Prince* to look after her, and her oil was extremely important to us. A lot of eggs in that one basket, you see." He frowned. "But the most delicate egg of all was the one in *Foremost.* I stationed her at the rear of the convoy, after we'd made the rendezvous and fuelled and settled down. She and the trawler, *Northern Glow.* I had my five destroyers spread across the van, one sweeper each side, and the merchantmen in seven columns, four to a column—with one empty billet after the Soviet oiler left us. Centre column was led by the commodore and tailed by the *Berkeley.* We had good, solid cloud at low level, and although we had aircraft on the radar screens often enough and quite a few times heard them overhead, they didn't find us. Well—there were a couple of half-hearted attacks by eighty-eights on the second or third day, which did us no harm—just happened to stumble on us by accident, lost us again at dusk, and by morning the cloud was thick again ... I suppose we were lucky. But I knew we had U-boats waiting for us."

He'd let his pipe go out. He paused now, putting a match to it. The sleight-of-hand was as impressive as before. I remembered him telling me, at our previous meeting, that to inquisitive strangers his story was that he'd had that arm bitten off by a giant mink. He glanced at me as he flicked the matchstick towards the fire.

"I had a very strong ambition indeed to get that convoy home intact. One always did hope and try to, of course, you could say this was one's raison d'être; but in practical terms one knew how the odds lay—certainly with the Murmansk runs. Down in the Atlantic, in quieter periods and then later when we'd broken the back of the U-boat threat, we did bring a very high proportion of convoys through unscathed. But we were at the climactic point of that Atlantic battle, just at the time we're talking about. In fact we were about to turn the tables very decisively, but for those few weeks it was—a close-run thing. And—here's what I was going to say—since it's states of mind and so on that interest you, my determination to get QP 16 through without loss was all the stronger for the notion that it was Nick Everard's convoy, that I had it as you might say on trust from him. And by that time he was talking all sorts of gobbledegook, didn't know where he was or why, or recognise anyone, or remember anything he was told for more than a few seconds—so Cramphorn told me, over TBS."

"He'd come out of his coma, then."

"Yes, he had, but he was ga-ga. I mean his mind was wandering.

Cramphorn said this was to be expected, and he hoped memory and mental processes generally would return to normal quite rapidly. But it could take months; and the worst possibility of all was permanent brain damage. The very idea of this—for Nick Everard of all people . . ."

"He'd sooner have been dead."

Trench looked at me. Silent, for a moment. Then: "I was also concerned for his wife. There was a certain horror in the idea of bringing home a man who mightn't recognise her, or make sense . . . I was—I suppose the word's involved. I was a devotee of his, you see. I still am." He fell silent, staring into the fire so absorbedly that he might have been reading the answer to his own question in it. I was assuming that such a question would be in his mind, just as it was in mine.

"Where was I?"

"Heading north towards Bear Island."

"Yes. Thanking my lucky stars for the cloud-cover and praying for it to last. Rather counting on it lasting, in fact, at any rate until we ran into foul weather, which was enough to ground the Luftwaffe anyway. The one threat to us, as I saw it then, was the U-boat line ahead of us."

"You never suspected there might be a surface threat?"

"Well, I'd been given reason not to!"

Paul asked Ozzie Steep, "If he's still unconscious, how can anyone know he's OK?"

"Cox'n says things like pulse-rate and temperature are all right by the book. He followed the instructions precisely—despite some nasty moments, one frightful panic-stations—and—well, he cut it out, and it all looked like the book said it should. He's keeping him drugged now because otherwise he'd be in pain, he says."

"When he comes round, tell him we're all delighted. And give CPO Bird our thanks and congratulations, would you?"

"Right." Steep asked, "How's your first lieutenant?"

"He's fine. Going off watch, about to crash his swede." Gimber was staring back at him, from a range of about three feet. Lank, blue-black beard, complexion greyish white. Jazz Lanchberry was in the first lieutenant's seat, and he was due for relief as well—by Brazier, who at this moment was making tea. Paul intended to spend the next hour checking insulations, but tea would be the first thing. They'd had corned beef hash for lunch, broken up in the gluepot and mushed with beans in it, but it had been very salty and everyone had a thirst although Gimber, who'd been duty cook, denied having added any. Paul told Steep, "Nice easy ride now. Even up top. Low swell, is all."

"Yes, the improvement's well timed." Steep sounded perfectly normal now, Paul thought. "Will you guff-through at six?"

"If we decide to, I'll let you know. Otherwise we'll stay down until dark."

Until it was time to surface, release the umbilical cord and set off to cross the minefield. *Setter* had made her landfall accurately during the night and was now paddling in towards the slipping position.

"That list still at five degrees?"

"Yes. It needn't worry us, I hope." Ditching some stores and shifting some engine-room gear had reduced the angle by one degree. A lot of work for very small results, but if it made her any easier to handle they might be glad of it later. Paul said, "All right, Ozzie. Give us a call at sunset."

"Right." But he seemed disposed to chat. "That panic-stations in the middle of Dick's operation—Christ almighty, he started coming-to, right in the middle of it, when the cox'n had both hands inside his gut! So Colbey here—you know Colbey, telegraphist?"

The grey-headed one. "Yes. What?"

"Cox'n had Number One as his theatre sister, as you might say, and Colbey as anaesthetist. Chloroform, on a pad. He moved like lightning, sloshed a lot more on, nearly asphyxiated himself and Bird as well!"

"I'd sooner have this job than that one."

"Who wouldn't!"

Hanging up, it occurred to him that if Eaton died now, MacGregor wouldn't let the news out. He'd veto bad news, just as Paul himself had kept from Gimber the news about X-ll and X-9. Gimber had been told now: he'd taken it in silence, abstractedly—Paul had guessed that he'd been seeing it, guessing at those last few minutes, the shape of the catastrophe you'd always known was on the cards. He'd told him about X-8 too, of course, so that only five boats would be crossing the mines tonight, out of the original eight. And without X-11, X-12 would be the only one using Rognsund, the narrower of the two approach fjords.

"Here, skipper." Brazier handed Paul a mug of the tea he'd been brewing. He put another within reach of Gimber, and leant over to pass one to Lanchberry.

Gimber swallowed some tea. His eyes, fastening on Brazier, looked like mud-holes. "What did you put in this? French letters?"

Brazier nodded. "Been saving 'em for you."

Lanchberry growled, "You're a dirty bastard, you are."

Brazier was shifting his bulk into a less cramped position. "Discipline's gone to pot already, skipper, did you notice?"

He was chattier than usual. He'd actually spoken several times without being spoken to; for the Bomber, this was the equivalent of anyone else having hysterics. There was a tension in them all, which they were trying to hide, or ignore. Nobody was looking more than they had to at Louis Gimber, either. Despite the rest he'd had in the last day or so, he seemed like a creature from some other world: you could sense his own awareness of the gulf between himself and them, and his resentment of it.

"You ready, Bomber?"

"Why not, indeed."

It was a gymnastic feat, Jazz edging out and Brazier having to make room for him but still be close enough to get into the seat quickly as soon as it was empty. There were trimming adjustments to be made as the weights shifted, and the hydroplanes couldn't be left untended. Brazier's size and strength were fine for his own specialised job of diver, but less so for acrobatics in confined spaces. Lanchberry made the change-round possible, doubling himself around the back of the seat: Brazier told him, "Quite handy, being a herring-gutted greaser, sometimes."

Gimber offered, from five or six feet for'ard, "Want to toss for the battery cover, Jazz?"

Lanchberry shook his head. He'd persuaded an amateur barber in *Setter's* crew to tidy him up, before they'd made the change-over, and the sides and back of it had literally been shaved. He said, "I'm not bothered. Better off aft, in fact." On top of the fuel tank in the engine space, he meant, with his feet protruding through the opening in the after bulkhead. Gimber repeated, "I'm quite prepared to toss for it."

"Too bleedin' late, old son." Lanchberry was crawling aft. "I'm 'ere."

Paul had put them into two watches—himself and Brazier, and Gimber with Lanchberry—each pair on watch for two hours at a time, and the two on watch could take turns at the controls and on maintenance chores. For the next two hours it would be himself and the Bomber working while Lanchberry and Gimber rested.

Brazier had the trim-pump lever pushed forward, shifting ballast to the for'ard tank to compensate for his own move and for the ERA having moved further aft.

Paul glanced for'ard. "While you're there, Louis, pass me the bucket and a swab?"

Gimber grunted, as he turned himself around. The bucket clattered. He complained, "Some lazy sod didn't wring this thing out. Here . . ."

"Thanks." On his knees, reaching for it. "You could have four hours off now, instead of two—if you like, Louis. I'm not tired at all."

"Nor am I. Thanks all the same."

"OK. Change your mind if you want to."

"Look." Gimber stared at him. "Let's get this straight. I don't need— don't want—any bloody privileges. I'm perfectly all right."

"If you say so, Louis."

"You wanted a first lieutenant, you've got one. Huh?"

Paul returned the angry stare. "Absolutely." He pointed. "And first lieutenants don't argue with their skippers. So get your head down. I'm not offering privileges, anyway, I simply want you fit and rested."

"All right." Gimber nodded: framed in the doorway of the W and D. "One thing, though. With only five boats going in now, couldn't we all go in through Stjernsund?"

Stjernsund, the passage between Stjernoy and the mainland, was the most direct approach to Altenfjord, and it averaged about three miles in width. Rognsund, which was to be X-12's route, was no more than two miles wide at any point, and had a much narrower bottleneck about half-way through. The reason this back-door approach had been allocated to X-11 and X-12—in fact to whichever boats were ordered to attack *Lützow,* and they'd turned out to be Paul's and Vicary's—was that with eight midg-ets all entering at more or less the same time, sending the whole lot through one channel might have increased the chances of detection. And in fact Stjernsund, being the main entrance and the one normally used by the German battle group, might be more closely guarded and patrolled. This might outweigh the hazards of the narrower passage.

"It's a toss-up." He told Gimber, "We may be better off than the others, for all anyone can tell. Besides, there's the timing factor."

Gimber hadn't taken that in. But he was on the defensive, unwilling to admit it. Paul remembered that he hadn't been briefed as operational crew, only for the passage . . . Behind him he heard Brazier mumble, "About right . . . Let's hope." Stopping the pump, he added, "Give or take a cupful." He was talking to himself about the trim; and he'd need to make another small adjustment to it shortly, when Gimber went through to the sleeping pallet. Paul explained to him, "Our target's closer than the others. But we have to start off together because we all need this same tide and moon. High tide soon after sunset for instance, so that we'll float over the top of the mines."

It was a longer route, through Rognsund. *Lützow* was in Langfjord, which led off from the top end of Altenfjord, whereas *Tirpitz* and *Scharnhorst* were right at the bottom, in Kafjord. The difference was about fifteen miles, and the plan was geared to the ideal of a synchronised attack, all three targets being hit at about the same time.

Gimber nodded. "I remember now." He turned again, to crawl though into the for'ard compartment. Paul squeezed out the swab, and stood up, only slightly stooped because at this point the dome gave added head-room, to dry the deckhead around the hatch and periscopes.

Gimber's state of mind worried him. So—slightly—did the fact that Rognsund was much shallower than Stjernsund. If you were caught in Rognsund you'd have a lot less water to hide in.

Brazier said quietly, "They were shut up in this for more than a week. And in rotten weather, plus sickness, must've been bloody awful. Have to make allowances, I'd think."

"You're right, Bomber."

Lanchberry muttered from somewhere near the after bulkhead, "He'll settle down. Give 'im time, you'll see."

"Get some zizz now, Jazz."

"Aye aye."

Brazier muttered, "Sounds quite hopeful for old Dick."

Drops of deckhead moisture dislodged by the swab, spattered down on Paul. The condensation had a sickly smell and taste, like sweat.

"Well, that's terrific!"

X-12 was at sixty feet, but *Setter* was up at thirty, her periscope depth. It was now just after sunset, and MacGregor was taking a look around. Or had been—he was on the other end of the telephone now, and he'd just told Paul that Dick Eaton was conscious and quite comfortable—except for pain when he moved, which according to the coxswain's medical handbook was par for the course.

Paul put his hand over the phone, and told the others. They'd all had some sleep, and they were at their diving stations, waiting for the sunset surfacing. MacGregor said, "Bird did a good job on him, it seems."

Paul thought this was the truth. He didn't think MacGregor could have lied so convincingly, not even for the sake of this crew's peace of mind. MacGregor was telling him now, "We'll stay down until nineteen-thirty. I want it good and dark. All right?"

He agreed. There was plenty of time in hand. He told them as he hung up, "Seven-thirty now. MacGregor reckons it won't be dark enough until then."

The only comment came from Gimber. "Don't know about anyone else, but personally I'll be glad to get on with it."

You wanted not only the next stage over, but to have the whole thing done. You wanted to have it finished—targets destroyed, and the X-craft out of the fjords, making their separate rendezvous with the parent submarines.

And when you'd got to that point, you'd still be looking ahead—to getting home to Loch Cairnbawn: then London, and Jane . . .

Daydreams. But the thought of Jane took his eyes back to Gimber—who looked about ten years older than he had a week ago. A shave and a hot bath would have made a difference, certainly, but the change was deeper than that. You could see it looking at you out of those dark holes in his head. Paul had decided, thinking about it during the afternoon, that most of the trouble might be Gimber's self-consciousness—being on guard against inadequacies in his own performance, and sensitivity to others' view of him. As Brazier had pointed out, you were dealing with a man who'd virtually been in solitary confinement.

He said casually, "It's astonishing how well you've come through it, Louis."

"Huh?"

Head twisting sideways: muddy eyes narrowed, suspicious. The blue-black beard gleamed with the moisture in it.

"Well, my God, you've been shut up in this tub for a week, and apart from growing that repulsive face-fungus you don't seem to have been affected by it. To be honest, I was worried whether you'd be in good enough shape."

Gimber blinked at him. Determined not to be fooled. Which sent the mind off at a tangent—the question of whether in another area he had been . . . Jazz Lanchberry helped, then, with a beautifully timed mutter of, "'Ear, 'ear." And Brazier boomed from the W and D, "He's not just a pretty face, is old Louis!" They were all laughing then; Paul felt as if the sky had lifted by about a mile.

Setter rose into the dark off shore night at exactly seven-thirty. A few minutes later Paul was on X-12's casing with the induction pipe up and opened: he called down, "Main motor half ahead." *Setter* was lying stopped, sternto, rolling sluggishly to the swell, and men were already climbing down the sides of her bridge and mustering on the after casing. Four of them—one would be the second coxswain. He called down the pipe, "Steer three degrees to port." Aiming her at *Setter*'s stern. The midget was moving ahead now, driven by her electric motor, plunging and soaring as the long swells ran under her. He called down again, "Steady as you go!" On *Setter*'s casing they were already taking in the slack of the heavy Manilla tow; it was much easier to get it in yard by yard as the gap closed than to have a big, heavy bight of it to drag in later. There was no question of just letting it go, having it dangle, 200 yards of tough rope on the loose so MacGregor couldn't move his screws for fear of having them fouled.

"Slow ahead, main motor."

Repetition of the order from inside was like an echo in a tin drum. The gap was narrowing fast, and his intention was to stop with a few yards between them, not so close as to risk the two ships being washed against each other, but near enough to make the evolution easy and quick. To lie stopped on the surface this close to an enemy-occupied coast was an uncomfortable experience; MacGregor would want to get under way as soon as possible.

"Stop the motor!"

Echo floating up: "Stop . . ." Vibration ceased. Only sea-noise now, the rush of it along her sides and the swells breaking around her, sluicing away in foam. He had a feeling almost of disbelief in what was happening: to be here, on the targets' doorstep, after all the months of preparation . . .

"Slow astern."

To stop her, keep her where she was. He had to leave this command position and go for'ard now, and he wanted to keep the gap as it was. When stern-power had taken all the way off her, he stopped the motor, waited to make sure it had stopped, then let go of the induction pipe and began crawling for'ard, through rushes of water that looked and sounded like fizzy milk and felt like ice. He crouched, right up on her snout—which was arcing through about eight or ten feet several times a minute—and let them see he was ready for the line to be tossed over. Coming now: the man nearest *Setter*'s stern leant back, and an arm scythed forward in a slightly round-arm swing: the heaving-line came soaring—well over, but falling across the midget's bow and over Paul's outstretched arm. When he'd gathered enough slack to double-up about a fathom of it, he leant over her beak and threw a rolling hitch of the doubled line around the much thicker Manilla rope. He could let go of the line now, and unplug the telephone connection. Hands near-frozen, but still functioning. Finally, with a wheel-spanner which he'd had on a lanyard at his waist, he banged twice on the pressure-hull, a signal to Jazz Lanchberry in the fore-end to release the tow.

He heard it go, and waved to the group on *Setter*'s casing.

"All gone!"

A yell of acknowledgement: then a shout of "Good luck!" over the crash of sea. Another yell had the words "bloody *Tirpitz*" in it. They were hauling in the tow itself and also the line bent to its end, getting the whole lot out of the water fast, while Paul cautiously reversed his position in order to return to the induction pipe. X-12 rolling like a drunken whale, the sea alternately thumping and sucking at her sides: but it was done now—the tow completed, communication severed, decisions taken and risks accepted. He called down the pipe, "In engine clutch!" Half a minute later she was turning clear of *Setter*'s stern, the Gardner diesel pounding throatily as it drove her across the swells on course for the inshore minefield.

An hour later she was among the mines. Or rather, over them. He'd picked up the island of Loppen half a mile to starboard, and turned her due east. The other four X-craft would be ahead and to the north, aiming for the gap on southeasterly tracks, across X-12's bows; some of them might already have cleared the minefield.

It was bitterly cold. He'd dressed for the weather, with an extra sweater on, but having his legs and arms soaked through had turned those into vulnerable areas. Frozen areas: he had no feeling in his feet at all. You had to ignore such things, and it was better not to think about the mines either. The fact there'd been no explosions up ahead was comforting: and thank God the swell was much lower, lower all the time as she closed in towards the fjords. It was more than just a matter of getting a smooth passage; it concerned the mines, the fact that heavy pitching such as she'd indulged in earlier could have nullified the safety-margin of the few feet of water between her keel and the horned mines swaying on their mooring-wires like long-stemmed flowers. She could have been dropped right on top of one, in one of those long bow-down swoops.

If she had been—he'd told himself earlier—you wouldn't have had time to feel sorry for yourself. You wouldn't have had time to feel anything at all. Just boom: four men in the explosion of four tons of Torpex.

He'd set a running charge, so that the Gardner was simultaneously driving her along and charging the battery, so as to have a full quota of stored amperes before they dived. Gimber and Lanchberry would be attending to other things as well—running the compressor, for instance, to top up high-pressure air in the bottles, and making final checks on all sorts of equipment. Brazier would be busying himself mainly with the W and D and his own diving gear and tools.

A dark mass forming now to starboard was Silden, an island shaped like a teardrop and running north to south, its sharp northern end adorned with a light-structure, black and skeletal, looming above a rocky headland which at sea-level was fringed white by the east-running tide. He'd memorised this approach—the distances, timings and landfalls—and had a chart of it in his mind; he knew for instance that when Silden had fallen back on the starboard quarter he'd have the southwestern extremity of a bigger island, Söröy, to port. There was a hill 1600 feet high on that point, and he was expecting to see it soon. There was also a lightening in the sky suggestive of moon-rise: he had this impression, without stopping to think about it very hard, and he was surprised—slightly confused, in fact—because he hadn't expected any sign of a moon for another ninety minutes or so. It bothered him, but he let it go—there were other things to think about and he was keeping a careful all-round lookout for ships. Fishing trawlers being the most likely: but there might be patrols as well, with those valuable ships in there. He'd thought he'd seen steaming lights once, about twenty minutes ago, but they'd vanished—a trawler passing behind land, or into some fjordlet, he'd guessed. But when the hill on Söröy's southwest point was abeam, which would be a ten-mile run from the point when Silden's light-structure was abeam to starboard, he'd turn her to a gyro course of

103 degrees, and then after another twelve and a half miles she'd be close to the northern entrance of Rognsund. She'd have dived before she got that far, to be out of sight before the sun rose a few minutes after 0200.

The wind was down to almost nothing; inside the barrier of islands, he guessed, the water would be like the surface of a lake. Not too good from the periscope point of view: a ruffled surface would have been infinitely safer. He was thinking about that—about running deep whenever possible, and coming up when necessary for quick and cautious peeps, when he realised that he'd been stupid, that that brilliance had nothing to do with any moon. It was Aurora Borealis, the Northern Lights, flickering above the Arctic icecap. The first time he'd ever seen it. Not that there was time now to enjoy the spectacle—any enemy to starboard would have this little craft in silhouette against those rising, shivering streams of gold. Please God, there'd be no enemy to starboard or anywhere else close enough to see them, and no observer with high-powered optics on the Silden cliff-top where the light-structure stood unlit and as unwelcoming and secret as the blank windows of an empty house ... It was, however, abeam; he called down the pipe to Gimber to check the log reading and make a note of it, so he'd know when they'd run the next ten miles. Straightening from the pipe—using it for communication was hard work, as you were competing with the noise of the diesel and the rush of air it was sucking in—he saw the hilltop he'd been looking for, in silhouette against the polar fireworks. Which was fine. Especially so since he knew, from having it on that bearing with the Silden headland just abaft the beam, that he had now left the mines astern.

He passed this news down to the others: among all the racket, he thought he heard a cheer. He felt good about things generally at this point: about progress so far, chances of success, and Gimber having adjusted—so it seemed—to new conditions. In which, incidentally, there was a lesson learnt—understanding of the doctors' preoccupation with individual psychology. Even that super-irritant Claverhouse ... He shouted into the pipe again: "Louis! Like to take over up here for an hour?"

"Right!"

He warned, "It's bloody cold ..."

It was no less cold when he took over again an hour later, but hot soup inside him acted as anti-freeze, and he'd restored circulation to his feet by pressing their soles against the warm casing of the gyro compass. By midnight he'd turned her on to the course for Rognsund, crossing the wide lower part of Söröysund; and soon after making this alteration a glimmer of brightness on mainland mountains confirmed that the moon was rising. Those heights were snowbound—even now, at the end of the months of summer. Remembering that briefing they'd had about the overland route to Sweden, the sight was daunting as well as beautiful.

Lights on shipping to the north, when he was out in the middle at about 0100, worried him for a while. If they'd been overtaking, as at first he thought they were, he'd have had to have dived her until they'd passed. But they began to draw left, and eventually disappeared. He realised that they'd first appeared just outside Kipperfjord, which was one of several wide inlets on that south coast of Söröy, and they could well have been fishing craft who'd spent the night in there at anchor and were now making an early start. From this point Rognsund would be roughly six miles ahead; he reckoned to cover two thirds of that distance before diving. Then he'd have the day's first light by which to steer her into that narrow gap, and the whole day in which to conn her through. He'd creep through, dead slow on the motor, to make no visible disturbance and as little sound as possible for hydrophones to pick up.

At 0140 he called down, "Diving in five minutes!"

Still thinking about Rognsund—its shallow areas which he'd steer around, and the headland which jutted from the right-hand shore to form a bottleneck, just the sort of place they'd have installed acoustic gear. You'd need to be very very careful, all the way. You'd have to show some periscope now and then, because of the twists and turns and tidal complications which could make for navigational problems. The tide was ebbing now, flowing seaward, but low tide would come at about 0500, and you'd have a slack-water period before it started again in the opposite direction. Even in Stjernsund the tidal flow would be something to be reckoned with, but in a shallower and narrower passage you might get something like a mill-race, at some times and places.

Stjernsund . . . Cameron, Place, Henty-Creer and Hudspeth would all be on their way through, by this time.

The entrance to the sund was a black hole about two miles ahead. Diffused moonlight washed the higher slopes of both Stjernoy and Seiland, but the gulf between them lay in deep shadow.

"Stop the engine. Out engine-clutch."

The Gardner's pounding ceased.

Silence was dramatic. There was only the swish of sea along her sides. A faint breeze from the west was barely enough to stir the surface. To the east, the high ground on Seiland was a black frieze against sky lightening with the first intimation of a new day coming.

From the direction of Stjernoy, a dog howled.

"Engine-clutch out!"

They'd disconnected the diesel, so as to change over to electric propulsion. Paul ordered, "Main motor half ahead." With the Gardner's racket silenced, the induction pipe was a reasonably efficient voicepipe. His watch's luminous face showed 0147. The motor started: he could feel its vibration and the renewed forward impulse. He called down, "Shut the induction." Shutting the valve on the pipe not only made it safe to dive, it also cut off his communications with the men inside her. He stooped, pulled the hatch up, slid in feet-first, dropped through; reaching up to slam it above his head and then swing the securing wheel round to dog it, he ordered "Open main vents. Thirty feet."

Ten minutes later, after Gimber had caught a trim and they'd put her through her paces—down to sixty, up to twenty, trim re-adjusted and no problems found—he ordered periscope depth.

"Take it easy, Louis."

Gimber grunted assent as he put angle on the hydroplanes, to ease her upward. The gauge showed seventeen feet when he shifted the trim-pump lever over to port, to flood water into the midships tank, ballasting her as she rose. Paul had the periscope-switch bag in his hand—thick rubber for insulation, and you had to feel for the right button to press: he watched the slow, carefully controlled ascent. The caution was vital—would be at any rate once it was light up there, and this was a matter of starting as you meant to go on. In that channel, you'd only need to make one slip, break surface once . . .

Twelve feet. Eleven. Ten. His thumb pressed the "up" button in the bag on its wandering lead, and the periscope rose silently, stopping with a jerk at its upper limit as Gimber reported "Nine feet."

"When we're inside, Louis, we'll try nine-foot six. I'll make do with about an inch of glass."

The gap between the two mounds of land was right ahead. He circled, checking all round, knowing there couldn't be anything very close but still doing it out of long habit, standard safety-drill. When they were in the fjord he'd put this scope up for just seconds at a time, despite the fact its top was no thicker than a walking stick. In that flat calm, anything that showed above the surface—particularly anything that left a wake behind it—would catch even the most casual eye.

Gimber had stopped the pump again.

A worrying thing was a slight misting in the lenses. There wasn't enough light yet to be sure, but the edges of the land seemed blurry. You'd tell better in half an hour or so, by which time the sun would have risen. Meanwhile she was on course and it would be an hour before she reached the entrance. He felt for the "down" button, and pressed it, sent the tube gliding down into its well, below the deck-boards.

"Sixty feet."

The hydroplanes tilted. Gimber's left hand on the pump lever, ready to make new trim adjustments as she nosed deeper. Brazier squatting in the W and D, watching Paul who was crouching over the folded chart, studying the detail of that entrance. You had to use the chart folded to the area you wanted, because there wasn't room to spread it out—no chart-table either, since there'd have been nowhere to put one.

Lanchberry yawning, eyes on the gyro reading, fingering the wheel. He yawned again. Brazier murmured, "Bastard's either snoring or yawning. Born tired . . ." He had his net-cutter beside him, and some tools he'd been using to service it. It was powered by water-pressure, so as not to send up bubbles.

At 0345 she was at ten feet again, and in the entrance. He'd have brought her up sooner but they'd heard propellers chugging and waited until a trawler had passed overhead, coming out of Rognsund. It was in periscope-sight now—well astern, and about to disappear westward behind Varneset, the headland on Stjernoy. The periscope was slightly foggy, not as bad as he'd feared it might be but certainly requiring attention when there was time and opportunity—tonight, perhaps, when they'd be holed-up for a few hours. He took some bearings, to establish their exact position, and set a course of 155 degrees, which would be good for three miles.

"Sixty feet, Louis." He told them, as the periscope slid down, "Nice and peaceful up there. Smoke drifting from cottage chimneys, some chaps mending a boat on a slipway, one horse-and-cart going somewhere very slowly, no signs of anything military."

Lanchberry said, "I never did like the military."

Paul decided that he'd come up for a check after two and three-quarter miles, measuring it by the electric log. At this low speed it would take about two hours. Slow movement not only made less disturbance, it also extended the life of the battery, and there was no certainty when it would be possible to run a charge. He'd get one in if he could, because you had not only the attack to think about, but also the withdrawal to sea afterwards. Or the hope of it. Maintaining slow speed like this would stretch the battery life to one hundred miles, but the snag was that in any kind of emergency it mightn't be possible to maintain low speed.

He cranked open the shutters that had been covering the viewing ports, port and starboard. They'd been shut because of the foul weather, mostly. There wasn't anything to be seen here, at the moment, but there would be later. Things like the underwater hull of a pocket battleship.

"Sixty feet, sir."

"Well done, Louis." He was acknowledging that "sir" as much as the report. It was right and proper—not Louis Gimber speaking, but X-12's first lieutenant—but not strictly necessary; Gimber's use of it had been in-tended to tell him something. Paul said, "We don't need four on watch. One man at a time could get his head down. Excluding me, that is ... Louis, old horse, this looks like being the easiest stretch ahead of us, and I'd want you to be on the job after the next change of course, so how about taking your stand-off now?"

He kept a log—detail on which to build the report he'd have to submit later—in a small notebook. Entries showed that when the tide was turning, around 5:00 a.m., he brought her up twice to take shore bearings and ensure safety from navigational hazards. Subsequent entries included:

> 0610. A/co to 123, having passed Stoergrd, shallow patch. Rock awash 3/4 mile stbd with iron marker.
>
> 0614. Small vessel ahead. Dived to 60ft. (Minesweeper?)
>
> 0622. Ship passed overhead. Turbines, 180 revs.

Gimber asked him, "How far on this course?"

"One point eight miles. We'll take a shufti after one and a half, though. We'll have the headland coming up then."

Jazz Lanchberry was off watch now. Brazier at the helm. They heard a ship's screws again just after seven—a reciprocating engine, this time—and after a while it overhauled them on the port side. It was probably a fishing boat. Then shortly afterwards:

> 0717. Fast H.E. stbd bow. More than one vessel, prob. E-boats.
>
> 0718. Dived to 100ft.
>
> 0729. H.E. drawing right. Two fast turbine craft, believe E-boats. Returned to 60ft then 40.

In the direction from which those enemies had come initially the chart showed a good anchorage in an inlet called Kvalfjord; he guessed it might be a base for patrol-boats, and made a note of this in the book. Then:

> 0746. Periscope depth. A/co 151 to clear Mjaanes Pt.
>
> 0748. 60ft.

This course would have taken her clear of the headland and right through, all the way. But he was wary of tidal sets in the bottleneck, and at 0820 when he estimated that Mjaanes Point should be abeam he ordered periscope depth to check on it. She was at twelve feet, rising very slowly under Gimber's cautious control, and Paul had pressed the "up" button for the scope, when they were all startled by the sudden thunder of propellers—from around the point of land, but loud, close and fast, closer and louder every second: and X-12 in its path, still slightly bow-up, lifting with her periscope rising too.

"Hundred feet!" Agony of waiting—only seconds, but seemingly an age, while Gimber got bow-down angle on her. Paul snapped, "Full ahead, group up!" Expecting the end at any moment: the crash, hull splitting open, finis . . . Then the wash hit her as she wallowed down: powerful as the blast of a depthcharge, enemy screws racing over and that huge thrust hitting her as she fought for depth, bow-down with twenty-four feet on the gauge but her stern higher than that, catching the major part of it. That sound—a destroyer's screws so close it had been touch-and-go whether you'd be ploughed open like a can ripped by the opener—he'd heard once before, in *Ultra* in the Mediterranean when an Italian had very nearly made it. X-12 flinging over, rolling right over on to her beam-ends, rammed not by the German's forefoot but by his wash: Paul had been thrown off his feet, the others almost out of their chairs: the ringing of the gyro alarm bell was subdued under a fresh crescendo of propeller noise, a second ship rushing over the top.

They'd come from behind the headland. That was why the noise had burst on them so suddenly, without warning. X-12 was at forty feet and rolling back. Loose gear had been sent flying—including the gluepot and the kettle, utensils, tools and buckets. Paul got to the gyro alarm switch and shut it off—remembering that the Brown's gyro would tolerate a twenty-five degree angle but no more. He told Brazier, as the second lot of screws receded, "Set the course indicator to ship's head one-five-oh." Near enough: their course had been 151. The course-indicator was aircraft-type equipment; it would be better than nothing for a while, until they could get the gyro working again. The magnetic compass would be useless in this fjord—or in Stjersund, for that matter—because of local magnetic anomalies creating wild variations. The chart, and the Pilot for the district, emphasized it.

"Fifty feet, Louis."

"Fifty: aye aye." Swinging the planes to get her bow up. Paul was still thinking about—or rather, reacting to—the extraordinary power of that first ship's wash. Admitting that this was a very small submarine indeed and that she'd been right at the crucial depth for it to hit her, and at extremely close range—even then . . . He told Gimber, "Group down, slow ahead." He'd needed full power to get her down, but in the last minute he'd been wasting amps. He heard Brazier comment: "Like going over Niagara in a barrel." Lanchberry was taking over the helm from him, having set the course indicator.

But—still rolling?

Lanchberry enquired, glancing back over his shoulder, that slanted, typically sardonic look as he slid into the seat in Brazier's place, "Anyone notice anything?"

Paul was checking the transverse spirit-level. His impression of a moment ago had been wrong: she hadn't been rolling, she'd been taking up a much more pronounced list to port than she'd had before.

He told Lanchberry, "Guess."

"Ten degrees?"

"Twelve."

It was giving Gimber problems with the trim. With this much slant on her, the hydroplanes could hardly be expected to function normally, since one was now lower than the other—therefore, in denser water, having more effect than the higher one—and also the slant giving an element of rudder-action to them, because they were so far off the horizontal. It needed only a few comments to establish this, for everyone to recognise the problem and the difficulties it presented. You could also understand how it had come about: the side-cargo, already loosened on its sealing copper strip to the extent that one of its buoyancy-chambers had been flooded, had been jolted looser still by the impact of the destroyer's wash. In fact Paul was wondering at this stage whether it had been a destroyer; the second one certainly had, and in retrospect a comparison between the two suggested that the first had been enormously more powerful. Lanchberry still staring

at him over his shoulder: he suggested, "Have to ditch the port side-cargo,
skipper. D'you reckon?"

The idea didn't appeal to him. He told Lanchberry, "Watch your steering, for God's sake."

Both those ships must have been destroyers, he decided. Recalling the
sound of their screws—even though the leading one had seemed so extraordinarily powerful . . .

Gimber reported grimly, "Fifty feet."

"Make it thirty."

After that, he'd take her up to periscope depth, get a fix and line up the
course indicator more accurately. Then—well, just south of this headland
there was an inlet three-quarters of a mile deep, called Lille Kvalfjord. Lille
meaning "little." The chart showed that it shelved to as little as ten fathoms
in there, and if it was empty or at least not crowded it might be a good spot
in which to lie on the bottom and set the gyro to rights, square off whatever
other defects might show up when one had time to look around.

Gimber muttered, working hard at the trim, "This is damn near
impossible."

"You're doing well, Louis."

Not all that well, though. And nearer the surface, controlling her was
going to be even trickier. Also, there'd be a slant on the periscope and you'd
get distorted bearings. It was quite probable that the periscope would have
flooded again, after that rough handling; he guessed the leak would be
either around the frame of the top glass, or in the metal casing itself.

It might be wise—although it went against the grain—to ditch the
flooded side-cargo. Set it to "safe" and release it. At least you'd be in shape
to carry out a successful attack with the other one—which on the present
showing certainly couldn't be guaranteed.

It seemed such a waste. Having brought the thing all this way . . .

Gimber reported, "Thirty feet."

"Nice work."

"I can't promise to keep her within a yard of any ordered depth,
though."

"Have to find a way to, Louis. Somehow. Try twenty, now."

"Christ." Gimber raised his voice to acknowledge more formally, "Twenty feet." Shaking his head, as he tilted the hydroplanes ... Paul still thinking about it—and realising that with trimming as it was now he wouldn't have dared to bring her up any higher than twenty. If they bungled it now, alerted the Germans to the threat of attack—giving them time to move their ships out, mount a hunt in the fjords, plaster the whole area with depthcharges ...

And if it happened, it wouldn't have been Gimber's fault. She was at twenty-two feet now and going down again: he'd been nervous of letting her overshoot upwards.

"All right. Twenty-five feet. I'll have to ditch the bloody thing."

Lanchberry's head inclined in a nod of approval. Gimber said, "Yes. I'm sorry, but it's just—"

"Can't be helped."

It still irked him to have to do it. Fifty per cent of her offensive potential down the drain. Facing facts, however, it could not be helped. And with six hundred feet of water here, it was as good a place as any to do it. He crouched at the port side fuse-mechanism. The pointer on the clock had to be turned through two stops to the left, to the one marked SAFE. Until it had been set there—or activated, set going with a delay-setting on it—the release gear couldn't be operated. He gripped the knob between forefinger and thumb, and twisted.

It wouldn't turn the whole way. It clicked to the intermediate stop, but no further. He returned it to the starting point, and tried again.

"The pointer won't go to 'safe.'"

She was at twenty-eight feet, and Gimber was still having to fight the controls. Paul beginning to appreciate that the problems were real and cumulative. He told them—Lanchberry, who was staring round at him, and Brazier's wide, ginger-stubbled face framed in the circular opening of the W and D—"It'll travel right, but not left. Not far enough."

So—next alternative ...

You could turn the knob to the right to the full extent of its travel, putting the maximum delay of six hours on the fuse, and then ditch it. The fuse would have to be activated, and after six hours it would explode.

Gimber had had the same thought. "Set a long fuse, and dump it?"

"Can't do that." He'd seen the answer. "Suppose we did it now. The bang would go off at three this afternoon. What chance would we—or any of the others—have of getting any attacks in tomorrow morning, d'you think? The Bosch wouldn't just say 'Oh, something's exploded in the Rognsund,' and do nothing about it, would they."

Gimber admitted, "No. You're right."

"So we're stuck with it, until tomorrow. Preferably until we find our target . . . Louis—let's try a bow-heavy trim, holding her on the planes?"

He thought that might answer the trimming problem. Instinct, the "feel" of her, suggested it. But even if it worked, you'd still have a periscope on the blink, a heavy list and a side-cargo malfunctioning . . . He was behind Gimber's left shoulder, studying the effects of the change of trim as it began to take effect. Thinking about that side-cargo—whether if it was defective in one respect it could be trusted in any other.

CHAPTER THIRTEEN

· · ·

Trench told me, "I'd arranged for the *Bayleaf* and *Arctic Prince* to divert to a new, closer rendezvous position. Two reasons: one, low cloud was giving us cover from the Luftwaffe and the forecast was for rough stuff ahead of us, the sort of conditions that make flying more or less impossible up there, so there was a good chance the bastards would be grounded. Normally I'd have gone right up to the ice and out of their range as soon as possible, but in these circumstances I thought I could take the risk of cutting the corner . . . Clear?"

It was not only clear, it was on the record.

"Second reason was we knew there were U-boats waiting up near Bear Island. I turned the *Bayleaf* to a southwesterly course—instead of southeasterly—and kept her clear of them. At the same time I altered the convoy's route so as to pass south of the island instead of north of it. We made the rendezvous, got on with fuelling the escorts, and altered again—to about two-five-oh degrees, leaving Bear Island sixty miles to the nor'ard."

Mrs Trench said, "If you leave your food alone much longer, it'll be stone cold."

He began to eat. She smiled at me. Eileen Trench was a good-looking woman, with a beautiful skin and good bone structure; in 1943 she'd have been what we then called a "smasher."

Trench told me with his mouth full, "As it happened, a U-boat on passage to join its chums ran into us by sheer chance. It dived well out ahead, *Leopard* thought she'd made asdic contact and pooped off a few salvoes of hedgehog, but—well, may or may not have been a sub contact, but if it was the Hun survived it. Within an hour or so we had him shadowing from astern, calling to his friends to come and join him. Some of them did—resulting in the loss of the *Lord Charles* and an American freighter—whose name I forget . . . Quite a lot of survivors, from the Yank particularly, thanks to a very quick rescue. But Martin Insole drowned. The vice-commodore who took over from him was also American—name of Claypoole, master of the . . ." he'd paused, with a forkful of mutton in mid-air: and got it ". . . the *Harriet Smith*. Odd how some names stick and some don't."

Trench seemed to be staring at his wife across the table, but his eyes weren't focussed on her and his thoughts, certainly, were a thousand miles away.

"We only lost those two. At dusk I made a drastic alteration southward. On its own this might have thrown them off, but in fact a strong blow from the northwest got up during the night, and by dawn—steaming west again by then—we had roughish seas with sleet and snow showers."

Trench continued, "My object had been simply to get away from the U-boat pack. This had been achieved, and we'd lost our shadower too—which was extremely fortunate. If they'd maintained contact and known exactly where we were, later events might have turned out quite differently. But anyway—the signal from London told me that *Lützow* and nine destroyers had been reported as having sailed from Altenfjord. It felt very much as it had on the outward passage with PQ 19 when they'd told us *Tirpitz* and *Scharnhorst* were at sea. Except we'd had a cruiser with us then—not that that alone could make a jot of difference, but she'd had a man commanding her in whom I had a lot more faith than I had in myself. I looked around and saw my handful of lightly-armed ships, as against twice as many Germans with much heavier guns—that's just the destroyers, let alone *Lützow* with her eleven-inch . . . I can tell you, I thanked God for the bad weather and for the fact we no longer had our shadower. But I still thought we'd come up against them, because we were so damn close."

"About—two hundred miles?"

"From Altenfjord?" He nodded. "About that, after we'd turned down to the southwest. I didn't know exactly when the Germans had sailed, but it would surely have been the night before, so we could have expected to run into them any minute. Their notion of my convoy's whereabouts might have been somewhat vague, based on U-boat reports twenty-four hours old, and I wasn't sure the U-boats would know which way we'd turned—they could have expected us to turn up towards the ice, you see, as we'd done before—I mean as Nick Everard had done. I had these imponderables in mind, and bad weather with very poor visibility as the one thing in our favour. Also, a fervent wish that Nick Everard had been on his feet and making the decisions."

"But he was still . . ."

"Yes." Trench put down his knife and fork. "C-in-C Home Fleet ordered the battle squadron out of Akureyri, and he sailed CS 39 as well—minus *Nottingham*, who'd been sent south to get her bomb damage patched up. Kidd had transferred his flag to *Rhodesia*. But they might as well have been on the China Station, for all the support they could give me from that distance."

I asked him, later, "The ship that nearly ran down Paul's X-craft and damaged her with its wash—would you agree that might have been *Lützow* on her way out?"

"Might've been. It's never been possible to establish for certain, largely because there's doubt about exactly when she did sail. We know she was at sea when the Admiralty made that signal—some hours before, in fact, because they'd had to take in and digest a report from our Norwegian friends first. And she certainly wasn't in the fjord when the X-craft made their attacks on the twenty-second: but Roskill in his official history gives her departure date as September twenty-third. So—"Trench helped himself to cheese—"you pays your money and you takes your choice. Bearing in mind that only Allah is perfect." He glanced across at me. "You knew Paul quite well, didn't you."

"Oh, yes."

Eileen Trench asked, "Were you and he contemporaries?"

"More or less. And we were both submariners."

"You weren't in X-craft, though, were you?"

"No. At a late stage I volunteered for it, but by that time they had all they wanted . . . One thing does strike me, about the ship that hit him with her wash. When he identified her as a destroyer, before he realised it might have been something much bigger, he had nothing to go by except the hydrophone effect." I explained to Trench's wife, "We called it 'HE.' It was the underwater sound of a ship's propellers. The noise a turbine made—which is tantamount to saying a small warship, as distinct from a cruiser or battleship—was quite different from a big ship's reciprocating engines."

She smiled at me as if she thought I was talking double Dutch. "Do go on."

"Well. That was the general rule, in 1943. But as it happened, *Lützow* was turbine-powered. Geared turbines, with diesels for cruising speeds. So turbine-driven screws is what he would have heard."

Trench nodded. "You could well have a point."

"And she must have sailed at about that time. But nobody had any sight or sound of her in Stjernsund. If she'd gone out that way, I think they would have, because X-10, commanded by Hudspeth, an Australian, was still in Stjernsund then, trying to make-good his boat's defects. He had no compasses, no periscope, several other major problems. In fact he had rotten luck altogether—in spite of the defects he got her right down to Kafjord, then had to abandon the operation. He spent a week hiding in the outer fjords, and eventually made a rendezvous with one of the towing submarines. If *Lützow* had steamed out through Stjernsund when he was there, he'd have heard her, for sure."

Trench agreed with me.

"You said," his wife broke in, "that this Australian had to give up. So besides Paul Everard's there were only—what, three X-craft left operational, when the time came?"

"Yes. Cameron, Place, Henty-Creer. All targeted on *Tirpitz*. Paul was supposed to attack *Lützow,* and there was nobody now to deal with *Scharnhorst.* Of course, none of the four teams who were in there had any way of knowing X-10 had dropped out."

•   •   •

The image of Louis Gimber sliding on to his seat at the hydroplane and main motor controls seemed to shiver, mirage-like. Paul blinked, to clear his eyes, and finished replacing periscope tools in their canvas roll. Jazz Lanchberry muttered, "Air's not too bad, considering."

He meant, considering they'd been shut down for nearly twelve hours now, and he'd only made the comment because the truth was that the air was extremely thin. It would have been intolerable by this time if they hadn't spread Protosorb on trays—Protosorb being Lithium Hydroxide, white crystals to absorb the poison with which four men's breathing was polluting the midget's damp, yellow-lit interior—and also doctored the atmosphere with guffs of oxygen from bottles stored in the engine-room. You had to go easy with the oxygen, because tomorrow might be a long day too. If you were lucky, it might be a long day.

Paul told Lanchberry, "It'll get worse before it gets better. We have a way to go yet." He gave the periscope a pat, and sent it down; he'd stripped it, dried its flooded lenses and reassembled it, but whether it would stay dry now, or for how long, was anyone's bet. He hoped it only flooded when she was banged around, as she had been in the ship's wash and before that by the bad weather. The leak, he guessed, would be either around the frame of the top glass or from a strained seam in the metal barrel that housed the optics, and by this time it might have opened up enough to make for a constant seepage.

Lanchberry and Gimber had got the gyro back into operation, and Brazier had attended to several minor items. The one thing nobody could do anything about was the flooded side-cargo, the list you knew she'd take up again as soon as she floated up off the bottom.

He held up the damp, discoloured chart. Its paper absorbed the moisture of the atmosphere, and there wasn't anything you could do about that either.

"Look here." Pointing, with a pencil. "If we find we have to do something about the air, at a pinch I'd surface her here."

"In daylight?"

Gimber had his mouth slightly open, like a dying fish. Paul added, "If

we had to, is what I'm saying." Pointing at an islet near the bottom end
of Rognsund—about a cable's length from the western shore, and with a
fringe of rocks and outlying reef. "We'd have cover there. Otherwise—
preferably—we'll carry on, come up about seven-thirty when it's dark,
then hole up here—this island, Langnesholm—until about dawn. Shove
off before sunrise, and you could be at work on *Lützow's* nets by four
a.m., Bomber. That'd give us plenty of time to lay the cargoes and sneak
out again."

Brazier nodded. "Right." Lanchberry said, "Give him a job, at last."
Bristling crew-cut, blue-jowelled, eyes showing their whites as he glanced
over his left shoulder. Brazier crouching like a caged but amiable Hunchback
of Notre Dame. Paul wondered what he looked like. Certainly like nothing to please the eye.

Depthgauge static at the figure 132.

"One hundred feet."

Gimber pushed the pump-lever over to starboard to open the midships
tank and set the pump's suction working on it, lighten her so she'd lift clear
of the sea-bed. They were in Lille Kvalfjord, and it was about four hours
since those ships had nearly run them down. The adjustment to the trim,
after they'd fiddled with it for a while, had worked quite well; she was
clumsy, and Gimber still had to work at it, but she was manageable.

"Ship's head?"

Lanchberry told him, "Oh-two-two."

"Steer that."

It would do well enough. He'd turned her before he'd bottomed her,
so she'd be pointing the right way—out—in case a quick exit had become
desirable. Movement now, heeling over. Like a whale starting to roll on
the fjord's rocky bed. The deckboards angled under his feet: then she was
floating up . . . 130 feet. When she reached 120, safely clear, he ordered
the motor slow ahead group down. X-12 was leaning woundedly to port
but was otherwise responsive to her controls as she paddled gently out to
re-enter Rognsund.

Back in business . . .

Gimber reported, "Hundred feet."

"Make it eighty, Louis."

The periscope leak worried him more than the list did, particularly as Gimber seemed to be managing the trim all right. To use the stub periscope, the short bifocal night one set like an alligator's eyes just above the casing, you had to be right up there, breaking surface, and with her slightly awkward handling now you'd be really breaking surface, off and on. So there could be no question of using the stub in daylight, and without the use of the main periscope you'd be blind. As for the list—well, the aim had to be to get rid of the flooded side-cargo as soon as possible. Once she'd shed it, she'd be back on an even keel. Safe withdrawal after the attack therefore wasn't compromised, except in the sense that a successful attack was the necessary first step in that direction and that the chances of completing an attack undetected had been reduced by the loss of manoeuvrability.

"Depth eighty feet." Gimber was adjusting the trim again. Lanchberry began to whistle between his teeth, then caught himself doing it, and stopped. Paul checked the log. One nautical mile—2000 yards—would take her far enough out into the sund, then he'd turn her to starboard to a course of 150 degrees on which a run of five miles would take her into fairly open water.

"Half ahead, Louis."

There was a need to conserve battery power, but he also wanted to get down near that little island, Stjernovoddholmen, so that if lack of air became a really immediate problem he'd be able to bring her to the surface with some hope of not being spotted. The foul air was already making him feel sick, and he was aware that his pulse-rate had risen. Brazier was sitting instead of squatting, with his head down between his knees, the accepted position for countering nausea . . . Problem followed problem: this whole thing was a gamble, and all you could do was press on, cope with each difficulty as it arose.

He was navigating by dead-reckoning now—using log-readings to get the distance run, and accepting the fact that the gyro was accurate only to within a few degrees one way or the other. He took her out to what he thought to be almost mid-fjord, and turned her to the southeasterly course before he could risk coming up and trying to get a fix. It would be a check on the state of the periscope, as much as on the boat's position; if the prisms had been flooded again, he'd get no more than a blur. He brought her up slowly, in stages, and at thirty feet he cut the speed from half to slow ahead—to reduce or even eliminate any "feather" at the tip of the periscope when it pushed up through the surface.

"Set the course indicator, Jazz. I'll turn her down-fjord, and we'll call that one-five-oh . . . Fifteen feet, Louis."

The hydroplanes tilted gently. There was no sound—which he was listening for, not wanting to be caught twice—of any other ship's screws. Only the purr of the main motor, and the water rustling along her sides. At fifteen feet Gimber seemed to have her in pretty good control.

"Ten feet."

He had the rubber bag in his hand, thumb on the feel of the "rise" button inside it. At ten feet the top glass would still be covered. His hope was to show no more than half an inch above the surface, if Gimber could hold her that steady—and in such calm water it would certainly have been possible if she had not had the list on her . . . He decided he'd order a depth just greater than the one he wanted, and use the upward variations, put up with periods of being blanked off.

"Depth ten feet."

He pressed the button. "Try nine and a half, Louis." The tube slid up, and stopped. Lanchberry looking back over his shoulder: Brazier with his head lifted, eyes slitted under the beetling ginger brows. Paul put his right eye to the lens. Bubbling, bright whorls, a kaleidoscopic medley of blues, greens and white, and diamond-like flashes through it all; the top glass was still covered when Gimber blurted, "Nine and a half. Can't be sure of holding . . ."

"Just do your best."

Rising now. He'd get some kind of a view, before Gimber forced her down again.

The prisms were fogged. But he could see enough to confirm that she was well out in the middle. The land-mass to port—a mountainous rise almost abeam, matched the same feature on the chart. To starboard, about thirty degrees on the bow, there was a higher one inland on Stjernoy. Between those features—ahead, beyond a vacuity of clear water—blurred heights with snow on them towered against a patchwork sky.

"Steer three degrees to port, and set the course indicator on one-five-oh."

"Three degrees to port, aye aye . . ."

The top of the periscope had dipped under. Water swirled, bubbling, then darkened into stillness. He pulled his head back and pressed the "down" button.

"Well done, Louis. Sixty feet."

"Periscope OK?"

"Far from it. But we're where we ought to be."

More or less. An accurate fix wasn't necessary anyway at this stage. He took a new reading of the log, from which to measure the run southeastward. Deciding at the same time that an emergency stop at Stjernovoddholmen wasn't really to be welcomed. To get in close enough to have cover from the island when you surfaced would require accurate navigation, to avoid the hazards of rock and reef around it. This thin, putrifying air was going to have to last until the sun was down.

"We'll treat ourselves to another shot of the oh-two, I think."

Approving murmurs . . . Oh-two meaning oxygen. The midget was nose-down, paddling lopsidedly down past fifty feet. He decided he'd re-new the Protosorb as well, since it might have absorbed about as much carbon dioxide as it could hold by this time. He told Gimber, "Half ahead," and Brazier, "Scrape up the Protosorb, Bomber, and spread a fresh lot." Lanchberry murmured, "Might as well be comfy," and they all laughed—laughter coming easily, when you needed it. Paul crawled aft into the engine space for another oxygen bottle.

It got worse again, of course. Worst of all were the last twenty minutes—having to resist the temptation to take a risk and surface before it was really dark. They were all sick, feverish, breathing in short gasps. The Bomber was asleep, but a better word for it might have been "unconscious." Paul had kept her on 150 for two hours, logging three point nine miles in that time, then altered to due south. If tidal streams had matched expectations, they ought by now to be in the wide upper part of Altenfjord. About an hour ago they'd have passed southward between Horsnes and Klubbeneset, and her immediate destination—Langnesholm, a very small island close to the entrance of Langfjord—would now be about three and a half miles on the bow to starboard. Driven by the diesel after she surfaced, she'd get there in about half an hour.

A quarter of an hour ago he'd brought her up to nine feet, but a quick glance through the blurred lenses had shown it wasn't dark enough yet, and he'd ordered her back to thirty feet. Since then, every few minutes he'd found either Gimber or Lanchberry staring at him. Once he'd snapped irritably, "No—not yet!" It was like being stared at by hungry dogs: and he didn't need their reminders, he'd been trying to keep his own thoughts away from that cold, fresh air. He was also worried about Brazier, but a man asleep used less air than the same man awake, and that one, being twice life-size, used a lot. So the temptation to see if he could be woken had also been resisted.

The needle was steady on thirty feet, motor slow ahead group down, time 1935, the others' panting intakes of breath irritatingly loud although one's own—oddly enough—were not. He thought he'd left it long enough, now. At his sudden move—he'd been sitting with his back against the gyro—the others glanced quickly round. He nodded. "Nine feet." The hydroplanes tilted sharply: he warned Gimber, "Take it gently, Louis." Gimber muttered something. Paul ignored it, and told Lanchberry to wake the Bomber; Lanchberry leant sideways from his chair, grabbed one of the large feet that were projecting from the W and D, wrenched it to and fro. "Wakey wakey, rise and shine!"

Bomber groaned. Lanchberry did it some more: there was another groan, and then a growl of "Oh, piss off . . ."

"We're about to surface, Bomber. You OK?"

Gimber croaked, "Nine feet." In fact she was at eight and a half. Brazier was on his knees at the heads bowl, retching into it. The periscope hissed up: Paul put his eye to it, circled right around, peering into blurry darkness in which an enemy would probably have been invisible even a yard away. But there was no sound of any.

"Stand by to surface."

Circling again—knowing the periscope was defective to an extent that made the exercise futile, and hoping to God that Brazier was going to be all right. Surprising it should have hit the strongest of them all the hardest. Bigger lungs having more room for poison in them, perhaps, bigger heart needing more oxygen to run on . . . He sent the periscope down and positioned himself under the hatch.

"Surface. Blow one and three main ballast."

The relief of getting into fresh air, then hearing the rush of it down the induction pipe when the Gardner thumped into action and began to suck it in, was so overwhelming that in those first minutes he didn't give any thought to the dramatic quality of the moment—that he was surfacing his boat in a German harbour and the one that accommodated the *Tirpitz,* at that . . . He did think about it later, though, while he was conning her southwestward at six knots to find that island. He was closer to it, in fact, than he'd expected; the ebbing tide—it would be flooding now, low water about an hour ago—must have been stronger than he'd allowed for. Land outlines were clearly visible, sharp enough to fix by, using the gyro and finding the results quite good. He had binoculars on the casing with him—in this dead calm water there was no problem using them—and that opening about a mile and a quarter wide could only be the entrance to Langfjord and *Lützow's* net-enclosed berth. Nets which Bomber Brazier would have to be fit enough to cut a hole in tomorrow morning. The feeling of nausea was wearing off: it was like beginning to feel better after a really terrible hangover.

He saw Langnesholm—or rather, a dark end to land that couldn't be anywhere else. His idea was to tuck X-12 in behind its southern end, so she'd be lying in the channel and in the island's shadow . . . He lowered the binoculars, and called down for an alteration of a few degrees to port: straightening from the pipe, his eye was caught by a flash of white—starboard bow ...

He whipped his glasses up. It had vanished—but it reappeared, and he was on it. A ship's bow-wave ... Small, but fast, travelling from left to right: he guessed it might be an E-boat, or some other kind of fast patrol craft. He called down to stop the engine. If necessary, he'd dive her, but by cutting out any motion through the water—and if the enemy held its present course—he crouched, knowing the midget would be virtually invisible, with so little profile ... The patrol boat would have entered through Stjernsund, he guessed, and from its present course might be heading for Leir Botn, the destroyer anchorage on the far side and opposite the south coast of Aaroy.

It had gone on, out of sight. He called down, "No problem. E-boat or somesuch, just passing. Half ahead main engine." Visualising the Germans in that boat's bridge—if they'd known there was a fox here in their hen-run. Highly explosive fox. But it was nerve-tingling too, in some ways— the racket of the Gardner, for instance, as she gathered way again, pushing through a surface that was rippling from a newly risen breeze: you could imagine Germans hearing this from miles away. The new wind was knife-cold—it made his eyes run, turned his damp clothes into an ice-suit. He shouted down the pipe, "Below—how's Brazier?"

Gimber answered that he seemed to be all right. It was a big relief. And there was a job for him, or would be in a minute ... "Tell him to put his rubber suit on." Gimber passed that message, then called again: "Get a hot meal ready, shall we?"

"Good idea!"

Hot anything ...

He'd been watching in case the patrol boat turned back, but there was nothing to be seen of it. He moved the glasses on, sweeping up the port side towards the bow. Down there at the southern end of the fjord, where in its offshoot Kafjord *Tirpitz* and *Scharnhorst* would be lying—tucked up for the night and feeling safe—X-5, 6, 7 and 10 would also be in wait.

Cameron and Place, he knew, had intended to spend the dark hours lying-up among the Brattholm islands, three or four miles from the Kafjord entrance. They'd quite likely be in sight and sound of each other, close enough to chat from boat to boat—just as X-12 would have had X-11 for company, if X-11 hadn't been at the bottom of the Norwegian Sea, with Dan Vicary and his crew kicking their heels on board *Scourge,* pretty sick with frustration, no doubt.

In another ten minutes he had her close to Langnesholm; an unlit light-structure on its southern end provided a good leading-mark. He nosed her in towards the opening between the island and the mainland coast—into deep shadow and a cliff's overhang. He called down, "Stop main engine!" The diesel's pounding ceased, and the rush of air stopped too; he didn't need to shout now, with only the swish of water along her sides. Silence emphasized the loneliness and the need for stealth . . . "Out engine-clutch. Main motor half ahead group down. Steady as you go." He was crouching, with the tube at a slant, half lowered. The gap between the island and the mainland shore was too shallow higher up, and too rock-strewn, to be navigable, and since there'd be no possibility of passing through that way in the morning he was going to hide her at this southern end. It was also more remote down here—roughly seven hundred yards from the other shore—and it was necessary to run a battery-charge while they were here.

X-12 gliding in, only the soft thrum of her motor and the wash of ice-water around her. The rocky coast of Langnesholm loomed against the sky on the bow.

"Stop main motor. Port five. Tell Brazier to come up." The gear Brazier was going to use was lashed inside the casing; he confirmed as he got it out that he was fully recovered . . . "Slight pain in the nut is all." There was a coil of steel wire rope and an anchor, and he was cutting the lashings off. Paul asked him, "Nut, or nuts?" The Bomber chuckled. The island coast was so near that any sentry up there might have been wondering what the joke was: Paul wondered how he could possibly risk running the diesel here, for the battery-charge . . . "Midships. Slow astern."

In a few minutes he had her at rest and, to all intents and purposes, hidden. Brazier went over the side, jammed the anchor in a rock-cleft and came back. He muttered, "You could have them aching soon enough in that stuff." Paying out the wire until her weight was on it; the end was shackled to the bull-ring, and they'd leave it here, simply unshackle it when they left in a few hours' time. Meanwhile it would hold her forty tons of deadweight stemming the inflow of tide.

"Nice work, Bomber. Glad you're OK. You had me worried."

"Took a little snooze, that's all . . . Skipper, there's corned dog hash below, when you're ready for it. Shall one of us eat first, then—"

"Listen . . ."

Music. From the mainland side.

It sounded like a fiddle. And voices now, singing. He concentrated—wanting to identify the language—there'd be all the difference in the world between a bunch of Norwegians having a hooly and some German garrison . . . Also, the question of how near or far, and the matter of the battery having to be charged—it was absolutely necessary. To move out into midstream to do it was an unattractive alternative, with likely interruptions by patrol boats or other craft . . . The singing and the accompaniment climaxed and stopped. X-12 moving to her wire, sea-movement loud among the rocks . . .

A male voice—making a speech . . .

It was drowned in clapping. Brazier said quietly, "Sounded Norwegian."

Paul thought so too; and the music hadn't sounded at all Germanic. A door slammed like a distant pistol-shot, and the fiddle struck up again, then quietened as a woman's voice rose—some kind of folk song, solo. There was no glimmer of light in that direction, or anywhere else either.

"Go on down, Bomber. Tell Louis to put on a standing charge. First man to finish his scoff can come up and relieve me."

The day's run south would have taken all the guts out of the battery, and they'd need all it had to offer tomorrow. With nets to negotiate you could expect to need bursts of full power; and having made the attack, the only way to withdraw would be dived, and perhaps at some speed, in the initial stages ... He heard applause now, cheers and clapping and a general hubbub of party noise. With luck, the rumble of the Gardner wouldn't carry that high and that far; another hope was that if anyone did hear it and stop to listen they might think it came from farther out, in mid-fjord or even from the far side.

It still sounded menacingly loud when it started. The rocky cliffs enclosed the sound, magnifying it ... Then Gimber came up to take over. There was no chance of hearing any party noise now.

"Bomber tell you about the singsong?"

"Yeah. We had a listen in the hatch. Think they'll be listening to us, now?"

"Doubt it. It'd be muffled, anyway, could be coming from miles away."

"Sounds bloody loud to me." Gimber added, "Plenty of hash left, you'll be glad to hear."

"Good." He pointed astern. "That's the danger sector. We could dive if we had to—trim her down right here and use the induction as a snort. Wouldn't even need to break the charge—just dive, on the wire that's holding us."

"That's a thought!"

According to intelligence reports, the enemy were developing a new class of U-boat that could run submerged on its diesels, using a tube called a "schnorkel" for the air inlet. One or two of the X-craft men had tried a similar technique using the induction pipe, but it was slightly hazardous because there was no automatic shut-off when the top of the tube "drowned," and the helmsman had to be quick to shut the valve by hand.

Paul slid into the hatch. Gimber asked him, "Will you be coming up again when you've eaten?"

He'd stopped, halfway in. Diesel fumes acrid, more noticeable down at this level. The lop on the water was more noticeable too: if the wind held, it would be good cover for periscope work tomorrow. If the periscope worked ... He answered Gimber's question: "Expect so. Why?"

"Something I'd like to talk about. While there's time and—" he'd checked, and caught his breath: "Christ, look!"

There'd been a flicker of light reflected in his eyes. Whipping round—to face into what he'd called the danger sector—Paul was looking into a blaze of it, just momentarily, then distant and changing, lengthening, the sword-like beam of a searchlight which as it swung round level with the sea had passed over them, illuminating and throwing a huge shadow from the light-structure above them: now it was silvering high ground on the island of Aaroy—which was four miles from here—and then, scything on clockwise, sweeping over the forepart and bridge superstructure of a warship. A giant warship. Immensely long, flared foc's'l, twin gun-turrets wide, flattish, powerful-looking; the forebridge behind them had a similarly squat look about it, and was dwarfed by the colossal director-tower.

Unmistakeably, it was *Scharnhorst*. At anchor, in the lee of Aaroy island.

"Is she under way?"

"No." Paul was recovering from the shock of that sudden glimpse, that enormous enemy just across the water. It had almost literally taken his breath away. The searchlight's beam fingered a steeply slanted funnel-cap, then abruptly switched off and died back, leaving them blinded in the dark, the diesel banging away . . . Gimber asked, "What's that island called?"

"Aaroy . . . Hudspeth's bound to have seen her there." He was thinking aloud, more than talking to Gimber. "At least, I'd guess he would have."

"Not if he made the southward run deep like we did. He could be at the Brattholms with the others, expecting to find her in Kafjord in the morning."

Pure conjecture. They might all four be there, or some of them might not have made it. And there was no way of knowing when *Scharnhorst* might have moved—when, or for that matter why—out of the protection of her anti-torpedo nets. 26,000 tons of battleship, in an unprotected berth . . . There was no shred of light now, where a minute ago the colossus had been floodlit. It was dark in all directions and there'd be enemies in most directions, X-12 in the middle of them with her diesel grumbling throatily to itself, ignoring all of them . . . As to that question "why?"—well, the X-craft had been on their own for most of the past twenty-four hours, and there could have been all sorts of developments they'd have no way of knowing about. The battle group might be putting to sea, for instance—the report of *Tirpitz* changing her gun-barrels might have been wrong, or the intentions might have changed. He couldn't imagine they'd leave *Scharnhorst* for long in such an exposed position: she'd have to be only pausing there, on her way either in or out . . .

Unless there'd been a scare, one of the other X-craft detected, and the Bosch at panic-stations?

"Give me a shout if anything looks interesting, Louis."

Below, eating his supper and chatting with the others, he decided that before he went up to join Gimber he'd strip the periscope down again and dry it out. You couldn't hope to do anything about the source of the problem, the leak—which would have been an external job, and you couldn't show a light up there—so it would soon flood again, but at least he'd be starting this next vital phase with a periscope that worked.

"Best hash we've had yet. Whose masterpiece was it?"

Lanchberry's eyebrows hooped. "Skipper, I'm amazed you'd find it necessary to enquire."

Brazier had been checking over various pieces of equipment, including the packs of overland escape gear. He'd also examined and tested his own diving gear and the water-powered net-cutter—so Jazz Lanchberry said, staring meaningfully at Paul.

"Well, for God's sake, how many times is that?"

Brazier looked embarrassed. Lanchberry said, "Every five bloody minutes, that's all. Right, Bomber?"

"Better too often than not enough."

"Ah, there's wisdom for you!"

"Leaks can develop, Jazz, and valves can seize up, and . . ."

Paul asked him, "How about our stuff?"

Brazier nodded. "The DSEA sets are on the top line, skipper."

DSEA stood for Davis Submarine Escape Apparatus, and sets comprising face-masks, harness, oxygen bottles etcetera were provided for the three non-divers. But all such equipment was in Brazier's care for maintenance purposes.

"What time do we push off, skips?"

He put down his coffee mug. The air was as bitingly cold down here, with the rush of night air feeding the Gardner, as it was up top. He told them, "About one-thirty. We'll dive right away to eight feet and keep the periscope right up as long as the light's dim. The leak's most likely near the top, in which case if I can keep it above water long enough to get a bearing on *Lützow* before we go deep, we'll be on the right track."

Lanchberry nodded. "Good thinking."

"Well." Paul looked at Brazier. "He's paying me compliments now."

"Because you liked his hash."

"Oh, that's it."

None of them felt like sleeping. Camouflaging taut nerves was a full-time job. For Paul it wasn't only the prospect of tomorrow's action—complicated by his boat's two-fold disability—it was the possibility of there being no action, if the battle group were putting to sea. He didn't mention this possibility to the others.

Gimber, on the casing a bit later, began abruptly, "Better talk about it, don't you think?"

"About what?"

"Her. Jane."

"Oh." There was a pause. The engine rumbling on, and the light-structure a black etching against paler sky. Moonrise would throw no light into this chasm. Paul thought that if Gimber knew about his own affair with Jane, he'd been nursing the secret very guardedly. He said, "If you want to, Louis."

"Remember what I asked you, that last night in the depot ship—about looking after her, if I bought it?"

"Yes, I do. But you're alive and kicking, so we can forget it, can't we."

"I was pissed. And I knew it, and I was being careful. Particularly as we were just off. It wasn't exactly a time to pick a fight."

He'd have been sitting up here rehearsing this speech. In the middle of an Arctic night, surrounded by enemies, with his mind on a girl who'd two-timed him. If he knew that much, and it had begun to sound as if he might.

"I wouldn't say this is much of a time for it, either."

"It's the only time we've got, though, for talking." Gimber added, "I had an uncle who was terribly proud he'd 'gone over the top' in the last war. He said you saw things more clearly, when you were waiting for the whistle, although at the time you might be practically shitting yourself."

"So?"

"What I tried to say that night was—well, if I didn't get back and you did, would you please either leave her alone or—well, look after her."

"I think you did say exactly that. But what exactly you meant . . ."

"You know damn well, Paul!"

"Sorry, but I don't. For instance, by 'look after,' d'you mean marry her?"

"If, as I said, you got back and I didn't—"

"Louis—we're in the same boat, the odds are that either we both get home or neither of us does. But supposing it did happen as you suggest, why on earth should she want anything of the sort? From me, I mean?"

There was a pause. Gimber was a black shape hunched against the standard of the stub periscope. He said, "She's fond of you. Despite . . ."

"For God's sake, I'm fond of her, but . . ." He did a double-take. "Despite what?"

"The fact you've spent the last six months trying to get her into bed?"

Trying . . .

"I—what?"

The diesel's steady rumble filled the darkness around them.

"When did you dream this one up?"

"She told me herself. So I know it. Every time you were with her on your own. You never stood a chance—but she's sorry for you, she thinks it's just because you're lonely. Lonely, for Christ's sake! But that's how she is, she's so—understanding, sympathetic. And she's dead straight, she doesn't make things up, Paul, so I do know. She's—decent, and loyal to the memory of her husband—all right, still in love with him, it's been my main problem. I can tell you, I've been learning patience . . . But you, Paul—all you ever thought of was getting her to sleep with you!"

"Wasn't it all you thought of? With all the others?"

If she'd told him—and she obviously had—there wasn't much point denying it. He asked Gimber, "Wasn't it, until you got involved with Jane?"

"You admit it, then."

"I suppose one does—make passes . . . But look here, if you've had some such notion, why on earth would you have wanted me to go on seeing her, whenever I was down south?"

"It was the last thing I wanted, after she'd written to me about it. You were seeing her behind my back, by then. Not realising that she and I have no secrets from each other. She told me everything, you damn fool!"

Not quite everything . . .

"I'm sorry. I didn't mean to be abusive. But I happen to feel very strongly about her."

"I think I gathered that much."

"And you had when you were doing your best to seduce her, too. You also knew she was still in a state of—I don't know, shock, perhaps—from her husband's death."

"Well, I wouldn't altogether agree with you there. But can we cut this short now, Louis?"

"Just like that? Just . . ."

"I don't want to go over and over the same ground. Jane, as I saw her, was a very, very attractive girl, and very much a party girl. Think of that first time you produced her—that night at the Bag o' Nails?"

"She could give that impression, but . . ."

"Right. She did. You happened to take a different view, but my own was—is, I suppose—pretty well how it's always been, vis à vis girls at parties. Same as yours was too—and the fact you've fallen for her doesn't entitle you to call the kettle black, either. A year ago, if you'd taken a shine to some popsie I was nuts about, you'd have jumped in boots and all the minute my back was turned!"

"Not if I thought you were really, deeply . . ."

"Oh, balls!"

There was a stir below the hatch—one of the others coming up. Gimber began quickly, "What I'm asking you—look, if I get back, OK, no problem, I'll look after her, and believe me you won't get a look in. But if I don't,

Paul—well, I don't want her treated like some cheap floozie. Either leave her alone, or—"

"Skipper?" Bomber Brazier was speaking through the open hatch. "Anyone want to get his head down? I'd quite like some freshers."

"Hang on, Bomber. Give us room, and Louis'll be right down." He told Gimber, "All right. You have my word for it."

"Swear it?"

"If that's necessary. But we're both going to get home, so it won't arise, anyway . . . Will you go below now?"

You couldn't have too many bodies on the casing at one time, in case you had to dive in a hurry. Gimber said, climbing into the hatch, "I'm glad we've had it out. No hard feelings, Paul."

"Of course not."

Jane obviously had fed Gimber that line of bull. Perhaps to hide the less acceptable truth behind it? And having her cake and eating it—enjoying the physical affair while still presenting Gimber with the image he treasured. And of course, if at some later stage Gimber had discovered that she and Paul had been lovers, it wouldn't be her he'd have blamed.

Not bad, really. Watching the Bomber heave himself up through the hatch, he thought, Not bad at all . . . But it was also possible she hadn't thought it out as purposefully as that, that she'd have done it on impulse—being as mixed-up as Gimber seemed to think she was, still in shock from the death of the fighter-pilot husband whom it was fairly evident she'd also two-timed. Happy memories tinged with guilt—but some sense of achievement too, because otherwise she wouldn't have talked about it as she had!

He told himself, Forget it . . . In this time and place, it had been an extraordinary conversation. Louis, of course, must have had it churning around his head ever since they'd sailed from Loch Cairnbawn. On top of everything else, poor bastard . . . He looked round, at the vaguely defined bulk of his diver.

"Bomber, I'll tell you something. True love's a killer."

"Ah." There was a pause. Then: "Are you in love, skipper?"

"Like hell I am."

Brazier asked him, after another pause, "Starting out at one-thirty, how will it go for the firing periods?"

The operation orders laid down a schedule of "firing periods" and "attacking periods." The object was to reduce chances of X-craft blowing each other up. Attacking periods, which were for making the approach and placing side-cargoes under the targets, were from 0100 to 0800, 0900 to 1200, and 1300 to 1600, and the single hours in which charges could be set to explode were 0800 to 0900, 1200 to 1300 and 1600 to 1700.

He answered Brazier, "It should work out all right. Slip from here at one-thirty, and it'll be an hour before the light's much good. By that time I'll have her round to the north of this island, and up to then it'll be dark or semi-dark enough to show a lot of periscope—amongst other things, keeping the wet out, I hope. By about two-thirty I'll have a clear view up Langfjord—I hope. We draw a bead on the target, go down to eighty feet, run in about two miles—so we'll be at the nets by half-three, roughly. Allow one hour for you to go out and cut a hole and get back in when we're through it, half an hour to lay side-cargoes, and another hour to get out . . . That's maximum, allowing for snagging in nets, and so on, and with luck we'll do better. But at the latest we should be clear by six o'clock, which leaves us two hours in which to bumble round the corner into Stjernsund. So we'll be on our way out, and we'll have the headland—Klubbeneset—between us and the whumpfs."

"Just the job." Brazier approved. "More so for us than for the others down in Kafjord."

"Yeah. But I'd sooner be having a crack at the *Tirpitz* . . . I'm afraid the wind's going down again."

It had risen suddenly, and now it was dropping just as quickly. He'd had hopes of a broken surface, but by present indications there'd be another flat calm.

CHAPTER FOURTEEN

· · ·

"There's a big oiler in that cove. But *Lützow* is not, repeat not, in evidence."
He pulled his head back, thumbed the "down" button—for the first time in
about an hour. Gimber had glanced round at him sharply, so had Lanchberry;
there was a scowl of anxiety on Brazier's wide, stubbled face. As a highly-
trained diver who'd never dived in action yet, he'd been longing for this day,
and now like the other two he was shocked by the suggestion that their target
might not be here. Paul told them, "Too bright now. And last night's wind's
gone completely." Too bright for the periscope to be kept up any longer, he
meant; he'd had it up ever since they'd left the Langnesholm hideout in the
dark fifty-five minutes ago, and its prisms had so far stayed dry and clear.

So far, and probably no farther. And he had not made any sighting of his
target. At this point he'd have expected to have taken a bearing and gone
deep for the approach.

That cove—checking it on the chart—was called Ytre Koven. Half a mile
wide, three-quarters of a mile deep. A mile southwest of it was where *Lützow*
should have been.

Gimber suggested, without moving his eyes from the depthgauge and
bubble, "Could've been her we saw off Aaroy in the night?"

"That was *Scharnhorst.*"

"But she could be there too."

"It's possible . . . Fifty feet."

"Fifty."

Paul took a log reading and made a note of it. That might even have
been *Lützow's* searchlight, for all anyone here could know . . . He decided,
"We'll run one mile in, then take another look. If she's not there we'll have
to think again."

X-12 nosed downward. The list didn't hamper this kind of depth change, it only made her awkward to handle when as little as a foot or a few inches counted, when she was up close to the surface. One of the satisfactions of completing an attack would be that getting rid of the flooded side-cargo would put things back to normal. She'd be on an even keel, in proper control again, for the withdrawal through Stjernsund. It would indirectly affect one's state of blindness too: when she was in full control, in certain circumstances one might be able to ease her up to a position where she was just breaking surface, so you could use the bi-focal stub periscope. You wouldn't do it in the open or close to enemies, but in bad light or where there was some sort of surrounding cover it would be something to fall back on. Escaping through the sund, for instance. In fact the stub periscope's most useful service was in net-cutting operations. You'd have the boat nudged up against the net, keeping slow-speed pressure on it while her diver cut a hole, and through the stub you could watch it happening.

Gimber reported, "Fifty feet."

"Half ahead."

From here, even if one could have risked showing enough periscope—and had one that wasn't flooded—to see across to Aaroy, the western bulge of the island would have hidden the berth in which *Scharnhorst* had been lying last night. It was conceivable that *Lützow* could be with her. Leir Botn was a wide, well-sheltered bay, and if the two big ships were on their way to sea and had wanted a quick departure without the delay of net-gates having to be towed aside, it would have been a convenient anchorage, during some waiting period.

He checked the log again. Wondering whether there could be much point in continuing deeper into Langfjord. *Lützow* was much more likely to have moved to some new berth elsewhere. This could turn out to be a waste of time.

"Slow ahead. Twenty feet."

He hoped to God that *Tirpitz* was still in her berth in Kafjord. But when one thing changed, you had to be receptive to the possibility of everything else having changed too. All the detailed planning could have been shot to hell.

If *Lützow*'s not here, go for the *Scharnhorst?*

There was no latitude in the orders for switching targets. On the other hand one wouldn't be going over to the other side of the fjord to attack *Scharnhorst,* one would be searching for one's own target, *Lützow.* It was a reasonably logical supposition that since *Lützow* wasn't in her own berth, and one of the others had moved into Leir Botn, then she might be there too.

From here to the south coast of Aaroy would be a run of five or six miles. Two and a half or three hours, say. You'd have to get there, make the attack and then get round to the other side of the island—for protection against the blast of the explosions—before eight o'clock, the start of the first firing period.

It should be easy enough. With no nets to deal with, it would be a quick and uncomplicated attack.

Touch wood . . .

"Depth twenty feet." Gimber added, "Main motor's slow ahead."

"Let's have her at fifteen."

Light from the surface was gleamingly visible through the viewing ports, the thick glass windows at shoulder height on each side. The light was brightening as she rose towards it. He picked up the folded chart again—limp as damp blotting-paper. The gap between Aaroy and the mainland, at the island's eastern end, was only about a third of a mile wide, but in the middle of it the depth was shown as nine fathoms. It would be possible to carry out an attack and then continue out that way, out northward through the gap.

If the target wasn't here in Langfjord.

"Fifteen feet."

"Make it ten, now. Don't try to rush it, Louis."

Gimber grunted acknowledgement, fractionally changing the angle of the hydroplanes. At the same time he pushed the trim–pump lever over to port, to let a few pints in amidships.

Use the flooded side-cargo on that oiler?

At first thought of it, he dismissed the notion of what seemed like a waste of two tons of explosive. But there was also an attraction in it. For one thing, while not even the largest oiltanker was a target to compare with a major warship, its destruction would be a lot more useful than simply ditching a defective charge. Which he'd have done earlier if it hadn't proved impossible. Also, in doing it you'd be ridding yourself of a handicap, returning to full efficiency and still with a lethal punch in reserve for a better target.

"Ten . . ."

Gimber cut the report short, muttered, "Sorry . . ." She'd risen to eight feet, seven . . . A few more inches, and the stub periscope standard would have broken surface. In broad daylight and with coastlines less than a mile on each side. Hydroplanes hard a-dive: and he was flooding the midships tank again.

Seven and a half, eight . . .

She'd dip now, before he could get hold of her and bring her back up, in control. Passing twelve now, nose-down: and he'd reversed the action of the pump, sucking out the ballast he'd just put in. Working like a mad organist: muttering, "Bitch . . ."

Looking like a mad organist, too. And entitled to. He'd been resident in this tin drum nearly a fortnight.

"Take your time, Louis. No rush."

He had her in hand quickly enough: she was rising towards the ordered depth then, with the fore-and-aft bubble amidships. Paul reached for the rubber bag on its wandering lead, and pressed the button to start the periscope sliding up.

"Let's have her at nine and a half, if she'll wear it."

"Oh, she's learning who's boss."

The organist was in a good mood, this morning. Having got that stuff off his chest last night might have helped. After such a long time cooped up and under stress . . . Ten and a half feet now, ten . . . He had his eye at the rubber-rimmed lens, watching the bubbling changing colours as the top glass rose: then the tip broke out, an inch of window above the flat surface, Gimber reporting, "Nine and a half feet."

"Brilliant."

He could see through it, too. It wasn't perfect but it hadn't actually flooded yet. Gentle treatment was what it needed. He made a quick all-round check, then began to search carefully over the area where *Lützow* had been when the Spitfires had last been over taking photographs.

She wasn't there now. Right ahead were the buoys supporting her net-cage, and there was a launch moored at its inshore end. Nets hanging empty like an unmade bed. That launch would be for opening and shutting the net gate, for letting the occupant or attendant craft in and out.

Nothing else. He dipped the periscope—down a couple of feet, then up again, standard drill that made it less likely to be spotted—then trained left for a look straight up the fjord. He could see about five miles, some-what hazily, but apart from some fishing boats anchored inside a headland about a mile west of the unoccupied nets, there wasn't anything afloat or on the move.

"At least the periscope's behaving." As he said it, bubbles frothed up to drown the top glass, cutting off his view just as he'd begun to train right, to find the cove that had the tanker in it.

"Sorry, coming back up . . ."

"All right." Waiting for it, he told them, "*Lützow* isn't here. Her nets are, but she's gone." He had a clear view again suddenly. And a need to come to a decision: you couldn't ruminate for long, you had to make up your mind and act . . . The bearing of the oiler in Ytre Koven was—318 degrees. It was at anchor, and in quarter-profile: he'd be on her port bow if he steered directly into the cove from here.

"Come round to three-one-eight, Jazz . . . Forty feet. Half ahead."

Studying the chart again. About one mile to go. He took a log read-ing . . . Plenty of water all the way in, except only fifteen fathoms off the western point of the entrance. You wouldn't want to be deep at that point anyway. But mental arithmetic, as one looked further ahead, revealed com-plications which at first sight looked bad. He put the chart down on the storage locker, and laid a parallel rule across it: he saw at once that the key to his problem was that gap between Aaroy and the mainland.

"Course three-one-eight, sir."

Formality, from old Jazz . . . Crises affected people in odd ways. He explained to them—after Gimber had reported the depth as forty feet and the motor half ahead group down—"Here's what we do. Our target having removed herself. She may be south of Aaroy, with *Scharnhorst*—we'll see. But meanwhile we have this large oiler in Ytre Koven—here." He pointed to it on the chart. "We'll move in there now and drop the flooded side-cargo under her. It won't be wasted, and our performance will be improved. Then we'll buzz over and see if our target's there, otherwise find some other good home for the starboard bomb, off Aaroy . . . Any better ideas?"

Gimber asked him, "With a fairly long trip over, what about the firing period? Will we make it?"

"Should work out." He explained, "Ten to three now. We'll be in there and slipping the side-cargo in half an hour. Away again by, say, three-thirty. Five-hour fuse setting, the thing'll blow at about eight-thirty—right in the middle of the firing period . . . The run over to Aaroy—six miles, roughly, say three hours if we go easy on the battery, so we'll get there around six-thirty. There'll be no nets to hold us up—at least, I wouldn't expect any. *Scharnhorst* must be there just temporarily, and so would *Lützow* be, if she's there. If she is, we'll attack her—otherwise *Scharnhorst* gets lucky. Then we push on through the gap at the eastern end of the island—which'll give us protection from whatever whumpfs are going off. Also, we'll be on course for an exit via Stjernsund."

He checked the log again. Less than half a mile to go.

"One last look now. Slow ahead, fifteen feet."

Up by stages again, a few feet at a time. A complication was that you had to reduce to slow speed so the periscope wouldn't make more feather than necessary when it cut through the surface, but slowing made her less responsive to the hydroplanes just when you needed maximum control.

The gauge showed nine and a half feet when the periscope's top window broke out. Paul searched all round once, then settled his single eye on the oiler. She was about fifteen thousand tons, deep-laden, and quite modern.

"Steer one degree to starboard."

"Three-one-eight . . ."

There was a lighter secured to the oiler's port side and some boats at a timber jetty on the shore, but nothing else afloat and no sign of watch-keepers. No line of buoys, either, from which an anti-torpedo net might have been slung. He sent the periscope down.

"Forty feet. Bomber, you're out of a job again. No nets." Lanchberry murmured, with a glance at Brazier in his rubber suit and with the weighted boots beside him, "All dressed up and nowhere to go." Paul saw that she was nosing down past fifteen feet; he told Gimber, "Half ahead." Because she'd got down far enough for the wash not to show up on the surface, with her stern up-angled. He'd noticed cloud was gathering in the north and northwest, and he guessed the calm weather wasn't going to last long; it would still be reasonably sheltered inside the fjords, but the passage out to join *Setter* might be a bumpy one. If one made it that far. But it was pointless to anticipate: you simply had to press on, cope with each problem as it came up. Here and now it was a matter of running in blind, all the way to the target; she was too close in now to risk showing periscope.

He guessed the oiler would draw about thirty feet, so forty would be a good depth at which to run in under her. He checked the release-gear on the port side-cargo, making sure the wheel was free to turn, and the time-clock of the fuse mechanism. You had only to make the switch, set the clock to a delay of anything from one to six hours, then turn the wheel to release the charge, which would fall away from the side and sink to the bot-tom. Even if it hadn't already flooded—which it had—it would sink when it parted company with the boat's side, as its buoyancy chambers filled and weighted it. On second thoughts, he set the clock now, for a five-hour inter-val; it was one thing less to be done later when he might be busy, and the fuse wouldn't start running down until the switch was made.

Dark water outside the viewing ports was lighter when you looked up-wards. Daylight shimmered there, through forty feet of sea.

When the log showed a hundred yards to go, he ordered "Slow ahead."
Gimber's right hand moved to the control wheel, but he didn't take his eyes
off the trim. She was porpoising a little, just a foot or two each side of the
ordered depth, and entering the cove he'd be alert for freshwater patches
from mountain streams. In the reduced density you could drop like a stone
if you weren't ready for it. The motor's hum softened as she slowed. Paul
was watching through the viewing port on the port side, and his first sight
of the target was a dark cloud growing, obscuring surface radiance as the
midget crept into its shadow.

"Target's right ahead . . ."

A clang—from the starboard side, for'ard. She jolted, lurched over . . .

"Stop main motor."

Rolling back. There was a scraping sound from outside, and vibration—as if her plates were rubbing against rock. But—not rock, it was more
metallic. It was moving aft, down the starboard side.

"Hard a-starboard."

Four faces, and no expression at all on any of them . . . Paul had realised
what it was. Lanchberry spinning the wheel. Her bow had begun to rise
and Gimber was working to get it down again—which was essential, as
the tanker's keel would be only a few feet above her now. He could see
the curve of one bilge through the viewing port. It was the anchor cable
they'd hit. He'd thought from the angle at which the ship was lying and
the direction of his own approach that she'd pass well clear of it, but he'd
miscalculated.

The scraping ceased. He'd turned her around the cable, swung her after-
part clear of it: which was desirable, since the projecting hydroplanes would
have snagged on it. X–12 was sinking, meanwhile, as she'd lost way through
the water and the planes no longer gripped.

"Slow ahead. Midships."

The shadow was out to port now, and dimmed by distance. This was the
oiler's port bow they were on, of course; X–12 had slid inside the cable,
between its long slant and the target's forefoot, and the turn to starboard
had carried her away from where he had to put her.

Thirty-five feet on the gauge. Thirty-six.

"Port fifteen."

"Port fifteen." Lanchberry muttered, "Cannon off the red." He added, "Fifteen of port wheel on, sir."

"That was her cable we side-swiped. Let's hope no-one was looking."

Brazier put his hands together as if in prayer, and murmured, "Arf, arf."

"Midships."

Now she'd turned back towards her target; its shadow extended from right ahead to about thirty on the port bow, filling half the area of the viewing port when he had his face close up to it. He moved to the stub periscope, through which as they closed in he'd have a clearer view.

"Wheel's amidships."

"Steady as you go."

"Steady. Two-four-one."

"Steer two-four-oh."

The outlines of the cloud hardened, became curved steel encrusted with marine growth. This oiler wasn't as clean underneath as she was up top, but X-12 was about to save her the trouble of dry-docking. Coming in on the target's port side and on roughly a forty-degree track. He checked the time—it was 3:19—and glanced from there to the side-cargo's fuse-clock, ensuring that he had it set right, to explode five hours after he activated it. Six hours being the maximum you could put on it, but five being right for the firing period. In a minute he'd need only to touch the switch, wind the handle of the releasing gear, and—away, the hell out, fast.

Well, not fast, exactly. This was a tortoise, no hare. And there'd be plenty of time to get over to Aaroy.

The oiler's shadow blotted out all the surface light. X-12 was right under her.

"Starboard twenty."

"Starboard twenty, sir."

"Depth's very important now, Louis."

Because with that much rudder on her she'd have a tendency to rise, and he didn't want to bump or scrape her on the target's bottom. There'd be people in there with ears—and nerves. Nearly all of them sound asleep, but a resounding clang right under them could change all that . . . Lanchberry reported, "Twenty of starboard on." She was turning rapidly, as he'd wanted just about under the centreline of the oiler. But he was going to release the side-cargo closer to her stern, where an engine-room might be the focal point for an upward blast into the ship's guts.

All those sleeping Germans: without the slightest notion of what they'd be getting for their breakfast.

"Midships. Meet her."

"Meet her . . ."

"Steady!"

"Steady—two-seven-eight, sir."

"Steer that."

He was back at the viewing port, close to the release gear of the side-cargo; with his face close against the port, to cut out reflections, he could see the barnacled curve of the tanker's belly as X–12 passed slowly under it. Gimber, looking up frequently at the other port, had the boat steady and level at forty feet. Paul said, "Here we go, then." He put the switch to "on": the light came on in the clockface. The fuse was now activated, and in five hours—eight twenty-five—it would detonate two tons of Torpex. He used both hands to turn the wheel, which was like a motorcar's steering wheel—anti-clockwise, to release the charge.

He'd turned it as far as it would go, and nothing had happened.

"Still there."

Turning the wheel back a little, he jerked it over hard, putting weight on the last part of its travel. It came up short and hard, and wouldn't budge another centimetre, but the side-cargo was still attached, with its fuse running. He tried once more.

No bloody good . . .

Almost as if this was only confirmation of something he'd expected. Recalling the doubt he'd had yesterday, when he'd wanted to set it to "safe," and a signal from *Sea Nymph* on the day before the crew-change: X–8 having had to ditch her side-cargoes, and one of them exploding and wrecking her. There'd have been some good reason for ditching them, and they'd surely have been set to "safe"—and still exploded . . .

"Give you a hand, skipper." Brazier, coming aft from the W and D. "Sharp kick may be all it needs." Gimber's left hand went to the trim-pump lever, to compensate for the transfer of that not inconsiderable weight. At least Brazier had taken off his lead-weighted diver's boots. He began trying to make the releasing gear work, as if he'd thought he had some magic touch which Paul lacked.

"Might try the rod."

It was a heavy bar with a screw-thread on it, which you could wind out through a special gland in the ship's side. It was stowed nearby, with a lashing on it, and Brazier was on his side, reaching between other gear to free it. X–12 was still under her target but about to run out under the target's stern.

Brazier got the rod free. He shipped it, fitting its end into the socket designed to receive it. It was a device intended for checking that the side-cargo had dropped away, not a tool for shifting it. Still, it might help—and God only knew what else . . . He was cranking it around.

"Main motor stop. Port twenty. Slow astern."

To hold her more or less under the oiler's screws, and turn her. The charge might release suddenly, and you wouldn't want it any farther away than this from the target. Taking a look through the stub periscope he could see the oiler's screws and the heavy black-painted rudder up there in shimmery, greenish water. It slid away to the left as the X-craft turned, stern-first.

"No joy, skipper." Brazier had the rod in but he couldn't turn it any further. "Won't budge."

Lanchberry muttered, "Bugger's bloody well got to budge."

Gimber working desperately at the trim . . .

"Far as it'll go." Brazier scowled at the rod, rubbed his head, as if to stimulate some alternative way of doing it. Paul told Gimber, "Stop main motor. Slow ahead."

"Thank God." Gimber's mutter was addressed to himself, expressing relief at being able to put the screw ahead again. The stopping and going astern, turning inside her own length with the oiler's screws only a few feet above the casing and Brazier's weight shifting aft at that same crucial time, had not provided him with much light relief. Brazier was having another shot at moving the wheel of the releasing gear, perhaps hoping that with the disengaging rod wound in there now it might have some effect. You could see—looking back and up through the ports—the glint of daylight receding, the oiler's screws against the last crescent shine of it, wavery like a mirage. X-12 was now creeping the other way, towards her intended victim's bow, but under her port side instead of the centreline.

"Come two degrees to starboard, Jazz."

"One double-oh."

"Switch it off, skipper, d'you think?"

"God, yes." He reached to the switch, and flipped it up. You couldn't turn the clock's fuse-setting back, but you could deactivate it by the switch. The fact you couldn't turn back the timesetting meant that whatever alternative plan you fixed on now, you'd be stuck with a five-hour delay on this fuse. Or six-hour: it could be advanced, but not retarded.

Brazier was still persevering with the wheel. Gimber, who'd been pumping ballast for'ard from the midships tank, had just pulled the lever back into its pump-stopped, valves-shut position, having compensated for the Bomber's move.

The Bomber said, "You didn't switch off, skipper."

But he had.

He'd also checked that she was middled under the oiler. "Come back to oh-nine-eight, Jazz."

The light still glowed on the fuse-clock's face. He flipped the switch the other way—to "on"—then back to "off" again. The light still burned; the fuse was still activated and running down. It was an enclosed circuit, you couldn't get at the wiring—which was just as well, because if you'd tried to you'd quite likely have short-circuited the clock and fired the charge.

Four hours, fifty-six minutes to run.

He announced, for the information of Gimber and Lanchberry, also as a start towards rationalising the situation in his own mind, "We have a side-cargo that won't leave us, and its fuse won't de-activate."

He'd had no nightmares since the crew-change. This was understandable, he thought: once you'd started, you were no longer projecting, anticipating. But this was the stuff of nightmares now—so much so that you felt there had to be some way of snapping out of it, waking up. Solutions ran through his mind like high-speed film. Bottom her here, set the other side-cargo to a shorter fuse, and abandon ship by DSEA. Well, you couldn't. You'd give the game away, wreck the others' chances—let *Tirpitz* off the hook. So—all right, drop the starboard cargo with a five-hour delay on it, get over to Aaroy with this port one still ticking, bottom under *Lützow* if she was there or *Scharnhorst* if she was not, and abandon—by DSEA, one at a time, through the W and D. You'd have lost nothing, that way—except all four of you in the bag, POWs.

"Skipper."

Brazier looked as if he'd had an idea. Paul was conscious of the others' eyes and ears on him: they were waiting for his decision, the way out. Conscious also of the oiler's bulk overhead, shutting out nine tenths of the filtered surface light. Gimber had more up-angle on the planes than she'd been carrying before; he'd overdone the flooding for'ard by a pint or two, must have decided to leave it alone until Brazier moved back to his kennel. Still dickering with that second plan, Paul was also troubled by his uncertainty about the gear in general: when so much of the system had gone haywire, should one trust in a five-hour fuse-setting giving you five hours before it blew?

He'd glanced at Brazier. "Yes?"

"I'll go out, skipper—release it from outside. It'll only be hanging on by an eyelash, all I'd have to do is prise."

"No."

It was his first mistake.

Trench said, "As everyone knows now, *Lützow* had avoided the submarines who were waiting just off those fjords by steering due west instead of northwest or north, which was what anyone would have expected. The submarines who'd towed the X-craft over were positioned in an arc designed to intercept a sortie aimed at interfering with QP 16—which was the whole object of the exercise, naturally."

He picked up a stalk of straw and drew it across the top of the wire cage. The mink dashed out of her nesting box, and the same hand that held the straw moved to insert a metal shield between the box and the wire run, thus shutting Mum away from her litter. You could see that this annoyed her. She was coal-black, with a glossy sheen to her slim, agile body, and small, furious eyes. Trench dipped his one hand into the straw of the box and brought it out full of what looked like very small chippolata sausages.

He was counting them. "Eight." He told the mother, "There's a clever girl."

"Eight's good, is it?"

This was May—kitting time for minks, worldwide. He nodded. "We get as many as eleven or twelve in a litter occasionally, but the average is about five." He'd put them back, and shut the lid. As he lifted the shield out, the mother whipped in like a streak of ebony. He made some cryptic note on the card above that box, and moved on through the shed.

"It's as well to bear in mind that one knows a lot more than one knew then. All I was aware of at the time was that *Lützow* and nine big destroyers were at sea and hunting for my convoy. Might run into them at any minute—or might not. As I've explained, the weather was deteriorating and visibility was rotten. One minute you'd see perhaps five or six miles, and the next perhaps not even fifty yards."

"Oddly enough it was clear and calm that morning in Altenfjord. There'd been some wind during the night, but it had dropped again."

"I dare say. Conditions are often highly localised, up there. But our weather was moving in towards the coast in any case . . . Oh, I did also know that our battle squadron had sailed from Iceland. The heavy mob's usual tactic, if they had nothing else to go on, would be to steer straight for the enemy's base—either to cut him off and force him to action, or scare him into thinking he'd be cut off if he didn't get the hell out fast. Which as you know he usually did—largely because Hitler's orders to his stooges effect-ively vetoed acceptance of any risk. They could attack only if they were in overwhelming strength. He hated his big-ship Navy, you know. Under the skin, anyway. Its commanders had always tended to be gentlemen—which Adolf so plainly was not. At the same time he was highly protective of it—any loss reflecting personally on him. The *Graf Spee* affair was a prime example, wasn't it—scuttle, so nobody could say they'd' sunk her. And *Lützow*—I suppose you know, her name originally was *Deutschland,* but the dread of having his *Deutschland* sent to the bottom, and the ridicule that would follow—well, he had her re-christened."

"She'd turned south, incidentally."

"Yes. But I had no way of knowing it. In fact all I had opposing me were the destroyers. Nine, against my five, and much more heavily armed—but you know all that. The first real news I had of them—and bear in mind I'd no doubt *Lützow* would be behind them somewhere in the sleet-showers—was an enemy report from *Legend.* She was on the starboard wing of the screen—and as I was expecting any attack to come from the south, it was rather a surprise. It was less than an hour after sunrise, we'd fallen out from dawn action stations and redeployed into day cruising formation. *Legend's* signal told me she had two ships in sight to the nor'ard—on a converging course, speed estimated as about eight knots."

"No radar contact?"

"No. Conditions were bloody awful, of course. And within half a minute of that signal, *Legend* reported the enemy had turned away and gone out of sight. I told her captain—John Ready—to investigate and *Leopard,* who was the nearest to her, to support her. I stayed with the convoy, but had *Laureate* and *Lyric* form line astern of me on its other bow, and for the time being I left *Foremost* where she was, astern. There was a minesweeper each side, and the trawlers were on the quarters. I'd alerted the new commodore—Claypoole—to the situation, of course, and the tactics we'd adopt if surface action did develop were all cut and dried. Of course it had to depend on which way the cat jumped—the cat, as I believed then, being *Lützow.*"

He'd stopped at another nesting box. The whole of the shed, which was about forty yards long, was noisy with the squeaking of baby minks, but somehow he could tell when he was passing a box that had a newly arrived family in it. He'd stop, put his ear to it for confirmation, then go through his counting and card-marking routine.

"Only three. Below par, you see. What we do is we take a couple of kits from one of the outsize litters and add them to the very small ones. If it's done in the first few days the mothers don't know the difference."

Walking on. This was only the second of about a dozen sheds. He told me, "It was three quarters of an hour before *Legend* established contact. I heard gunfire before *Ready* came through on TBS. Two signals—first his own saying he and *Leopard* were in action, engaging four enemy destroyers who were on a parallel course, range four miles; then a report from *Leopard* that a larger but unidentified ship astern of the destroyers had opened fire. Only its gun-flashes had been seen, from *Leopard*'s director tower. To me, this could only mean one thing—*Lützow*. In fact it must have been a destroyer who'd become separated from those others, but in the circumstances it was a natural enough conclusion to jump to. It left five enemy destroyers not yet accounted for, but I obviously had to move out and join in. I told Crockford of *Foremost* to act in accordance with previous orders, and invited Claypoole—the American vice-commodore who'd taken over Insole's job—to make a ninety-degree diversion to port. Crockford knew what his job was—as the convoy turned away, if there was an enemy in sight he'd lay smoke between them. The sweepers were also to make smoke, but they were to stay with the convoy, chivvy the lads along and see they hung together. *Foremost* would hold the middle ground—and she had the speed, of course, to put herself and her smoke wherever it might be needed. One thing I ought to tell you. Crockford had talked to me that morning, over the radio-telephone, when we were all at dawn action stations. Around two a.m. that would have been. He told me Nick Everard had been up and dressed and wandering about the ship. He still didn't know what was happening, or why. He had some impression that he was taking passage in order to take up a new appointment—a cruiser squadron, Crockford said he'd mentioned, and he was disturbed by a belief that he hadn't been able to say goodbye to his wife. Anyway, they'd got him back to his cabin and persuaded him to turn in, and so on. That young doctor I'd had transferred into *Foremost* to look after him, unusual name, but oh, Cramphorn—got it rather heavily in the neck from me for having let it happen. He was as shocked as anyone, I think; he'd fallen asleep or gone to the heads, I don't remember. He was responsible, but well, I gave him hell, I'm afraid. It wasn't fair—he couldn't have slept for about a week, poor fellow. But Nick could have gone over the side, you see, in the state he was in—that was what made me tear Cramphorn to shreds over TBS. I'd told Crockford to put him on. Crockford was rather a quiet, easy-going sort of man—I made up for that." He shrugged. "You know how I admired Nick Everard. And it was his life I was concerned for."

Pausing near the door at the far end of the shed, Trench was obviously deeply concerned about the way he'd treated the young doctor. I could well understand his anger: he'd picked Cramphorn himself, as one who'd do a good job conscientiously and keep his—Trench's—hero alive for him. I liked Trench already, but I found myself liking him the more for this display of a nagging conscience over what was really quite a small thing. Cramphorn would surely have accepted the blame, and he'd have seen the rebuke as justified, particularly so from Trench; and he'd soon have forgotten it altogether. Whereas Trench had never forgotten, and still blamed himself for having been too harsh.

As a matter of fact I've encountered this kind of thing before. Old men's pigeons coming home to roost, and in their transit of the years changing into vultures.

I said, "Cramphorn would hardly have expected congratulations."

Trench pushed the door open. He said without looking round, "I was tearing a strip off him at two-thirty. By seven he was dead."

I caught on, then. Like a punch on the nose. Astonished that I'd been so stupid. Because obviously. I'd known . . .

"Where was I . . . Oh, yes. Belting out north-westward, *Laureate* and *Lyric* astern of me, thirty-four knots across a long, flattish swell and with a gusty snowstorm in our faces. Impossible to use binoculars—half the time you couldn't even see your own foc's'l. I had *Legend* and *Leopard* on radar by that time, I think—must have had—and I was getting frequent reports from John Ready over TBS. His exchange of gunfire with the four Huns—or five, counting the one astern of them that was supposed to be a heavy cruiser and which I was intending to attack with torpedoes if I could get into position to do so—well, those exchanges had been brief and sporadic, just a couple of salvoes snapped off between snow-showers. Well, you can imagine."

I could, indeed ... *Moloch, Laureate* and *Lyric* in line-astern, thrashing across the long rolling swells with spray sheeting back from high-curving bow-waves, their stems plunging and then soaring, tossing green sea back across the guns; snow blinding, driving horizontally, the ships racing directly into it and into the icy wind carrying it. Guns' crews and torpedo crews, oilskinned and tin-hatted at their weapons, needing to hold on and to watch footing and balance on steel decks often awash and constantly tilting, lifting and dropping through thirty feet or more a dozen times a minute. Trench was on his high seat, in the port for'ard corner of *Moloch*'s bridge, with—behind him—his first lieutenant and torpedo officer, Henderson, at the torpedo director sight, navigator Jock McAllister at the binnacle, Sub-Lieutenant Cummings taking reports from plot and radar, yeoman of signals Halliday and other bridge staff—a signalman, lookouts, messengers, communications numbers—crowding the pitching, jolting, spray-swept platform. Abaft and above their heads the director tower trained slowly to and fro, searching out gaps in the surrounding curtains of foul weather—Gareth Williams, gunnery officer, with his rate officer beside him, presiding over director layer and director trainer in the front seats. If and when there was anything to shoot at, all the guns would be aimed and fired from here.

Cummings had answered a call on the radar voicepipe. He reported, his voice pitched high over the racket of ship and sea, "Radar has three surface contacts, oh-two-one to oh-three-seven, six point five miles, sir!"

Trench leant against a supporting pillar, doing his one-handed pipe-stuffing act. He told me, "They could only be Germans, of course, split

off from the bunch who'd been in action with *Legend* and *Leopard,* I presumed. I had them—John Ready's two ships—fine-ish on the bow, on the
radar screen and liable to come in sight any moment if the visibility lifted.
They'd lost contact with their Germans at that point. I was trying to get
some more detailed information out of radar when John piped up on TBS;
he was in action again, with two destroyers who'd appeared out of a snowstorm ahead of him, crossing his bows—steering something like south, in
fact. So it was obvious this enemy force had divided. And there were still
some who hadn't shown up at all. My guess was they'd be screening *Lützow,*
and I had a nasty premonition: half the enemy destroyer force, *Lützow* with
them, attacking from the south with nobody except *Foremost* and those tid-
dlers between the convoy and annihilation, I and my lot having been lured
away northward, distance between us increasing every minute . . . But the
enemy were here, you see, and what's more at least one group of them was
steering south towards the convoy, very clearly couldn't be ignored. I had
no evidence of attack coming in from any other quarter, remember: in fact I
still reckoned *Lützow* was somewhere up on this side . . . Anyway—two lots
of Germans, *Legend* and *Lyric* sparring with one team, and the other—radar
now informed me, or the plot did—also steering south. I did about the only
thing that seemed to make sense and answer obvious requirements—told
John Ready to drive his pair away from the convoy, close the range and
either sink them or force them to turn away but for Christ's sake not to
let them work round to the south of him and get at the convoy—and I
turned away to starboard to intercept the others. In fact I turned my three
ships into line abreast—a Blue turn, happened to be a convenient way of
doing it, and also put me in a position to attack with torpedoes if these
contacts should happen to include the *Lützow*—which seemed possible,
even likely, in view of that earlier report from *Leopard.* Radar range had
come down to something like eight thousand yards, we were closing fast
and I knew we might suddenly find ourselves looking right up the barrels
of those eight-inch guns."

Tubes were turned out and ready, with depth-settings of sixteen feet
on the torpedoes. In each of the three British destroyers one quadruple

mounting was turned out to port and one to starboard, allowing for immediate reaction either way, depending on when and where the enemy appeared. All three ships beam-on to the swell, and rolling—Trench said—"like buggery." Guns as well as tubes were ready—shells in the loading-trays, layers' and trainers' pointers following the director's. Below, in the transmitting station they were waiting for information from the director tower and radar, figures for enemy course, speed, range and inclination; one's own ship's course and speed were fed automatically into the computing system, and already in it were such factors as wind direction and velocity, atmospheric pressure and temperature, all the things that complicate the problem of translating the sighting of an enemy into straddling him with your shells.

Trench observed—breaking into my mental reconstruction of a scene he'd just lightly sketched—"All be over by Monday. As you'll have noticed, only a very few haven't kitted yet."

We were talking about minks again. It took a moment to readjust. I said, "They seem very efficient, reproductively. Don't you ever get any that are sterile?"

"Well, they get weeded out, you know. But ninety per cent of it's simply a question of diet. And at mating time every female gets covered twice, by two different males." He shut that box, withdrew the shield, and marked the mother's card.

"Your records have to be kept very accurately, I suppose—which ones have bred with which, and so on?"

"Certainly." He turned, and moved on down the aisle; a big, shambling figure, ears apparently tuned to the squeaks even when he was talking. But it was only the cages with unmarked cards that caught his attention, I realised. He told me, pausing again, "When I was just starting in this business, an old mink hand told me that if a pair of his animals didn't react too enthusiastically to each other, his method was to put 'em together in a sack and whirl it round his head for a minute or two. When he let 'em out, they'd be at it hammer and tongs." He checked a card, put it down again. "Don't know if that's ever been tried on human beings. For impotence or frigidity, what have you." He glanced round at me as he started off again between the ranks of boxes and cages. "Where were we?"

We were in the Barents Sea.

"Visibility opened up as suddenly as drawing curtains, and we were about three thousand yards short of a line-ahead formation of Narvik-class destroyers steering south at about ten or twelve knots. Three of them. No sign of *Lützow*, of course. We opened fire and turned to starboard, parallel to them—I'd no thought of wasting torpedoes on such a chancy target as destroyers, even big blighters like these, when I had reason to believe there was much bigger game in the offing, but it must have looked to those Krauts like a torpedo attack, and they turned away and increased to full speed. At least I imagine it was torpedoes they were scared of. They heeled away, cracking on full power and opening fire a few seconds after we had. Our first salvoes were only from A and B guns, of course, and one reason for turning was to open the A-arcs, get X and Y guns into action. The range was close, and I saw a hit almost immediately on one German's stern; I was told afterwards there'd been two or three, just from the for'ard guns before we'd got ourselves round. Most of the enemy's splashes went up short—very large splashes too, compared to our own—but I heard a few whistle over, and *Laureate* took a direct hit on her A gun. It wiped out the gun's seven-man crew and of course wrecked the mounting. Those five-inch bricks played hell with a destroyer's light armour—as we were to see demonstrated much more clearly very soon afterwards. But it was over almost as soon as it started, this phase. The Narviks could easily have out-run us, and they were running, and I wasn't prepared to be drawn any farther away from my convoy. I was in the process of turning my three ships back, then, when Batty Crockford of *Foremost* came up on TBS rather excitedly to tell me he was in action against another four enemy destroyers who'd come belting up from the southeast. Very close to that premonition I'd had, you see. Except no *Lützow*—this far. I was still expecting her to show up at any moment, and the likely place for her to appear now seemed to be in the south, behind these newcomers. I remember thinking I should have backed that hunch . . . Anyway, Claypoole had turned the convoy ninety degrees to starboard, now. Back to its original course, in fact. *Foremost* was laying smoke and from time to time nipping out through it to loose off a few shots at the enemy—one of which might even have been *Lützow,* for all I knew, and in that bad visibility. As you'll know yourself, in conditions of that kind and the mild confusion one tends to get when a number of ships are in action here and there, reports have to be," he shrugged, "sorted out, interpreted . . . But Crockford was actually talking to me on the radio-telephone when *Foremost* was hit by one of those five-point-ones. He turned back into his own smoke—they had his range, and they'd surely have finished him in the next few minutes if he'd held on as he was. They were holding off, for the moment, presumably wanting to eliminate him so they could then move in unopposed to do a thorough job on the convoy. Rather typical of their tactics, actually. But—well, my three ships were under helm, turning south—our little fracas being over, those three Huns high-tailing it into the sleet, and the convoy under close, immediate threat. *Foremost,* too. Which as you can imagine was very much in my mind. I told John Ready in *Legend* to get himself and *Leopard* down there fast—if by this time he wasn't otherwise engaged—and there we were, split-arsing south."

"This must have been about four o'clock?"

Trench considered it: then nodded. "Something like that."

CHAPTER FIFTEEN

· · ·

Time: 0343. The flooded side-cargo still clung to her, and its fuse was still active. He'd been manoeuvring her for the past fifteen minutes or so under the oiler's deep belly, keeping her in its shadow so that if the cargo should suddenly give up and slip away its later eruption wouldn't be wasted. He'd considered trying to wipe it off by running the midget's port side against the anchor cable which she'd hit during the approach, but there'd be a risk of raising an alarm—there might also be a limit to the rough treatment to which you could subject a two-ton charge of high explosive.

He was looking up through the viewing port, seeing the target's propellers and rudder pass slowly overhead again. Gimber had been doing a very good job, considering how clumsy she was to handle with this list on her, and the close confines of the space in which he was having to turn her.

You couldn't hang around forever, though. Times, distances, firing-periods—and other side-cargoes that might already be lying on the bottom of the fjords with their fuses running—all contributed to a sense of urgency.

"All right. Listen."

Heads turned. Gimber's face like a death-mask, Lanchberry's drawn but calm, the Bomber's questioning. He still wanted to go out through the W and D in his diving gear and try to free the side-cargo from the outside, and he didn't understand why Paul had refused the offer.

Paul told them, "Only one way out of this balls-up. We dump the starboard side-cargo here, with a five-hour delay on it. Then we nip over to Aaroy and bottom ourselves under *Lützow* if by chance she's there, or otherwise under *Scharnhorst.*"

Scharnhorst would be a much more satisfying target, but they'd been detailed for *Lützow* and if she was within reach she was the one to hit.

He finished, "Then we abandon ship by DSEA, giving ourselves plenty of time to do it in good order, with the Bomber out first to give us a hand out and shut the hatch behind each man as he emerges. The good side of this is that we make the best use of ourselves we can—in the circumstances—with neither side-cargo wasted. The drawback is we become POWs, instead of getting away, which would have been very nice but I personally wouldn't have put any money on it."

Gimber said, "Nor would I." He nodded. "I'd say you're right, Paul. No option, really."

Lanchberry nodded. Brazier continued to look puzzled, like a student in class who doesn't want to admit he hasn't understood. Paul was troubled for the moment by a new thought. The hope of taking plenty of time over the DSEA escape—it might not be all that practicable. They'd have to get out not too long in advance of the firing period which began at eight o'clock, because abandoning too soon could give *Tirpitz* time to shift out of her berth and dozens of patrol boats could start dropping depthcharges. One had to think of the other X-craft, not only X-12. He didn't say anything about this, as it wasn't strictly necessary at this stage, but he could foresee that waiting around on the bottom under the target until nearly eight, with their own charge set to explode at 0825 but on its recent showing hardly the most reliable piece of equipment—well, there'd be more comfortable situations.

Even without that thought in their heads, the others weren't looking too happy. Too many things had been going wrong, and not knowing where their target was didn't help.

"Stop the motor. Starboard twenty."

New technique for turning her in the restricted area. When the screw stopped and she lost most of her forward impetus so that her planes ceased to grip the water, her tendency—since Gimber had her trimmed slightly heavy for'ard—was to sink. There was plenty of water between the oiler's keel and the bottom of the cove, so there was room for this, and there was just enough residual way on her to push her round to the reciprocal of her previous course. You accepted a change of depth and the turn was made in silence—and deeply enough so that any German crewman leaning over the rail up there would be unlikely to spot the whale-like intruder.

Lanchberry said, "Twenty of starboard wheel on . . . Skipper—question?"

"Go ahead."

"Why not let the Bomber have a go at shifting the fucking thing?"

He explained. It would take too long and it might not work. It might even explode it. By the time Brazier had gone through the routine of shutting himself in the W and D and then flooding it, equalising internal pressure with that of the sea outside so that he could then open the hatch and climb out, and had then done his stuff with the side-cargo—which might or might not have been effective—and come back inside, drained down the W and D into its operating tank so he could then open up and reappear among them—well, you'd have lost valuable time, possibly achieved nothing at all. He explained also that time was precious because the trip over to Aaroy had to be completed long enough before the start of the firing-period for the job to be done and the DSEA escape completed; it would take between three and four hours at normal dived speed, conserving battery power, or as little as two hours if it didn't matter what happened to the battery.

"If your effort didn't pay off, Bomber, we'd be a lot worse off than we are now. Besides which you might blow us up."

It was 0348 now. Twenty-three minutes since he'd activated the firing mechanism on the flooded side-cargo. That fuse now had four hours, thirty-seven minutes to run. If the clock could be relied on . . . It could be given an extra hour, of course, by increasing the delay to its maximum of six hours, but that would trigger an eruption in the middle of Altenfjord in a "safe" period—just when Don Cameron, Godfrey Place, Henty-Creer and Hudspeth might be withdrawing northward.

"Main motor slow ahead."

Gimber wound the hand-wheel clockwise. X-12 had drifted down to nearly fifty feet—to very near the bottom—and also outward, away from the target's side. You could see its shape up there still but it was no longer black, vague and shimmery-green against surrounding silver.

"Bring her to two-nine-five, Jazz."

"Two-nine-five, aye aye . . ."

He wondered if this other side-cargo was going to release, now. When one part of the equipment failed, you tended to distrust the rest of it. He edged over to that side, casting a glance over the releasing wheel and the fuse-clock, then looking up through the viewing port at the hardening underwater outline of the oiler as they rose closer and turned in under it.

"Course two-nine-five."

And still coming up. Gimber was flooding compensatory ballast into the midships trim-tank as she approached the depth ordered.

"Forty-five feet will do."

"Forty-five."

Allowing an extra margin overhead so there'd be less danger of scraping or bumping the hull above them. Gimber eased the pump-lever back. The reason she became lighter as she rose was that in shallower, therefore less dense water, the hull expanded enough to increase the volume and weight of the water she displaced. As had been discovered by Archimedes, a body immersed in water experiences an upthrust equal to the weight displaced; so the increased upthrust now—"upthrust" meaning buoyancy—had to be countered by taking in more ballast. Conversely, on her way down he'd had to pump a few gallons out, or the dive would have got out of control. Paul had learnt about the Principle of Archimedes originally in a physics class in Connecticut, USA, then had it driven home to him in the first hour of the submarine training course. This, now, was a practical application of the classroom lesson—under an enemy ship in an enemy anchorage while a time-fuse buzzed away the minutes.

"Forty-five feet."

She was under the oiler and near enough in the middle—or would be, after a slight drift onward as she turned. He told Lanchberry, "Port ten, and steer two-seven-eight."

"Port ten . . ."

He set the clock to the five-hour mark. Gripping the releasing wheel then, staring up through the port at the dark swell of the oiler's bilge. It seemed to swivel very slowly as the midget completed her turn. And now was as good a time as any. He had to switch on, to activate the clock, then turn the wheel: and if this one didn't separate either . . .

But the switch surely wouldn't fail as well. Unless the whole lot were defective. The other boats—the *Tirpitz* lot, too? It wasn't impossible: one of the things nobody had been able to rehearse had been live firings. But if this one didn't release it wouldn't make all that much difference, except to the oiler, in which at this moment—0351—a whole crew would be asleep, oblivious of the threat beneath them. They'd be spared and that was the only real difference there'd be; you'd be taking two un-detachable side-cargoes across the fjord instead of only one.

He pressed the switch. The light on the clock came on, and its motor started.

"Now here goes."

Lanchberry raised his crossed-fingers hand. Gimber murmured, "God bless." Bless whom, Paul wondered as he pushed the releasing wheel around. He heard the securing links snap away, then the rip of the copper sealing-strip peeling off; this was a sure indication that the side-cargo was actually separating from the hull, its buoyancy chambers filling to drag it down. He might have imagined it, but it felt as if it gave her a small nudge of encouragement as it went.

Bad luck, for those slumbering tankermen. Really very bad.

"Port fifteen."

The course to get her to the south coast of Aaroy but clear of a one-fathom hazard on the island's southwest corner would have been 110 degrees. But the tide had turned about an hour ago and would now be ebbing strongly. A course of 115 would offset the tidal drift, and still just clear Langnesholm if he happened to be overcompensating: there were no guaranteed-accurate figures for tidal flows available. He thought he'd bring her up in that area—about 3000 yards out from this cove—for a check, but the periscope might have flooded completely by that time and you had to be prepared to make the whole transit blind. And then—well, play it off the cuff.

"Steer one-one-five, Jazz."

It would be safer to stay deep the whole way over. If there'd been any alarm raised—one of the X-craft sighted, or submarines' presence even suspected—there'd be a lot of sharp eyes busily looking for periscopes. He thought his estimates were safe enough to rely on.

"Course one-one-five. Sir."

"What makes you so respectful all of a sudden, Jazz?"

"Thought you'd like it." Lanchberry glanced to his left, at Brazier. "Can't please some people."

"Eighty feet, Louis."

"Eighty . . ."

Battery power did not need to be conserved. It went against one's natural submariner's instincts to be profligate with it, but these were unusual circumstances. For X-12, they were terminal circumstances. They were going to abandon her with the side-cargo in place, there was absolutely no chance of getting her away to sea now, so it would make sense to get over there fast and have the extra time in hand.

He explained this to Gimber. "So we might as well step on it."

"Skipper?"

Brazier: his head was lowered, eyes showing their whites under matted brows—the attitude of a bull about to use its horns. "Yes, Bomber?"

"Sorry to harp on about it. But I reckon I could shift it. I'd guess it's gone like it has because with the weight of one buoyancy chamber flooded there's been distortion on one or more of the links. If I just prised it away slightly—at the heavy end, whichever that may be—"

"Depth eighty feet."

"Keep her grouped down for the moment, Louis." Paul squatted against the slight warmth emanating from the Brown's gyro. "Bomber, the snag as I see it is the time factor. If we dash over there flat-out, giving you the time you'd need for this, then we'd have a flat battery and we couldn't get away anyhow. If we crossed at economical speed, I doubt you'd have nearly enough time."

"Might split the difference? Say group down full ahead? And I'd be all set and ready to go out the minute you got us under here. I could have the chamber flooded before you bottomed her. Half an hour at most—probably much less—and I'm back inside!"

"Isn't that somewhat optimistic? It might take you up to—well, seven-thirty. And the firing-period begins at eight."

"But," Brazier gestured towards the side-cargo, "it's set for eight twenty-five."

"Come on . . . It's not only ours, Bomber, is it. Hudspeth could be under *Scharnhorst* this very minute, leaving his two bombs set for eight sharp. We might bottom ourselves right on top of them. How's that for larks?"

Lanchberry chuckled. Brazier glanced at him, then back at Paul. One large hand passed around the wide, ginger-stubbled face. "Well, that's all true, skipper, but . . ."

"Even if *Lützow's* there and we go for her, X-10's charges under *Scharnhorst* would still blow us to Kingdom Come."

"But your time of seven-thirty, skipper—that would be the very latest, absolute limit of it. I'd hope to finish long before that. And once I'm back inside and have the hatch shut, you could be on the move right away. I mean, why should you wait for me to drain down?"

He was talking sense. You wouldn't need to wait. The wet-and-dry was flooded from, and drained down into, number two main ballast, which was right under it. The operation in either direction was an internal one, with no effect on the boat's weight or trim.

Paul reached for the chart, to check how far it was from *Scharnhorst's* last-observed position to the exit at the island's eastern end. The answer was a mile or a mile and a half, depending on exactly where she was berthed. That glimpse of her floodlit forepart last night, at a distance of three or four miles, hadn't exactly pinpointed her. He doubted whether she could have moved since then, either to sea or back into her netted berth in Kafjord, without sight or sound: and the fact was that Brazier's proposals weren't all that crazy, after all. If the diving sortie went smoothly, a lot of problems might be removed.

"You may be right, Bomber. It could work. After you're back in and the side-cargo's on the bottom—latest seven-thirty, and set to go up at eight twenty-five . . ." he was thinking aloud ". . . but we'd have to be clear away, and really legging it, at that."

"Group up, full ahead!" Brazier's eyes were gleaming. "Run like a rigger for that gap!"

He laughed, out of excitement at the prospect of having his own job to do—and more than a routine net-cutting operation, at that. Paul nodded slowly. "Yes . . . But then we'd have to wait there—in the gap, until 0900. Otherwise—well, if we were out in the middle, the blast even from the one we've just planted . . ."

He was thinking aloud again. Gimber broke in, "Must say, I don't go much on the prospect of barbed wire for the rest of the duration. I mean, if there is a chance we could skin out of it."

Paul saw Lanchberry nod. And obviously he felt the same way himself. Glancing round, out of habit checking depth, angle of the planes, ship's head . . . He said, "It all hinges on whether you can get the side-cargo off, Bomber. And how long it takes. If it didn't work we'd be in a hell of a spot—you realise that?"

A nod. But then a grin. "I could do it with my bare hands, skipper. There's no other way that thing could be stuck to us."

"Jazz. You know more than the rest of us how the side-cargoes are fixed. D'you agree with him?"

"I'd say I do. I'd say it's a good chance, any road." He glanced sideways at Brazier. "I'd be dead sure of it if it was me doing the job. Instead of a cack-handed bloody ape."

Brazier murmured amiably, "Remind me to put you on a charge, you sod."

"Louis." Paul had made his mind up. "Put main motor to full ahead grouped down." He looked back at Brazier. "Bomber, how d'you like the thought of breakfast?"

"Oh, just the job!"

"Your job, then. Tinned fruit, coffee, biscuits and jam. OK?"

Lanchberry muttered, "Bugger coffee, I'll have tea."

"You can bugger the jam too, while you're at it." Vibration increased as Gimber wound her up to full ahead. He added, "Marmite, I'll have."

Spirits shooting up. Having been rather thoroughly depressed, the upturn was all the sharper.

Off Langnesholm he brought her up to nine feet for a look around. The periscope was fogged internally but he could see enough through it to take rough bearings of Korsnes, Klubbeneset and Aaroy's left and right-hand edges. He sent the periscope down again and told Gimber, "Eighty feet." There'd been some fishing-boats rounding Klubbeneset, and what looked like a tug chugging north from the lower end of the fjord, but he couldn't see anything of *Scharnhorst*: she'd be hidden, just, by the island's western bulge. The intersection of his position lines from the bearings he'd taken wasn't all that neat—he'd known it wouldn't be, because of the twelve-degree angle on her and also the fogged-up prisms—but he chose the most dangerous position in the spread of the "cocked hat," one from which the present course would just about have scraped her past the one-fathom patch, and played extra safe by altering two degrees to starboard, to 117.

Time now: 0439. Estimated time of arrival at Aaroy's southwest corner: about 0600. But the tidal set out in the middle might be slacker than it had been up here where it channelled into the two sunds. When he was off that corner of the island he'd come up for another check, he decided—navigational, and also because from there he'd have a clear view of *Scharnhorst*, possibly of *Lützow* too. He'd have steered farther out from the Aaroy coast—particularly because of the danger of showing periscope so close to land in these millpond conditions—if he'd had more time in hand; but as things were, a shortcut was essential.

Gimber reported, "Eighty feet." He looked round over his shoulder. "How long, to get over there?"

"Hour and twenty minutes."

"And on the fuse-clock?"

"It's set for eight twenty-five. Should make—three hours and forty minutes to go." He checked it, and found the delay left on it was exactly that. "Keeping good time. That's something."

Gimber had another question. "Supposing we make it—out through that gap—how far to the rendezvous with *Setter*?"

"Well. Eight miles to get into Stjernsund." He had the distances in his head. "Then twelve through the sund, and another thirty to get out and across the minefield."

"Total around fifty. Say forty-eight hours' passage."

Paul nodded. He'd have to time the exit to coincide with high water, to carry them over the moored mines. He said, "You'll be stir-crazy by then, Louis. If you aren't already."

"Pain in the arse is the only problem at the moment. This bloody chair."

"Well, come out of it. I'll take over for an hour."

Brazier, aided by advice from Lanchberry, was selecting the tools he'd take out with him, but he took over the steering now so Jazz could ease his chair-cramped muscles too. As well as tools he was going to take a heaving-line, which he'd use for slinging himself down over the midget's side. At a quarter to six they all changed round again; Lanchberry had made more tea. Then at five minutes to the hour Paul told Gimber, "Twenty feet. Slow ahead."

It was a relief to see her upward movement on the depthgauge. For half an hour he'd been visualising her approach to that rocky coast, and particularly the shallow patch. Having made your calculations you had to trust to them, but flying blind in unfamiliar territory required a certain control of nerves.

"Main motor's slow ahead."

And still nosing up . . .

"Are you fit, Bomber?"

Brazier lifted one rubber-gloved hand, from his position in the W and D. He'd got into his diving gear—rubber tunic, weighted boots on wader-type leggings, oxygen equipment harnessed to his back with the distributor in front and the face-mask dangling. The tools were on his belt, which also had lead weights in it for ballast. X-12 rising past the thirty-foot mark, leaning clumsily to port.

"Depth twenty feet."

"Make it fifteen."

Then ten. And when it was clear he had her in good control, nine and a half. Paul felt for the button in the rubber bag, and pressed it.

Greenish water swirling, with diamonds flashing in it. Then surface flurry and a liquid glare of daylight.

"Depth?"

"Nine feet—"

"Christ's sake!"

"Nine and a half. Sorry . . . "

Aaroy's rocks loomed alarmingly close to port. He could see them as if he was looking through a glass of water, but one small section of the lens was clearer than the rest. Circling slowly to the right . . .

"Wow."

Scharnhorst. Bow-on, enormous, about a mile away. Maybe more—maybe 3000 yards. She was lying parallel to the shoreline and—as far as he could tell—on a single anchor. If that was the case, one might guess she wasn't planning to stay here very long. A second thought was far from cheering: when the tide turned, she'd swing with it—away from any ground-mines laid under her.

Wait for the turn of tide? But it wouldn't be until—seven, seven-thirty.

Bloody impossible, then . . .

Panic flared. He told himself, Hold on, now. Think it out.

No *Lützow.* Over against the far shore—the other side of Leir Botn—a minesweeper lay at moorings. And *Scharnhorst,* of course, might have her stern secured to a buoy, or a stream anchor out. It was wishful thinking, from here you couldn't see at all, but it was none the less quite possible. Other moorings over on that side were empty. Some small stuff right inshore—motor launches, he thought. There was certainly no target other than *Scharnhorst,* anyway. He wondered where X-10 might be: Hudspeth could be making his approach at any moment, and *Scharnhorst* was his target. X-12 was a poacher in his territory.

But they were all poachers. And so far the gamekeepers seemed to be asleep. *Scharnhorst*'s bearing down here was—082 degrees.

"Take down some bearings, Jazz."

Lanchberry had a pad and pencil beside him. Paul gave him bearings of Aaroy's edges, of Langnesholm back on the quarter and the mainland point directly south. Four bearings instead of three, to make up for the fact they'd all be distorted anyway.

"Port ten. Steer oh-nine-oh." He squeezed the rubber bag to send the periscope down, and told Gimber, "Sixty feet."

"Sixty . . ."

"Full ahead group down." He took a log reading, and told them while he was putting that fix on the chart, "*Scharnhorst*'s at anchor, no nets I can see, about a mile, mile and a half away. We'll call it two thousand five hundred yards." It wasn't really a fix, in the true sense of the term, more a good indication of their position, and it was as much as he needed, anyway.

"Bomber, you can relax for a while."

He glanced at the depthgauge: she was passing fifty feet, and Gimber had the trim-pump working on the midship's tank. Reporting now, "Main motor full ahead, grouped down." Paul told them, "I'm going to run in one thousand yards by log, then sneak up for another look from broader on her bow. It's getting towards low water and she may swing with the tide, unless she's moored aft, which I can't tell yet. You'll still have plenty of time, Bomber."

The last half-mile would have to be covered at slow speed, though, to avoid visible disturbance of the water or sound-levels audible on asdics.

He explained, "I can't afford to wait for the tide to turn. Earliest she'd start swinging is half-seven. Bomber wouldn't be able to get inboard again by eight, so it's out of the question. If she's only anchored for'ard I'll have to guess at how she'll lie by eight-thirty, and hope for the best."

Hudspeth would be facing the same problem, of course. He might already have done so. X-10's side-cargoes might already be lying on the bottom. Wiser, perhaps, not to speculate on that, when you were going to have to bottom there yourself by and by.

But almost certainly—he saw this suddenly—*Scharnhorst* did have a stream anchor out, holding her stern. Because she was lying the same way she'd lain last night—and last night when they'd seen her the tide had been flooding, whereas right now it was ebbing!

Except she might not have been at anchor, at that moment. Might have been in the process of anchoring—hence the illuminations?

Brazier asked, "What's the depth there, skipper?"

"About nine fathoms."

"*Scharnhorst* draws—what, twenty-five feet?"

"That's her mean draft. Call it twenty-seven, to be safe. And nine fathoms. We'll have a clear twenty-five feet of water under her."

The tidal problem, the single anchor complication, was a snag he hadn't foreseen when he'd accepted Brazier's arguments. He studied the chart now, trying to see any others that might arise, now or later. And there was one. The withdrawal—distance, time, air supply—particularly as so much of the bottled oxygen had been used . . . After the explosions there'd be an enormous hue and cry, charges dropped, and so on; the crossing to Stjernsund would have to be made deep and at slow speed, sparing the battery as much as possible, and it wouldn't be dark enough to surface until about 0800 . . . It would mean a hell of a long time shut down. In fact, impossibly long!

He got the answer. Or an answer. Right in that gap between Aaroy and the mainland—or just close to the north of it, near the island's tapering eastern end—he'd bring her to the surface for a very quick guff-through. Then down again very smartly, with a full load of fresh air. There'd be some cover there, and with luck the Germans would be chasing their tails, at that stage, coping with their destroyed or damaged ships.

But all you could establish in advance was a general intention, a delineation of what was feasible and what wasn't. When the moment came—each moment, one on each other's heels—you'd adapt to circumstances. As he'd been realising during the recent hours, nothing was cut and dried.

"All right." He'd checked the log. "Twenty feet. Slow ahead."

He asked Gimber when she was at ten feet, "Can you manage a stop-trim, while I take a fast shufti?"

"Well." Gimber's mud-coloured eyes didn't leave the controls in front of him. A stop-trim was a state of accurately neutral buoyancy, a trim so good that you could stop the motor and just hang there. "Might manage a few seconds' worth."

"That's all I'll need. When you're ready, nine and a half feet, and stop."

She'd have no way on, or almost none, so the periscope would poke up with no feather, no rippling wake to it even. This close to the target, in broad daylight and with barely a wrinkle on the surface, it was about the only way you'd get away with it. Gimber had made his adjustments to the trim: his right hand moved to the control-wheel and wound it anti-clockwise to its stop, then pulled out the field switch. Paul had the periscope sliding up, trained on the bearing where he expected to locate his target. Snatching the handles down, pressing his right eye against the rubber.

"Bearing—oh-six-four. I'm thirty on her port bow, and—she has a wire out to a buoy astern!"

He'd squeezed the bag, and the tube was rushing down. Lanchberry muttered, "Good oh . . ." Brazier clapped gloved hands together. Gimber said, "Can't hold her, she's so bloody skew-whiff—"

"Slow ahead. Fifty feet. Come to port to oh-six-four, Jazz."

Seeing that wire out to the buoy under her counter had felt like one of the best moments of his life. X-12 was already slanting down, trembling very slightly under the slow-speed thrust of her screw. As if she, too, were a little excited now.

Too slow-speed, though. He wanted to be there, now, getting on with it. Then, best of all, getting out.

"We'll hang on until we're really close, Bomber. Five minutes short of bottoming. Otherwise by the time we get there you'd be frozen solid."

Brazier nodded. It wasn't going to be any fun in the wet-and-dry chamber, and he knew it better than any of them.

"Course—oh-six-four."

Gimber reported, "Fifty feet."

The slow creep of the approach was galling. He was constantly check-ing the distance by log as the minutes passed, and he could see signs of the tension in the others. The temptation to increase to half ahead was difficult to resist: using up so much time like this, when you knew that once you'd shed the side-cargo you'd need every minute of it, was maddening. There was also—when your head was close to it—the purring fuse-clock on the flooded side: and your distrust of it.

It was six forty-two when he saw *Scharnhorst*'s huge shadow through the viewing port. The time, and the log reading, checked exactly.

"Come to oh-six-oh, Jazz."

"Oh-six-oh . . ."

"Target's in sight." He tapped the glass. "Forty feet, Louis." There might be as little as eight fathoms where she was lying. Gimber took his eyes off the starboard side viewing port. It wasn't easy to stop looking—*Scharnhorst*, one of the most powerful ships afloat, about a hundred yards ahead and at their mercy.

Not that "mercy" would be quite the word for it.

"All right, Bomber. In you go, and flood up. Don't touch the hatch until I give two bangs on the bulkhead—then carry on out, quick as you like. Take care you aren't under the side-cargo when you free it—all right?"

Brazier nodded.

"Three bangs on the bulkhead would mean emergency of some kind, stop everything and drain down." Paul leant over with his hand out. "Bomber—good luck, now."

"Yeah." Lanchberry also reached to shake his hand. "Best of British, Bomber." Gimber was too far away and too busy for handshaking; he said, "Bomber, first night back in Cairnbawn, I'll buy all your drinks."

Brazier grinned round at them all. "Arf, arf." He backed into the W and D, and slammed its steel door, and they saw the clips hinge over. Lanchberry muttered, "Dunno what we're fussed about. He'll do it on his ear."

Brazier would have shut and clipped the other door as well, the one leading into the fore end. So he was now enclosed in a space in which he could only crouch with his elbows in contact with both bulk-heads and the closed hatch above his head. He'd put on his mask, and start breathing oxygen from the counter-lung strapped to his chest and fed, via the distributor valve, from the bottles on his back. Equipped like this, being the size he was, he'd only just pass through the hatch when the time came for his exit. In preparation for that outing he'd now be setting about flooding his steel cell by pumping water up from number two main ballast tank. He had a pump-lever in there, similar in operation to the trimming-pump control; the first part of its movement opened the valve from the W and D to the ballast tank and also the vent they shared, and the next started the pump, which was a powerful one producing up to fifty pounds to the square inch. By now the water would be roaring in, flooding up around him, deafening him with its noise as the level rose and the pressure increased. He'd adjust his flow of oxygen, the pressure of it in the lung, to balance that rising pressure. The flooding process lasted about four minutes, unpleasant minutes—and more so than usual, here in seventy degrees north latitude, by the fact of it being only fractionally above freezing point. The worst moment came when the inrush of water, having already closed over Brazier's head, hit the roof of the chamber—the underside of the hatch. At this point the vent lost the battle and pressure jumped suddenly to equal sea-pressure outside. For the diver it was like being slammed against a wall. Brazier would have softened the blow, and saved the counter-lung and his own lungs from being squeezed flat, by stopping the pump just before the chamber filled.

Those controls inside the W and D were duplicated here in the control room. You could do all of it from here, except of course for opening the hatch. That had to be done by the man in the chamber. When the time came he'd reach up, grab the central handwheel above his head and wrench it round so that the dogs would disengage on the rim and allow him to push it up. Brazier wouldn't be doing that yet: he'd be hunched in there now, enclosed in icy water under pressure, waiting for Paul's signal.

Paul waited too—watching the shadow fill the viewing port and darken, its wavy edges firming as the midget crept in under it. *Scharnhorst* was nearly 750 feet long and 100 in the beam; she carried twelve-inch armour on her sides, but the vast expanse of underwater hull now exposed to X-12 had no such protection.

Fifteen hundred men up there inside her. Probably having breakfast.

Rippling silver ended where her great bulk shaded the water under it. The approach had been at an angle of thirty degrees to the battleship's fore-and-aft line, and the small alteration of course he'd made five minutes ago would have brought them in just about amidships, under that funnel with its rakish cap. It was probably the best place to leave a single charge, he thought. If X-10 had placed—or was placing—her two side-cargoes, she'd drop one at each end, a tactic designed to break the ship's back. Another in the middle, therefore, would make a real job of it.

"Stop main motor."

"Stop . . . Motor's stopped."

"Port twenty."

"Port twenty." Lanchberry span the wheel. "Twenty of port wheel on, sir."

"Take her down slowly, Louis."

A nod. Gimber's left hand moved the pump-lever to port, then centred it again. Forty-two feet. Forty-four . . .

"Give her a touch astern."

Gimber put the motor to slow astern for just long enough to feel the screw churn, taking the way off her. Looking upwards through the ports it was as if an enormous steel shutter stopped sliding over them. It was lifting now, going out of focus. Gimber had stopped the motor. The gauge showed forty-eight feet—eight fathoms. At fifty-four there was a bump for'ard: she lurched, bumped again.

Hard. Too hard.

"Rock."

As expected. A crunching sound from under their feet lasted for about ten seconds while she settled. The needle was on fifty-four and a half feet, and there was no movement on it at all now. The fore-and-aft bubble was on the centreline, but she was leaning a few degrees to port, canted by the flooded charge's weight although not as much as she had been when she'd been waterborne. She'd be resting on her heavy, level keel, kept upright by the buoyancy in her compartments and in some tanks.

Paul took a wheelspanner from where it was hanging on the deckhead, rapped twice with it on the door of the W and D. The metallic crashes were startlingly loud. Then he went to the stub periscope, the short bifocal one. He was looking into a dim, shifting haze, water and water-movement distorting the overhead view of *Scharnhorst*'s bilges extending into what looked like miles, wavery like sinews in it flexing themselves. He couldn't see X-12's fore hatch until it opened; it was below the periscope's field of view, set down in a short well inside the casing. But he saw its rim appear now—a curve of black at the very bottom of the glass; the hatch had been flung back, and that was the top edge of the lid standing open. Now Brazier was rising into view, ungainly undersea creature dramatically emerging, rising and inclining forward—this way, leaning towards and over the stub periscope—hooking black rubber-gloved claws into the casing's apertures to hold itself down and drag itself aft. Boots loud on the casing's steel, ringing clangs, and bubbles rising in a thin stream from his breathing exhaust.

Astonishing to think you knew that sinister-looking creature—had talked, eaten and drunk with it.

"He's out, and moving aft."

They'd have known from the fairy footsteps, but he'd forgotten to tell them, in his own fascination with the sight. Lanchberry said, "He'll have it done in five minutes. Anyone want to bet?"

Gimber took him up on it. "I say ten minutes. Starting now. Five bob."

"You're on."

The periscope window went black as Brazier loomed over it. Water displaced by that large body's passage through it danced mirage-like above him. You could hear every shift of the leadweighted boots; other metallic sounds would be from the tools slung on his belt. Paul checked the time: six fifty-four. Leaving one hour and six minutes to have the job done and get her through the gap to the blind side of the island. It would be all right as long as the Bomber did take as little as five or ten minutes. Paul was at the viewing port, and he could see Brazier handling his line, letting himself down over the side; he'd have secured it to the periscope standard, or thereabouts. Gimber and Lanchberry had both swung round on their seats to watch—or rather, to catch glimpses, which was all you'd get—and Paul stood aside to clear their view. Then Brazier's body was covering the outside of the port, so there was nothing to be seen at all. Paul had looked round to make some remark to Gimber, when it happened.

An explosion: like a distant rumble of thunder amplified immediately into a deafening clap of it right overhead. Paul's thought was, Side-cargo . . .

(He was right, although he had no idea at the time whose or where it was. Later reconstruction from sources including German naval logs make it clear that it was the charge left by X-12 herself in Ytre Koven and which should still have had two hours' delay left on its clock.)

In the first impact of the shock-wave, Brazier was wiped off the midget's side. Paul saw him receding into blackness, cartwheeling head over heels; his mask had been blown off and trailed on its pipe. Brazier's limbs were extended—the legs at any rate in their heavy boots, whirling by centrifugal force as he turned over and over—in an attitude of crucifixion, whirling away. It was more horrible than any of the nightmares, and now X-12 was on the move too, crabbing side-ways, angled over to starboard, at first just sliding but then grating, bouncing, crashing over rock. Paul had been sent flying. Gimber was clinging to his seat but Lanchberry had been ejected backwards, torpedoing head-first into machinery behind his chair. Struggling up, imposed over the sight of Lanchberry's head gashed and blood streaming in a scarlet curtain over his face was the image still in Paul's brain of Bomber Brazier in that maelstrom, drowning if the concussion hadn't already killed him. Which it would have. The boat was on her side, grinding over the rocky bed of the fjord, and the obvious countermeasure—to blow main ballast—wasn't on the cards, because you'd have been blasting her to the surface under the eyes and guns of fifteen hundred Germans—under *Scharnhorst's* guns. Gimber had the pump running on the midships trimming tank; Paul had crawled to the lever to do it himself—acting blindly, on instinct, as it were buried in the noise—and he'd found the lever already over to starboard, Gimber holding it there with one hand and clinging to the hydroplane control with the other. Lanchberry shouted in Paul's ear, "Blow one and three?" Paul yelled back "No!" He saw astonishment in Lanchberry's face, and allowed himself second thoughts: you could blow enough ballast out just to get her off the rocks, before she smashed up completely. He'd got himself half to his feet: he shouted "Jazz!" Lanchberry staring at him with a hand to his head and blood still pouring, just about all over him by this time. Paul yelled, "Blow one and three, but only one short guff in each!"

The motion was easing: these were only dying residues of blast now, and noise diminished with it. Lanchberry opened the two high-pressure blows, paused for a count of three and then jammed them shut again. X-12's bow lifting: but not her stern . . . He shouted, "Another guff in three!"

The angle had increased alarmingly. She was bow-up, with an angle of about twenty degrees on her. Her stern, obviously, was still resting on the bottom—you could hear it, the grinding contact with rock—as if that tank hadn't been blown at all. Lanchberry had opened the blow again: Paul heard the thump and rush of air through the pipe, then the noise of it escaping, whooshing out. Lanchberry heard it too and shut the blow.

"Stern tank's holed."

So it could not be blown. A minute ago, in that deafening cacophony, they hadn't been able to hear the air escaping.

Gimber had stopped the ballast pump. He saw Paul turn to glance at the position of the lever, and explained, "Wasn't doing any good." Pointing at the depthgauge: "Seen that?"

The needle was static at 238 feet.

So she'd been washed away from the Aaroy coast into much deeper water. And at 238 feet the pressure would be something like—he forced his stunned brain to work it out—125 pounds to the square inch. It made the prospect of escape by DSEA somewhat unattractive. But X-12 was stuck here, finished; there was nothing to do except abandon her.

That same sensation swept over him: that this couldn't be true, couldn't really be happening—you'd wake up suddenly . . .

But it was happening. Had happened. And now had to be coped with. He heard Lanchberry mutter, "Poor old Bomber."

The enemy might or might not know there was a submarine down here.

It depended on whether those large escapes of air had been seen when they'd frothed the surface.

Gimber said, "I suppose the side-cargo's still attached."

The time was eight minutes past seven.

There was an intermittent scraping from the stern, where she was grinding her tail on rock, but also—he was noticing it now for the first time—an internal trickling. He saw Lanchberry also listening to it while he dabbed with a handful of cotton-waste at his gashed head. X-12 resting on her tail, snout pointing upward at the surface, Lanchberry and Gimber both in their seats while Paul crouched with an arm hooked round the barrel of the periscope. Lanchberry said, "Leaking in aft." His thin lips twisted. "Be bloody amazing if it wasn't."

It would be through some loosened hull-valve, or possibly more than one. It was hardly worth looking for, though, because sooner or later they were going to have to bale out. Sooner, rather than later. But at least with this stern-down angle on her, the water that got in would take a very long time to reach the battery. There'd be no chlorine gassing to worry about, in the short term.

Small mercies . . . Particularly as there couldn't be a long term.

"DSEA then. This depth's going to create problems, but . . ."

He'd checked. He'd been about to tell them, We'll go out through the W and D, one at a time. The first step would have been to operate its valves—its connections with number two main ballast—from here in the control room, in order to drain it down. Then each man would have gone out—Gimber first, then Lanchberry, and finally himself, and each of the first two would have had to shut the hatch behind him before allowing himself to float up to the surface with the rubber apron of his set extended, like a parachute in reverse, to slow the ascent and reduce the likelihood of "bends." But you couldn't do it—couldn't use the W and D at all. Because Brazier had left the hatch standing open. Paul remembered it distinctly. It had been only minutes ago, yet already remote in memory—that dream-quality again—but he could see as if he was looking at it now the rim of the open hatch, and then the Bomber like some weird apparition rising out of it, a spectral being from another planet. There was a side thought at this point, a thought within the other one—that the weighted boots and belt would sink the Bomber's body, hold it down at least for quite a long time ... But he'd left the hatch open because he'd been set on doing a quick job out there and getting back inside within minutes.

Paul hauled himself up to the stub periscope, to check this, but of course at such a depth as this there wasn't any light to see by. Only the roofing shimmer of the surface.

"What's the drill now, skipper?"

"We can't use the wet-and-dry, unfortunately. Bomber left it open."

A slow blink, slow enough to be a temporary closing of the eyes. Lanchberry said, "Ah."

Gimber whispered, "Shit . . ."

"So we'll have to flood her through the seacocks, and use this hatch."

"Christ, how long'll that take?"

The short answer was too long. For a variety of reasons, none of them hard to see. The system he was proposing just happened to be the only way out there was. They'd strap on their DSEA sets, and start breathing from them when the water got to about shoulder height. Or so high you had to anyway. You wouldn't use the sets before you had to, because unlike Brazier's proper diving gear a DSEA set was only meant to support life in a man on his way up to the surface, and the oxygen capacity was quite limited. The flooding process would be complicated, too, by the midget's bow-up position. At this angle—if she stayed like this, when she'd taken in that great weight of water—and she might, because the stern compartment would be the first to fill—the air pocket would be up against the top of the W and D bulkhead, not under the hatch as would be normal. The hatch, in fact, would be drowned long before the pressures equalised. That was another factor—the pressure would be huge, really killing, increasing as the flooding continued and finally balanced sea pressure so the hatch could be opened.

By anyone who was still alive to open it.

Well—you could open the door to the W and D, at that stage, and use the fore hatch. Easier than having to dive down and locate the main hatch and open it. But exactly the same applied, of course, about equalising pressure. In fact you could open that W and D door now—you could knock its clips off and allow it to fly open with sea at more than a hundred pounds to the inch behind it, and in the second that it opened you'd all be killed by that blast of pressure.

Hardly profitable.

Lanchberry answered his own question. His sweater was soaked brownish with his blood. He'd stemmed the flow, with cotton-waste stuck to the gash.

"Take an hour, or more. Much as two hours, even."

Gimber checked the time. Seven-thirteen.

"Firing-period starts at eight." He nodded towards the boat's port side. "And that thing's set for twenty-five past."

At 0800, or at any time thereafter, there could be other side-cargoes exploding. Not that you'd need them, from X-12's point of view. If she took an hour or more to flood, the three of them would probably be dead from cold long before they'd be in a position to open up and get out. It would have been bad enough for the Bomber in his rubber suit, but without such gear, standing for an hour in ice-water slowly rising until it covered you . . .

"How long's the oxygen last in these?"

Lanchberry was pulling the DSEA sets out of the storage locker. Paul admitted, "If she floods that slowly, not long enough."

Forty-five minutes, he was remembering, on the main cylinder. Then you could switch to the reserve and get another five.

"Can't do it, can we."

"What we can do," he'd just started talking, spouting thought aloud, "is get her up to the surface, abandon ship—and she'll go down again on her own with the hatch open. As she's going to blow up, there's no problem about secret equipment in enemy hands, so . . ."

"Skipper—how?"

"Just listen to me, Jazz." He leant with a hand on Louis Gimber's shoulder. "First we'll lighten her as much as we can." He pointed at the trimming pump. Gimber interrupted, "Pump's got a hell of a pressure to work against." Paul nodded. "Sure, it'll be on the slow side. But we'll start by emptying the stern trim-tanks and comps, shift that weight to the bow or amidships. It'll at least help to balance her. Then we'll blow one and three."

"Skipper—"

"Hang on. We'll lose air through three, I know, but the blowing will still have some effect, from the air as it passes through. It did start to—remember? Before we heard it escaping and you shut off? Then as soon as she shows signs of stirring, full ahead group up. Planes hard a-rise. Surface. At this angle, and keeping her at full ahead and blowing like hell—well, she ought to get there, and although she won't stay up for long there'd be time to evacuate . . . Right?"

"Ten to one against."

"Balls, Jazz. But that's better odds than we've got down here, anyway."

Gimber agreed, "It's the only hope we've got, isn't it?"

"Exactly. We can pump out number two main ballast too, Jazz. I was thinking we couldn't—for some reason . . . But we do have a chance, you see." There was a glint of hope in Lanchberry's eyes, at last. Paul told him, "I'll take over as helmsman, Jazz."

"Yeah?"

Gimber looked surprised too.

"Because I want to control the blowing myself."

It would make enough sense—just enough—for them to accept it. In fact he wanted to change places so the two of them would be under the hatch and first out. If she reached the surface. Lanchberry had been near enough right, he thought, with his estimate of the odds against.

CHAPTER SIXTEEN

· · ·

Trench said, "That's the lot. Those top sheds are empty, at the moment. Until we disperse the litters, you see."

Trying not to show my relief too plainly, I pushed the door shut. When you've seen a few thousand minks, you have a fair idea what a mink looks like. I thanked him for the guided tour. "Fascinating."

"Really?" He was genuinely surprised, "D'you think so?"

Unspoilt Norfolk countryside lay around us. There was a village in a dip, thatched cottages clustered round a church with a square stone tower; in woodland between us and the village the trees were in new leaf. Some fighters had roared over at something like Mach 2 while we'd been in the shed, but all was quiet now and it looked as it might have done fifty years ago.

Trench told me as we strolled towards the farm's office building, "*Foremost* was hit a second time, and stopped, just as we got down to support her. The enemy destroyers, in line ahead, had turned towards her and the convoy—which they couldn't see yet, on account of the smoke she'd been laying, but obviously knew where it was . . . They had *Foremost* pretty well for target practice, steering to pass her at close range and no doubt blow her out of the water on their way to make hay with the convoy. Having had their friends lure me away to the north and northeast, you see."

"D'you think it was a deliberate plan they'd followed?"

"No, I don't. Visibility was too bad, for one thing. I don't think they had much idea of anything until they actually ran into us. They were scouting in separate divisions, that's all, and it's how things happened to turn out."

"So you were steering south—with the enemy and *Foremost* in sight."

"The Germans didn't spot us until it was too late—too late for them—and by that time we'd fired torpedoes. It was too late for poor *Foremost* too, of course. She was quite obviously done for, but they were still bombarding her. At times you couldn't see her for their shell-spouts, and the smoke pouring out of her, and fires—and the vis being what it was anyway . . . I was—well, you can imagine. I'd put him in that ship—then left her, gone swanning off on a wild goose chase, and . . ."

He paused, shaking his head. "I know. I couldn't have stayed down there, ignored the enemy reports from *Legend*. Still . . . *Foremost* was helpless—stopped, burning, one gun firing at irregular intervals—and those bastards methodically completing her destruction. Their job, of course—but there seemed to be a certain Germanic precision about it that got my goat. In fact they were preoccupied with it to the extent that our fish were on the way to them before they knew we were there. I'd have thrown the galley stove at them, if I'd had it handy. What I mean is—I told you earlier I'd intended saving our torpedoes for *Lützow*, obvious thing to do, of course. But here were these swine in a neat line like fairground ducks just waiting to be knocked over, and the long and short of it is, my three ships each fired four torpedoes—holding another four in reserve—and only then opened up with our guns. Of course the very patchy visibility helped, but they should have seen us long before they did. It cost them two destroyers. I've no idea whose torpedoes did the damage, but out of the twelve we'd fired we got three hits, and sank two of them, second and third ships in the line. It left numbers one and four well separated and no doubt shaken to the core—this being their first awareness of our presence. Extremely lucky, of course—unseen approach, snap attack, two enemies destroyed—that's luck, all right. The two survivors turned and ran, in opposite directions. I went after number one, the leader, and told *Laureate* and *Lyric* to attend to the other; and mine, when after a mile or so he saw he had only me on his tail, decided to have a final crack at *Foremost*. He was between me and her, you see. When he turned to run, he crossed my bows at about seven thousand yards but he was closer than that to her. I couldn't see her all the time, only glimpses of her out beyond this Hun; I was turning to starboard to bring my guns to bear on him. I suppose he reckoned he could polish off *Foremost* with a salvo or two—well worth it, for a Knight's Grand Cross or whatever and then throw a few at me as he took off. He had the legs of me, he'd know that, and he'd also be well aware he out-gunned me. In fact he'd good reason to expect to get away with it."

Moloch's four-sevens firing as fast as they could be reloaded: every time the four "gun-ready" lamps glowed in the director, the director layer, with his crosswires on the target, would press his trigger. He'd got the German's range and straddled: one hit glowed and smoked amidships, shell-spouts lifting all around: the fire-gongs clanged again and another salvo crashed away. Trench, with his glasses on the enemy, saw his stern guns swinging round, shifting target: he still had his glasses trained there when *Foremost* blew up. A huge streak of flame, then the eruption . . .

"I felt it." He touched his head. "Like something in here, exploding."

The German's guns were all directed at *Moloch* now. Most of the first salvoes went over, but one shell hit aft, smashed the searchlight and killed and wounded some torpedomen. *Moloch* scored too, with a hit below his bridge, and he was swinging to port.

"Turning away, sir!"

"Port fifteen! Full ahead both!"

Trench told his engineer over the telephone, "I want every ounce you can give me, Chief! I don't care if you burst the bloody boilers!" He slammed the phone down. "Midships!" He had to repeat that order—it had coincided with the crash of the four-sevens. He'd displaced his navigator at the binnacle now. "Steer—" sighting over the gyro repeater, "Oh-eight-three!"

Moloch at full stretch, hurling herself across the swells, spray sheeting aft as she cut through them. He'd turned her enough to follow on a course roughly parallel to the enemy's but with all his guns still bearing. Shellspouts lifted: and she was racing into them . . .

Then, the bridge was engulfed in flame, deafeningly concussive noise.

"Where I got this." He touched the empty sleeve. "Or rather, lost it. Didn't know it at the time, hardly felt a thing. There was a sort of knockout effect, I knew we'd been hit, of course, but this arm was like—well, just a blow, no more than that. The amount of bleeding became noticeable soon afterwards—the arm wasn't severed so much as smashed. They put a tourniquet on it, up near the armpit, while I was still too busy to take much notice. I'd got one in the jaw as well. I was still conning the ship, you see; I'd been knocked down but only for a moment, it didn't seem to me I'd been seriously hurt at all. We'd had one shell in the bridge and another in the director tower, all four of them killed up there, and radar gone, and wireless—well, a lot of damage. The bridge was a shambles too. McAllister—my navigator—had had his head blown off, Cummings—sub-lieutenant—was dead too, and my yeoman—excellent man called Halliday—was very badly wounded. He survived, I'm glad to say—thanks to Dicky Rudge, my quack—who undoubtedly saved my life as well, with that tourniquet. He was about to give me an injection of morphine, I'm told, but apparently I knocked the thing out of his hand and used some highly abusive language. I don't remember any of it, myself. But the voice-pipe to the wheelhouse was intact, Henderson had got the guns into local control—done it by messengers, since the telephones to the TS and the guns themselves had gone to hell—and we were still intact, mobile and manoeuvrable, a fighting unit."

He paused. Reaching into memory, or putting memories into order. His recollections—as he explained now—were only patchy, in some areas.

"What follows is less from my own remembering than from what they told me. And it's not always clear to me which is which—if you see what I mean. But some bits—visual flashes—are as clear as anything. Above all else I remember an absolute dread of the possibility that the German might get away from me. It was an entirely personal feeling, like wanting your hands on a man's throat, and obviously it was because of *Foremost*. They told me I was—berserk, was the word Dicky Rudge used, and Henderson was honest enough to agree with him. I certainly wasn't rational. I had a bit of that German shell in my jaw, you know—here. Scar doesn't show much now, but I still feel it. I'd barely noticed it at first, but I knew it by this time, and it was distorting my speech as well as giving me a lot of pain. But—sticking to what matters—the German had turned back towards me, for the simple reason he'd found his retreat cut off by *Legend* and *Leopard* and I suppose he preferred to face one rather than two. My guns were still banging away at him, but in local control the shooting wasn't all that good and we'd just been straddled again. So I—"

He'd checked, turned and thrown me a glance. Then looked away again. "I steered to ram. Straight into those guns of his, which unlike mine were in director control and shooting accurately. It was a lunatic thing to do, of course. Suicidal, and quite unjustifiable. All those bloody great five-point-ones blazing in my face. I jinked her a bit, dodging, turning towards the fall of shot each time—so I'm told—so I couldn't have been completely off my head, but it was madness all the same. The dog in the fight, you know? The pain inflicted being what matters, not the wounds received? And my aim—contrary to everything that's gone on record—was to ram him."

I began, "It's understandable . . ."

"Then you don't understand. I had five destroyers under my command. All of them present, intact and fighting fit. I also had a large convoy to protect. What I was doing was indulging a personal hate—revenge—whatever you like to call it, and it was tantamount to throwing my own ship away. The fact she stayed afloat wasn't my doing. Half the for'ard guns' crews were killed, the foremast went over the side, we had a fire amidships and a shell went clean through the upper seamen's messdecks without exploding—and none of it was necessary. D'you see, now?"

"But you headed him off. He'd have got clean away—as you said yourself, he had the legs of you—but you forced him to turn back into the arms of *Legend* and *Leopard*."

"You've been reading too many official histories." Trench smiled briefly. "That was the fortunate end-result of an act—no, period—of lunacy. Which in the record went down as tactical brilliance, forthright leadership and—well, you've read it all. Coolness and courage in the face of the enemy. Coolness, my God!" He shook his head. "I don't have to tell you about our casualties. Fortunately, I passed out. Loss of blood, Rudge told me afterwards. I don't know, perhaps he got one of his damn needles into me. Henderson took over, and turned her under the German's stern, and we came off a lot less badly than we would have done if I'd been on my feet to see it through. *Moloch* was in almost as bad a state as *Foremost* had been: except we could still steam. As you say, we'd forced our Hun to alter course again and we'd hit him a good few times, and then John Ready caught him on the rebound and applied the finishing touches. That was how Ready described it. *Laureate* and *Lyric* had meanwhile polished off the other one. I was on my back, being shot full of morphine—came round eventually in my bunk with an arm missing, jaw strapped up, couldn't say a word, only listen to Henderson's report. Which, as you'll have guessed, covered for me. Then, and afterwards. All was well, convoy intact and on course for Iceland—the RAF had photographed *Lützow* at anchor somewhere off Narvik—"

"On her way down to Gdynia, I think. Either to refit or pay off."

He nodded. "And there were nine survivors out of *Foremost*. Nick Everard, of course, not one of them. I had that to lie there and think about, too." He added, after a silence, "I interviewed every one of those nine, not many weeks later, in the hope of finding out what had happened to him."

I'd spoken to two of them myself, quite recently. From one, a man who'd been the loader on *Foremost*'s B gun, I'd heard the same story he'd told Trench nearly forty years earlier—the story Trench repeated to me now. How Nick Everard had last been seen leading a blinded signalman aft in order to get him into a Carley float before she sank or blew up. Leading this signalman by the arm, helping him down the ladder from the foc's'l break, telling him he was going to be all right, plenty of room in the floats and other ships at hand who'd pick them up, and how eye surgeons could perform marvels these days—that sort of stuff, shouting in the man's ear because *Foremost* had been under fire at the time, on fire, one gun still sporadically in action.

"Apparently he'd turned out and got dressed when she went to action stations. He was on the bridge with Crockford to start with, then helped organise Cramphorn's first-aid and stretcher parties. He was wearing a tin hat with MID painted on it; *Foremost* had no midshipman serving in her at the time, so that one was spare and he wore it. Cramphorn was among the missing, and I wasn't able to establish to what extent Nick had recovered, whether or not he knew who he was or where, or why." Trench pushed a gate open. "All we do know is that the end became the man."

It was a matter of fitting the pieces together—times, and the events which are explainable now but weren't then, to the participants. Such as *Lützow* being on her way south to Gdynia, and *Scharnhorst* anchored not in her usual berth but off that island—Aaroy. In fact *Scharnhorst* was out there because after the raid on Spitzbergen her captain, Hoffmeier, had decided his ship's gunnery wasn't up to scratch, and arranged for some practice shoots. This was why he'd moved her out of her protected berth, and on the morning of the twenty-second was only waiting for permission to proceed to his exercise area up in the wider reaches of the fjord.

"It's running."

The trimming pump—sucking on number two main ballast. Gimber kept his hands on the pump's casing—getting some slight warmth from it, or hoping to. The bottom of Altenfjord was freezing cold.

Unlike numbers one and three main ballast, which had open holes in the bottom through which when you blew the tanks with high-pressure air the water was expelled, number two had a Kingston valve at the bottom that could be opened or shut. So you could keep this tank full, for trimmed-down ballast and bodily weight at sea, or empty for buoyancy and safety in harbour. It also made possible its use as a reservoir for the flooding or draining-down of the W and D.

Which was unusable because its hatch was standing open.

You could hear the pump's soft whine. It was having to work hard against outside sea pressure. You could also hear the trickling noise from aft where water was seeping in. Then—something quite new . . .

Lanchberry pointed a long forefinger upwards. His eyes were turned up towards the deckhead. Lips drawn back exposing teeth whiter than the whites of his eyes. Face black with stubble, and dried blood in it, bloodstains all over and the soaked cotton-waste, hardening and black, adhering to his scalp. The overall effect was barely human. He said, "Weighing anchor."

"Scharnhorst?"

"Wouldn't know what else."

It was so familiar a sound—that steady, rhythmic clanking—that there was no question of not recognising it. The clanks were made by each link of the anchor-chain as it crashed over the lip of the hawsepipe, with enormous strain on the cable as it hauled the 26,000-ton battleship up to her anchor. They'd have taken the wire off the buoy astern before they'd begun heaving in for'ard.

Gimber said, "Doesn't make much odds, since we didn't leave a bomb under her."

"X-10 may have done."

"Could be just shortening-in. If it's timed for eight she may still be there."

Paul looked at Lanchberry. Thinking, Let's hope we're not still here.

It was 0720. In forty minutes' time this end of the fjord might erupt. And in a sense you had to hope it would—if it didn't, the operation would have been a failure. But if it did, and you hadn't been able to lighten her enough to get her to the surface . . . He frowned, not wanting to see so far into the future, not liking as much as he could see.

Gimber suggested, "We could try it now, I suppose."

Staring at Paul from about a yard away. Lank beard, dull eyes, grey damp skin. If Jane had seen a photograph of him as he looked now she'd have said, No, that's not Louis . . . Paul began, "Trouble is, if we give it a go too soon and it doesn't work—"

"We'd have used up all the air."

"Exactly, Jazz."

"So we'd 've had it, chum." Lanchberry said, with apparent equanamity and back into pidgin Arabic, "Malish, Sidi Bish . . . " He nodded to Gimber. "Gyppo for 'best carry on pumping,' that is. I'd say pump the bastard right out, then try."

Paul thought he was right. This was the only hope they had of getting out, and you could only attempt it once. When you started you'd either have her on the surface in a matter of two or three minutes or you'd know you weren't going to make it at all. So the sensible thing to do would be to continue pumping either until the tank was empty or until the time was just about running out. He told Gimber, "Every pint we get out of her improves the chances. We'll pump it dry, or until ten to eight."

"Isn't that cutting it a bit fine?"

He shrugged. "Quarter to, if you like."

He was remembering Gimber leaning against the jamb of his cabin door, in the depot ship in Loch Cairnbawn, mumbling drunkenly "If you get back and I don't . . ." He told him, "I'll be your best man yet, Louis. There's no reason this shouldn't work. I just don't want to go off at halfcock."

Gimber's eyes showed fear, suddenly. Before, there'd been anxiety, and perhaps a lack of hope, but now suddenly you could see—sharp apprehension, might be the way to describe it. As if, looking into that kind of distant future at Paul's invitation, he'd realised it probably did not exist. He blinked, as he looked away. "Good. I'll hold you to that."

"Better clean up a bit, before you pop the question."

He'd glanced back, frowning. "You light-headed, or something?"

"Light conversation. To pass the time, old horse."

Brazier cartwheeling, helpless as a leaf in a high wind, in the vortex of that underwater blast . . .

Gimber, making an effort to play the game, asked Lanchberry, "Come to my wedding, Jazz?"

"Yeah." Lanchberry snorted. "I'll sit in the back row and laugh."

"I'm serious."

"So 'm I. Laugh me bloody head off."

Scharnhorst still shortening cable. Clank, clank, clank . . .

"Skipper—if we get her up there—"

"When we get her up."

"Yeah. When we do, and start piling out, Gerry's going to start shooting—right?"

"From *Scharnhorst*, if she's still there. Yes, I suppose—"

"Depending on how far we got carried, we wouldn't be all that far from her, would we?"

"If she's weighing, not just shortening-in, she might have buggered off by then. But," he nodded, "I suppose otherwise they'd get some guns manned pretty quick."

"So how about the first man takes out a white flag with him?"

Paul nodded. "That's a good idea."

It also allowed him to make a point that might otherwise have been difficult.

"In the locker, Jazz—you'll find my spare shirt. Pass it to old Louis there—he'll be first out, and . . ."

"Who says so?"

Gimber looked affronted. Paul said, "I do, as it happens. That's a good enough reason on its own. But I'll give you two more—one, you're nearest to the hatch; two, as you've just pointed out, you have a fiancée."

"No, I don't, not . . ."

"A potential fiancée. It's more than I have, or Jazz. Anyway, you're detailed for it now. Just be sure when the time comes you move like a scalded cat." Lanchberry found the white shirt and tossed it to Gimber. Paul told him, "Wave it over your head as you climb out, then drop it so the next man," he looked at Jazz, "can do the same . . . Pass me the chart, will you?"

To estimate, if he could find clues that helped, which way and how far they'd been washed, in that explosion. Two hundred and thirty-eight feet being about forty fathoms . . . And he saw it at once. They'd been shifted southeastward. Soundings there, perhaps seven or eight hundred yards from where they'd started under *Scharnhorst*, gave thirty-five fathoms to the west and forty-one about a mile east. They were in just under forty here, so interpolating roughly he was reasonably sure X-12 had to be lying about half a mile south of the island's eastern tip. In fact it was a very small off-lying island, so small it wasn't even named, about two hundred yards southeast of the tip of Aaroy and with rock shoals in between. East of this islet was the gap through which he'd been planning to get away northward.

There were twelve fathoms in the channel, but it shelved up to rocks edging the mainland shore. Out here the charted depths varied sharply over quite small distances—eight fathoms, fifty-seven, forty-nine . . . It did seem certain that this was the only place they could be, bottomed in just on forty fathoms.

"Here." He reversed the chart, for the others to see. "When we were under *Scharnhorst* we were about here. We travelled about seven-fifty yards. See this sounding?"

After a minute's close inspection, Gimber agreed. "Not much doubt of it."

Jazz shrugged. "Take your word for—"

Open-mouthed, listening . . .

Listening to silence. The clanking had ceased.

"She's finished shortening-in, is all."

"I guess you're . . ."

It had begun again.

Paul thought, visualising the scene up there, cable was up-and-down so they stopped, reported it to the bridge, and got the order "Weigh!"

It was wishful thinking, of course. He wanted *Scharnhorst* out of it, before he made this attempt to reach the surface, because with no-one up there with guns trained on them there'd be a better chance of one or perhaps two of them surviving. As POWs, of course. He didn't expect that he himself would survive. He didn't have either time or inclination to analyse his own feelings, but he was aware of a sense of surprise and relief in not caring all that much. It might be accounted for by his being preoccupied with the hope of getting the boat up there and these two out of her. He had no suicidal tendencies at all, but as the boat's CO his primary duty, now that no other useful purpose could be achieved, was to save their lives. He'd been well taught, and he'd had not only the recent months of X-craft training but a long and quite intensive period of submarine patrols before that, and awareness of the always-present chances of disaster had caused him to give a lot of thought to the control and direction of his own impulses and reactions. The worst fear of all, as so many had discovered throughout the history of war, was fear of fear, horror at the thought of personal failure in the final emergency; he'd always known this and vaguely recognised it as the main ingredient of those nightmares. The dreams might have helped, even, in a sense rehearsed him for this. Whatever the basis of it, anyway, he was all right; the urge to survive was intact but not predominant.

The clanking stopped again.

He saw hope in Gimber's half-smile. The grounds for it were confirmed then, as the battleship's screws began to churn. She'd weighed anchor, and was on the move.

"Nice timing." Lanchberry glanced at his own watch. "Half past."

It was 0731, to be exact. If there'd been a side-cargo under her she'd be moving clear of it now. So that attempt—costing Brazier's life and their own predicament now—had been futile. But you couldn't have known and it would have been inexcusable not to have tried. He began, "Quarter of an hour, then—"

There was a crack like an outsize Christmas cracker being pulled, a puff of blue smoke and a stench of scorched metal. From the ballast pump.

"Just what we needed." Gimber muttered it to himself as he pushed the lever to its neutral position and switched off the power connection to the pump. Lanchberry said, "I'll get a spare." Spare fuse, he meant. "Get the bloody cover off, will you?" He tossed a screwdriver to Gimber.

0732. Twenty-eight minutes left, in which to fix this pump, get some more weight out of her, then try to beat the odds. Paul felt half inclined to accept the chances as they were now, get on with it. But in principle the earlier decision had been the right one: every ounce out of that tank now was a step in the right direction.

The doubt was whether, even if you got it completely pumped out, there'd be enough difference to her buoyancy—or lack of buoyancy—to make it work. Another reason for accepting delay, in fact, might have been reluctance to put it to the test. Knowing that if it failed there'd be nothing left: whereas until you tried it, you did have that small hope.

Lanchberry was back with his tools and spares. Gimber had un-screwed one bolt, but there were four in the plate that had to be removed. Lanchberry took the screwdriver from him and crouched over the job, hissing between his teeth. The sound of *Scharnhorst's* propellers was reced-ing. It was a confused sound, and Paul guessed she might have a tug with her, perhaps to push that long bow round against the tidal stream. He realised that his impulse to attempt surfacing a minute ago had been an undisciplined one: with those enemies on the move the obvious thing to do was to wait, and use the time for pumping.

Lanchberry dropped the screwdriver. It clanged off the pump's casing and disappeared under a twisted mass of piping underneath. He grabbed another, took out the last bolt, and prised off the rectangle of metal. Removing the burnt-out fuse now, gingerly muttering "Bloody hot, can't hardly touch the sod . . ." Scraping the contacts clean, then pushing in the spare fuse. Like a wheel-change in a motor race, every second counting. Slamming the cover-plate back on and fumbling a bolt into one of the holes: his hands were shaking. Gimber tried to help by putting another bolt in at the same time, but he was in Lanchberry's way.

"Christ's sake . . ."

"Sorry."

"Too many fucking cooks . . ." Second bolt: driving it home, teeth bared in a snarl as if he hated it. But glancing up now: "Two'll hold her. Switch on?"

Seven thirty-seven. *Scharnhorst* must have rounded the western end of Aaroy; there was no propeller noise to be heard. Gimber had closed the switch: he moved the lever to its "pump from for'ard" position. The pump started to work on the tank again, a throbbing whine.

Paul said, "Seven minutes more."

The pump's fuse blew, exactly as before.

The impulse was to scream. He saw Gimber's face clench—eyes screwed shut, mouth compressed within the beard. Lanchberry on his knees at the pump again, swearing viciously; Paul getting a grip on his own reeling mind . . . "It'll blow again, Jazz. Let's get her up."

It was sheer luck, *Scharnhorst* departing when she had. Not that her pres-ence would have stopped them surfacing—or trying to . . . His thoughts were on the mechanics of it now—or rather, the hydrostatics. Picturing and dreading the waste of high-pressure air, his boat's life-blood pouring out of her as she struggled to get up. Lanchberry suggested, "Have a decko at the chart, so we know which way to swim?"

"Sure. Here."

The mainland coast would be as near as the islet, he thought. Whichever looked to be the closest, he told them, would be the one to make for. It might be a swim of a thousand yards or it could be as little as three hundred; and anyone who succeeded in getting out might be fit to make it, or might not.

"If they see us when she breaks surface, there'll be boats out to us. Might not need to do much swimming."

You could spin coins till the cows came home, with so many "ifs" around. But the odds were she would be spotted. He remembered seeing small craft in the destroyer anchorage off Leir Botn's south shore, which was only two miles away, and there'd be a huge disturbance of escaping air to herald the arrival of the boat herself. He was leaning over to point out charted features that were relevant. Eight p.m. was the earliest you'd expect side-charges to go off, and you'd want to be out of the water before it happened, but if there was even as much as three hundred yards to swim you'd end up like the Bomber—like a stunned fish.

And even that was looking too far ahead. If any of them got as far as facing that problem, they'd have had enormous luck first.

Lanchberry still clutched the chart in both hands, as if it was a talisman with some power of its own to save his life. Gimber's eyes, the expression in them, were telling him, We won't make it. Or that might have been his own thought, Gimber's intent stare only a search for reassurance. It was the loss of high-pressure air through the holed main ballast tank that worried him most, the probability that with 238 feet to wipe off that clockface she'd use it all, empty the groups of storage bottles long before she came even near it.

You still had to try. The only alternative would be to sit and do nothing—until eight twenty-five at the very latest. X-12 was saddled with her own inevitable destruction.

"Are we all set?"

They both nodded. Lanchberry tossed the chart aside.

"Group up, full ahead." Paul flopped into the helmsman's seat, put his hands on the blowing valves for the two main ballast tanks and looked back over his shoulder at Louis Gimber; he saw him make the field switch and start winding the hand-wheel clockwise to put full battery-power on the main motor. Paul turned back, and wrenched the blows open. Thumping rush of air and its vibration quivering the pipe, the sound of it like sand-paper on steel but drowned now in the speeding of the main motor, its thrumming getting louder as revs built up. He was scared for the rudder as he felt her move, the first lurch.

"Main motor's full ahead, grouped up!"

"Hydroplanes hard a-dive, Louis!"

"Dive angle" on the planes tilted them so as to force the stern up in or-der to push the bow downward. There was no chance of the bow turning down, with the for'ard tank blown, but he hoped it might lift her stern up off the rock. The propeller was reasonably well protected, the rudder being abaft it and the rudder's supports like horizontal guards above it and below; but a lot of her weight would be on that rudder now, on its lower pivot. Noise was increasing: air bubbling from the after tank, a grinding of steel on rock back aft where the danger was, the boat shuddering and rattling from the full power of her screw . . .

Seven forty-four.

If the rudder support collapsed, the screw would crumple, smash itself against the rock, about one second later.

She'd lifted by a foot or two, then dropped back; there'd been a clanging impact aft. She hadn't been designed or built to stand this kind of treatment. He was waiting for the next ringing crash from that battered stern—and dreading it, knowing each one could be the last . . . It hadn't come, though. Not yet. He was holding his breath, every nerve and muscle taut . . . Gimber's report came instead, in a triumphant yell—"Two-twenty feet!"

But how much air had just eighteen feet of climb used up, he wondered. Admittedly it was something, to have her stern off the bottom. Twenty-five degree angle on her, and she was shaking like something palsied. Number one main ballast indicator light flashed on, telling him the tank was blown right out, empty; he shut the blow. Wishing to God he could shut the other one as well. Her entire store of HP air was gushing out through the stern tank now—maybe giving her a little buoyancy aft as it ripped through.

"Two hundred feet!"

Slightly better. Thirty-eight feet off the bottom, and the time, seven forty-five.

"One-eighty!"

Rising faster, gaining some upward impetus. He looked back, and saw Gimber had set the planes level now, no "dive" or "rise" angle on them. It was probably the best bet—minimal resistance to the water. One hundred and fifty feet ... But the vibration was increasing—she was finding the struggle too much for her. He had his hand on the blow to number three main ballast: the dilemma was whether if he shut it off now he'd slow or even stop the rise, or whether it would make no difference except to save some air. Then his brain cleared: there'd be no use for HP air after this: either this succeeded or it failed, and if it failed that would be the end. He took his hand off the blow. Gimber reported, yelling to beat the noise, "Hundred and twenty feet!"

She was half-way to the surface. Ship's head on 050. It was surprising the gyro hadn't toppled, with this much angle on her. Not that it mattered. The wheel moved in small jerks this way and that, from the force of the sea against the rudder, and he left it to its own devices. Time now: seven forty-six. Coming close to the hundred foot mark.

"Jazz!"

Lanchberry hauled himself up the incline and put his head near Paul's.

"When we hit the surface, you open the hatch, push Louis out, then follow him, quick as you can. I'll be right behind you but for God's sake don't wait for me. OK?"

"Aye aye, sir!"

Lanchberry was tops, he thought. Just as the Bomber had been.

"Ninety feet!"

But the flow of air was slowing. He put his hand up to the pipe connection to three main ballast. A minute ago he'd have felt it, the tremble
imparted by the rush of air. Now, he felt nothing except the ice-cold
wetness of condensation on the pipe. The noise from the stern was also
lessening. He glanced round at Lanchberry and Gimber. Lanchberry's face
was set hard, his eyes glaring at the depthgauge: Gimber's head turned
this way.

"Ninety."

Hanging. Holding that depth but making no upward progress. If there
was any air still flowing it could only be a dribble.

Lanchberry grated, "Ninety-one." His hand came up, pointing accusingly at the gauge—as if it had let him down, as he'd known it would.
"Bloody hell . . ."

Here it was: the final and—he'd known it, really—inevitable outcome.
Ninety-two feet. She'd begun to slip back, stern-first. Slowly, at the moment, but the fact she was sinking instead of rising, despite the motor full
ahead grouped up, spelt "curtains." He'd foreseen it in his imagination, en-
visaged it, so the event itself now was a replay, the opening stages of a dream
he'd had before—another of those nightmares but this time it was real.

It wasn't easy to accept—despite having recognised the facts and prob-
abilities and having had quite a long time in which to think about them.

"Ninety-five feet."

A full stop on all hope was as difficult to hoist in as the concept of
limitless space. The two were similar—you felt there had to be something
beyond the full stop . . . Another peculiar fallibility of the human psyche
was that you could see it in black and white and still try to convince yourself it wasn't true.

Ninety-eight feet. Gimber said, in a perfectly normal tone, "We've had
it, haven't we." X-12 still trembling, straining to fight the downward drag
of her own weight. She'd exhausted her reserves of air and now she was
using up all her battery-power. At full grouped up it wouldn't take long.
Seven fifty now. In ten minutes the world would end: at least, they'd be on
the fjord's rock bottom waiting for it to end, with nothing to do but wait.

Might say prayers, he thought. Open the last tins of fruit. Pray, or tell dirty jokes, sing hymns . . .

There'd been a few narrow squeaks before this. In the Med in *Ultra;* and in his first ship, the destroyer *Hoste*—he'd come very close to drowning, that time. You couldn't go on throwing sixes forever. As this thought appeared in the back of his mind he recognised it as one he'd entertained before, but not of himself, always in thinking about his father and his narrow squeaks.

"Hundred feet."

Gimber's report brought him back to earth. Or rather, to this limbo. "Limbo" was how it felt, how it was and would be—because this was perdition, no one could ever know the details of X-12's loss. In that sense one might be dying—about to die—on another planet.

He'd seen the wheel move.

Light had flashed on its rim as it jerked to port. It struck him that although she was sinking, and at a steeply stern-down angle, she must still have some forward way on—possibly a significant amount, was travelling forwards at fair speed as well as losing buoyancy and sinking: would as likely as not respond to her helm if he applied some.

His brain did a double-take on that . . . and woke up.

Ship's head was 054. Course to the shallows on the far side of the channel would be roughly 030 . . . He grabbed the wheel, flung it round to put on twenty degrees of port rudder. If there were only a few hundred yards to go to get her into those shallows—if you could drive her on to them—up them—and if she'd hold herself together while you did it, while she crashed along the bottom, after first hitting the bottom at some point and surviving that . . .

How many "ifs" was that? But she was answering her rudder, swinging to port.

"Hundred and five . . ."

Crash!

She'd struck stern-first—in seventeen and a half fathoms. She was ploughing on—lurching, staggering, stern scraping over rock.

"Hundred feet!"

Lanchberry was clawing his way back up the incline of densely-packed machinery. He'd been knocked down again and he was growling obscenities. Paul had her on a heading of 030: he shouted, with one hand extended for it, "Chart!" A hundred feet was about seventeen fathoms. And the point was, she'd risen, she'd been at a hundred and five, struck rock and bounced, finished at a hundred. Well, not finished, not as long as there was still some juice in the battery: and that might be the next thing, sound of the motor slowing . . . The wheel was jumping in his one hand: the imminent danger now was to the rudder, which at any minute could be smashed in one of those clanging impacts on rock.

"Ninety feet!"

Lanchberry pushed the chart over Paul's shoulder. Paul told him as she struck again, the whole body of the boat jarring from it but still driving on, "Get Louis here—both of you—"

All along the coast opposite the island the bottom shelved quite steeply. So if she could be kept moving that way—uphill—as long as the rudder and propeller could stand up to it—which was a toss-up, second by second—and as long as the side-cargo could endure this battering—the cargo and its running fuse, which was another thought altogether . . . Gimber was close behind him, Lanchberry at his left shoulder: he shouted, having to scream to be heard over the racket as she ground over rock—bow falling slightly as her tail-end crashed against some outcrop and flung upwards— "East side of the channel—I'm steering for the shallows. Dotted part on that coastline—see?"

"Got it!"

"When we're there—if we make it that far—not much water over us. Abandon by DSEA—OK?"

Lanchberry shouted, "Still take a bloody hour! More—she'll flood slower!"

He shook his head. "Through the wet-and-dry. Get sets on, breathing from them, hold on tight and I'll knock the clips off, let the door blast open . . ."

"Christ Almighty!"

He yelled at Gimber, "Depth now?"

He'd craned round to see the gauge. Clinging to overhead pipes. Sixty feet . . . Ten fathoms. You could see that patch on the chart. A hundred yards to travel—if she got that far before breaking apart. Steeper incline here. She felt and sounded like a tin can being used as a football, noise and motion both stunning, really frightening: she'd split clean open any moment . . . "Get the sets out, Jazz!" He heard Gimber's scream of "Fifty feet!" There was a period of savage, penetrating grinding from the stern, the length of her keel touched again, lifted, bounced in a crash and an up-ward spasm that felt as if the keel had fallen off, to leave (his imagination saw it) her belly unprotected, to be opened on the next bounce like a can ripped by the knife . . . He told himself, teeth gritted, that she'd make it. Her bow had swung up again as if she was trying to push her snout up out of water. For which he wouldn't have blamed her . . . Another crash-ing impact aft rang her like a gong: she rose, came down again stern-first and—this time—crumpled.

He heard steel ripping, somewhere underneath. Lanchberry let himself go sliding and bouncing to the engine-room bulkhead, slowing his prog-ress by grabbing at fittings as gravity took him aft. He slammed the hatch on the crawl-hole to the engine space, and forced the clips over. Gimber shouted, "Thirty-three feet!"

She was still driving on . . .

But the rudder had gone. The wheel was stuck, immoveable. She could be turned, deflected into deeper water. He thought, Stop her, then . . . He was turning his head to pass the order: Gimber shouted, "Twenty-eight feet!" And simultaneously he heard the screw go. A noise like throwing a lump of metal into a meat-grinder, and a violent trembling right through her frames. It lasted about five seconds, by which time the propeller could have no blades left on it: the main motor raced, its hum rising to a howl which cut off as Gimber broke the field-switch.

X-12 sliding on over rock: slowing, but still sliding, sounding like a heap of scrap-iron under tow.

She'd stopped. Still with bow-up angle on her, and a list to starboard instead of port. Time: seven fifty-six.

"Depth?"

The swirl and lap of sea were the only external sounds. But there was water-noise inside her too, internal flooding. Gimber told him, "Twenty-one feet."

"Check the side-cargo's still there."

Lanchberry did so. Panting . . . He turned back, nodding. "Bastard . . ."

But Paul wanted it to be still there. He'd only questioned it because of the list being to starboard instead of to port now—but that would be caused by the incline of the rock shelf she was resting on. He wanted it there, and to have it blow at eight twenty-five, so it would destroy the boat and all her contents, including equipment that was on the secret list. The orders had been to abandon in deep water, if at all, or otherwise to smash up that gear before leaving, and there wasn't time for such attention to detail now.

"DSEA sets on, boys. Quick as you can. Chuck mine over, Jazz."

The crunch would come with the opening of the W and D door. Even at this depth, opening up to outside pressure at one blast would be like getting yourselves run over by a truck. But if you could survive it—by hanging on like grim life itself and—essentially—preventing your oxygen mask from being knocked off—then you'd only have to crawl into the W and D and climb out through its open hatch, float to the surface.

With the mainland shore only yards away. He talked to the others about it while they were strapping-on their DSEA sets.

"When I see we're all ready, I'll knock the clips off. See you lads up top. Good luck."

"Same to you, skipper." Lanchberry said, "Done a bloody good job, I'd say."

"Seven-pound hammer, Jazz. For the clips."

Gimber began, "Paul . . ."

"Talk later, Louis. Let's get cracking."

Lanchberry produced the hammer. Seven fifty-eight. Twenty-seven minutes left on the clock on the port side-cargo, and possibly as little as two minutes on others.

Lanchberry was the first to be breathing from his mask. He settled himself against the after bulkhead and raised a thumb towards Paul. Gimber joined him at that end. Paul fixed his own mask over his mouth and nose and opened the distributor valve; the bag inflated, and he was breathing oxygen. They'd all been through the drill a dozen times in the practice tank at Blockhouse; that tank was a hundred feet deep, but you started in a chamber at the bottom of it that was flooded gradually—rather like the flooding-up of the W and D—not just suddenly flung open . . . He braced himself with his back against the bulkhead beside the W and D door—on the side away from the hinge, so the door would open away from him. There was a small space here in which it had been suggested a half-size chart-table might be fitted, and it gave him room in which to press himself back into the corner. He put his left hand up to his face, grasping the mask by its snout where the flexible pipe joined it from the bag. He glanced at the others, saw they were doing the same, and they both signalled "Ready." He raised the hammer.

One clip off.

They could be put on or taken off from either side of the door. Normally you'd do it by hand, but with such sea-pressure in the chamber, forcing the door against the clips, you needed some power to shift them. Only one clip held the door now. He took another quick look at Gimber and Lanchberry—saw they were ready, watching him, like Mickey Mouses in their masks. He aimed the hammer, swung it down.

The blast flattened him against the bulkhead. He couldn't breathe in or out: he was dizzy, reeling—down on his knees in a roaring, leaping torrent. Struggling up . . . Left hand still pressing the mask to his face. Then the noise was stopping, and his main impression was of the incredible viciousness of the cold: it was like ice hardening around him. There was a numbness already growing through his arms and legs, but as the roar of inflooding sea quietened he was thinking, That wasn't so bad . . .

As long as one didn't freeze.

He thought afterwards that he might have been unconscious for a few seconds. But he was breathing normally by this time and searching for the others, in darkness relieved by a diffuse radiance entering the viewing ports. He'd expected the control-room lights to stay on, even under water, but they must have shorted out. He half walked, half swam towards the after end of the compartment where they'd been when he'd last seen them. It would be eight by now, he guessed, and shut his mind to it, to the possibility of a new, huge eruption hitting them at any moment. There was only one that he knew for sure was coming, and he had twenty minutes to get away from it.

A hand closed on his arm.

He moved his other hand to the arm of whichever of them this was. Then felt the face and head. Sharp stubble surrounded the mask, not Gimber's beard which in water would be like seaweed. A stubbly scalp, too. Identification positive—Jazz Lanchberry. He was pulling at Paul's arm, trying to lead him. Paul allowed it, went that way, and had his hand placed on the body of Louis Gimber. It was limp and there was no mask on the face. Paul made himself breathe lightly and regularly—through the mouth: there was a clip on his nose to hold the nostrils shut—as per the Blockhouse drill book. There was no point in putting Gimber's mask on for him: he was unconscious, his mouth and windpipe would already be full of water, the only way to save his life would be to get him out and give him artificial respiration as soon as possible. If he could be got out. Recollections of old nightmares had to be held at bay: the feeling of tight enclosure, the hoarse, frighteningly loud sound of your own breathing rasping in the mask, the sensation of being trapped in the bubbling laughter of drowned men. He had a grasp on Gimber, sharing him with Lanchberry, both of them moving awkwardly for'ard with the burden between them. It was likely to be difficult getting him through the crawl-hole into the W and D: one of them would have to be in there with him, and there wasn't space for two. It had to be done, though. Old Louis, to be returned to Jane, if only so she could cheat him for the rest of their natural lives. The mind wandered, vaguely recognising the miraculous fact of being alive and the distinct possibility of suddenly becoming dead. Lanchberry slid into the crawl-hole like a sea-snake entering its cave, then lugged Gimber in after him, with Paul helping from outside, or trying to. They managed that part of it all right, but now Jazz would have either to push the body up through the hatch above him, or get up through it and reach down to pull it up behind him. Limp bodies were extremely difficult things to handle in such circumstances and in very confined spaces. Limbs tended to catch on hatch-rims and in other places, and there'd be a danger of getting him stuck in it. Such things had been known to happen in DSEA escapes, or attempted DSEA escapes. Very much on their side in this one, of course, was the extremely shallow water.

The cold was painful, like heavy ice squeezing, gripping, and you couldn't afford to be delayed for very long. Paul adjusted his distributor valve to give himself a better supply of oxygen, and after what seemed like about ten minutes but was more likely sixty seconds he put his head through the hole and saw Lanchberry's legs disappearing upwards. He could see it because of the surface light showing through the open hatch, a light that was temporarily eclipsed as Lanchberry's body filled the hatch on its way through. Paul was in the W and D by then, crouching, keeping his mask out of the way of Lanchberry's feet, looking up and waiting for the exit to be clear. Then he climbed up into the hatchway. As Bomber Brazier had done only about an hour ago, an hour like half a lifetime.

Thinking of Brazier: and that if a side-cargo went up now, when all three of them were in the sea . . .

Please God, ten minutes more?

Having got this far, he was sharply conscious of the urge to live. It had never really left him, but he'd had to subdue it when there'd seemed to be no hope. He was out of the hatch, holding to X-12's casing to stop himself floating straight up. Breathing loudly, and bubbles streaming from each exhalation. But Lanchberry had gone on up with Gimber, and there was no reason to make himself wait. He let go, arched his body in the approved DSEA training tank position, but didn't bother with the apron in only about twenty feet of water.

Daylight exploded in his face. And the sight of a mountainside with snow on it. Treading water, he wrenched the mask off and gasped cold air into his lungs. Some salt water came in with it, and he was choking for a while. Lanchberry was supporting Gimber. The sea lapped a fringe of rocks that lined the shore, very much as he'd expected. In not much more than a minute, the two of them sharing Gimber's weight again, they were among the rocks and wading. They were floundering towards the shore itself, with only a few yards to cover—but then an almost vertical rock climb, which wouldn't be too easy, with Gimber—when Lanchberry stopped.

"Bloody hell . . ."

Gimber's head lolled on a broken neck. It must have happened inside the boat when the rush of water hit them. They'd brought a corpse out with them.

"Leave him here."

The body would be better hidden here than it could be up on the shore. It would be a disadvantage to have it found too soon. He didn't quite know why, but in fact he realised later that his thoughts must already have been turning towards escape as distinct from surrender to the Germans. This was crazy, of course—since they were both frozen, wet, exhausted, half-drowned and hadn't been able to bring any of the overland-escape gear with them.

Lanchberry let Gimber's body down into the shallow water, where it would be contained by the surrounding rocks until some Norwegian fisherman, or German soldier, came across it. Except that when the side-cargo exploded . . .

"What's the time?"

Lanchberry had an expensive, waterproof wristwatch of which he was extremely proud. He glanced at it now. "Eight-ten." He shook his head. "I don't believe it. I thought—"

"Hey! Hey!"

On the rock edge above them—a boy. Kid of about twelve, in rough, warm-looking clothes and a woollen cap on his head. Blunt, freckled features and an expression of excitement.

"English?"

Paul nodded, shivering. "Yes."

Lanchberry muttered, "Well, fuck me!"

"Kom!" The boy beckoned. Looking around—across the water, and back at the coast road behind him. There were cottages in sight, Paul found when he got up there, and he remembered the chart had shown some settlements along this coast. The boy had a sack with him, in which he stowed their DSEA sets when they shed them. He seemed to be quite sure of what he was doing. Paul hoping it wouldn't turn out to have been all on the kid's own initiative, that there'd be some adults around as well. In any case this was the best bet, the only chance of warmth and perhaps a hideout. The boy slung the sack over his shoulder; he'd beckoned again, and he was leading them towards the road when from somewhere in the south and some miles away the explosion of a side-cargo came like a clap of thunder: then, right on its heels, two more, overlapping—a triple-barrelled eruption that went on echoing for half a minute from snow-clad mountainsides. The boy laughed, and shouted back over his shoulder, "*Tirpitz!* Boom-boom-boom!" he beckoned again and broke into a trot.

Eight twelve.

CHAPTER SEVENTEEN

. . .

Trench confirmed, "Wielding Christofferson, the boy's name was. I suppose you know Paul became godfather to his first child?"

I did know. Paul had gone over there quite often, after the war—combining a visit to those people with some salmon fishing. They'd been wonderful, he told me, those Norwegians. They hid him and Lanchberry until most of the fuss was over, then kitted them up and briefed them and sent them up the mountain with a guide to point them in the right direction. They had luck in another aspect too. What remained of Louis Gimber was found somewhere up on the shore where the surge from the explosion had dumped it, and the Germans for some reason assumed he was the only one who'd got out before X-12 blew herself to pieces. So they weren't looking for any other survivors.

Don Cameron and his crew, and Godfrey Place and his diver, Aitken, were prisoners on board *Tirpitz* when the side-cargoes from X-6 and X-7 went up. Place's other two crewmen drowned, and X-5 was lost, probably destroyed by gun-fire outside the nets. The battleship had been warped aside on her cables before the charges went off, but they still lifted her six feet out of water and put her out of action for six months. Then a Fleet Air Arm strike crippled her again, and finally the RAF sank her with new, much bigger bombs.

Cameron and Place were both awarded the Victoria Cross.

Trench pulled a pipe out of his pocket, looked at it, put it away again. We were almost at the house. He said, "Paul was as tough as old boots, and I suppose his ERA must've been too. And they had a lot of help from the Lapps they met along the way. It was still a hell of a journey to have survived."

Paul's war hadn't ended there, either. He commanded one of the midget submarines—XE-craft, the improved version—which acted as markers for the Normandy assault waves. As we all know, D-day was postponed by twenty-four hours because of bad weather, so the midgets had to lie in exposed positions off those beaches for an extra day and night in near-impossible conditions, and still played their part to perfection when the time came. After that he came back to ordinary submarining, was selected for COQC—Commanding Officers' Qualifying Course—and had been given his first full-sized command shortly before the war ended in the Far East.

And was killed, with his wife Lucy, in a crash on the Ml motorway ten years later.

He'd been married less than a year, and they'd had no child, so the title went to Hugh, Nick's son by Kate. (Who remarried, in Australia, not long after the end of the war.) Hugh took over Mullbergh, the Everard estate in Yorkshire, and farmed the land—as Paul had done—living in the Dower House because Mullbergh itself, that old monstrosity, had been sold long before and turned into a country club. He still lives and farms there. The Dower House had been, of course, Nick's stepmother Sarah's home for many years. She died in 1944. She'd been knocked sideways by the news of her son Jack's death—as prisoner of war on the run in Germany—but she had her first stroke when she heard about Nick. Despite the fact she'd hated him—or had seemed to—since about 1920. In the West Riding of Yorkshire there was less surprise at this than an outsider might have expected. It was no secret in certain houses up there that Sarah's son Jack had been Nick's, not his father's. There had always been scandal around the Everards, and the funny thing was they'd never seemed to appreciate that their neighbours had eyes, ears, tongues and brains.

There was never anyone called "Jane." There was a girl of another name, widow of a serving officer in another service, whom Louis Gimber had hoped to marry, but that was not her name, and Gimber's was neither Gimber nor Louis. This last piece of disguise is simply a matter of discretion: "Louis" was killed in X-12, and he was the only child of parents who are now dead too.

When Paul told me about "Jane"—quite soon after the end of the war, and years before he met the girl whom he eventually married—he also told me that after his return to England he only saw her once. It was at her wedding to a then serving officer who has since become internationally famous as well as extremely rich. The engagement had been announced before Paul's return via Sweden, apparently. Paul said, I remember, "By God, she was fast on her feet, that girl!" He laughed for about a minute, then sobered and added, "Would have been tough on old Louis, though, wouldn't it."

Strange as it may seem, that marriage is still in being and the family quite numerous.

At the house, I thanked Eileen Trench for her hospitality, the meal she'd given me, and so on.

"Won't you stay and have some tea? Or a drink?"

"You're very kind. But I've a long way to go."

Trench walked out with me to my car. I thanked him, too, for the help he'd given me, filling in the gaps.

"That's all right." We shook hands. "I know you'll do them justice."

By "them," of course, he meant the Everards. I've tried to—warts and all. And that's about all there is.

POSTSCRIPT

· · ·

I should like to thank a one-time shipmate and former X-craft CO, Commander Matthew Todd, Royal Navy, for his kindness in providing answers to technical questions.

Only six X-craft took part in Operation Source. X-11 and X-12 are fictional. Nor was there any convoy PQ 19 or QP 16; the last in that series were PQ 18 and QP 15, after which the prefix letters for Arctic convoys were changed from PQ/QP to JWIAR.

Adding fiction to fact has not been allowed to alter the facts as they are recorded. For instance, Karl Rasmussen was caught by the Gestapo and tortured, and did kill himself rather than betray his colleagues Torstein Raaby and Harry Pettersen. And *Lützow* did leave Altenfjord just before the X-craft arrived, just as *Scharnhorst* was at anchor off Aaroy—moving on the forenoon of the attack into the netcage vacated by *Lützow.* Donald Cameron saw *Scharnhorst* in that vulnerable position when he was on his way south to the Brattholm islands in X-6, but his target was *Tirpitz* and he was not to be deflected. I knew Cameron, and feel sure he would not have objected to my using his "magnificent feat of arms"—Admiral Sir Max Horton's description of the operation—as a background to this last Everard story.

A. F.

The Halfhyde Adventures
Philip McCutchan

The Halfhyde Adventures Series follows the remarkable, rollicking adventures of the headstrong Royal Navy Lieutenant St Vincent Halfhyde. Acting as a virtual Agent 007 in the early years of the 20th century, Halfhyde's forté is performing risky special missions for the Admirality. In action set against a background of rapidly shifting alliances, Lieutenant Halfhyde triumphs as Her Majesty's Royal Navy challenges Russia, Japan, and Germany for control of the seas.

"Halfhyde is a fine hero,
insubordinate and ingenious."
—The New York Times

"Riveting and authoritative, with flashes of dry humor and bawdiness to lighten the strain." *—Savannah News*

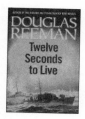
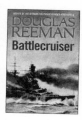
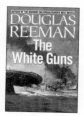
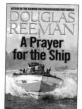
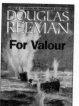